A CONSPIRACY OF
DRAKES

DRAGON MANIFESTOS BOOK 1

Kathleen Nelson

KATHLEEN H. NELSON

A CONSPIRACY OF DRAKES

DRAGON MANIFESTOS BOOK 1

KATHLEEN H. NELSON

Paperback ISBN 978-1-77400-011-3

Ebook ISBN 978-1-77400-010-6

www.dragonmoonpress.com

DEDICATION

In memory of Mom.
With gratitude to Les.

ACKNOWLEDGMENTS

Small press publishers don't get the accolades they deserve. Gwen Gades is no exception. She has taken Dragon Moon Press from a near-pipedream to a well-known, well-respected house that publishes award-winning fiction. She wears all the hats. She never quits. And she makes Dragon Moon Press feel like family. I am proud to be one of her authors. Thank you, Gwen, for everything. Here's to the next twenty-five years.

Thanks to Melissa Carrigee as well for her insightful remarks and direction.

Last but not least, heartfelt thanks to my extended village for all the love and support. I am a truly lucky woman.

CHAPTER 1

DRAKES

From dreaded god of darkness and magic to ignoble crime-lord—that's how far the great drake Tezcatlipoca's fortunes had fallen. He often brooded about that. Indeed, he was brooding about it now when he was supposed to be preparing himself for the event that might well restore him to his former glory. How utterly humiliating it had been to be so abruptly deposed—and by humans, no less! Such filthy, arrogant creatures!

And it was all his sister's doing! Tezcatlipoca might well detest men, but he absolutely abhorred Quetzalcoatl.

Younger, lesser drakes did not appreciate the depths of his hatred toward his sibling. If a dragon did not like a clutch-mate—and such was often the case—then one simply forgot that he or she existed. But no dragon ever had suffered the kind of betrayal that Quetzalcoatl had visited upon Tezcatlipoca. She'd torn his very godhood away from him, and with it, his dominion over the world. How could anyone who had never been divine understand what a profound scar such an injury would leave?

Tezcatlipoca rumbled, commiserating with himself, and then shook the thought of his treacherous sister out of his head with a full-body shudder. In the ensuing moment of peace, he decided to get on with his preparations. All he had left to do was Change—a process he would have gladly skipped under other circumstances. A young drake could reshape himself in a few minutes with no ill-effect. As a drake aged, however, his bones set like stone and transformation became a misery. Tezcatlipoca ached for days after taking another form. But dragons lacked the capacity to vocalize their thoughts, and trying to address a crowd of drakes mind-to-mind would quickly devolve into bedlam so he had no choice but to shift into something more garrulous. He inhaled deeply through his nostrils, savoring the smell of his brimstone musk one last time, and then concentrated on the form that he had created for himself back when he was young.

His body went rubbery first and then semi-molten. The row of spine guards that ran from the base of his skull to the tip of his tail melted back into his backbone. His neck shrank. His tail disappeared. Then his hind legs straightened out, his muzzle receded, and the small sharp bones in his head began to rearrange themselves. Moments or hours later, he dropped to the stone floor as a tender-skinned man. As he lay there panting from pain and exertion, his perceptions shifted, too. The floor felt hard and cold. The air smelled frigid. The darkness seemed suddenly denser.

Oh, how he loathed this feeble form!

As he struggled to regain his equilibrium, a sharp buzz disrupted the chamber's stillness. It was followed by another and then another. Tezcatlipoca snarled, a jaguar-like curl of the upper lip. He disliked being disturbed while he was recovering from a Change. And no matter where he was or what he was doing, he thoroughly resented being disturbed by the man-magic known as cell phone. It was unnatural, intrusive stuff. He had to admit, however, at least to himself, that it was an extremely convenient way to communicate with those who were not in his presence. The cell phone buzzed again; he groped for it in the darkness. As soon as it fell into his soft, clawless hand, he thumbed the talk button and snarled, "What?"

"Great One." The voice was that of his high priest, Carlito. "Grishka Rasputin is here."

His upper lip relaxed. Grishka was his closest ally and co-conspirator, and was slated to play a critical role in the upcoming conclave. "See that he gets what he needs," he said, and then as an afterthought, added, "Is everyone present now?"

Carlito's response was immediate. "No, Great One. Drogo Channing and Vern Pendragon haven't checked in yet."

Tezcatlipoca hissed, reflexive distaste for the late-comers. Drogo Channing had no doubt planned to arrive late as a plausibly deniable show of disrespect. That ill-tempered fire drake was bold. And ambitious. It was no secret that he saw himself as Tezcatlipoca's equal even though he was younger by ages. Tezcatlipoca intended to deal with the upstart at some point, but not yet, not while his own ambitions hung in the balance. Upstart or not, Drogo got things done. He had coerced at least a dozen drakes into coming all the way here to Juarez, and most drakes had no desire to venture beyond the boundaries of their territories.

"Some of the attendees are growing restive," Carlito said then. "Would you have me start the feast?"

"No!" Tezcatlipoca was quick to reply. "If they eat now, they will curl up around their full bellies and sleep through the conclave." Then, mindful of how resourceful a hungry drake could be, he added, "Make sure the meat is secure."

"Already done," Carlito replied, proving himself an able high priest yet again. A moment later, he added, "Grishka wonders if your paths will cross before the conclave begins."

The message was pure Grishka: perfectly respectful on one level, indefinably sly on the next. Most of the other drakes disliked him because he was as peculiar as he was intelligent, and they didn't trust either of those qualities. But Tezcatlipoca appreciated the lesser drake's wit and considered advice. His idiosyncrasies had their uses, too. So even though he would've preferred to keep to himself until his post-transformation pains subsided, he pushed himself onto his flat, fleshy feet and said, "Where is he?"

"Mid-level warming chamber," Carlito replied.

Without another word, Tezcatlipoca ended the call. Then he wrapped himself in a cloak made of black jaguar skins and shuffled forth from his resting chamber.

The passageways leading to the middling levels were rough-hewn mine shafts, ancient remnants of an Aztec gold mine. As he made his way up the stony grade, he thought about the upcoming conclave to distract himself from the spangling pain of walking upright. It was to be an unprecedented event: every kind of drake from every part of the world convening to elect the course of action most likely to secure the next age for dragon-kind. It was an exciting prospect—but not without its challenges. Drakes had evolved as solitary, independent creatures. Convincing a score of them to converge on the same spot had been difficult. Convincing them to cooperate in the name of a common goal would be harder still. There would be contrariness. There would be factions. There would be Drogo Channing.

The combustive stink of torches began to displace the cold, mineral-laden smells of the lower regions. A short time later, the shaft's gold-flecked walls began to glimmer with firelight. The kaleidoscopic dazzle confounded Tezcatlipoca's eyes. He blinked, trying to acclimate to the light. As he did so, he thought he saw Quetzalcoatl staring at him from the rockface.

He opened his mouth to roar at the hateful visage, but the sound that came out of him was closer to a squeak. His sister's shadow-self mocked him with a snort and then receded into the rockface. He stared at the spot for a long moment, daring the drakena to return, but the wall remained a blank—more mockery, it seemed.

The pseudo-sighting left Tezcatlipoca in a prickly mood, and when he finally arrived at the warming chamber and saw Grishka Rasputin occupying the choicest spot in the room, his disposition grew even more peevish. Grishka was ungainly for a water drake, narrow of shoulder and hip but bulky in the middle as if he had swallowed something whole. His left hind leg stuck out at an unnatural angle. The back of his long, pointy skull was scarred. He sat squarely on his haunches in front of the warming stone, toasting his distended belly like a dog.

"Move!" Tezcatlipoca growled.

Grishka's head swiveled in Tezcatlipoca's direction. His S-shaped neck arched as if with surprise, but Tezcatlipoca knew it was an act by the sly sparkle in the lesser drake's murky green eyes.

"Great One!" he exclaimed, mind-to-mind because he was still in dragon-form. *"I did not expect you so soon. You honor me with your promptness."*

"Move!" Tezcatlipoca said again. "That spot belongs to me."

"My mistake, Great One," Grishka said, and then, still upright, waddled like a duck to a less desirable patch of stone.

Tezcatlipoca grimaced at the sight and growled, "Could you possibly be any more undignified?"

"I do not know, Great One," Grishka replied, projecting respect. *"Permit me to try."* His eyes crossed and then rolled back in their sockets. His pink fork of a tongue slid past his front teeth and hung in mid-air like a dead thing. The pose was so absurd, it made Tezcatlipoca forget his pique.

"Enough," he said. "Drogo already complains about your un-dragon-like demeanor. If he sees you like that, he will surely insist that I kill you."

"He does seem particularly ill-disposed toward me," Grishka replied blandly. Then, as he settled back into his basking pose, he said, *"So tell me: how are the wyrms doing?"*

Tezcatlipoca's nostrils flared, a show of surprise. "Is that why you wanted to see me?"

"Why does that surprise you?" the lesser drake asked, cocking his misshapen head like a puzzled cocker spaniel. *"It's been months since I last saw them. I'm eager to know how they're developing, especially given their extraordinary origins."*

"They're doing well, remarkably so as you will see," Tezcatlipoca said, too casually for Grishka's liking. "But I do not understand your peculiar attachment to them. You didn't sire them."

"It is true that there is no proof that they are my offspring", Grishka countered, *"but I did find them in Siberia, which is my territory. And I did conjugate with a wild drakena at the turn of the last age. So it could well be that I sired those wyrms. My interest in their development has nothing to do with their paternity, however. They are a gift to us from the Divine, a sign of Her favor and willingness to finally forgive us. They must be treated accordingly."*

"The wyrms are being given everything they need, Grishka," Tezcatlipoca crooned. "You worry too much."

Grishka gave the man-drake a probing once-over, then shook off his doubts and snorted. *"You are right; I tend to overthink things. I will make an effort to be less cerebral."* He shifted his weight then, revealing a lumpy homespun sack which he then tail-flicked in Tezcatlipoca's direction. *"I almost forgot. I brought you something."*

Tezcatlipoca scooped the sack up and snuffled its contents. As he did so, his amber eyes acquired a nostalgic gleam. "Spanish coins," he said, "made from Aztec gold. How delightful." He plucked a tarnished disc from the bag and rubbed it between his thumb and forefinger—a slow, dreamy caress. "How did you come by such a treasure?"

"One of my agents found the cache in a cave that he was scouting as a hideout," Grishka replied. *"He brought it to me, but I have no interest in such things so I brought it to you."*

The gleam in Tezcatlipoca's eyes acquired a roguish cast. "Some would say that a drake who does not keep a hoard is a drake who should not be trusted."

"I would not disagree," Grishka said, perfectly deadpan. *"I would merely point out that one can hoard things other than gold."*

Tezcatlipoca rumbled—a rare show of appreciation that was cut short by a familiar buzz. As he pulled the cell phone out of a pocket in his cloak, Grishka warbled a confession. *"I must admit: the sight of you using man-magic still boggles me. When we first met, you crushed my phone when it went off and warned me to never bring any kind of technology near you again."*

"Yes, well," Tezcatlipoca said, as he retrieved the message that Carlito had left him. "My high priest persuaded me to set my preferences aside during this time of transition." He started to say more only to interrupt himself with a violent hiss. "That thick-headed earth-wyrm! He's not coming!"

"Which thick-headed earth-wyrm would that be?" Grishka inquired politely.

"Manos Pequenos," the Great One grumbled, using his derogatory nickname for Vern Pendragon. "He says there's no money in the conclave for him. He says he has lots of irons in the fire right now. He says no hard feelings, OK?

"What kind of a drake talks like that?"

"Most kinds, actually," Grishka observed, but Tezcatlipoca was still fuming and did not hear.

"He sounds like a human. He's been masquerading as one of them for so long, he has forgotten what he really is. The only thing still draconic about him is his capacity for hot air." Grishka disagreed. He had only met Vern Pendragon once, but the Divine had seen fit to gift him with a sharp eye for character and so he had seen right away that the drake was vain and not overly bright and mainly interested in amassing a hoard. Which made him no different from the majority of other lesser drakes. Unlike most other drakes, however, he did not insulate himself from human society. Instead, he lived loudly, proudly, and lavishly at its pinnacle—and humans admired him for it! Tezcatlipoca had believed that such a skill could play an important but as-of-yet undetermined part in securing the sixth age. Grishka thought that was expecting too much from one so unevolved.

"The Divine favored us by exposing his untrustworthiness now rather than later," he said, gingerly intruding on the mandrake's ongoing tirade. *"But if you are set on having him with us, then perhaps you should send Drogo Channing to talk to him. I hear he has exceptional powers of persuasion."*

Tezcatlipoca sneered. "Drogo Channing is obnoxious. And he only acts in his own best interests."

"Yet he is an ally, is he not?"

"On the surface perhaps. The bad thing about Manos Pequenos is that he is frivolous. The bad thing about Drogo is that he is not. Neither one of them will be easy to trust. Or control."

"If anyone can do it, you can," Grishka said, the silkiest of reassurances.

The mandrake sneered again. "Flattery, Grishka?"

"Nothing of the sort," Grishka replied, projecting sincerity and maybe a single subliminal strand of coyness. *"You are eldest. You were a god. You are capable of anything."*

More flattery, Tezcatlipoca supposed, but it mollified him just the same. And the message that he received a moment later further improved his mood. "Finally!" he said, as he squinted at his cell phone. "Drogo has arrived. We can begin."

Carlito stood in an alcove at the high end of the underground grotto, discreetly hidden from view. A score of drakes in man-form had amassed in the cavern's fire-lit bowl. The more dominant among them had claimed spaces around the numerous firepits. The lesser drakes were hunkered down on cold bare bedrock, squabbling over scraps of warmth and turf until someone more powerful decided to shut them up. Carlito observed the goings-on intently, trying to discern a pecking order for future reference. Tezcatlipoca appreciated information like that.

The hair on his nape bristled: a sixth sense stirring. Heartbeats later, someone sniffed the back of his head. The moisture seeping from his armpits turned suddenly cold. At the same time, his mouth went dry. The sniffing moved to his left ear and then down to the base of his neck. A sharp-nailed finger plucked the collar of his shark-repellent chain-mail shirt like a guitar string, catching a little flesh, too.

"Do you really think this flimsy suit will save you from someone like me?" a leathery voice wondered.

"No, Great One," Carlito replied, going with flattery because that sometimes sweetened up a sour drake. "I'd need to be encased in a battle tank to survive someone like you. And even then, I wouldn't like my odds."

His inquisitor snuffled the back of his head and then said,

"You reek of Tezcatlipoca, so you must be his pet. Tell me, Pet. Do you spy on the conclave for your master or for your own miserable kind?"

"I am not a spy," Carlito said.

"Then why are you here?"

Carlito shrugged, a show of nonchalance that belied the on-alert beehive in his belly. "If you wish to know, you should ask Tezcatlipoca."

The man-drake stepped into view. A casual observer might have taken him for a retired heavyweight prizefighter. He was shorter than Tezcatlipoca by a few inches, but what he lacked in height he more than made up for in vigor. His skin was still supple; his musculature, robust.Like most drakes, he despised hair and so only manifested a slight fringe over his hooded grey eyes. He leaned in close, all but rubbing cheeks with Carlito, and said, "Do you know who I am?"

"You are Drogo Channing, CEO of Black Dragon Enterprises," Carlito replied. "It is said that you can turn a man into a king just by whispering in his ear."

"Yes," Drogo said, stretching the word into a hiss, "it is said. Yet your master keeps me at a distance. Instead of consulting with me, he conspires with that cripple. I would know what secrets those two are keeping, human. I would have you tell me."

Carlito's pulse fluttered in his throat: his feigned nonchalance taking flight. For there was no upside to a situation like this. If he dished on Tezcatlipoca, the Great One would kill him. If he kept his mouth shut, Drogo Channing would feel justified in tearing his throat out. The loss of his high priest would irritate Tezcatlipoca, but Drogo would almost certainly survive the Great One's dyspepsia. He needed to act, and act fast! Problem was, he didn't know what to do. As he fumbled for a move, the shadows disgorged another man-drake. This one was clad in a heavy woolen robe like a monk and would have been considered hirsute even by human standards.

"Drogo Channing," he said, running gnarled, yellow-nailed fingers through the tangles of his chest-length beard, "why do you menace this human for information? You might as well menace a mosquito for blood."

Although the mandrake's manner was as humble as his garb, Carlito caught a ripple of something in his voice far below the surface—a ripple of amusement perhaps or scorn. Drogo sensed that fleeting ribbon, too, and chose to be offended by it. His upper lip curled. His nostrils flared. An instant later, he was huffing in the newcomer's face instead of Carlito's.

"Grishka Rasputin!" he said, turning the other drake's name into an accusation. "Are you spying on me, too?"

Grishka reared back as if he were trying to focus on something that had just landed on the tip of his nose. "Why would I spy on you? We are not enemies."

"Are we not?" Drogo asked, sniffing at Grishka's aura. "Sometimes I wonder. You hide much behind that repulsive overgrowth of hair, I think. I question the nature of your secrets, and mistrust your obsession with the Divine."

"Would that we could all be as open and upfront as you," Grishka purred, playing with a long strand of hair just to raise the other drake's gorge. "But if I am otherwise, it is because the Divine has made me so."

Drogo spat—a spattering of venomous droplets that sizzled for a second when they hit the cold stone floor. "Maybe you're not a threat. Maybe you're just addled."

"I will be honest with you," Grishka said in a vaguely confidential tone. "My mind is sharper than it has ever been. I see things that others overlook. I hear things that are only said in whispers. For example, I heard that while quail hunting with a group of diplomats recently, you shot one of them in the face and then made him apologize for getting in your way."

Drogo looked down as if to admire his longish but otherwise perfectly manicured nails. "The apology was his idea," he said. "And he was only in my way after the fact."

"A masterful work of terrorism," Grishka said. "But tell me: what purpose did such an act serve?"

A sneer chased the smugness from Drogo's blunt-nosed face. "If nothing else," he said, "it shut everyone up. And that was a good thing because their arrogant blather was eating at me like acid. There they were, pretending to be the mightiest, most intelligent creatures to ever walk the earth. And all the while they were hunting tiny birds with automatic weapons!"

Grishka cocked his head at the other mandrake and warbled. "You shot a man in the face because you think humans are less sporting than dragons? That sounds a bit contrary to me."

Carlito feigned a sudden and urgent interest in his cell phone so Drogo would feel less inclined to punish him for Grishka's irreverence. But even with his back to the drakes, it was impossible for him to completely ignore their squabble. He heard Drogo shove Grishka—a two-handed thrust. He also heard Grishka absorb the blow without moving an inch.

"One day, Rasputin," Drogo said, "you will go too far with me."

"I do not doubt it," Grishka said, sounding resigned and maybe a little bored. "Such is my nature."

"Your nature will get you killed some day," Drogo said, delivering a perfunctory second shove. "From what I have heard—and from what I can see—you should be dead already."

"It is true," Grishka replied, and now his voice was striped with faint regrets. "There is no hiding that which was done to me that night. I arrived at the Yusupov Palace with a straight back and supple limbs and a visage that was not terrible to behold. But the poison that those would-be assassins fed me ravaged my face. The bullets that they pumped into me later rendered my arm useless, and the clubbing that came next shattered my leg. Had they stopped there, I would have surely died. Instead, they dumped me into the life-sustaining river."

With a subtle shift of his weight, Drogo removed himself from Grishka's personal space and then reached into his suit jacket for a cigarette. As he lit up, he eyed the other drake over the butane flame and asked, "Were your attackers drakena agents?"

"I never thought to ask," Grishka said, raising his right shoulder in an approximation of a shrug. "I was younger then, and ignorant. More likely, I simply attempted too much too soon and reaped the rewards of impatience. I will not make the same mistake again."

"That does not preclude you from making others," Drogo said, and blew a thin ribbon of grey smoke at him. "So I ask again: why does Tezcatlipoca prefer your counsel to mine?"

Grishka shrugged again, an inflammatory show of indifference. "Perhaps it is not my counsel that interests him. Perhaps he seeks guidance from the Divine."

"Fool," Drogo said, bathing the word in more smoke. "The Divine is an ancient relic, useful only as a prop for nostalgic weaklings like you."

"You should not say such things," Grishka said, letting his restless fingers run through his untrimmed beard again. "You will attract Her displeasure."

Drogo hissed. "Are you threatening me?"

"Certainly not," Grishka said. "I am only the messenger."

Carlito was sweating sheets in his chain-mail shirt, and not because of the extra bodies in the vicinity. The air in the alcove was thick with dragon musk and menace. If violence broke out in this small space, he was sure to catch the worst end of it. But he couldn't leave his post before the appointed time. If he embarrassed Tezcatlipoca in front of the entire assembly, the Great One would have him for lunch. He shuddered at the thought. An instant later, his forgotten cell phone shivered, too. The message was from Tezcatlipoca. Carlito was happy to relay the message.

"The Great One is on his way. He wants to know if all is in readiness." He glanced at the mandrakes, who were still posturing for each other. "What should I tell him?"

Grishka was the first to break eye-contact—a casual concession graciously made. "I am ready," he said, and then looked again at Drogo. "I fear, however, that I am distracting you."

Drogo gave Grishka a scornful once-over, then took one last drag from his cigarette and flicked the still lit-butt at Carlito. Streaming smoke from the corners of his turned-down mouth, he then stomped off to join the other congregants. Carlito watched him descend into the grotto, kicking and slinging lesser drakes out of his way. In the innermost chamber of his heart, a place where he alone had ears, he heaved a massive sigh of relief. To his surprise, Grishka made the same sound aloud.

"That one has a vile disposition," he said ruefully. "I must remember to pray for him."

The thought provoked a snort from Carlito. Grishka arched a wooly caterpillar eyebrow and asked, "Do you scoff at me for wanting to pray?"

"Not at all," Carlito said, kicking himself inwardly for that fleeting loss of control. "It's just that I think of praying as a human thing."

The mandrake rumbled disapprovingly. "That, to me, is the height of human arrogance," he said. "You think you are the only beings worthy of The Divine's blessings."

"No," Carlito said, holding up a hand as if to fend off Grishka's indignation, "that's not it. I don't believe there's an all-mighty being who watches over us. I thought your kind felt the same way."

"Ah," Grishka said, lapsing back into his former state of disheveled pensiveness. "Then I must remember to pray for you, too."

A sudden hush fell over the grotto, disrupting their conversation. They shifted toward the bowl in time to see Tezcatlipoca make his entrance. His man-form was saggy of belly and jowl, but still firm of chest and back. Although he must have been in great pain from his Change, he moved like the magnificent jungle cat that had once been his preferred avatar. Across the grotto he strode, heading for the bowl's most prominent lip. When he reached that ledge, he settled onto it with no sign of unease and then looked down upon the gathering for the first time.

"In the beginning," he said, in a voice that filled the grotto without booming, "there were only dragons and The Divine. The Divine granted us dominion over all of the earth, and we lived according to our nature, doing as we pleased when it pleased us.

"Then men shinnied down from the trees.

"At first, they saw us as gods, and all was well. But my sister and the other drakena soon grew weary of the natural order. They thought it was cruel. They lamented 'the waste'. So they began to meddle in mankind's evolution. They taught men how to think and reason. They taught them ways other than fear. In return, those wretched creatures turned the Divine against dragon-kind and then began to hunt us down. The drakena despaired and went into hiding. We drakes fought back tooth, nail, and flame, but were wildly outnumbered. By the end of the fourth age, most of us were dead—and the still-bitter drakena would not reconcile with the survivors so we could not replenish our numbers. We had no choice but to go into hiding, too. That is where we remain to this day.

"The Year of the Dragon is coming. With it comes the dawn of a new age. My question to you is: do you want to spend the next cycle skulking in mankind's shadow? Or would you rather reclaim your birthright and restore the natural order?"

Pandemonium erupted: a cacophony of clapping, snapping, whistling, and shouting. A few of the attendees—the youngest perhaps or perhaps the weariest—lost control of their forms and morphed back into roaring, steam-snorting dragons. Carlito could not help but marvel at the singular sight.

"I know what you are thinking," Tezcatlipoca said, willing the crowd to silence. "You are thinking that we are too few. You are thinking there is nothing that any of us can do to turn the next age in our favor. And do you know what I am thinking? I am thinking you are right. There is nothing that any one of us can do." He paused for effect and then added, "But if we work together—"

An older, scar-faced mandrake who had claimed one of the firepits for his own snapped at a less substantial changeling for infringing on his space and then returned his attention to the Great One. "What's this? Drakes working together? Like humans? I don't like the sound of that."

"When you phrase it like that," Tezcatlipoca fired back, "neither do I. But if we want things to change, then we must change our ways—leastwise for a while."

Grishka stepped into view, obviously on cue, and said, "What would you have us do, Great One?"

Tezcatlipoca bared his teeth in a feral grin. "We are all engaged in activities designed to disrupt human society. I deal mainly in drugs and slavery. Wo Long, Azi Zhahhak, and Imugu are arms dealers. There are politicians among us, and terrorists, too. That is all to the good, but we need to go further.

We need to dedicate ourselves to a single, pre-determined goal, one that will tip the sixth age in our direction."

"I know the way we must take, Great One!"

The claim came from a small, sleek, bronze-colored mandrake who held a moderate scrap of territory in the center of the bowl. Carlito didn't recognize him, but guessed that he was Persian by his Punjabi pants and shalvar. And any fool could tell that he was young by the way he flaunted his excess energy.

"That sand snake is Drogo's thrall," Griskha remarked to Carlito. "You would do well to avoid him."

If Tezcatlipoca felt the same way about the sand-snake, he guarded his inner thoughts well. "Speak your mind, Azi Zhahhak," he said, graciously yielding the floor. "All will hear you."

If Grishka had not clued him in, Carlito might not have noticed Azi glancing in Drogo's direction before springing to his feet. "Brothers," he said, in excellent, Farsi-flavored English. "The answer to this riddle is simple. To claim the sixth age, all we have to do is get rid of the humans. To do that, all we have to do is call extinction down on them."

"The idea is not without merit," Tezcatlipoca said, "but you underestimate their capacity for recovery. If we don't kill them all at the same time, the survivors will breed themselves back into a problem in a wingbeat."

"Exactly," a new voice bellowed. "That is why we should loose Armageddon on them."

All heads swiveled Drogo's way. He was on his feet now, and posturing in front of a fire pit so everyone could see him. In profile, he looked like a raptor with a rounder head and slightly longer arms.

"The ancient Mayans predicted that the fifth age would end with Fire," he said. "We now have the means to fulfill that prophecy."

"Elaborate," The Great One said.

"I have spent the last forty years cultivating the trust of the most powerful men in western government," Drogo said. "As a result, I now have access to a stockpile of nuclear weapons. Azi Zhahhak," he said, acknowledging his underling with a nod, "is in a similar position in The Land of The Peacock. And Imugi," he added, gesturing at a pale Asian drake who had lost control of his man-form in the initial excitement and not bothered to Change back, "is responsible for the build-up on the Korean peninsula. On our own, we have the potential to wreak great havoc on the world of men. But to achieve maximum destruction, we need the rest of you to join us. Wo Long," he said, pointing at a handsome, thinly-mustachioed mandrake who was sucking on a hookah in the shadows, "Your base is in China. Will you join with me?"

Wo Long blew twin spirals of smoke from his nose and then leaned forward into the light so his face at least might be seen. "I am an arms dealer," he said, "not a politician. It would take me years to infiltrate the PLA's nuclear weapons program and even longer to steal what you want from it. It is my understanding that we do not have the luxury of that much time."

Drogo's nostrils flared as if in response to a bad smell. For once, however, he kept his vitriol to himself and looked toward the overlook where Grishka and Carlito were ensconced. "What about you, Rasputin?" he said, in a voice ringing with false comradery. "Although you have been removed from the Motherland's politics for over a century, I am sure you could use your unnatural way with people to slip back into the inner workings of the Politburo. Russia is very well-armed."

Grishka pulled himself to his full, twisted height, an effort that sent pain coursing through his veins like white-hot lumps of lead. He sucked in a breath, imagining the lumps coming to rest in a pool of cool water. Fortified, he then declared. "I would not do such a thing—not even if the Tsarina herself invited me back to the Kremlin."

Several drakes hissed, Drogo loudest of all. "Why not?" he jeered. "Are you afraid that those vodka-addled apelings will try to kill you again?"

Carlito gritted his teeth, half-expecting Grishka react badly to such a cheap shot. But the drake remained unflappable. "My near-assassination was by no means a pleasant experience," he said. "But I would risk a thousand deaths for a worthy plan to secure the next age."

Drogo reared back as if trying to arch his neck. "My plan is perfect!" he snarled. "It is the final solution!"

"It is an offense to the Divine," Grishka countered. "It would turn the whole world into a radioactive wasteland."

"What of it?" Azi Zhahhad said, bounding back to his feet uninvited. "We are immune to radiation. We would survive."

"To what end?" Grishka asked. "The drakena will not reconcile with us if we destroy everything they cherish."

"On the contrary," Drogo said, through a terrible smile. "They will not reconcile with us as long as they remain snug in their human-infested nests. If we take everything away from them, they will have no choice but to start over with us."

"You assume that they will survive your final solution," Grishka said, refusing to back down. "For that, you would need to find a suitable number of them and remove them to a place of safety before Armageddon comes to pass."

"Where does one find drakena?" one of the younger mandrakes wondered. "I have never seen one."

Drogo sneered at the question. Grishka was quick to furnish an answer. "Drakena are secretive by nature and ward their lairs well. They do not mark their hunting grounds, either so they are ridiculously difficult to track down.. And even if you did happen into one—" He paused; the effect was one of stifled amusement. "Drakes stop growing shortly after we sex, but drakena keep on growing until they die. An ancient could be ten times your size. I do not think you could move her if she did not wish to be moved."

"Then she would die," the young mandrake declared, "and the world would be rid of a stubborn old female. I have heard the older ones are no good for breeding anyway."

"If you would destroy that much wisdom simply because you cannot conjugate with it," Grishka said, "then Drogo Channing was right to scorn you for a fool. The old ones know much that would otherwise be lost. The old ones must be preserved!"

To Drogo, he said, "You would exterminate the humans only to become just like them."

To Tezcatlipoca, he said, "Killing drakena offends the Divine. Surely there is some other avenue we can pursue."

"As it happens," Tezcatlipoca said slyly, like a cat with a mouthful of feathers, "I believe there is. What if we did not need to go hunting for drakena?"

The conclave fell silent for a moment as if hit by a stun grenade. An instant later, a fury of rumbling broke out. The Great One encouraged the commotion for a moment, knowing that it spelled the end of Drogo's hopes, and then signaled Carlito with a nod.

As soon as he saw the Great One's cue, Carlito pushed down a lever that he had shielded from Drogo Channing's view with his body. The wall to his rear shuddered and then split down the middle. An instant later, the two halves fell away from each other and the real reason for his shirt-mail came snapping, snarling, and screeching into the grotto. Although they were only the size of wolves, the wyrms were daunting creatures: all claws and teeth and mindless hunger. As they launched themselves toward the cavern's upper reaches, he stood ready with the shock collar controls just in case one or more of them decided to double back and try to make a snack out of him. Grishka shouted glad tidings at them as they went streaking past him.

"How is this possible?" Drogo asked, as he gaped overhead at the swarm. "Where did they come from?"

"Grishka found them in a giant sinkhole that opened up in the Siberian outback a few years ago," Tezcatlipoca said. "They were frozen, of course, but the Divine told him that they might be revived, so he brought them here to me. These are the ones we managed to thaw."

"But to what purpose?" Azi asked, as he swatted at a black-scaled wyrm who had taken a liking to his turban. "They have no control over their forms or their behavior. They do not listen, they will not obey, and they have the attention spans of gnats. Until they sex, they are brainless eating and playing things."

"True," the Great One said, cheerfully conceding the point. "They are of no use to us as they are. But—" His teeth flashed, a sly display. "Imagine if all or at least the majority of them sexed female. Right here. In this compound."

The collective rumbling sheared off into silence as the conclave caught a glimpse of the shiny white light at the end of Tezcatlipoca's tunnel. "Our plan for the sixth age would not hinge on a reconciliation with the drakena," Azi warbled. "We would have our own breeders."

"Breeders who have not tasted the poison of decadence," Drogo said, seemingly intrigued by the idea, "and who have inherited no fondness for humans or their society." He ran his tongue over his teeth and then spit out a false compliment. "A clever strategy, Great One," he said. "But it hinges on them sexing as female. How do you plan to manage that essential and oh so random detail?"

"By eliminating the randomness from the process," Tezcatlipoca said triumphantly. "These wyrms are being treated with high dose female sex hormones."

Grishka started at that, clearly taken aback. But it was Drogo who voiced the gathering's collective consternation. "What? How?"

"I own a bootleg lab in Juarez," the Great One said. "It manufactures designer drugs for my cartel. One of the biochemists in my hire isolated the necessary estrogens from a sample of my blood and learned how to synthesize them. Then he created high-dose hormone patches. The wyrms get a fresh patch every week, which means that they will be feminized long before they start to sex. As a bonus, we should be able to manipulate their hormones post-sexing so we can breed with them more than once an age."

A gamy musk rose up from the grotto floor—the smell of draconic excitement. The only drake who wasn't oozing approval was Grishka.

"Great One," he said, all but twitching beneath his heavy robe. "When we first discussed how we might use this clutch, there was no mention of trying to sway its sexual orientation with man-made hormones. That is not natural. That is not our way."

"Nothing will change if we do not dare to try things that we have not considered before," Tezcatlipoca replied. "And I, for one, am weary beyond measure of stumbling around on two legs with no tail for balance. If we do not go this way, then we must go Drogo's way. These are the only two options available to us."

Grishka sighed—a loud, steamy exhalation. "Both options have a human stink to them," he said. "But if I must embrace one or the other, then I will hold firm with the wyrms. But mark my words, Great One: The Divine is uneasy. This is a perilous path."

"As are all paths leading into the unknown," Tezcatlipoca said, and then bared his teeth as one of the wryms let out a peevish honk. "The young ones grow hungry. I do, too. I propose we pause to feed and then reconvene later to make our final decision. Does anyone object?"

"No indeed," Drogo said, hoisting himself to his feet with gusto. "Important decisions should never be made on an empty stomach. What are you serving?"

"Mexicans," the great drake said, and then signaled once again. Carlito rang an old dinner bell. In response to the mission-like clang, the wyrms beat an eager retreat for their holding pen and the supper that was waiting for them there. As Carlito closed the gate behind them. Grishka shook his shaggy head and said, "This is not how it was supposed to be, Carlito. I fear no good will come of it."

Carlito made no reply. What reassurance could he offer that a drake would want to hear?

CHAPTER 2

ROSALYN

Rosalyn Vanderbilt and her gang of three were strolling down Grant Street in Chinatown on their way to a late lunch. The sidewalk was a mass of bodies in motion, locals and tourists all doing their best not to make contact of any kind with one another. The locals were sensibly clad in jeans and jackets. The tourists were wearing shorts and tees and sun-screen. One blue-lipped young woman in a barely-there halter-top provoked a sympathetic wince from Roz's best friend, Mara.

"I went to San Francisco," she said, as if she were reading a tourist-bait tee-shirt, "and all I got was hypothermia."

Mara's husband, Max, draped his arm across her shoulders and then spouted a quote that was commonly attributed to Mark Twain. "The coldest winter I ever spent was a summer in San Francisco."

"Oh, come on, you guys. It's not that cold," Roz said, and then gestured at a nearby bank LED display. "Look, sixty-four degrees. That's practically balmy!"

At that, her boyfriend broke into a full-throated song-and-dance routine. "We're having a heat wave, a tropical heat wave. The temperature's rising, it isn't surprising. She certainly can can-can!"

"Aldo," Roz said, *sotto voce*, "not now, OK?"

He ignored her like he usually did when he was showing off. "She started the heat wave by letting her seat wave," he sang, pointing Rosalyn's ass out to leery Asian passersby. "And in such a way, that customers say, she certainly can can-can. Gee, her anatomy makes the mercury jump to—sixty-four!"

Mara rolled her eyes at Aldo's theatrics and muttered something under her breath. Max gave her a discreet, don't-start nudge and then skidded to a stop in front of a window brimming with discount electronics. "Holy crapola," he said. "They're practically giving Wiis away. Look! We paid almost double that for ours."

"That's because you had to have it the same day it hit the stores," Mara said, in a tone as arch as her eyebrow. "Two hundred percent mark-up be damned."

Max's dark eyes went wide with disbelief. "You're going to hang that on me? Really? You're the one who's been hinting around for a Wii U for Christmas! And that system hasn't even been released yet!"

"Geeks," Aldo sneered, as he admired his reflection in the window.

Roz reached out as if to drape an arm around his neck, meaning to give the backside of his head a mind-your-manners flick. Before she could make contact, though, the enormous TV that was on display inside the store distracted her. The black-and-white image on the screen was of a span of water that featured a fuzzy serpentine jut in the background. The accompanying caption read: New Loch Ness Monster Sighting?

Roz whirled to face her friends and crooned, "Who's up for a road trip to Scotland? I so want to see Nessie firsthand."

Aldo laughed and then snaked in to give her a closed-mouth kiss. "I love that about you," he said afterward. "I really do."

"What's that?" she wanted to know, linking arms with him as they started down the walk again.

"You still believe in monsters," he said in a marveling tone. "At your age, in this century, with satellites and Google drones mining the darkest places of the world for the last of its secrets, you still think there's such a thing as a Loch Ness Monster. That's fucking adorable."

If anyone else had damned her with such fluffy praise, Roz would've taken umbrage. But since it had come from Aldo, she took it as a compliment. The love of your life was supposed to find you adorable, right? That was one of the rules of romance—and Aldo Whimsey Baker had a romantic streak in him a half-mile wide. He was also an actor, so a certain amount of hyperbole was to be expected. Complimentary or not, though, she was not about to let the discussion end on that note.

C'mon," she cajoled. "How can you deny the possibility that there might be something in that lake that mankind hasn't discovered yet? You saw the image."

"All I saw was a tree branch sticking out of the water," he said.

"What about you guys?" she said to Max and Mara. "What did you think it was?"

"I saw a blob of pixelated fuzz," Max said. "It could've been anything: a tree branch, an elephant's trunk."

Mara sneered. "An elephant's trunk? Seriously, Max?"

Max held up his hands as if to ward off her scorn and said, "Hey, it was an honest-to-God theory back in the '30s. Look it up."

His wife dissed him again with a haughty toss of her head and then joined forces with her best friend. "Well, I'm with Roz," she said. "I saw a long, S-shaped neck with an angular jut of a head. It looked reptilian, possibly saurian. That's the Loch Ness monster in a nutshell."

"Mara says nutshell, I say just plain nuts," Aldo quipped, and then pressed a hand to his moderately chiseled abs. "Speaking of which, is anyone besides me hungry?"

Resentment rippled through Roz like a sonar ping, lighting up all sorts of sore spots. OK, so he didn't enjoy speculative banter like she, Max, and Mara did—he'd made that clear early on in their relationship. But he could at least play along once in a blue moon just to make her happy. Yet even as she bristled, an inner voice leapt to his defense. It wasn't his fault. He'd been raised on a steady diet of movies and television whereas she'd grown up at science fiction and fantasy conventions, events where people of all ages stayed up till the witching hour talking about things like Cthulhu versus Godzilla: Who Would Win and Why. This wasn't him being selfish. This was cultures clashing. As they grew closer and their worlds merged, that conflict would disappear.

"I'm starving," she said, resolving to be more patient. "Do you want to see if we can get seated early? Mom won't mind us getting a head-start as long as we pre-order some pot-stickers for her."

"I could eat," Max said, and then half-turned to solicit Mara's vote only to realize that she was no longer by his side. "Uh-oh," he said, tracking her back to a storefront that they had left in their wake. "We're screwed. She made the jump to shopping mode."

A half-block downstream, Mara was standing in the middle of the sidewalk and waving for Roz's attention with the enthusiasm of a kid on Christmas morning. "C'mere!" she shouted, indifferent to the scowls she was drawing from passing strangers. "You have to see this!"

"Don't," Aldo said—half-plea and half-command. But before he could turn their linked arms into an arm-lock, Roz was off, weaving her way through oncoming foot-traffic like a star running back. She passed a jasmine-scented tea shop, the mouth of a graffiti-scrawled alleyway, and a two-for-ten tee-shirt shack—all Chinatown classics. The next store was a standard, too: a gift shop that sold faux Ming vases, jade Buddhas, cloisonné, and other touristy objects d'art. A statue of a Chinese dragon guarded the shop's brass-belled door. It stood at least seven-foot tall, and had been rendered in painstaking detail from its horned head and lion-like mane to the tip of its tufted tail. Even its hooded eyes seemed to gleam from within.

"Oh my God," Roz said. "Mom would love this."

"I know, right?" Mara said, gloating over her discovery.

The dragon's bronze scales glistened in the midday sun—an invitation to touch. But even as Roz stretched her hand toward the bow of its belly, someone swatted her hand away and said, "What, you stupid? Sign say, 'Don't touch!' That mean you."

"Sorry," Roz said, as she tried to rub the sting from her knuckles. "I didn't see the sign." Then she got her first look at the woman who was chastising her and blurted, "Whoa."

She towered over Roz by at least a foot and was built like a rugby player: lots of muscle, a bit of a gut, and a tree stump for a neck. Her face was long and narrow, with wide-set, slightly protruding eyes, a pug nose, and a thin, almost lipless mouth. The shock of coarse black hair that she wore long and down gave her a horsey appearance. Although Roz was sure that she'd never met the woman, she was equally certain that she knew her from somewhere. And the odd thing was, the woman seemed to feel the same way.

"You know Naga?" she said, returning Roz's searching look. "You—dragon people?"

Ah, that explained the feeling of deja vu. The woman must be a fan of her mother's work. Roz had probably bumped into her at a signing or convention. Fleeting or not, an encounter with a giant like Naga would've made a subliminal impression.

"Sorry," she said, "you must be thinking of my mom. She'd love this statue, by the way. How much is it?"

The woman narrowed her eyes as if she were trying to see through Roz and then loosed a dismissive snort. "For sale only to dragon people," she said. "You bring mama to Naga, we talk."

"Not likely," Roz said. "Mom doesn't like to—"

'Shop', she was about to say. But before she could get the word out, Aldo came barging up the sidewalk looking like he'd been sucking lemons for the last five minutes. "I thought you said you were starving," he said, without excusing himself to her or Naga. "If you don't wrap up this little gab-fest right this instant, Max and I are going to leave for the restaurant without you."

Naga snorted, a gust of disdain. Aldo refused to acknowledge her in any way and instead honed his churlish glare on Roz. "Well?" he asked. "Are you coming or not?"

"Lead the way, darling," she said, gesturing broadly. "Mara and I are right behind you." Then, as he set off in a huff, she shared a helpless shrug with Naga. "What's a girl to do? He gets cranky when his blood sugar drops." Then she offered an elbow to Mara and said, "Shall we?"

Once again, Naga laid hands on her, this time clutching her by the round of a shoulder. When Roz tried to pull away, the woman tightened her grip to the point of pain and then leaned in close. "You bring mama to Naga," she said. Her breath smelled of jasmine and fruit tobacco. Her skin smelled of smoke. She inhaled deeply as if savoring Roz's perfume and then added, "I want talk with her."

"You let go of me right now," Roz replied, in a tone that was both soft and fierce, "or the next person you'll be talking to is the ambulance guy who will be asking you which hospital you want to go to."

An amused smile spread across Naga's flat-line of a mouth like a crack in thin ice. An instant later, she swooped in and brushed cheeks with Roz. "Naga is not the enemy, little one," she purred, as she withdrew again. "Remember this."

An instant later, she was gone. The clamor of shop-door bells celebrated her departure.

"Jesus," Mara said, as she and Roz hastened to catch up with their men. "Did she hurt you?"

"Not really," Roz said, rubbing her shoulder where Naga had gripped it. "But I have the feeling that she could have snapped me in half if she had been so inclined. No way she's getting anywhere near Mom."

They rejoined Aldo and Max, but Aldo was still miffed at Roz for keeping him waiting so he gave her the silent treatment all the way to the restaurant. Roz made no effort to jolly him out of his snit. She was too busy thinking about Naga. Nothing about the woman struck Roz as particularly fannish—and she had met enough of her mother's fans to recognize the type. But if she wasn't a fan, then why was she so keen on seeing Aurora? And what had she meant by, 'I am not the enemy?'

"Oh, yay! You're just getting here, too!"

Roz started out of her thoughts to see her mother striding across the marble-floored lobby. She looked both windblown and pleased.

"I kept telling Elizabeth that I had to go," she said, as she closed in on the group, "and she kept saying, 'Just one more thing.' I was certain I was going to find you upstairs at a table littered with half-empty dishes."

She group-hugged Mara and Max, nodded curtly at Aldo in passing, and then gathered Roz into her arms. In mid-embrace, she sniffed at Roz's neck. Roz reared back and snapped, "Why'd you do that?"

"I like the perfume you're wearing," Aurora said, looking at Roz as if she had grown an extra head. "What's it called?"

"'Flight,'" Roz said, embarrassed she had been so easily spooked.

The elevator opened with a ding, inviting everybody to step inside. Six floors later, they arrived at The Empress of China Roof Garden Restaurant. As they spilled out of the elevator, a wizened, red-jacketed waiter came shuffling toward them, collecting an armful of menus on the way. When Aurora greeted him in Mandarin, he broke into a gummy smile and then gestured for the group to follow him.

The dining room was a study in contrasts: opulent Han Dynasty décor and threadbare carpets; silver service and greasy, take-out smells. "Honestly, Aurora," Aldo said, as he trailed after her. "I don't know why you're so fond of this place. It may have been a celebrity hot-spot back in the sixties, but now it's just a rundown tourist trap."

"I'll admit, the old girl isn't as grand as she used to be," Aurora said. "But Duncan and I used to come here all the time when we were first married, so the Empress will always have a sweet spot in my heart."

The waiter brought them to a table in the center of the room. The wall next to them was all window. On a foggy day, diners might only be able to see a smattering of buildings and Coit Tower's old-fashioned fire-nozzle profile from this vantage point. But on a clear day like today, even the vision-impaired could see all the way to the bay. Aurora allowed herself to be seated at the head of the table. Mara sat to her left; Roz, to her right; the men settled down next to their respective partners.

"I already know what I'm having!" Roz declared, and tossed her menu aside. Then, as the rest of the table began thumbing through the selections, she turned to her mom and said, "So was it a productive meeting?"

"I guess that depends on your definition of 'productive'," Aurora said, with a weary smile that made her look more middle-aged than usual. "She did manage to talk me into a mini-tour."

"Local?"

"Regional," Aurora said, and then took a sip of freshly-brewed oolong tea. The fragrant steam seemed to rejuvenate her. "I told her I'd get the new book out sooner if I just stayed home and worked, but she wouldn't have it. 'Readers are fickle', she said. 'They need to be reminded that you're still around.'"

Roz made a sympathetic face. "No fans, no Ferrari."

The quip caught Aldo's ear. He leaned into their space and said, "What's this, Aurora? You're getting a Ferrari? Sweet! I always thought that Lexus of yours was a little hokey." Roz kicked him under the table. At the same time, Aurora fixed him with a blasé version of the evil eye. "Not that there's anything wrong with hokey," he hastened to add. "It's just not very sexy." Roz kicked him again. "I mean glamorous." A third boot toe to the shin ensued. He shot Roz a bug-eyed threat display and then blurted, "C'mon, it's a pink sedan. You can't get any more Mary Kay than that!"

"And what, besides my daughter's car, do you drive?" Aurora asked, a concisely worded query that might have passed for polite under different circumstances.

"As it happens," he said loftily, "I'm between vehicles at the moment."

"It's weird how quiet it is in here, isn't it?" Roz said, trying to engage Mara and Max in loud conversation before her mother could press her attack on Aldo. "Most restaurants pump in music to cover up eating noises and the blank spaces in the table-talk."

"I know, right?" Mara said gamely enough. "Would you say that's passive or aggressive? What do you think, Max?"

"I think I'm going to get the braised tofu," he replied, glancing from her to the menu and back again. "What about you?"

As if on cue, their waiter reappeared to take their order. His arrival seemed to sweeten everyone's mood. "Lunch is on me," Aurora announced, "so get what you want. And let's start with some pot stickers, shall we?"

As soon as the waiter shuffled off again, Aurora leaned toward Max and said, "So how's the new job? Do you like working for a start-up?"

"Well," Max replied, "I'm not crazy about the hours. But the work is super-interesting."

"I hear the pay is pretty good, too," Aldo said.

Mara snorted. "He doesn't care about the money. He'd work for free if the idea at hand tickled his fancy." She reached over and pinched a fleck of napkin fuzz from her husband's dark, neatly trimmed beard. Afterward, she added, "I think he was an alchemist in a former life. I can see him locked away in a castle turret, trying to change lead into gold by candlelight."

"Me, too!" Roz said, and then roped Aurora back into the conversation with a grin. "His nickname in high school was Mr. Wizard."

Aldo laughed. "High school kids can be so mean."

"Actually," Max said, "I thought that was an awesome nickname. I even had a tee-shirt made with that printed across the front. I still have it somewhere."

"If it still fit," Mara said as an aside to Roz, "he'd still be wearing it."

"What about you, Mara?" Aurora asked, happy for the chance to grill her 'con-kids'. "How's business?"

"Terrible," Mara said, taking a sip of tea as if to rinse the bitterness from her mouth. "In this economy, there's not much of a market for custom-made costumes. If it weren't for Max,

I'd have to shut down my website and get a regular job."

"If you ever get to the point where you're seriously thinking of packing it up," Aurora said, "talk to me first and we'll work something out because losing you to the mainstream fashionistas would be a tragedy of the first order. You're not just ridiculously talented. You have vision. The Lady DragonJoy gown that I saw on your website not too long ago was perfect down to the last stitch."

Mara fanned a hand in front of her face as if she were trying to cool herself down. "Oh," she said, fanning herself with a fluttery hand, "why thank you. Thank you very much."

The waiter appeared the first course: a cauldron of hot and sour soup. "Look, Mom," Roz said, pointing to the steam rising from the bowl. "Dragon's breath!" It was an inside joke, a reference to a moment they had shared long ago. "Remember?"

Aurora responded with a nostalgic sigh that survived a surly, "I don't get it," from Aldo. "We were at our cottage on Lake Siskiyou at the time," she said, in a tone as dreamy as her look. "Roz had just finished reading my first Esmerelda novel and was suddenly a dragon fanatic. 'I want one, Mommy,' she kept saying. 'I want my own dragon friend.' I didn't have the heart to tell her that there was no such thing as dragons, so I made up a story instead. I said that dragons were very, very particular about their friends and searched all over the world for the one person they liked more than anyone else. I told her that all she could do was watch and wait and try to be the best little girl she could be. She scrunched up her face as if she suspected me of trying to trick her into being good, but then nodded decisively and said, 'OK, Mommy. If that's what it takes.' I congratulated myself on a parenting job well done and thought no more about it. The next morning, as I was getting ready to go for my daily walk around the lake, Roz announced that she was going with me. I was surprised because she wasn't exactly an early bird, but glad, too, because I'd been bugging her to spend a little more time in motion. So off we went—out of the cottage and toward the trail. The morning was warm and still. Tendrils of fog were rising up from the lake. Suddenly, Roz let out a gasp and tugged on the hem of my sweatshirt. 'Mommy, look!' she whispered. 'What is it?' I asked, thinking she'd seen a snake. She pointed at the fog and said, "Dragon breath! A dragon is watching me!"

Everyone at the table chuckled at the tale. "And the funny thing is," Aldo said afterward, "she hasn't changed a bit." To Aurora, he said, "She wants to go kiting off to Scotland in search of the Loch Ness Monster."

"Really?" Aurora asked, casting a curious glance at her daughter.

Roz shot Aldo a scalding look—possibly for outing her, possibly for making her sound like a flake in the process. But the expression she turned on her mother was level. "Why not?" she said. "There's a new image of Nessie going around these days and it looks real enough to me. If it's been seen once, it can be seen again—and I'm just the girl to do it."

Aurora peered at Aldo as if she were about to thank him for bringing such madness to her attention, but then returned her gaze to Roz. "Sounds like fun to me," she said. "While you're in the area, keep an eye out for long-lost relatives. Your father's mother's family used to live in the highlands around Inverness, you know."

"Why don't you come with me?" Roz said, voicing the idea even as it popped into her head. "We could do research for a new book. Ezzie and Francine could learn about bagpipes. And haggis! We'd have a blast."

"We would indeed," Aurora agreed, as she stirred the soup that the waiter had set in front of her. "But as I mentioned earlier, I just agreed to do a series of appearances. I also just started working on a new book so it's too soon to begin researching the next one." When Roz implored her with her best, please-Mommy look, she shook her head and said, "Sorry, sweetie. Not this time."

"What about you?" Roz asked, catching Aldo's eye. The idea of going to Scotland had her in its teeth and wouldn't let go. "Come adventuring with me!" When he balked, startled by the impetuous offer, she felt compelled to sweeten it. "It'll be my treat." Aurora coughed up a bit of hot and sour at that, but Roz ignored the maternal reproach and upped the ante again. "We can hike the highlands and golf in Edinburgh and maybe catch some of the Festival. It'll be that romantic getaway we've been talking about." When he continued to stall, she made one last appeal. "Do this with me and I'll wear that Princess Leia costume that you've been bugging me about for Halloween."

"Oh, dear God," Mara muttered, and hung her head as if she were suddenly in pain or in mourning. Max rubbed her back as if in consolation while Aurora scowled at her soup bowl. The only one who looked pleased was Aldo.

"As it happens," he said, "I'm between engagements at the moment. And as it happens, I've never been to Scotland. So I would be most honored to accompany you to the land of your ancestors, lovely lady."

Roz sprung to her feet with a delighted squeal and then flung herself at him. "This. Is. So. Awesome!" she said, punctuating each word with a kiss. "We're going to have so much fun."

"That we are, milady," he said, basking in the attention. "That we are."

Roz spent the rest of lunch in an excited daze. Holy shit! She was going to Scotland! She didn't know why she was so thrilled, exactly. As a child, she had traveled all over the world with

Aurora. As an adult, she'd done her fair share of adventuring on her own. It was just that this trip felt so right. Maybe it was because she was, as Aldo said, returning the land of her ancestors. Or maybe it was because he had agreed to go with her. She'd never gone away with a boyfriend for more than a long weekend. When asked why, she used to say that men were like fish: after three days, they started to smell. But Aldo was different. Aldo's scent made her heart race.

"Roz?" Aurora asked. "Do you want something else to eat?"

The query was pointed enough to penetrate her happy little bubble, but not sharp enough to wound. She returned to the here-and-now with no hard feelings. "Thanks," she said, "but I'm about ready to pop." Then, as her mother handed her credit card off to the waiter, she added, "Do you have something else on your dance card this afternoon? Or can you bop around the city with us?"

"I'm going home," Aurora said. "There's a story fragment banging around in my brain that needs to come out before it gives me a headache."

"Do you really get headaches if you don't write?" Mara asked, ever and always curious about her favorite author's process.

One corner of Aurora's mouth quirked upward: affection for Mara's literal-mindedness. "It's not as simple as all that," she said. "Although at times it does feel like an idea is pressuring me for release. For the most part, however, I find pent-up ideas distracting. All I want to do is think about them, play with them, dress them up or down until they look just right. When I'm in that kind of head-space, I do stupid things like leave my glasses in the mailbox, wash reds with whites, and leave doors open at night so raccoons can get into the house. Doing stuff like that makes me cranky. And that's what gives me a headache."

45

Aldo leaned toward Max to share a chuckle. "I heard about the raccoons," he said. "They ransacked the pantry and then tossed the sitting room—all while Aurora was working in the next room. It took her and Roz days to clean up the mess."

"Sounds dreadful," Max said, with a fastidious scowl.

"It was," Aurora said, as she signed the credit card receipt. "So perhaps you can see why I like to empty out my head as soon as my Muse calls." She got up. The rest of the table followed suit, voicing their appreciation for lunch as they rose. "Thank you for the company," she replied, and then latched on to one of her daughter's forearms with foreboding firmness. "Would you mind walking me to my car?" she said, as they strode toward the elevator. "It's parked just a few blocks from here in the Portsmouth Square garage on Kearny."

"Sure," Roz said, trying to sound chipper even though she had no doubt that her mother meant to drag her out of earshot of her friends at some point and lambast her for the taking-Aldo-to-Scotland thing. "We can cut through the park."

"Maybe we'll catch some of the old guard practicing tai chi," Mara said, oblivious to the tension between Roz and Aurora. "I've always wanted to try that. It looks so serene."

The elevator dropped them in the lobby. There, Aldo stopped to check out the wall of old black and white photos—headshots of dignitaries who had dined at the Empress of China back in its prime. "Hey," he said, "check it out! Clint Eastwood was here. I ran into him at the Monterey Jazz Fest a few years ago. Did you know that he plays piano? I tickle the ivories a little, too."

Roz wasn't listening. She was too busy anticipating the argument she was about to have with her mother. It was one they had had several times already. 'I just don't see what you see in him,' Aurora would say. Roz would reply, 'I know, and you refuse to even try!' Aurora would follow with either, 'He's just using you,' or 'He's shallower than a Serengeti mud puddle in the summertime.' And Roz would say—

Someone bumped into her, jarring her out of her thoughts. She looked up to see an old Chinese lady glaring at her over her shoulder as she shuffled down the sidewalk. Only then did she realize that her group had relocated to the street and she was blocking the flow of foot-traffic.

"Sorry!" she called after the woman, only to be slammed from behind again. At the same time, she felt her purse being ripped out of her hand. The thief was a young Asian man, and damned fast on his feet. By the time Roz processed what was happening, he was halfway down the street. "Hey!" she shouted then, to the public at large. "Stop that guy! He stole my purse!" When no one made a move to help, she swore under her breath and took off after the perp. Over her shoulder, she said, "Max, call the cops!"

"Dammit, Roz!" Aldo shouted after her. "Don't be stupid!"

She couldn't see the thief anymore, but he had left a daisy-chain of jostled people in his wake—an easy trail to follow. It led her past a dingy blur of storefronts and into the mouth of an alleyway. There, she stopped to catch her breath and appraise the situation. The alley was dimly lit, a squalid communal outlet lined with back doors and graffiti-scrawled dumpsters. All of the entry level entryways were barred and locked. None of the fire escapes had been accessed. Either the thief had used the lane as a shortcut and was long gone or—he was hiding behind one of the dumpsters.

It never occurred to her to not look.

As she prowled toward the first garbage bin, the smells of frying garlic and plum sauce that had followed her in from the street gave way to a miasma of rotting vegetables and urine. Litter and broken glass added texture to the floating stench. She rounded the far side of the first dumpster ready to do battle only to find no one there. She rounded the second in the same state of readiness only to be disappointed again. An adamant inner voice that sounded a lot like Aldo declared the thief out-of-here and urged her to quit this hare-brained chase before she stepped in something unspeakable. But even though she supposed the voice was right, she couldn't stop herself from looking behind the third dumpster. There, she found a twenty-something Asian woman crouched in the shadows. She was wearing the thief's clothes and rifling through Roz's purse. She seemed as surprised to see Roz as Roz was to see her.

"I believe that's mine," Roz said, gesturing at the wallet in the thief's hand. "Give it back right now and we can leave the cops out of this."

The woman dropped the wallet onto the ground and then rose out of her crouch like a flowering tea blossom. She had pretty eyes and a kittenish jawline, broad shoulders, small breasts, and narrow hips. Roz forgave herself for mistaking her for a man from behind.

"You should not have come here," the woman said, in soft, southeastern-Asian-flavored English. "This is not a place for tourists." She pulled a flip-knife from the back pocket of her faded, low-rise blue jeans. "This is a place where tourists get hurt." She snapped the blade open with a practiced crack of her fine-boned wrist. "Go home while you still can."

"Not without my stuff," Roz said, and then shifted into the fighting stance that she had learned while her mother was researching self-defense techniques for her third Ezzie and Francine book. Aurora had only studied the Dragon Form long enough to get a feel for the moves, but Roz had taken classes for three years and still practiced regularly.

"You were warned," the thief said, and then lunged, thrusting the knife at Roz's midsection.

Roz stepped back to her right, and then used the Dragon's Tail—both arms sweeping in parallel to the left—to knock her attacker off-balance. But the thief was quicker on her feet than Roz anticipated and so instead of falling to the ground, she merely stumbled.

"Lucky," she said, as she positioned herself to menace Roz again.

"Not really," Roz said, and then had to jump back as the thief rushed her. She thought she had cleared the accompanying knife stroke cleanly, but the sound of tearing fabric told her otherwise. She glanced at her left biceps and caught a glimpse of the tattoo that spanned the length of her arm. "Shit!" she said. "This was my favorite jacket. That's going to cost you, bitch."

The thief sneered. Roz responded with Dragon Feints, a three-step rope-a-dope move that tricked the thief into leaving herself open to a round-house kick to the solar plexus. The force of that blow drove the air from her lungs. As she stumbled backward, trying to catch her breath, Roz swept her legs out from under her with Dragon Drop. Roz meant to kick the knife out of the thief's hand as she hit the ground but she bounced funny and Roz wound up kicking her in the groin instead. The thief curled up like a shrimp on a super-hot skillet.

"Chhke nhi," she hissed through gritted teeth. "It's just a purse."

"You were ready to kill for it," Roz said, gliding back in ready position. "What makes you think you'd be the only one?"

"It's just a purse!" the thief said again.

"Maybe to you," Roz said. "What did you take from it?"

"Nothing."

"Really?" Roz said. "Empty your pockets."

The thief rolled onto her back and turned both of her pants pockets inside out at the same time, a defiant gesture. A smattering of loose change hit the ground along with a crumpled tissue. "Happy?"

"Not yet," Roz said. "Your hoodie has a pocket, too."

The thief's eyes narrowed into sullen slits, but she sat up in one fluid motion and then made a show of cleaning out the hoodie's pouch. She extracted a baggy of what looked like marijuana shake, then a set of keys, a cylinder of lip balm, and a credit card. As she flipped the card at Roz's feet, she did a reasonable job of palming something else. If Roz hadn't been on the look-out for some kind of funny business, she would've missed the sleight of hand.

"Nice try," she said, "but no cigar. Hand it over."

"You are quicker than you look," the thief remarked, and then added Roz's driver's license to the hodgepodge of surrendered items. "Now what?"

"Take off your pants," Roz said.

"What?" the thief blurted, shifting from snotty to shocked in the span of a blink. "Why?"

"Do it and I'll call us even," Roz said. "Refuse and I'll call the police." When the thief snuck a peek at the far end of the alley, obviously calculating her chances of escape, Roz added, "Try to run and I'll treat you to a real ass-kicking and then call the cops."

The thief scowled at Roz's well-worn boots and then dragged a dirty sleeve across her pretty mouth. "Please," she said. "There's something you don't know."

"I don't doubt it," Roz said, "and I don't care. You pick: pants or police. The pants option goes away in thirty seconds." She pulled the cell phone out of her back pocket and tapped the '9'. "Twenty seconds. I'll even let you stand up so you don't have to drag your ass across the garbage-crusted asphalt."

"Do not—make me do this," the thief said, baring her teeth in a desperate snarl. "You do not know what you're asking."

"Fifteen seconds," Roz said, and tapped a '1'. "Did I mention that I have a friend on the SFPD? If I ask, he'll lose your paperwork and you'll spend the whole weekend in a holding cell." The thief continued to scowl at her, a laser-tight glare brimming with resentment and fear. Roz dismissed the look with a shrug and said, "Ten seconds. I hope you like Friday night drunks puking all over you." Then, as she went to tap in the last '1', the thief shot to her feet as if spring-loaded.

In one angry, fluid motion, she undid her belt and shoved her jeans to the ground. An instant later, she jerked her hoodie down to hide her pretty pink panties— but not before Roz caught a glimpse of a distinctive bulge. She blinked. Her jaw dropped.

"Holy shit," she said, locking eyes with the thief. "You really are a dude."

"Chkke nhi," he snarled, and then bolted. Roz let him go, but didn't shift out of her fighting stance until she was sure he was truly gone and not coming back. As she relaxed, she gave her head a go-figure shake.

"Now that's a first," she said, and wondered what Aurora would say about this odd little adventure.

The thought of her mother conjured an image: Aurora standing in front of the Empress of China, gnawing at her lower lip as she tried to see past the chaotic parade of foot-traffic. Aldo loomed to one side of her, and sported a thunderhead scowl. The vision sent Roz scurrying after her scattered belongings. She stuffed everything into her bag willy-nilly, and then seized the thief's knife and the bag of marijuana, too, because you never knew when one or the other or both might come in handy. Then she folded his jeans and set them on top of a stray plastic bag along with the keychain and loose change.

"Why you take pants if you no want?"

The hair on the back of Roz's neck bristled, a primal reproach for letting her guard down in an unsecured place.

51

She straightened out of her crouch with feigned nonchalance and then pivoted to face her questioner. Although some part of her had recognized the soft, slightly sibilant voice, she was still surprised to see Naga standing tall in the shadows. Her all-too-substantial presence felt imposing rather than threatening, but her shaded expression gave nothing away.

"You were watching?" Roz asked, trying to figure out if she should be alarmed or not.

Naga nodded, a bare-boned acknowledgment. Roz decided to respond in kind.

"He stole from me," she said. "Such things should not go unpunished."

"Just so," Naga said, nostrils flaring as if in response to a savory smell. "But that was 'she', not 'he'."

"Maybe to the casual observer," Roz fired back. "But trust me, I had a better view. That thief was definitely a dude."

"Only outside," Naga said, waving a long-nailed hand in front of her torso. "Inside, she female. Inside more important than outside."

"Very liberal of you, I'm sure," Roz said, capping the conversation simply because she didn't want to chat about the nature of transsexualism with a complete and rather daunting stranger in the middle of a squalid Chinatown alley. "But the bottom line is: he, she, or it, a thief is a thief is a thief. And I don't take kindly to people stealing from me."

Naga responded with a congested rumble that could have been a chuckle or the beginnings of a smoker's cough. "I like you, little one," she said, "You have strong heart. What is that on your arm?"

Roz made a sour face. "It used to be a jacket. Now I guess you could call it a rag."

Naga scowled—a forbidding expression. "I do not like you

that much, so desist with the impudence and show me what you have inked onto your skin."

An almost overwhelming urge to tear the ruined sleeve off seized Roz. It was all she could do to push the material up instead and angle the tattoo in Naga's direction. "Six hours of hell," she said, "and a fifth of tequila. My mother was furious when she saw it."

"What mother would not be?" Naga said, trading her scowl for something softer as she admired the exquisitely detailed dragon tatt. "Yet it is beautiful work, and very telling." She reached into her jacket and pulled out a packet. "Drink this," she said, and tossed the packet at Roz. Roz snatched it out of the air. "Then come see Naga again."

The first thought that popped into Roz's head was: yeah, right. But before she could get the words out, Naga turned away and disappeared through a door that Roz hadn't noticed when she first set foot in the alley. She gaped at the entryway for a long moment, thinking whiskey tango foxtrot, then stuffed the packet in her purse and headed back the way she had come.

True to her vision, Roz found her mother fretting outside of the Empress of China building. Mara was at her elbow, chattering like a squirrel on methamphetamine. "See?" she said, as Roz came striding up to them. "Here she is, looking none the worse for wear."

Aurora gave her daughter a critical once-over, checking for damage. When she saw the slashed sleeve, the color drained from her cheeks and pooled in her neck. "Are you OK?" she asked, probing the tear for traces of blood. "Should we call an ambulance?"

"I'm fine, Mom," Roz assured her. "There's not a scratch on me—thanks to the Dragon Form."

"Seriously?" Mara asked, displaying relish where Aurora

showed only relief. "You got into it?"

"Kicked his ass," Roz said, admiring her fingernails. "And got my stuff back." Then, realizing that she was only posturing for half of her party, she glanced up and down the street for Aldo and Max. When she didn't see either of them, she asked after them.

"Max went looking for a cop," Aurora said. "Aldo went looking for you—or so he said. My guess is that he's hiding in some nearby tee-shirt shack waiting for the KNTV news truck to pull up. As soon as he sees a camera, he'll come waltzing out with every hair in place and a harrowing, almost-had-him tale to tell."

Mara snorted and then shot Roz an apologetic look that wasn't even close to sincere. Roz made a mock-sour face and shook a finger at her two favorite women. "You guys need to cut him a little slack," she said. "Not every man has the temperament to be a hero, you know."

"I don't expect Aldo to pull children from burning buildings or disarm dirty bombs in his spare time," Aurora said. "I don't expect him to work with HIV patients or the homeless, either. I do, however, expect him to treat you with decency and respect—and not just when the doing suits him."

Roz started to defend Aldo's behavior only to be cut off by a buzz from her cell. She fished the phone out of her back pocket and then broke into a vindicated smirk when she saw who was calling. "Oh, look," she said, flashing the number, "it's Aldo—no doubt calling to see if I'm OK. Is that decent enough for you?"

"Hey, babe," she said, deliberately taking the call in their presence, "thanks for checking in. I'm fine—not a hair out of place. I got my stuff back, too. Me and Mom and Mara are hanging out in front of the Empress of China, waiting for you and Max to return. Oh, wait—here's Max now. Where are you?"

"My agent pinged me a few minutes ago with word of an audition," he said, "so I'm in a taxi on my way to Fort Mason. Good news about you getting your stuff back. I knew you would, that's just who you are."

"Thanks for the vote of confidence," she said, trying to sound chipper despite the irritation that was crackling in her back-brain. "Do you have any idea how long you're going to be?"

"Not a clue," he said. "And it's a closed audition so I can't invite you to come and watch. You'll just have to try and have fun without me. Call you later, OK?"

"OK." The line went dead then, but Roz continued to hold the phone to her ear. After a moment's pause, she cocked her head and said, "No. Absolutely not. There's no need to ditch the audition. I'm fine. Really. Go. Break a leg, knock 'em dead, or whatever it is that you theater types say. Yes, I love you, too. Bye." As she slipped the phone back into her pocket, she offered her modified gang of three a stoic shrug and said, "Looks like it's just us. His agent got him an audition."

"Sorry," Mara said, trying to sound earnest. "But I guess that's the way show business works."

"It's for the best, actually," Roz said, rubbing the spot just above the bridge of her nose. "Because now that the thrill of the chase is wearing off, I'm getting a headache that promises to be monstrous."

"MSG and adrenaline," Max said. "Bad combination."

"No shit," Roz said ruefully. "If you guys don't mind, I'm going to take a rain-check on the rest of the afternoon and catch a ride home with Mom."

Mara closed in immediately for a parting embrace. "We don't mind at all, sweetie. You need to get horizontal in a dark room ASAP."

"Feel better soon," Max said, as he delivered his hug. "We'll call tomorrow."

They extended their farewells to Aurora, too, and then merged with the foot-traffic. As they bobbed out of sight, Aurora arched a dubious eyebrow at Roz and said, "Are you sure the problem is MSG?"

"What else would it be?" Roz replied irritably.

Aurora shrugged, conceding the conversation but nothing else. Then she shouldered her purse and started toward the parking garage. Roz followed in sullen silence, kicking thoughts around in her head like stones. *I'm in a taxi heading to Fort Mason.* Would it have killed him to call before he got in the cab and at least pretend to be a little worried about her? She could've gotten lost or hurt—or hell, even killed. Her mother was right. The only one he really cared about was himself. And if he thought she was going to pay his way to Scotland, he had another think coming. The whole idea of Scotland left a sour taste in her mouth now. If she wanted to see a monster, all she had to do was look at a head-shot of Aldo. Forget Scotland. She'd go adventuring elsewhere—Morocco maybe, or maybe Cancun.

Just try and have to have fun without me.

Watch me, asshole.

By the time Aurora pulled up to the gates of their home in Saratoga, Roz's headache had receded into a crabby little knot in the space between her eyes. Her resolution to get a new boyfriend and new travel plans—and maybe a new haircut, too—had soothed her ego but now her id was in mourning. She had really believed that Aldo might be 'the one'. Letting go of that tender hope was sad work.

"How's the headache?" Aurora asked, as she pulled the Lexus into its spot in the garage. It was the first thing she'd said since they'd left Chinatown. "Any better?"

"A little," Roz said, expressing the words as a sigh. "I'm really tired, though. I think I'm going to make myself a cup of tea and lie down for a while."

"Good idea," Aurora said. "If you need me, I'll be in my office. And if it's not too much trouble," she added, as she climbed out of the car, "I wouldn't mind a cup of tea, too."

"No trouble at all," Roz said.

By then, Aurora had already cleared the garage and was presumably making a beeline for her computer. Roz snorted, venting a microburst of amusement and affection. That was her mother in story mode—laser-focused to the point of distraction. It could be days before she returned to regular Mom mode. Which was fine by Roz. She preferred to do her processing in private.

She made her way into the sprawling gourmet kitchen that she and Aurora shared. An instant after she tossed her handbag onto the granite countertop, the latch sprung open, exposing the bag of marijuana that she'd confiscated. The sight prompted a happy, "Oooh!" A hit or two of that might go a long way in curing the Aldo-didn't-love-her blues. She extracted the baggy, meaning to roll herself a joint then and there, only to curse out loud when she got a better look at the contents. The dried brown leafy matter that she had mistaken for pot was actually loose tea.

"Crap, it's just not my day," she said, and then remembered the packet that Naga had tossed her.

She pulled the packet from her jacket and pinched a sample of its contents between her thumb and forefinger. It was definitely tea, she decided, and definitely not Lipton. The leaves felt dry but supple and maybe even a little spiny. When she rubbed them together, they did not rustle or crumble, but rather made a faint hissing sound. She raised the sample to her nose. A mélange of aromas registered: lychee, licorice, forest floor, wood smoke, a hint of umami. She had never smelled the like, and she considered herself to be an aficionado. And the weird thing was, Naga's tea smelled just like the thief's tea. What were the odds?

A smart woman would have tossed both packets out and been done with the day's strangeness. But Roz couldn't resist scratching an itch. She turned the electric kettle on and then pulled two tea pots down from a cupboard. She loaded the first one with Darjeeling and the second with the mystery tisane. While she was waiting for the water to boil, she assembled a plate of nibbles for Aurora: a wedge of hard cheese, some sliced apple, a handful of Triscuits. If her mother didn't have sustenance on hand while she was working, she simply didn't bother to eat.

The teas were still in the early stages of steeping when Aurora came shuffling into the kitchen. "What is that?" she asked, sniffing at the air like a hound on the hunt. "I've never smelled anything quite like it."

Aurora's appearance inspired both surprise and a flash of concern in Roz, for it was so very unlike her mother to vacant her office so soon after taking up residence in it. But she didn't seem ill in any way, just a bit bemused and distracted. And the kitchen did smell rather intriguing—like wood-smoke and peat and open water after a thunderstorm.

"Must be the tea I picked up in Chinatown this afternoon," she said, fully tongue-in-cheek.

"Can I have some?"Aurora asked.

"I made you a pot of Darjeeling," Roz said.

"I see that," Aurora said. "But I'd really like to try the other one. May I?"

"Sure," Roz said, because she couldn't deny her outright without a good reason. "But just so you know, I've never tried this blend so I have absolutely no idea what it's going to taste like. And to tell you the truth—" A little of it, anyway. "I'm kind of leery about the source."

"I'm sure it'll be fine," Aurora said, grabbing a tea cup and holding it out. "And if it's not, you can say I-told-you-so when we recover."

"All right then," Roz said, in an arcing, so-be-it tone. She poured a drib for her mother and then a slightly larger measure for herself. Fragrant steam rose from the cups—fat, lazy tendrils that reminded her of that long-ago pre-dawn morning on Lake Siskiyou. As she raised the cup to her lips, she said, "Here's looking at you."

The first impression that hit her when she took her first sip was of heat—a seemingly scorching eruption that belied the brew's temperature. But before she had a chance to suck in a cooling breath, the heat dissipated on its own, leaving a floodplain of flavors in its wake. The top stratum was woody and bitter; the first sub-layer had a rich, meaty tang. Then came the rain-washed floral notes that coated her throat as she swallowed.

"Wow," she said, savoring the lingering after-notes. If nothing else, Naga had amazing taste in tea. She felt refreshed, even a little energized. Her concerns about possible toxicity were a fading memory. "That was amazing."

"No kidding," Aurora said, and looked as transfixed as Roz felt. "This is the best tea I've ever had. Can I have more?"

"Sure," Roz said, and filled her cup to the brim.

"Thanks, sweetie," Aurora said, and started back toward her office. "See you later."

"Take the cheese plate, too," Roz said. "You know how you get."

"I know," Aurora said, but never turned back to collect the food. Roz shook her head and smiled. That was her mom in writer mode: nothing but words in her head. She snagged the plate and carried it into the office. If Aurora noticed her in passing, she didn't let on. That brightened Roz's spirits. So did the kitchen's ambience upon her return. It felt warm and cozy, and the mystery tisane had filled the air with its exotic breath.

We're having a heat wave, a tropical heat wave....

All of a sudden, Roz saw how wrong she had been to be mad at Aldo. It wasn't his fault that he had gotten a casting call while she was chasing down a purse-snatcher. He was an actor; those calls were his life-blood. And his seeming lack of concern for her safety had actually been confidence in her ability to handle herself in a pinch. He believed in her. What was so wrong with that?

She took a sip of tea. Its warmth cascaded through her, infusing her with positive energy. The trip to Scotland was back on, she decided. She and Aldo were going to have the time of their lives.

CHAPTER 3

AURORA

The woman is sitting in the shade at the edge of the jungle, watching as the last embers of the clearing fire smolder like devil eyes in the midday sun. Although the smoke-thickened air burns her eyes and nose and throat, she will not pray for a wind for fear of offending the god of hot-and-muggy. Instead, she wishes for something to eat. There is a trove of gourds filled with seed corn and beans buried in the ground on the other side of the clearing, but that cache is for planting, not eating. If the gods did not kill her for devouring the future, her mate surely would upon his return from his hunting trip. She murmurs a prayer, begging for divine forbearance and a scrap of food.

A cloud passes over the sun's face. She recognizes this as an omen, but does not know if it is good or ill. Such divinations are a man's domain; all a woman can do is hope. She hopes it is a good sign— the leading edge of a rainstorm perhaps or perhaps a god guiding her mate toward a hunting grounds rich with prey. Her mouth moistens at the thought of meat: monkey, weasel, deer, even bird. She would be happy for any kind of morsel, raw or cooked. Even the dragonfly that is dipping and wheeling over the clearing would do. She sits stone-still, willing the insect to come within reach, and then tries to snatch it out of the air as it buzzes past her ear. But she is slow, too slow, and the dragonfly darts away. She covers her eyes and starts to cry. The need to eat is so strong it leaves the rest of her weak.

A shadow engulfs her as she weeps. She dismisses the shade as another cloud until she hears a massive thud and crunch. Clouds do not fall from the sky. But gods do. The Jaguar God in particular likes to drop in on the unsuspecting and feast on their flesh. The thought provokes fear in her, but also a profound pang of relief. Life and misery are joined at the hip; death is the only release. She listens for a cat's padded footfalls. What she hears instead is a throaty warble. The sound confuses rather than frightens her. Jaguars bark and jaguars growl, but as far as she knows, they do not warble. Is the god teasing her? Or is hunger playing tricks with her ears? She hears another warble. This one sounds like Look-At-Me. Conditioned since birth to obey, it does not occur to the woman to refuse. She uncovers one eye and then the other. An instant later, she throws herself onto her belly and grovels like the lowliest of worms.

"Get your face out of the dirt," the god commands, in a voice that the woman can only hear in her head. "Sit up and look at me."

She shifts onto her knees. Then, although she has only been told to look, she cannot help but stare. For the god that has settled in the clearing is no jaguar, but rather a magnificent pink serpent with a frill of feathers around its throat. Its eyes are the color of jade. Its fangs are long and curved. Its neck is as long as its muscular tail and its wings are like massive palm fronds. This cannot be The Jaguar. This god is beautiful like the quetzal. This god inspires fear without dread. Being eaten by this god will be the highlight of her life.

"I have not come to eat you," the god says, baring its fangs as if in distaste.

Disappointment flares within the woman like a wind-blown ember. And while she knows it is wrong to question a god, the thought takes shape anyway. "Why then?"

"I have been watching your kind," the god says. "You are capable of intelligent thought, yet you live like beasts. This is my brother the Jaguar's doing. He does not want you to thrive."

The woman does not understand 'thrive'. Nor can she imagine any other way of living. "Your brother is a god," she says. "He stands between us and the end of the world."

The pink-frilled Serpent spits, causing small plumes of ash and flame to rise up from the blackened ground. "He also stands between you and your potential. I have come to free you from his narrow-mindedness."

The woman knows all too well that The Jaguar is a hard, demanding god, random in his cruelties. He took her firstborn son one night while she was sleeping. He took her second child while it was still growing in her belly. Good, bad, or indifferent, however, gods are gods. She cannot imagine being free of them or their whims. Yet in the secret part of her heart, she has to admit that she likes the idea of The Jaguar being gone.

"How?" she asks, daring to hope. "What will you do?"

The Serpent rears to its full height and spreads its wings—a magnificent display. It looks big enough and strong enough to defeat a jaguar. As it postures for the woman, its body starts to shimmer and change. First, its wings disappear. Then its neck and tail contract, leaving a stubby torso. The next thing the woman knows, she is gaping at another woman, one with jade eyes and a pink-feathered headdress. The sight crushes her fragile, fresh-formed hope.

"Why?" she, on the verge of tears.

"I will live among you," the god says, "and guide you to a better life."

The woman collapses, deboned by sudden despair. She is as distraught as she was the night she lost her son to The Jaguar. Her sobbing confuses the god.

"Do you not want a better life?" the god asks.

"I do," the woman wails. "But you cannot free us from your brother as you are."

The god makes a warbling sound that is equal parts curiosity and irritation. "Why do you doubt? Did you not behold my might?"

"I did," the woman says, too mired in disappointment to care if she has offended the god. "But your brother walks the world as a jaguar. You mean to walk the world as a woman. Men do not fear the things they fuck. If they do not fear you, they will not listen to you. Men fear other men—and jaguars."

"Then I shall be seen as a man," the god says, and again wills the woman to look up. She does so without enthusiasm only to gasp at the changes she sees. The god's breasts are muscular pads now and there's a sturdy penis where before there were only curly hairs. And while the god is still wearing a head-dress of pink feathers, it seems fierce now instead of decorative.

"Only you will know the truth," the god says. "If you keep my secret well, I will see that your daughters flourish."

"No one else will know," the woman says, and then faints from hunger and joy.

Aurora woke with a drowning man's gasp to find herself seated in front of her computer. The screen was dark, and the tea that she had fixed for herself had gone cold. She leaned back in her Herman Miller chair, raking her fingers through her short, mostly dark hair at the same time. What the hell, she thought, as she struggled to reorient herself. She never dozed off at her desk—not for a minute, never mind an hour! She hadn't even been tired when she sat down.

And that dream!

She was famous for saying that she did her best work in her sleep. And that was true. The inspiration for Esmerelda, her copyrighted little pink dragon, had come to her in a dream.

So had the ideas for Ezzie's many adventures. But those had been vague, free-form imaginings, nothing like the vividly detailed daydream that she'd just experienced. The smell of humidity and charred earth still lingered in her nose. The ache of starvation still clung to her ribs. And there had been an underlying sense of urgency to the dream that continued to pluck at her subconscious. What was her brain trying to tell her? The Serpent God was obviously a variant of Ezzie. The woman might be an adult version of Francine. Were her characters trying to tell her that after twenty years in a fantastical stasis they were finally ready to grow up? The idea of exploring more mature themes and situations both troubled and excited Aurora. Her publisher wouldn't be thrilled with a change of direction. Ezzie and Francine were perennial best-sellers, a working gold mine with their own line of merchandise: little pink dragons and purple-winged pixies on everything from pajamas to lunch boxes. She wasn't going to get that kind of visibility with adult characters. She could lose a big chunk of her fan-base, too, for few who believed in Peter Pan wanted to see him grow up. Nevertheless, this new storyline had a strong hold on her. She wanted to see how it played out.

"So get back to work already," she told herself. "No story, no fans."

The thought made her smile, because it was something that Roz might have said. But an instant after her mouth acquired that tender bend, her brow furrowed because at the moment, her beautiful, intelligent daughter was traipsing around Scotland with that narcissistic rear-end, Aldo. Aurora prided herself in her ability to let Roz make her own mistakes, but—dear God! Aldo was such a bitter pill: all looks and no substance, a textbook case of arrested development. She kept waiting for Roz to wake up and see that, but sadly, her darling girl had a blind spot for handsome men with hard bodies. She thought to wash the pasty taste of disgust from her mouth with a swig of tea, but her mug had long-since gone cold so she got up to brew herself a fresh one. She really liked this tea. It energized her without making her wired like caffeine did. Thief's Blend, Roz called it. Aurora was going through the stash in a hurry.

A hand-written sign dangled from the kitchen-way lintel: 'EAT SOMETHING!' That was Roz's doing. She had hung several others around the house. As if she feared that she would come home to find Aurora's shrunken, ice-cold corpse flopped over her keyboard otherwise. Silly child. Aurora was perfectly capable of not just living but living well on her own. And to prove it, she was going have some wine and cheese instead of another cup of tea. It was Friday afternoon, after all. Why not splurge?

As she headed for the fridge, she flicked on the kitchen radio. 'Bad Romance' by Lady Gaga came spilling forth, one of Aurora's favorites. She boogied to the tune's driving beat as she pulled cheese and fruit from the refrigerator, and sang the chorus at the top of her lungs. "*I don't wanna be friends! I don't wanna be friends! Want your bad roh-mance!*"

Next came the news—a welcome respite after such a long, energetic song. The lead piece was about hundreds of women from Juarez going missing. "Most are presumed to be victims of drug-related crimes and domestic violence," the dee-jay said, "but that doesn't account for all of the disappearances. Cries for an international investigation are mounting."

"Unbelievable," Aurora muttered. "Those poor women."

The second report was on the Deepwater Horizon disaster. The good news was, the well had finally been capped. The bad news was, over 40,000 barrels of crude oil had gushed into the Gulf of Mexico every day for over two months. Scientists worried that the scope of the damage done wouldn't be known for years. BP's CEO, Tony Hayward, on the other hand, was quoted as saying, "You know, I'd like my life back."

Aurora sneered. "You poor thing you."

"And," the dee-jay went on, "our favorite doomsayer is at it again. This time, Brother Baine and his end-of-the-world devotees held a rally in Golden Gate Park, urging tourists and other passersby to repent before the end of the world sends them straight to hell. According to Baine, we can expect the apocalypse on December 21, 2012, which is the day that the Mayan calendar comes to an end.

"What do you say, listeners? Think it's time to change your evil ways? I've got a pair of free tickets to Death Metal Duel for the caller who comes up with the best slogan for Brother Baine's end-of-the-world campaign. You can reach us here at—"

She had no desire to listen to an onslaught of puerile apocalyptic catchphrases and so killed the radio. The whole Mayan calendar thing was bogus. Brother Baine was probably just trying to generate a little hysteria so he could cash in on it further on down the road. She added a few finishing touches to the cheese plate in contented silence and then went to pull a bottle of sauvignon blanc out of the Sub-Zero. As she did so, the security system buzzed, announcing a presence at the front gate.

"Must be the FedEx guy," she mused aloud, shifting in mid-reach toward the monitor. "He's late today."

But the man standing at her gate wasn't wearing a uniform. Nor was he anyone that Aurora recognized. She supposed he could be one of Roz's friends. They called on her unannounced all the time. Very few people, however, dropped in on Aurora, mainly because she discouraged such visits. Writing was solitary work. Interruptions were costly in terms of time and focus.

"Go away," she told the grainy image, figuring that he'd think there was no one home if she didn't answer. Instead, he pressed the buzzer again. Such an irritating sound. She rapped the intercom as if it were the interloper's nose. "What?"

"Hi," the man said in a chipper tone, seemingly undaunted by her snarl. "I'm your new neighbor, Charles Weber. Sorry I didn't call first, but your number's unlisted. And apparently, no one in town has ever heard of you."

It came as no surprise to her that he hadn't been able to wangle a phone number from any of the locals; they'd always been very protective of her privacy. And since no one had called to let her know that someone was asking around after her, she supposed he might actually be a new neighbor rather than some overenthusiastic fan. Even so, Aurora was inclined to keep her distance. Good fences made good neighbors. So did a good stiff-arm.

"So what brings you?" she asked, with cool civility. "Did you need a cup of sugar or something?"

He chuckled—an easy, amiable rumble. "I'd like to introduce myself," he said, "and maybe chat for a bit over a TGIF cocktail. I brought wine." He held a bottle up to the camera. "It's local, but I hear it's OK."

The label surprised her. Local or not, Ridge Monte Bello was world class wine and pricey to boot—not something that one usually shared with a stranger on a Friday afternoon. And she was willing to bet that this fellow was well aware of that. She gave him a second look, taking in details this time. He was dressed in jeans, a hoodie, and tennis shoes, but he wasn't a young man or even on the south side of middle-aged. He looked fit but not super-athletic. She found herself tempted to let him in, and not just because she had a sudden yen for expensive wine.

"Where did you say you live?" she said, because despite her craving and curiosity, she wasn't a fool.

"I bought the Stevenson property," he said. "My realtor is Susannah Lee. Her cell phone number is 408-871-9909 if you want to call her to confirm."

Thorough. She liked that. "All right," she said, activating the gate. "Come on in. I'll meet you out front. If that bottle is a fake, I'll sic the dogs on you." She didn't have any, but he didn't need to know that. "I'll be the one in the camp shirt and jeans."

"Good to know," he said. "See you in a few."

She rounded up a pair of wine glasses and a corkscrew. As an afterthought, she grabbed the cheese plate as well and then headed for the front porch. She often sat out there to catch the afternoon sun. The chairs were comfy; the mountain view, spectacular. And she felt a lot safer meeting a strange man out in the open air.

To her surprise, he was still working his way up her driveway when she got to the porch: walking, not driving. Although the gate was almost a quarter-mile away, he had made good time at what seemed like a leisurely pace. His chin-up, shoulders-back carriage suggested a degree of military training. He stopped well short of the porch, a polite gesture, and tipped a non-existent hat to her.

"Charles Weber," he said. "At your service."

"I'm Aurora," she said. "Welcome to the 'hood."

He was a striking rather than handsome man, perfectly landscaped from his capped teeth to his fashionable five o'clock shadow. His thick, chocolate-colored hair had just the right touch of grey at the temples, and his equally thick eyebrows had been expertly trimmed. "Thank you," he said, and then handed her the wine bottle that had been tucked under his arm. "It's a gift," he said. "Please don't feel like you have to open it now."

She smirked, reflexive scorn for such a ridiculous suggestion. "You're under no obligation to join me in a glass," she said, "but this bottle is definitely getting opened."

"As you wish," he said gallantly, and then gestured at the corkscrew. "Want me to do the honors?"

"I can manage," she said, with a self-empowered smile, and then motioned him toward the chair next to hers. He sat down and crossed his legs in one fluid movement. For a large man, he took up very little space.

"Nice view," he said, as she went to work on the cork. "Nice cheese plate, too. Are you always this hospitable toward strangers?"

"Just ones who come calling with Monte Bello," she said, and then handed him a glass.

He gave the contents a swirl and then said, "Great color."

"Great bouquet, too," she said, holding her glass under her nose. "I'm getting hints of cassis and dark chocolate and maybe even a little forest floor."

He scoffed. "Seriously—forest floor? I don't even know what that means."

"Of course you don't. You just moved here. But take a hike in those hills one of these days," she said, nodding at the mountains that dominated the horizon, "and you'll understand what I mean. The Monte Bello vineyard is just a few ridges from here."

His mordant smile took a self-mocking bend. "Touché," he said. "And you're right—I don't know much about this part of the world. I guess I'm going to have to find a knowledgeable native to show me the ropes." He took a sip of wine that left his expression reverent. "I may not know what forest floor smells like," he said, "but I know good wine when I taste it. And this is very good."

"I agree," she said. "Thanks for sharing."

"My pleasure," he said, and then offered a toast. "Here's to good wine and good neighbors."

"I'll drink to that," she said, and did so—an appreciative, eyes-closed sip. Afterward, she sank back in her chair like an afternoon talk-show host and politely began to grill her guest. "So what brings you to this part of the world if you know nothing about it?"

"What's not to like?" he said, gesturing at the surroundings. "There's the gorgeous views and perfect weather. There's San Francisco for food, wine country for drink, and almost no bugs anywhere. And the price of land hereabouts keeps the tweakers and other undesirables out."

Aurora would've added proximity to the ocean and ski slopes to that list, but otherwise, he had pretty much covered all of her favorite things about this region—even the part about it being too expensive for low-end criminal types. She took another sip from her glass and then pressed on.

"So where were you before you came to California?" she said.

"Oh, here and there and everywhere in between," he said, swirling his wine like an old pro. "But mostly Asia and Central America."

"I've always wanted to visit Asia," she said. "What's your favorite country there?"

"Thailand," he said, without a moment's pause. "The food's great, the beaches are beautiful, and there's lots of wilderness. Bangkok's an armpit, but so are most third-world cities."

"What about China?" she asked. "Have you been there?" At his nod, she said, "How is it? I've heard mixed reviews."

Again, his response was immediate. "As far as I'm concerned, it's a festering boil on the planet's backside. The air pollution in most of the cities is as toxic as cigarette smoke. Acid rain is killing the forests. The Yangtze used to be the most beautiful river in the world. Now it's been dammed up and everything that lives in it is dying. If you give a ripe fig about the natural world, you'll stay away from China unless you want your heart broken."

His passion for the environment impressed Aurora. Too many men of his age and probable tax bracket considered nature to be superfluous. She recalled a dinner party that she and Roz had attended recently. Over pre-dinner cocktails, Roz had mentioned climate change in passing. The jowly middle-aged man who happened to be standing next to her responded with a raspberry and said, "All this jibber-jabber about global warming is a waste of time," he'd said. "I mean, face it. Everybody in this room is going to be dead and buried long before it comes to a head." Roz had been aghast. "You have four kids, dude," she'd said. "What about them?" He shrugged and then helped himself to another canapé. "Every generation has its challenges. They'll cope, just like everyone before them did."

She nibbled on a piece of Manchego to rid herself of the memory's bitter taste and then asked, "So what takes you all over the world?"

"Business mostly," he said. "I was what you might call a facilitator. But," he added, a dramatic after-note, "that's all in the past. I'm officially retired now."

"Ah," she said. "So you're going to spend the rest of your life exploring the Santa Cruz Mountains."

"Maybe," he said, flashing another of his perfect smiles. "If I can find the right guide." Wait. Was he flirting with her? Or was it the wine playing tricks on her? Either way, the tops of her ears were burning. Then he added, "I'm also going to try my hand at raising exotic animals."

"Oh?" The thought of a Wild Kingdom in her backyard chilled her down in a hurry. She let her tone get a little cold, too. "Like what—lions, tigers, and bears?"

"No, no, nothing like that," he said, dismissing the

possibility with a wave of his hand. "I'm talking ungulates. You know—antelopes, zebras, gazelles. Don't worry," he added, before she could form an intelligible objection, "I'll take care of all the fencing. And every animal will be properly inspected, inoculated, and declared disease-free before it sets hoof on the property. All you have to do is call if you have any complaints or concerns." He whipped a business card from his back pocket with scripted aplomb and presented it to her with a flourish. "I don't want this endeavor to have any impact at all on my neighbors."

"I appreciate that, Charles," she said, slipping the card into her back pocket after giving it a cursory glance. "But why exotic animals? You don't look like the zoo-keeper type."

He ran a hand over his perfectly cut hair and then cracked a self-deprecating half-smile. "No, I suppose I don't. And to tell you the truth, I've never owned any kind of animal in my life. I've always been busy or on the move or invested in other things. But I've been around enough, and seen enough, to know that some of these animals are going to be extinct rather than merely exotic in the very near future if someone doesn't do something to protect them. So I'm going to start a little game preserve and see how things go from there. At least, at the end of the day, I'll be able to say I tried to do something."

Wow. She couldn't remember the last time she had been so impressed with a man. Or, if she was honest with herself, so attracted. She'd had her fair share of suitors—her relative fame could be quite an aphrodisiac, especially to men of a certain age. And it wasn't like she'd turned into a sexless drudge after Duncan's death. But her late husband was the gold standard by which she judged other men, and so very few measured up. It was both exciting and unnerving that this Mr. Weber was doing such a good job of making her forget that.

"Do you have pets?" he was saying now. "You look like a dog person to me."

She started to run her hand through her hair, but then thought better of it and reached for more cheese instead. "I had horses for a while," she said, although in truth, they had been Roz's animals, another of her daughter's manic passions that had come and gone at Aurora's expense. "Unfortunately, I couldn't give them the attention they needed, so I sold them to a neighbor. I'd have the same problem with a dog. I just travel too much."

A gleam danced its way into Charles' eyes. "Ah," he said, "a fellow globe-trotter. Do you travel for business or pleasure?"

"Business mostly," she said.

"What kind of work do you do?"

The question surprised her, for she had assumed that he already knew who she was when he rang her buzzer. Her name, after all, was fairly well-known. And he had been asking around about her like fans sometimes did. But while she wasn't used to it, anonymity agreed with her. She felt free to be herself rather than a celebrity. Eventually, somebody would fill him in on her particulars, but for now, they were going to remain her little secret.

"It's all contractual," she said, tongue-in-cheek. "It pays the bills and supports my vices, but it's what I do, not who I am."

He nodded approvingly. "Well said. And I share the sentiment. Shop-talk should stay in the shop. What should we talk about instead?"

A number of things leapt to Aurora's mind, including the possibility of another glass of wine. But even as she thought about offering to refill his glass, her internal governor kicked in. She was always telling Roz that less was more when it came to first impressions and men. It was time to practice what she preached.

"Actually," she said, mustering an apologetic tone, "I'm afraid I have to ask you to leave. I've got a conference call in twenty minutes and I'm not quite ready for it."

He reared back, a parody of shock. "What kind of a slave-driver schedules a conference call for happy hour on Friday?"

Ooh, he was sharp. She liked that. Fortunately, she was good at making things up on the fly. "A potential client," she said. "One with lots of money and no spare time."

"Ah, one of those," he said, in a knowing but still playful tone. "Then I'll take my leave so you can prepare." He stood up. As he did so, a postcard slipped out of his hoodie's pouch and fluttered to the ground. The photograph on its face was of a handsome, bare-chested Scotsman in a kilt.

"Is that mine?" she wondered, as he went to pick it up.

"It is," he said, and then handed the card over along with several other envelopes that he pulled from his pocket. "The mailman pulled up just as you buzzed me in so I convinced him to give me the day's delivery. I meant to give it to you right after I introduced myself but then we started talking and drinking wine and I totally forgot that I had it until now. I'm sorry, Aurora. I only meant to save you a hike out to the mailbox."

"I appreciate the thought," she said, although she might not have been as charitable on any other day. The wine had left her mellow, forgiving of near-strangers and the mailmen who succumbed to their charms. And Mr. Charles Weber was very charming. "But just so you know, I don't mind the walk." She stuffed the mail into her back pocket without inspecting it first, and then held out her hand. "It was nice meeting you. Thanks again for the wine."

He clasped her hand and gave it a gentle squeeze. Afterward, he was slow in letting go. She didn't mind. His hand was manicured but not soft. The combination pleased her.

"If it's OK with you," he said, "I'd like to stop by again sometime."

"That would be nice," she said. "However—"

He arched an eyebrow, inviting her to drop the other shoe. She grabbed a pen that she had left on the side table while doing bills two nights ago and used it to write her phone number on the label of the wine bottle. "Next time," she said, as she presented the half-full bottle to him, "call first."

The corners of his mouth quirked upward, and for a moment, she thought he might lean in and kiss her. Instead, he looked her over one last time and said, "It's been a pleasure, Aurora. I'll see you soon."

Then, shoulders back and head held high, he started on his way. Aurora watched, pulse pounding in her ears, as he strode down her quarter-mile driveway. When he reached the gate, he half-turned and waved—a single languid sweep of the arm. An instant later, he was gone and the gate was swinging shut again.

Holy guacamole, she thought, as she headed into the house with the glasses. What was going on here? Her wrist was still tingling from when his fingertips trailed over the skin as he released her hand. Her heart was still slamming into her ribcage. The wine must have gone straight to her head, because she wasn't the one who got all hot and bothered by men. That was Roz.

And speaking of—

She fished the mail out of her back pocket and shuffled through it until she came to the postcard. The bare-chested Scot in the photo had a smirk on his face, teasing or perhaps taunting her for being so easily inflamed. She fanned herself with the card and then flipped it over. The sight of Roz's handwriting calmed her down.

'Wish you were here!' the message read. 'The Edinburgh Festival was a blast—lots of music, eating & revelry. Tomorrow, we're off to Inverness & Loch Ness. The weather has been fabulous & so has Aldo. Traveling brings out the best in him. Don't be surprised if I come home with a ring on my finger! He's going to propose, I just know it. See you soon. Love—R'

"Oh, you foolish, foolish woman," Aurora grumped, and then flapped the postcard at the heavens and her dead husband, Duncan. "This is all your fault, you know. If you had been here when she was growing up, your daughter wouldn't be such a rotten judge of men!"

Duncan's ghost laughed. *Says you.*

She responded with a sigh. "I miss you."

As she washed and dried her stemware, she wondered, as she often did, what different turns her life might have taken if Duncan hadn't died in that car crash. They would have almost certainly had more children. 'The more, the merrier!' he liked to say. But would she have found the time to write the Ezzie and Francine series with a large brood clamoring for her attention all day and night? Or would she have gone the soccer mom route instead? Maybe if she had been a better, more traditional mother, Roz wouldn't have the issues she had now.

So—are you saying that Aldo is your fault?

"Ha-ha. Funny. Not," she said. "Now go away, I've got work to do."

She turned on the electric kettle, meaning to make herself a fresh cup of Thief's Brew. As the water heated up, she filed through the rest of the mail. Most of it was junk: two catalogues, a pack of coupons, and a realtor's pamphlet. There was also a bill from her dentist and a flyer from a local Aztec dance troupe. The advertisement gave her an idea: why not use ceremonial dancing in the new book? She checked the fridge calendar—there was nothing going on for the weekend of the advertised Festival. She could go and do a little research, and, as a bonus, spend some time in the great outdoors.

A creak ghosted into the kitchen. The haunted-house sound was a familiar one: a loose floorboard on Roz's side of the house. Aurora didn't think anything of it until the board squeaked again.

"Roz?" she called, absurdly hoping that Roz had gotten homesick and come home early. "Is that you?"

The house seemed to go extra-quiet, as it were holding its breath. Aurora hitched up her jeans, readying herself for only God knew what, and then nearly hit the roof as the kettle reached its boiling point and began to scream.

"Jesus," she said, and was suddenly very glad that Roz wasn't here to see how jumpy a glass of wine had left her. She switched off the kettle and then filled her mug with boiling water. An instant later, fragrant steam infused the air and coaxed her pulse back down to normal.

"That tea is not for you."

A second jolt of adrenaline sizzled through Aurora, leaving a coppery taste in her mouth. Nevertheless, she managed to fold her arms over her chest and pivot in the speaker's direction. The woman standing on the far side of her kitchen was Asian, Roz's age maybe or maybe a bit older, with long, black hair and hard eyes. Although she was wearing a hoodie, Aurora could tell that she was broad-shouldered and narrow through the hips. She didn't appear to be armed, but her proximity to the block of kitchen knives made that a moot point.

"Who are you?" Aurora asked, trying to sound calm. "What do you want?"

"I am Lee," the woman said, in crisp, accented English. "I am here to see Roz-a-lin. Naga sent me."

"Who in hell is Naga?" Aurora asked.

Lee dismissed the question with a shrug. "Naga is Naga. No words suffice."

"Great," Aurora muttered. "And what does she want with Roz?"

"That is for Roz-a-lin to know."

"Rosalyn isn't here at the moment," Aurora said. "So if you don't care to leave a message, then I suggest you get the hell out of here. Unless, of course, you'd rather I call the cops."

"Call if you must," Lee said, seemingly unfazed by the threat. "They will not catch me." Then she nodded at the steaming cup of tea and scowled. "You should not drink that. It is not for you."

Aurora's gaze bounded from her to the mug and back again. "You know what this is?"

"Dragon tea. It is only to be consumed by those who have bonded with a dragon."

"What makes you think I don't qualify?" Aurora asked, looking to throw this cocksure intruder an inside curve.

Lee's eyes widened for an instant and then narrowed into suspicious slits. She sniffed at the air like some wild thing searching for an elusive scent. "This place bears no dragon-trace," she noted. She sniffed in Aurora's direction and added, "You bear no dragon-trace. And yet—" She took a step toward Aurora only to rear back and raise her eyebrows as Aurora shifted into a fighting stance. "You know the Form, too. How confusing. Are you Roz-a-lin's mother?"

"Why?" Aurora asked, wondering just how much more bizarre this situation was going to get. "What business is that of yours?"

"Naga says the bond passes from mother to daughter," Lee muttered to herself, "but only when the mother dies." She shot Aurora a look that was both puzzled and aggrieved. "You are still alive, so Roz-a-lin cannot be bonded. Yet—how can you be so old and bear no dragon-trace?"

Aurora bristled at the ageist remark. But even she opened her mouth to assert her relative youthfulness, Lee cut her off. "Does the tea give you dreams?"

"I dream all the time," she replied, doing her best sullen-teenager impression.

"Are your dreams of a dragon?"

"Of course," she said, another snotty salvo, then hastened to burst the woman's peculiar bubble. "A little pink-frilled dragon. I've dreamed of her for over twenty years now."

Lee recoiled as if from an electrical shock. "A dragon has been calling you for twenty years and you still do not bear her scent? Aaaiiii! You must be a very broken woman!"

"That's it!" Aurora said, thoroughly fed up with the insults and this completely ridiculous situation. "You're done here. If you don't leave right this minute, I'm going to call the cops and have you arrested for breaking and entering."

"I will go now," Lee said, suddenly quite eager to be on her way. "Naga must hear of this. Naga will not be pleased."

"Yeah well," Aurora said, as she ushered the woman toward the front door, "tell Naga to leave me alone."

"Naga is not the enemy," Lee said, and then bounded down the front steps with sure-footed grace.

"I'll make a note of it," Aurora said, matching the woman step for step, intent on escorting her all the way to the front gate. "In the meantime, forget you were ever here. I don't appreciate trespassers, and I guarantee that I won't be as charitable if there's a next time."

Nothing more was said until they reached the top of the driveway. There, all tight lips and mock-politeness, Aurora pulled the pedestrian gate open and then gestured for Lee to pass through the gap. As she did so, she speared Aurora with a look, and in a low voice, said, "The Year of the Dragon is almost here. It will not go well for us if we are not prepared. Seek out the drakena who calls you!"

An instant later, she was off and running down the road.

Good riddance, Aurora thought, as she pushed the gate shut again. And: what a weird experience that had been. She had run into her share of overzealous fans on the convention circuit over the years—excitable, semi-obsessive souls who wanted to talk dragons with her all night long—but this was her first bona fide stalker. Happily, she had been nonviolent. Hopefully, this would be last she heard of her. Nevertheless, the first thing she did when she got back to the house was lock all of her windows. Then she went online to upgrade her security system—just in case.

CHAPTER 4

Grimy and hot from a long day's hike in the Santa Cruz Mountains, Carlito strode into the confines of his house with a newfound appreciation for its natural coolness. He had not cared for the place when he bought it. It was rather overdone for his tastes—a rich man's interpretation of rusticity, with a double-wide stone hearth in the great room, a kitchen like a landing strip, and lots of empty space. The man who had owned it before him had hosted hunting parties here, and there had been animal heads and automatic weaponry mounted on the paneled walls. The walls were bare now. The man was dead. As far as Carlito was concerned, both changes were for the better.

The remnants of a case of wine sat on the granite-topped kitchen island that served both as a dinner table and a desk. He snagged a bottle and uncorked it, then suffered a jolt of surprise as he inhaled the wine's bouquet. Damned if he hadn't caught a whiff of forest floor! He thought of the woman who had assured him that such a moment would come. Of all the neighbors he had met in the process of securing his perimeter, she had been the most intriguing: scruffy yet self-confident, aloof yet oddly engaging, a hard nut to crack. While snooping through her mail, he had discovered that she supported a dance troupe that bore Tezcatlipoca's name. Was that pure coincidence? Or a sign from the Divine? Either way, he intended to see her again. In fact, he rather liked the idea of seeing her tonight! Maybe he could entice her into joining him for dinner.

As he reached for the bottle on which she had written her phone number, his cellphone buzzed. The call-sign belonged to

Tezcatlipoca. Shit. The Great One never initiated a call unless something bad had happened or he was hungry for news. He considered dodging the call because neither conversation was going to begin or end with the drake in a good mood. It was, however, a fleeting thought, one that was banished by the knowledge that screening the call would surely compound the drake's aggravation. He had no real choice but to pull the phone out of his pocket and answer the call.

"Carlito here," he said, doing his best to sound nonchalant rather than resigned.

"Where is She?" Tezcatlipoca asked.

Carlito knew exactly who the drake meant by 'She'. Even so, an image of Aurora flashed in his mind's eye first. "I do not know yet, Great One," he said. "This piece of the world has lots of mountains. Her lair could be anywhere."

The mandrake hissed, an ominous sound that made Carlito glad that they were separated by over a thousand miles. "Find men to help you search!"

"I have a crew," he said. "They are combing the countryside with drones as we speak."

"'Drones?'" Tezcatlipoca asked, in a suspicious tone. "What are drones?"

"They're unmanned aerial vehicles," Carlito said, knowing full well that the Great One wouldn't even try to understand what he was saying. "Flying mechanical spies." When the drake continued to menace him with silence, he resorted to his standard explanation. "It's man-magic, Great One. Drones can cover more ground than a man on foot and penetrate some bad-ass bush. They're more effective than men."

The Great One didn't care. "It's been six weeks already since my sister tried to plunder my dreams," he said sourly. "I want her caught before she tries again."

"I understand—"

"Perhaps this task is beyond you. Perhaps I should send a drake to oversee the search."

Privately, Carlito hated the idea, for even the most tolerant of drakes would have him walking on fire and eggshells from the moment he arrived until the moment he departed. But disagreeing with Tezcatlipoca was a tricky thing, one that had to take the drake's massive pride and scorn for humanity well into account. He'd have to try and sneak his preferences in through the back door.

"As you see fit, Great One," he said. "Who will you send? Wo Long? Or what about Azi Zahhak? That one is Drogo's thrall, so calling him into play would annoy both drakes at no cost to yourself."

The suggestion nudged the Great One into a less caustic frame of mind. "I like the way you think," he said. "And if we were hunting a lesser drakena, I would consider the idea. But my sister is a Great One, too, Carlito, and she rides the Dreaming like no other. Azi Zahhak may be sly, but he does not guard his thoughts well. If she were to come upon him in his sleep, she could strip every secret we have from his head and none of us would be the wiser."

Carlito did not understand exactly how the Dreaming worked. But the idea of a dragon having access to the innermost reaches of his mind made him squirm. "Is there no way to shield our thoughts from her?"

"You need not fear my sister," Tezcatlipoca said, "for you are human and male and therefore immune from her scrutiny. Even if she wanted to seek you out, the Dreaming would not take her to you. It is otherwise with us drakes. The only thing that will keep her away if she comes nosing around in the night is a strong mind."

"Grishka has a strong mind," Carlito said, thinking that he could live with that drake if he absolutely had to. "Perhaps he should lead the search for your sister."

Tez dismissed the suggestion with a rumble. "I want Rasputin to help with the wyrms. They are growing restive as they mature, and he has a calming influence on them."

"Ah, so he is in Juarez," Carlito said. "I thought he was in Siberia, searching the wilds for more wyrms."

"You need to listen more carefully," The Great One said, growing agitated again. "I did not say Grishka Rasputin was here, only that I wanted him here. He says he is on his way, but who knows when he will arrive. Can you believe it? In this age of long-distance air travel, he insists on crossing the great waters of the world by boat because he believes that doing so pleases the Divine. Over land, he travels by train for the same reason. So even if I thought he was the right drake to task with finding my sister, I cannot trust him to get where you are in good time.

"But Grishka is not the drake for this task," he went on, sounding less aggrieved now that he had aired his gripe against his closest ally. "I know already that he will not do what needs to be done once my sister has been found."

"And what is that, Great One?"

Silence ensued, sly and vee-shaped like a drake's smile. "She must die, Carlito. Elsewise, she will find a way to compromise our plans for the sixth age."

Carlito could not contain his surprise. "But—she is your sister! You would kill one of your own?"

"Why not?" Tezcatlipoca wondered. "We have always been enemies, even in our youth. Shared blood is often bad blood, you know. Besides—" His voice deepened into a cat-like purr. "I will not be the one slaying her. You will."

CHAPTER 5

"I love the highlands!" Rosalyn declared, as she and Aldo stood side by side on the rim of the Suidhe Viewpoint. Twelve hundred feet below them spanned South Loch Ness, a blue-green jewel glimmering at the feet of slope-shouldered mountains. "I love Scotland!" The air smelled of rain-washed heather. The hills wore rough-spun kilts of bracken and heath. "I feel so at home here."

"That makes one of us," Aldo said, petulantly swatting at a bee that had taken a shine to his aftershave. "I want to go home. Or at least back to Edinburgh. I've had more than my fill of friggin' Brigadoon."

She slipped her hand into his and then hugged his arm, trying to cuddle him into a better mood. "C'mon, baby," she cajoled. "All I'm asking for is twenty-four more hours. That will give us time to tour Urquhart Castle this afternoon and take the Nessie cruise tomorrow morning."

He tsked, a sound like a tiny whip cracking. "I've already told you that I'm not going on that stupid cruise."

"I know," she said, still coaxing even as she admitted her guilt, "but I'm hoping you'll change your mind. For me." When he didn't soften, she threw in a girlish, "Pretty please?"

"Not even with sugar on top," he said. "The Loch Ness Monster is a hoax perpetrated by the locals to suck money out of tourists. I'd rather spend our money on something of value—a night out for instance, or an amazing bottle of single malt."

She released his arm as if it were on fire and then shoved her hands in her pockets as if they had been burned. It wasn't like it was his money that they were spending! Part of her recognized the thought as unfair. 'What's mine is yours,' she often told him, because that's how it was supposed to be when two people were in love. Still! He didn't have to be such a dick about it!

"Fine," she said, "I'll do the cruise. You can sleep in."

"And then we'll head back to Edinburgh."

Telling, not asking, she noted. That irked her, too, but she tried to be reasonable. "Sure," she said. "Why not? Maybe we can visit a distillery or two along the way."

"Yeah," he said. "Maybe."

She realized then that he must be getting hungry. How else to explain such a lackadaisical response to an afternoon of whiskey sipping? One of these days, she was going to learn to pack a snack for him when they went adventuring.

"C'mon," she said, gesturing toward the trail. "Let's get cracking. We don't want to miss lunch!"

He took off like a power-walker: chest out, legs straight, head held high. Roz followed at a slightly more casual pace, happy to give him his space and admire his well-formed backside in peace. She knew he probably wasn't going to be happy until they returned to Edinburgh because he hadn't really been happy since they'd left. Sure, they'd had fun there, wining and dining and listening to live jazz at the city's annual festival. But she liked this, too—hiking the Highlands, a rugged, windswept region steeped in history and blood. Something about the place spoke to her. Something about it tugged at her head and heartstrings.

The thought made her think of Mara. 'To the only girl I know who can play tug-of-war by herself,' she had written in Roz's senior class yearbook. Roz readily admitted that she was restless by nature. Being in motion—mentally and physically— always felt better than being still. That made her good at a lot of things. It also made her seem a bit ADHD sometimes. According to Aurora, her dad had been the same way. Roz had to take her word for it, for she'd only been three years old when Duncan Vanderbilt died. The only thing she still remembered about him with any clarity was his voice, deep and rich, the sweetest of all sounds even when it contained a frown.

'Rosalyn, get down from there!'

'Rosalyn, don't play with that!'

'Rosalyn, come to Daddy!'

'Rosalyn, give Daddy a squeeeeeze!'

Perhaps the reason she felt so drawn to this place had something to do with the fact that his mom hailed from these parts. According to family legend, sixteen year old Sheila Maclachlan had been a ginger-haired free spirit who cared little for customs or conventions. An instant after she laid eyes on the handsome young American who had come to hunt fallow buck on the moors, she offered to be his guide. Then she kissed her parents goodbye and never looked back. Devon Vanderbilt brought her to America and gave her everything she wanted: a son, exotic excursions, a place to call home. She stayed with him until the night he died and then died herself four hours later.

Rosalyn smiled to herself, savoring the taste of such enduring devotion. If you had to die, that was definitely the way to do it. She tried to imagine what it would be like to go out that way with Aldo. They'd be nestled together in bed, spooners to the end, and while they'd be aware of each other's breathing and body temperatures, they wouldn't be alarmed by the changes that they were sensing. Indeed, it would feel like they were slipping out of their skins and into a new dimension—

"Jesus, Roz," Aldo griped, from somewhere further up the trail, "would you put it in gear already? At this rate, we'll never make it back in time for lunch. If I miss lunch, there's no way I'm touring that stupid castle."

Her imagination lurched. Now all she could see was Aldo in his deathbed. She supposed she must be a little hungry, too. "On my way," she shouted. "Race you to the car park!"

Back in Drumnadrouchit, they bought fish and chips from the first take-away shack they came to and ate right there in the street with their fingers. Rosalyn's mood improved with every passing bite. Aldo seemed to perk up, too. As they ate, their eyes met. They shared a fishy smile. She laughed, delighted, for this seemed to her like a scene right out of a romantic comedy. All of a sudden, she got the urge to turn this into an afternoon that they could tell their kids about some day.

"Listen," she said, as she licked the last delicious molecules of grease from her fingers. "I know you don't want to tour Urquhart Castle, so screw it. Instead, let's find a bottle of wine and take a stroll along the lake."

He made a sour face. "I've had enough walking for one day, thank you."

She rubbed herself against him like a cat and then hugged one of his arms. "C'mon," she said, "it'll be fun. We'll find a secluded little beach and—" She waggled her brow suggestively. "You know. Be naughty."

He looked at her for a long moment as if he were weighing the thrill of hanky-panky against the onus of another hike. Then he pulled his arm free and in a perfectly deadpan voice, said, "You know, if you had made me an offer like that this morning, I might have gone for it. But it's too late now, Roz. I've had it. I'm going back to the room and packing."

The first word out of her mouth was, "But—" But what she was thinking was, 'Really?' Had he really just chosen packing over sex on a beach? That was so unlike him! This morning's hike hadn't been that strenuous! "What's the rush? We've still got another day here."

"You've got another day here," he said. "I'm done with this place. I believe I'm done with you, too."

Again, the first thought that popped into her head was, 'Really?'

"I'm taking the car because the rental agreement is in my name," he was saying now. "Capable as you are, I'm sure you'll have no trouble finding your way back to Edinburgh—or wherever it is you want to go next."

Bitterness sluiced through her, leaving a bad taste in her mouth. Leave it to him to start complimenting her now on character traits that he had never really appreciated. Next he would be telling her how much he liked her golf-game.

"Are you sure about this?" she said, giving him one last chance to change his mind. "I know this hasn't been the ideal vacation for you, but—"

"C'mon, Roz," he said, "admit it. Our relationship was going south even before this trip." Now that he had dropped the bomb, he was much more relaxed, and as cheerful as she had seen him in over a week. "You're fun and all, but we just don't have that much in common. And your friends are just plain weird."

The cheap shot about Max and Mara sparked a burn in her back-brain, but she contained it for the moment, preferring to focus on the southbound nature of their relationship. "If you were so unhappy," she said, letting a little edge creep into her tone, "then why did you come to Scotland with me?"

"I didn't say I was unhappy," he said, verbally splitting that hair. "I just said we don't have much in common. I thought some time away in a foreign country would fix that. But as it turns out, it only made things worse. You always do what you want to do, Roz—and that's never going to change. I need to be with someone who takes my needs into consideration."

"Really?" This time, the thought popped out of her mouth—an incredulous half-gasp that both mocked and condemned him. An instant later, a realization struck her squarely between the eyes. "Dammit! Mom was right again." A volatile cocktail of anger and embarrassment welled up within her, bringing with it the threat of tears. She turned her back on her spanking-new ex before he could see the shimmer in her eyes. "You have an hour to clear out of the hotel room," she said. "If you're there when I get back, I'll have you thrown out. Have a nice life."

"Wait!" Aldo said, as she squared her shoulders to leave. In spite of herself, she paused. In spite of her roiling emotions, part of her actually hoped that he was about to fall on his knees in theatrical apology and beg for a second chance. Instead, he asked, "What exactly did Aurora say about me?"

"They were big words," she drawled. "You wouldn't understand." Then she frilled her fingers in an over-the-shoulder farewell and walked away. She didn't look back, not even once. And as soon as the glimmer was gone from her eyes, she went in search of a bottle shop. There, she asked the proprietor for a bottle of his finest single malt. He was a wiry old gent with iron in his beard and steel in his stare, and as he reached for a dusty brown bottle on a nearby shelf, he gave her a critical once-over that struck her as borderline rude. Ordinarily, she would've ignored such behavior. But at the moment, she was in the mood to be rude back.

"You got something against women drinking whiskey, mister?" she said, doing her best Clint Eastwood imitation.

His iron caterpillar eyebrows arched, a Scottish WTF. "Nae, lass," he said, his accent thicker than winter wool. "A've always thought tha women got more call ta drink than men." As he dusted the bottle off, he casually added, "Special occasion?"

"Yes," she said, extending her credit card. "It's Independence Day."

"Good fer you," he said, and slipped the bottle into a bag. "Freedom's a good thing, it is." He ran her credit card then. As he waited for the company to authorize the charge, he gave her another extended once-over. When she took him to task with a terse, "You're staring again," he started like someone who had been caught daydreaming and then waxed sheepish. "Ai," he said, "A suppose A was. It's just that ye look like a tanner version of someone A used to know a long, long time ago. She ran off with a Yank when A was just a boy. A always thought she'd come back, but she never did."

It occurred to her that he was talking about her grandmother. It occurred to her to say so. But she knew it wouldn't end there. He'd want to know more and she'd feel obliged to tell him and she just didn't have it in her heart to be social at the moment. All she wanted to do was find a place to be alone with her bottle and the open wound formerly known as Aldo.

"People tell me I look like someone they know all the time," she said. Then she stuffed the bottle under her arm and headed for the door. On her way out, she added, "I'm sure she and the Yank had a great life together."

As she headed for the lake, she heard a set of giant engines thrumming toward an unseen dock. She figured it was the Nessie Hunter returning home with a load of tourists, and wondered if anyone had seen anything. She wondered if she would when she went out tomorrow. Because she was, by God, going on that cruise. The Urqehart Castle tour was the very last thing she was going to miss out on because of Aldo.

The town beach was empty except for a mob of twenty-something Japanese backpackers who were smoking cigarettes and posing for selfies at the water's edge. "Hey, sexy lady," one of them said, as she and her bottle marched past the group. "You want some help with that?" The rest of the mob laughed. She kept on walking—down the beach, past an outcropping of fringing rocks, and onto a narrow pathway of pebbled hardpan that led her into the woods. She followed the trail until the terrain turned rugged and then made her way back to the lake. There, she came upon a dimple in the shoreline: a cozy little cove that appeared to be some fisherman's favorite spot. He or she had dragged a length of fallen tree trunk onto the inlet's narrow, muddy shoulder. To the right of that, just out of sight, he'd built a primitive fire-pit and laid in a stash of wood.

"How perfect is this?" she said, settling down on the log. "A jug of Scotch, a place to sit, and thou."

Up close, the lake had a grey cast to it. Or maybe that was just a reflection of her mood. She had nurtured fantasies about Aldo being Mr. Right. But he had been playing the part of Mr. Right-For-The-Moment all along. What was it that made her such a poor judge of men and their feelings toward her? What was it about men?

She shed her backpack and then cracked open the bottle without bothering to discard the paper bag first. The fumes that wafted up from the sack reminded her of moldering Band-Aids, but she knocked back a man-sized swallow anyway. The lining of her mouth ignited. An instant later, her throat began to burn. Then, as the splash hit her stomach, she gagged on a clot of heat and liquefied bog. Her eyes watered. So did her mouth and nose. For a moment, her diaphragm refused to work.

"Holy shit," she gasped, when she could breathe again. "They must call this stuff Scotch because napalm was already taken!"

And that suited her just fine. This was just the sort of thing she needed to cleanse her of All Things Aldo. She took another swig and managed not to cough it back up. Her face started to tingle. The tip of her tongue went numb. A half-swig later, she developed a terrible yearning for consolation and pulled out her cell phone. Max answered on the second ring. The sound of his spritely tenor made her tear up.

"Roz, hi!" he exclaimed, his usual cheerful self. "What a wonderful surprise! When did you get back?"

"He dumped me, Max," she blurted in reply. "He came all the way to Scotland to dump me."

A moment of confused silence followed and then: "Wait. Where are you?"

"Highlands," she said morosely, staring out at the lake. "All washed up on the shores of Loch Ness at the ripe old age of twenty-seven."

"Really?" he said, in a tone that both worried for her roaming charges and marveled at the quality of her service. A heartbeat later, he added, "Wait. Have you been drinking?"

"Didn't you hear me?" she yowled, instantly indignant. "Aldo dumped me! Of course I've been drinking!" She reached for the bottle, meaning to illustrate the point with a loud glug, but then opted to leave it nestled in the fire-pit. "'I'm done with this place,' he said. 'I believe I'm done with you, too.' Quote, unquote. And he called you and Mara weird."

"Us? Weird?" he said, an indignant echo. "I told you he was a jerk."

"Yes, thank you ever so much for that," she drawled, not meaning a word of it. "Is Mara there?"

"Sorry," he said. "She has an early morning yoga class on Wednesdays. Want me to send her a text telling her to call you?"

An image flashed before her semi-drunken mind's eye: Mara in a child's pose, beaming like a Madonna as she immersed herself in her practice. Miserable as Roz was, she could not bring herself to disrupt her friend's reverie simply to cry on her shoulder. "No thanks," she said. "Let her enjoy her workout."

"Well," Max said, a dangling, bait-like sound, "I'm not doing anything that can't wait. I can listen if you want to talk."

His unflinching willingness to put her needs ahead of his own made her tear up again. Why couldn't Aldo be like that? "Thank you so much, you dear sweet man," she said, sincerity itself this time, "but this talk cries out for estrogen. Just tell Mara what happened when she gets home and let her know that I'm OK, OK?"

"Are you?" he asked. "OK, that is?"

"Yeah, sure." She scrubbed the tears from her eyes with the back of her hand and then rubbed her nose as well. "This isn't the first time I've been thrown by a bull."

"Aldo Whimsey Baker isn't a bull," Max said, in a serrated tone. "He's a shallow rodeo clown. And just so you know, I'm sending some seriously bad juju his way. I hope he loses his pretty boy hair and his pretty boy teeth and his pretty boy waist-line, too!"

The vehemence with which Max cursed Aldo into middle age wrenched a laugh out of her. "I love it! I love you, too! Now get on back to what you were doing. Talk with you soon. Bye!"

She hung up then, but her hunger for solace had not been slaked. She wanted soft, cooing sounds. She wanted now-now's and there-there's. Aside from Mara, however, she only had one friend who knew how to soothe her overwrought inner child. She scrolled down to her mother's number. But even as she went to click on it, she balked. Aurora had despised Aldo from the very start. So while she might start out sounding sorry about the break-up, sooner or later, she'd slip and crow about him being gone or like Max, let out a well-meaning 'I-told-you-so'. And the last thing she wanted right now was to be reminded that absolutely everyone in her life had seen this train-wreck coming except her.

"It's for the best, baby!" she said, doing a decent if somewhat caustic imitation of Aurora's voice. "Hopefully, you'll learn something from the experience."

She started to shove the phone back into her pocket only to decide to take a few pictures of the loch first. She had to have something to post on Facebook when she got back, right? The only problem was, a weather front was rolling in from the north. Rain was already falling in the hills, and fog was rising up along the shoreline. A smart woman would head for the hotel before the worst of the weather got here, she told herself. A smart woman wouldn't be reaching for that damn bottle of Scotch again.

"If I were a smart woman," she said, shouting that inner voice down, "I wouldn't have gotten involved with an actor in the first place. If I were a smart woman, I would've listened to my mom. But here I am and here I'm staying. Fuck the weather."

The fog quickly moved south. In those spots where it ran aground, the tree-line broke it into patches of thin, drizzly mist. Out on the water, however, it remained swirly and dense like a cloud. As Roz watched the bank's progression, thinking nothing but why, why, why, a shadow appeared in its midst, upright like a sailboat mast. She scowled at the sight. It just figured that the fisherman would pick now to return to his favorite spot! She stood up, meaning to be gone before Captain Crummy Timing sailed into the cove. An instant later, her Scotch-wobbly knees spilled her back onto her butt. In the span of that up-and-down moment, the mast in the fog sprouted a triangular crow's nest that resembled—ha-ha, how funny—a lizard's head. Funnier still, there did not seem to be a boat attached to the mast. Instead, it was being followed by three sizable humps and some very fat ripples.

Shit!

She scrambled back to her feet and retreated a few steps so she'd be able to bolt into the woods if the situation turned dire. Until then, though, she meant to soak up every moment of this honest-to-God Loch Ness Monster sighting. Nessie was swimming toward the cove at a leisurely speed, streaming fog from slotted nostrils. She had a sleek, saurian head with slender horns and dainty, seal-like ears. Her close-set eyes were the color of heather in full bloom. From a distance, her hide seemed to be bluish gray, but as she drew closer, it acquired an iridescent shimmer, possibly from all of the moisture in the air.

Incredible, Roz thought, drunkenly transfixed. Mara would be speechless with envy when she heard about this. And Max—well, Max would require proof. The realization punctured Roz's daze. Gun-slinger quick, she whipped out her cell phone. As she thumbed it to camera mode, she made full-on eye contact with Nessie, who bared a jagged mouthful of teeth in response.

No feckin pictures!

The command popped into her head, loud as Scottish thunder. She was so startled by the clap, she fumbled the phone. For one oh-shit moment, the whole of her attention was dedicated to catching the phone before it hit the ground. Somewhere within that tiny span of time, the Loch Ness Monster turned into an overcast patch of bubbles.

"No!" Roz cried, a distraught howl. The opportunity of a lifetime and she'd just bumbled it away! "Come back!"

The water at the mouth of the cove erupted as if an ICBM had just been launched. An instant later, a massive redheaded woman splashed down on the beach in her birthday suit. She shook herself off like a wet dog and then flashed Roz a carnivorous grin.

"Failte," she said. When Roz stood there gaping, she added, "Walcome."

She was curiously built, with a long neck, narrow shoulders, a muscular torso, and stubby legs. She made no attempt to cover her mannish breasts or her hairless groin, but neither did she flaunt them. Her lavender eyes were fixed on Roz.

"Took ye long enough tae get here," she remarked. "A was beginning tae think that ye dinna exist."

Roz's incredulity eroded, exposing a strange, surreal sense that she had been waiting for this moment all of her life. "Funny," she said, overcome by a sudden wave of giddiness, "but I could say the same about you."

Nessie's grin shifted into something slyer. "So ye've figured out who A am, av ye?" At Roz's nod, she gave her curly seaweed locks a toss and said, "What gave me away?"

"I think it was the tail," Roz said, pointing to the stubby jut that was protruding from the changeling's backside.

Nessie whipped her head around to see the offending appendage, forgetting that her neck was a mere stump of its former self. "Feck, tha hurt," she rumbled, and then tried again at a more appropriate speed. "Ah, well," she said then. "'Tis usually smaller than tha, but A were a wee bit concerned that A'd scared ye off so A rushed the Change.

"Is tha usquebaugh?"

"What?" Roz asked, looking around for something that resembled the phlegmy sound.

"Usquebaugh. Whiz-kay," Nessie said, breaking the word into two exaggerated syllables. "Is tha whiskey?"

"Oh," she said, zeroing in on the firepit, "yeah. Want some?"

"Thought ye'd never ask," Nessie said, and snatched the proffered bottle from Roz with a slightly webbed hand. In one enthusiastic pull, she guzzled more Scotch than Roz had swallowed over the course of an hour. Afterward, she blew a set of fog-rings from her prizefighter nose, scratched her brawny belly, and then tucked the bottle under her arm. "Right fine droppa."

"It's all yours," Roz said, fully aware that she wasn't getting the bottle back regardless.

Nessie's nostrils flared again, this time in Roz's direction. "Ye smell a wee bit chill. Fancy a fire?"

Roz sniffed, ever so discreetly, trying to discern the scent she was giving off. But her nose really was 'a wee bit chill' and the only thing she could smell was her high octane breath. "Good idea," she said, and dragged a log into the fire pit. As she leaned back toward the wood pile to pick up some kindling, the changeling spat through her teeth. The spittle hit the log with an explosive splat. An instant later, the log whooshed into flames.

"That's a handy little knack," Roz said, trying to hide her surprise.

"Tis tha Divine's gift tae dragons," Nessie said off-handedly.

Roz was halfway to letting the statement slide when she finally realized what she had heard. "Wait," she said then. "Are you telling me you're a dragon?"

"Ai," Nessie said, looking puzzled. "A thought ye knew."

"Nuh-uh," Roz said, dumbstruck all the way down to her toes. "I thought you were The Loch Ness Monster."

Irritation tugged at the corners of the changeling's eyes and mouth. "Feck," she said. "A hate tha name. Do A look like a monster?"

"Not at the moment," Roz admitted, studying her visitor through the curls of gray smoke that were rising up from the fire. "But unless I'm drunk to the point of hallucinating, you looked a wee bit different when you were in the water."

"Ur not tha drunk, are ye?"

"No," Roz said, squinting now, trying to see through the strapping, heather-eyed woman with wild red hair. "I don't think so."

"Gud. Because it's gahn tae be a rough road fer both of us if ye canna hold ur drink. Wat's ur name?" When Roz balked, Nessie flushed pink like an irked chameleon and said, "Ur not daft, are ye? Answer me!"

"Only if you tell me your name first," Roz blurted.

"Ye know who I am," the changeling asserted. "Ye said so yerself."

"You said you hate being called the Loch Ness Monster," Roz countered. "So I doubt that's what you call yourself. And I read somewhere that there's power in a dragon's true name. Those who know it may call upon it for protection."

The next thing Roz knew, the changeling was in her face, so close that Roz could feel the chill radiating from her outsized body. "Tha power's in the dragon, lass, not tha name," she said, in a soft, low voice that could've been construed as menacing. "Ye need to start reading a better brand of books."

Roz hadn't expected the bulky changeling to be able to move that quickly. Nor had she grasped how precarious her situation was until this very moment. This wasn't some elaborate cosplay game based on characters from her mom's fantasy series. This was a close encounter of the real kind, and she had no idea what to do next.

"Look," she said. "This is a mega-first for me. No offense, OK, but I was hoping that if I had your name, you wouldn't be able to eat me."

"Why would A want tae eat ye?" Nessie wondered, and then inhaled deeply, smelling Roz from head to toe. "Ur not a virgin, are ye?" When Roz recoiled, an involuntary reaction, Nessie let out a throaty guffaw, then sat down on the fallen tree and had herself another drink. "Ha!" she said afterward. "Ye should've seen ur face! As if A'd go tae all tha trouble of Calling ye here just tae make a meal of ye! A swear, humans can be so ridiculous."

"Yeah, right," Roz said, warm in the face from embarrassment rather than the fire. "Ridiculous. My name is Rosalyn, by the way. Rosalyn Vanderbilt. Roz for short."

The changeling's forehead furrowed; at the same time, her neck arched. "Van-der-bilt? Tha's nae a highland clan."

"My father's mother was a MacLachlan."

"Ah, the MacLachlans," she said, switching to a more approving tone. "That's a name A recognize. Ye come from hardy stock, Roz Vanderbilt. And since ye asked, A'll be glad tae tell ye my name. Most assume it's Nessie because of my association with tha loch. But in fact, A've had many names over the ages. The one I like best is Brigit: She of the Sacred Flame and the Hearth."

"Is it OK if I just call you Brigit?"

Brigit guffawed and then patted the span of wood next to her, an invitation to sit. "A like ye, Rosalyn Vanderbilt," she said, as Roz complied with the request. "Ur a quick wit. And the fact that ye didn't run away when ye first saw me tells me tha ur brave as well. There's just one thing more A need tae know."

Roz licked her lips. They tasted of whiskey and mist and a hint of uncertainty. "What's that?"

"Do ye trust me?" Before Roz could reply, she went on to say, "A know ye have no call to, and A'd not be keen to declare myself so quickly if A were sitting where ye are. But there are things you need to know; things A need to tell ye. And the telling of these things canna be done out here in the open. A would take ye back to my lair, but we canna get there from here by ways ur used tae takin'. If ye agree to go with me, ye must do as A tell ye—no questions asked. Can ye do that?"

Don't do it!

That's what Aurora would have said, that and a footnote: you know you always put your trust in the wrong places. Sage as the advice might be, though, Roz had no intention of heeding it. Not only was she thoroughly convinced that the dragon meant her no harm, she also believed that their friendship was preordained. Indeed, she only had one reservation at the moment and she was quick to voice it.

"It's not that I don't trust you, Brigit," she said. "I do. I just don't know if I can follow anyone anywhere blindly or in silence. That's simply not my nature."

Brigit plucked a blazing coal from the fire-pit and twiddled it between her fingers as she considered Roz's objection. Moments later, she pitched the coal back into the fire and said, "A understand what saying, lass, as A much prefer leadin' ta followin' myself. But in this case, A believe ur better off not knowin' what's comin' till yer on the other side of it. So just this once, I need ye ta do as yer told and ask questions later. Can ye do that?"

"I suppose," Roz said grudgingly. "But just this once!"

"All right then," Brigit said. "Let's get crackin'."

She hopped to her feet and began to stomp the fire out with her bare feet. Roz watched, appalled at first and then increasingly delighted. Aurora was going to flip when she heard about this!

"What's so funny?"

The question startled her out of her reverie. She phased back into focus to find Brigit scowling down at her.

"Are ye laughing at me?"

"No!" Roz said, adding 'thin-skinned' to the list of things she was compiling about the dragon. "I was just imagining the look on my mother's face when I tell her about you."

"Telling people about me is nae a gud idea," Brigit said. "They'll mock ye fer a fool even as they mob the loch tae look fer me."

Roz dismissed the warning with a wave of her hand. "Mom wouldn't mock me. She's the one who predicted that you'd find me."

Brigit reared back, forgetting yet again that her neck measured in inches now rather than feet. "Ye said yer Maclachlan on yer father's side, nae?" At Roz's puzzled nod, she asked, "Then how'd yer mum know tha A'd be Calling?"

"I dunno," Roz said. "Mom's been writing stuff about dragons since I was a kid."

"'Stuff'?" the changeling warbled. "What kind of 'stuff'?"

Brigit's agitation flustered Roz. For one heart-pounding moment, her thoughts scrabbled like a dog on glare ice. She didn't know where to look or what to say or recall so much as a word from any of her mother's books. Then Ezzie popped into her head, squawking like a little sister, and brought her a measure of traction.

"Books," she said. "She writes books about a pink-feathered dragon and her fairy friend."

"A've never met one of the fairy folk," Brigit said, waxing thoughtful. "A've never seen a pink-feathered dragon, either. Then again, A dunna get around much. Where'd yer mum see this dragon?"

"In her dreams," Roz replied. "She likes to say she does her best work in her sleep."

Brigit let out another warble and then leaned in close. Her breath smelled of whiskey, brimstone, and fish. The innermost part of her nostrils were an ominous shade of red. "In her dreams, ye say?" She inhaled deeply as if trying to sniff out the truth. "An ye say she's nae a Maclachlan. Could she be from some other highland clan?"

"Not even close," Roz said, trying not to be distracted by the changeling's proximity. "Her father was Spanish-American. Her mother's family came from Mexico. But—what difference does it make?"

"If she were a highlander," Brigit said, "A'd be talking tae her right now instead of ye."

"What?" Roz blurted, feeling instantly and absurdly betrayed by both mother and dragon. "Why? Did I fail some kind of test just now?"

Brigit snorted, expelling twin streamers of fishy-smelling mist into Roz's face. "Tha Calling's not a competition, lass. It always finds its way tae the eldest female of tha blood."

"Sorry," Roz said, starting to feel rather depleted and tired. "I'm not following. Calling?"

"Damn," Brigit said, and then spat into the fire-pit, causing the smoldering embers to flare up again. "A canna believe ye know nothing of these things." She snatched up the whiskey bottle and drained it in one long swallow. Afterward, she said, "This meeting were no accident. A Called ye here. A've been Calling fer years. Did ye not feel me tugging at the corners of yer mind?"

Roz's first impulse was denial. No way! Couldn't be. This trip had been her idea. She'd thought of it, organized it, and made it happen. Hell, she'd even brought that jerk, Aldo, with her. A dragon would've made sure that he stayed home.

"Not necessarily. A've got a soft spot fer pretty faces, too."

It took a moment to realize that Brigit hadn't said that aloud. In that moment, she became aware of a presence nestled at the bottom of her subconscious. It was subtle yet familiar, an alien energy that had been with her for as long as she could remember. She'd called it wanderlust and ADHD. Occasionally, it had seemed like fear of commitment. It was much, much more than that, though. It was a link both magical and genetic. It was an honest-to-God bond with a dragon. The realization hit her like a religious experience. She felt both humbled and exalted.

"OK," she said. "You Called. Here I am. What next?"

Brigit backed into the loch, staring at Roz all the while. As her knees disappeared beneath the water, she doubled in size. A few steps later, her legs shrank back into her lengthening torso and she submerged with a weighty splash. When she popped back up a few moments thereafter, it was as the Loch Ness Monster in all of her serpentine glory.

"If ye call me a monster again, A will eat ye even if yer not a virgin."

"Touchy, touchy," Roz said, feeling secure enough to tease.

"Come tae me," the dragon instructed. *"Press your back against my chest."* When Roz balked, a natural reaction to the thought of water-logged jeans, Brigit added, *"Quickly now. We've a ways tae go."*

An instant after Roz set foot in the water, a shiver skittered up her spine and set every hair on her body on end. "Shit," she said, through gritted teeth. "If this water was any colder, it would be frozen. Why don't we fly instead?"

"We canna."

"Why not?"

"A dunna have wings".

"What?" Roz barked, even as she tried to keep her teeth from chattering. "What kind of dragon are you?"

"A water dragon," Brigit said, splashing her tail for emphasis. *"Now come. Quickly. All will be well. A promise."*

Roz slogged forward, grumbling every step of the way. She shuddered as the water came to her knees. Icy tears sprung to her eyes as it rose over her hips. "I don't think I can—" Do this, she meant to say, only to gasp instead as the dragon reached out and pulled her close. An instant after she made contact with the dragon's chest, all but the faintest chill melted away. Even her legs, which were still underwater, warmed up.

"Wow," she said, amazed. "How'd you do that?"

"Water dragon magic," Brigit said matter-of-factly, and then began streaming fog through her nostrils. Moments later, they were engulfed in a pillow of gray mist that then followed them like a tethered balloon out of the little cove and into open water.

"Where are we going?" Roz asked, trying to peer past their personal fogbank.

"Quiet!" Brigit ordered. *"We may be disguised, but sound carries across water and dusk is tha time when fisherfolk head home. If ye have questions, learn to ask them through the bond."*

Through the bond? What was that supposed to mean? She almost wondered that aloud, but caught herself at the last second. Dragon's stomping grounds, dragon's rules. If she wanted quiet, then quiet Roz would be.

"Smart choice."

Roz beamed at the praise only to be struck by an afterthought. *"Wait. You heard that?"*

"Ai. Why so surprised?"

"I thought telepathy would be harder than that."

The dragon snorted, incidentally thickening their fog-bank. *"Some things are only as hard as ye make them, lass."*

"If that's so," Roz replied, *"then why haven't I heard anything from you before today?"*

"Maybe ye weren't listening," Brigit suggested. *"Or maybe ye live too far away. Now that yer here, though, and speaking through tha link, who cares about yesterday?"*

"I do," Roz began, only to pause as she caught a glimpse of the far shore through the fog. The coastline was a series of tall, sheer cliffs. There was no suggestion of a beach or any other place to go aground. She waited for Brigit to veer off in one direction or the other, but the dragon continued to swim straight ahead, picking up speed as she went. Finally, unable to bear the suspense any longer, she asked: *"So what do you know that I don't?"*

"Quite a bit, A'd imagine," Brigit replied, and then abruptly changed the subject. *"How long can ye hold yer breath?"*

"Why?" Roz wondered, and then realized that they were starting to submerge. *"Really? Fine time to ask, dragon!"*

"Just close ur eyes and fill ur lungs. A willna let ye come tae any harm."

Grudgingly, Roz did as she was told. An instant after she blocked off her windpipe, the dragon dove. The shock of perma-cold water rushing over her head nearly made her cough up her air. The sensation of being carried into the depths did nothing to assuage her comfort levels. She clung to Brigit's forearms, willing herself to be calm. The presence at the back of her mind urged serenity, too. A trickle of bubbles leaked from a corner of her seam of a mouth. Heartbeats later, a second trickle escaped from her nose. She tried not to think about her growing hunger for air. Perversely, oxygen was the only thing on which her brain wanted to focus. A third trickle broke free. Panic began to set in. She had never held her breath this long! She didn't think she could go another second without a breath of fresh air.

"Hurry!"

At that very moment, Brigit lunged: a muscular, vertical thrust. Something rough and hard scraped Roz's knee in passing. She let out a mental yowl that turned into a full-on stream of bubbles. All at once, the feeling of being underwater disappeared. She gasped—a blustery, blind reflex. The air tasted of algae and damp rock and things that lived in the dark.

"Oh my God," she said, gagging on a backwash of adrenaline and Scotch. "I think I'm going to be sick!"

Quick as a thought, the dragon dropped her.

She landed feet-first on a rocky floor that was slick rather than wet. She had the sense that they were in close quarters but all she could see was pitch-darkness.

"Where the hell are we?" she asked, starting to feel cold as well as water-logged.

"Home," Brigit said, speaking aloud so Roz would know that she had shifted back into human form.

"Nice place," Roz grumbled, as she wrung loch water from her sodden clothes. "Entertain much?"

"Ye'd be surprised," Brigit said "We've still got a ways to go, though, so c'mon. Follow me."

Roz wondered how she was supposed to do that when she couldn't see anything past her nose. But before she could give voice to the thought, a tiny tongue of red flame appeared ahead of her. Its faint light reflected off Brigit's blue-grey back and made her seaweed curls glisten.

"This way," Brigit said, and the flame began to bob forward. "Mind ur step."

The reason for the warning soon became apparent. The floor was uneven, broken into steps that climbed upward into more darkness. The steps were uneven, too, time-worn footholds formed by giant-sized strides. Roz tripped more than once on her way to the unseen top and was on the verge of throwing a righteous temper tantrum when the flame disappeared. An instant later, a crack of gray bisected the blackness and then expanded into an opening.

"Finally," Roz griped, and then followed Brigit into the light.

If Roz had had to guess what a dragon's den might look like, she would have imagined a dark, rough-hewn space cluttered with old bones. Brigit's home looked more like a traditional Scottish cottage. It had a fireplace with an enormous stone hearth. It also had a kitchen of sorts, with a pump for water and an old-fashioned icebox. Although there were no tables or chairs in sight, an oversized heap of floor pillows had been piled in front of the fireplace. And a bookcase filled with books and memorabilia occupied the far wall. On any other day, she might have remarked on that curiosity, but as soon as she caught sight of the cottage's other entryway, she forgot about all else.

"This place has a front door?" Roz asked, lancing Brigit with an incredulous glare. "And you brought me in through the loch and damn near drowned me in the process? What's wrong with you?"

Brigit deflected the grievance with a shrug. "There's no way tae open tha door from the outside when it's been locked from within," she said. "It's got a proper warding on it."

"A what?" Roz said, feeling entitled to badger the changeling.

"A warding," Brigit said, showing remarkable patience. "Dragon magic, ye would call it. Tis how we protect tha which we hold dear." She eyed Roz critically then. "Ye should get ur wet togs off before ye catch a chill." When Roz balked at the advice, the changeling cocked her head and snorted. "What? Ur shy? After A've been socializing with ye in me nuddies all afternoon?"

Roz wanted to deny it. She had done her fair share of nude hot-tubbing with Aldo. She'd flashed her boobs for beads at Mardi Gras that one time, too. But there was something unsettling about the thought of stripping down in front of a dragon.

"Oh fer Divinity's sake!" Brigit said, and then spat into the fireplace. As the pre-laid fire roared to life, she added, "Do as ye will. A'll be back inna few."

With that, she stomped off to an adjoining room.

In the changeling's absence, Roz scurried over to the blazing hearth to warm herself. As she stood there shivering, she scolded herself for being silly. It wasn't like there was anything to be ashamed of here! She peeled off her wet clothes and laid them out on the hearth-stones to dry. As she did so, the fire's sweet, billowing heat began to soften her up like a triple-cream brie. The next thing she knew, she was eying the nest of pillows. It had been a brutally long day. A snooze in front of the fire sounded like the perfect antidote.

"So ye do have a bit o' sense in that head o' yurn after all. Gud."

Out of reflex, Roz raised her arms to cover herself. The changeling started to sneer at that only to nod approvingly as she caught sight of the dragon tattoos on Roz's arms. "Nice work, that."

"Thanks," Roz said, consciously exposing herself so she could display the ink to full effect. "I'm planning on getting one on my back as well."

"This is a good sign," Brigit mused, as she studied the artwork. "Ye knew who ye were before we connected." She took one last look at the tattoos and then tossed a large green cloth in Roz's direction. Roz thought it was a towel at first, but as it flew through the air, it unfolded, exposing fur on the edges. The material was antique velvet, and smelled of dust and whiskey.

"Damn," Roz said, as she wrapped the sumptuous cloak around herself. "Where'd you get this?"

Brigit was similarly cloaked, albeit in black. The color offset her brilliant red hair. "Ye live in a place long enough," she said, "ye accumulate things. These belonged tae an English earl who thought he could rule tha highlands. He quickly came tae think otherwise.

"Now if ye don't mind—or even if ye do—A need tae sleep fer a spell. A'm too old tae be switching back and forth between shapes like a freshly sexed wyrm. While A'm out, ye may do as ye please so long as ye dunna disturb me."

"I think I can manage that," Roz said, snuggling deeper into her wrap. "I'll probably grab some shut-eye, too."

"Gud idea," Brigit said. "A'll nae be out long—a day or two at most. Then we can have a natter."

Roz's first impulse was to object. Two days? That sounded a bit excessive! On second thought, though, one that was accompanied by a massive yawn, two days sounded just about right. The next thing she knew, she was curled up among the pillows, fast asleep in a dragon's lair.

Roz roused slowly, luxuriating beneath velvety covers. As she lounged in the arms of semi-consciousness, she extended her left leg, expecting to make dreamy contact with a warm, muscular calf. When all she encountered was cool, empty space, alarms went off in her head.

Something was wrong.

Aldo was missing.

Her dream bubble burst and she popped fully awake—not in a posh hotel bed with all the trimmings, but in a pile of pillows that smelled of wood-smoke. Her sumptuous covering was an old-fashioned cape. She wasn't wearing any clothes. She ran her fingers through her stringy hair, suffering a moment of Mardi Gras déjà vu. Then yesterday's events resurfaced like bubbles in a black lake. Aldo was gone—*I believe I'm done with you.* She had gone to the loch to get drunk and had met a dragon instead. This was that dragon's home. The dragon was asleep in the next room.

Shit!

It had been so much easier to accept everything that had transpired when she'd been a little pickled. Stone-cold sober, she didn't know what to think. Denial was impossible, for here she was. Yet belief was slow to show its face.

Perhaps her break-up with Aldo had induced a psychotic break.

Her stomach rumbled—a sharp, hungry pang that wanted to know what psychotic breaks kept in their iceboxes. She climbed to her feet, still wrapped in the cape, meaning to have a look only to spot her clothes. They looked like pieces of jerky now, all dry and heavily wrinkled, but she traded the cape for them nonetheless, savoring their infused warmth. The fire was still ablaze in the hearth. The log didn't look as if it had burned at all. As far as she was concerned, that was another arguing point for a psychotic break.

Her stomach growled again. "Yeah, yeah," she said, and headed for the icebox only to slam the door shut an instant after she tugged it open. Meh! She didn't know what she had been expecting, but it sure as hell wasn't salmon carcasses, some of them quite gnawed upon and none particularly fresh. It occurred to her to look elsewhere for something to eat, but before she could act on the thought, she was struck by a more urgent need. Where was the bathroom in this place? There were only three doors that she could see. The front door was magically locked, the second led back to the loch, and Brigit was sleeping behind the third. The first two options didn't seem at all promising, so she went scurrying toward door number three. At this point, she didn't care of there was a whole nest of sleeping dragons on the other side of it!

The smell of Scotch enveloped her as she eased the door open—not a stray puff of stale morning-after breath, but a full miasma of distillery effluvia. The reason for this became obvious as her eyes adjusted to the room's barely there lighting. It looked like a mid-sized whiskey cellar, with barrels on racks and bottles in crates and drinking glasses on dusty shelving. Some of the barrels bore very old time-stamps. Under less urgent circumstances, Roz would have stopped to take a closer look at this single malt wonderland. As it was, she hurried through it with barely a second glance—only to skid to a stop in front of a massive mound of gold coinage and jewels. The sight was so stunning, a word slipped past Roz's lips before she could stifle it.

"Whoa."

The mound shifted ever so slightly, revealing a patch of black velvet. The thought that accompanied the shift was not pleased. *"A told ye nae ta disturb me."*

"I know," Roz said, projecting an image of herself dancing in place. "And I didn't mean to. But I thought there might be a water closet or midden or something of the like back here."

Alien comprehension flared in her mind, that and possibly a hint of sympathy. *"Outside. To the right of the cottage."*

"What about the lock?" Roz asked urgently.

A moment's pause ensued—the drakena removing the spell. *"Go,"* she said then. As Roz took off running, she added, *"When ye are relieved, return tae me."*

The outhouse was dilapidated and reeked of rotting fish, but Roz didn't care. She didn't even mind that the paper was old and waxy. Under the right conditions, she decided, anything could feel posh. Even so, the first thing she did when she finally rejoined Brigit in her private chamber was offer a little unsolicited advice.

"Indoor plumbing," she said. "Think about it."

The changeling was perched atop of her treasure trove now. When she shrugged, human-style, her velvet cloak slid down, exposing a blue-white shoulder. "If a dragon shits in tha loch and no one sees, what need has she o' plumbing?" Before Roz could respond, she dismissed the matter with a wave of her hand and said, "Tis nothing ye have to concern yerself with anyway as we'll not be staying here after all."

"What?" Roz blurted. "Why? I thought there were things I

needed to know. I thought you were going to school me."

"There are," Brigit said. "And I was. "But last night as I was pondering tha mystery of ur mum, A was swept up into the Dreaming and brought to an understanding."

"OK," Roz said, "I didn't understand a word of that. What's this about my mom?"

"She writes about a dragon that comes to her in her sleep!" Brigit said, growing animated with excitement. "Think about it! The answer's obvious. She's being Called by a drakena!"

Roz's first impulse was to dismiss the claim. Seriously? Mom? That was crazy! But even as the denial popped into her head, logic sounded off. Why not Aurora? As far as Roz knew, there was no rule restricting a family to one dragon. And the thought of Esmerelda being real was actually kind of cool.

"OK," she said, "I'll bite. My mom is being Called. What's that got to do with us?"

"A got the sense tha her dragon is a Great One," Brigit said. "And that tha Great One needs our help."

"How are we supposed to do that?"

"A willna know till A meet ur mum."

"And how do you propose to do that?" Roz wanted to know. "She won't come here; I already asked."

"Then we'll go tae her."

Roz loosed an incredulous laugh. "Do you have any idea how far away California is from here?"

Brigit shrugged, projecting an air of haughty insouciance. "What is distance is this age of sky-travel? A may spend most of my time in tha water, but A have eyes and ears and know about aero-planes. We will fly tae ur homeland."

"Oh?" Roz said, waxing snotty in turn. "Do you have a passport? Do you have any kind of identification at all?"

"Of course not!" Brigit said. "A'm a feckin' dragon!"

"You could be Mary, Queen of Scots for all the good it would do you!" Roz fired back. "If you don't have the proper documentation, you won't be allowed to board any plane bound for the United States. And even if we managed to sneak you aboard, you'd be nabbed upon landing, because they check your papers on both ends."

"A dunna think they could hold me if A dinna want to be held," Brigit said, glancing slyly at her nails.

"Maybe," Roz countered. "But you wouldn't get away without drawing a ton of attention to yourself. Is that what you want? Because that's what you'll get if you try to gate-crash the US. Your face will be plastered on every newspaper and television on the planet. You'll have to find yourself a brand-new secret identity."

Brigit rumbled, clearly disturbed by that prospect. She twirled a lock of fiery hair around a forefinger for a thoughtful moment and then asked, "What if A didn't travel in human form? A could Change into something else."

"Like what—a dog maybe?" The thought of Brigit as a fire-breathing Chihuahua with a red mane tickled Roz. "That might work. I could call you a rare Scottish Gryphon and keep you under my seat."

Brigit nixed that idea with a sorry shake of her head. "A can Change my form, but not my mass. So while A can make myself smaller than this," she said, gesturing at her body, "A canna get any smaller."

"OK," Roz said, "so you're too big to pass for a dog. You can't go as a horse, either. I've had some experience in equine transport and in addition to the proper papers, there's bloodwork involved and quarantine. I'm telling you, Brigit, there's no way you're flying across the Atlantic unless you sprout your own wings."

"Would that A could," Brigit said. "But for better or worse, A am made for water, not air."

"Then why not swim across the Atlantic?"

Brigit sighed, expelling twin rings of steam from her nose. "A've never crossed the Great Water," she confessed. "Indeed, A've never crossed anything larger than the Irish Sea—and that were back in my younger days. So A canna say A canna swim it because A've never tried. And A canna say how long it would take me because A dunna know where A'm goin'."

"Maybe we could fit you with a GPS or some other kind of small craft navigational system," Roz said, thinking out loud. "Or maybe—" A set of smokestacks emerged from the fogbank in her brain. An instant later, a massive, wave-splitting bow appeared. "Holy hotcakes," she exclaimed, tapping herself on the forehead. "That's it!" When Brigit looked at her askance, she said, "A cruise ship. That's the ticket. Why fly when you can sail?"

"What about documentation?" Brigit asked dubiously. "Surely the same transportation rituals apply."

"They do," Roz said, oozing satisfaction. "The difference is, a plane is a self-contained vessel that flies at 35,000 feet. Once it's in the air, there's no getting inside it until it lands again. A cruise ship, on the other hand, sails at sea level and has all sorts of open air decks."

The changeling's nostrils flared—her liking the smell of that idea. "Ah, of course! A'd be able ta climb aboard the ship after it sets sail. Brilliant!"

"Wait, maybe not," Roz said, backtracking after a moment's thought. "Most of those ships are over a hundred feet tall. I don't think climbing up the side of one is a viable option."

"Then A'll jump onto it!"

"I dunno," Roz said. "That's a pretty steep trajectory."

"Not fer me. Water dragons canna fly, but we can jump like fleas." When Roz continued to balk, Brigit body-surfed down the side of the treasure trove and grabbed her by the hand. Her grip was as fierce as the gleam in her lavender eyes. "Just wait, ye'll see," she said. "This is goin' tae work."

"If it doesn't," Roz countered, "you get to swim all the way to the States."

CHAPTER 6

The woman is pulling weeds away from the corn plants that are sprouting up on her family's chinampa. The stalks look healthy and strong. The squash crop on the next islet is doing well, too, as are the tomatoes and beans. Thriving: at last, the woman knows the meaning of that sound. Her belly has not growled at her in a long, long time, and her breasts are heavy with milk for the child whom she has left sleeping beneath an anchor willow. He is a robust boy with quick hands and a bold voice. Since his birth, her mate has found few reasons to hit her—and not just because the god-in-disguise disapproves of such behavior. In the midst of such abundance, he has become a more forgiving man. The woman is grateful for that; thankful. Yes, she has come to know the meaning of those sounds, too.

Thanks to Quetzalcoatl.

All of the villagers sing his praises now, but when the god-in-disguise first came to them with his plan for a better life, they thought he was crazy. "Listen to me," he insisted. "Why fight the jungle for food when you can farm the lake-bed instead?"

"Show us," the woman said, because she knew that hungry people didn't trust anything but their own eyes.

So Quetzalcoatl constructed the first chinampa.

Everyone watched as he staked out a square plot on the lake's shallow south shore and fenced it in with wattle. Everyone watched as he layered the plot with mud, lake sediment, and rotting vegetation, and planted precious seed. But no one except the woman believed that corn or anything else would grow on that boggy plot—until the first tender shoots burst forth from the muck.

Now the south shore is blistered with floating gardens. Each chinampa has its own trees, one on each corner, and their roots secure the plot to the lake-bed. The chinampas are separated by channels so canoes can come and go freely at harvest-time. So far this year, the canoes have come and gone four times, ample harvests all, and the fifth is in the ground. Everybody believes now. Everybody wants to offer sacrifices so the harvests will keep on coming. But Quetzalcoatl does not permit sacrifices to be made to him or any of the other gods. 'Let your sweat be your sacrifice,' he tells them. Tezcatlipoca does not approve of such instructions. The woman has often heard him barking in the jungle at night, protesting the lack of respect. But fear of reprisal no longer robs her of sleep because she knows that the god-in-disguise will keep The Jaguar at bay.

The soft, fussy sounds of a baby waking up attract the woman's attention. She pushes to her feet and stretches to relieve the weedy kinks in her back. Then she strolls toward the willow tree. As she looms over the wattle basket that serves as her son's bed, he breaks into a smile that is as broad as it is toothless and kicks his pudgy legs in a joyful greeting. She smiles back, the only time she ever shapes her mouth like that, and then lifts him to her breast. As he starts to suckle, she closes her eyes and savors the sensations of life.

The dream-memory of being suckled was so intense, Aurora had to stop typing to see if her breasts were leaking even though she hadn't nursed anything other than the occasional hangover since Rosalyn was a baby. The thought of her wayward daughter further distracted her. She had called from Scotland last night. Finally. After the opening niceties, she dropped a bomb.

"Aldo and I broke up."

That should have been the best news ever, but before Aurora could compose an appropriately sympathetic yahoo, Roz delivered another bunker-buster.

"I couldn't bear the thought of being on the same plane with him all the way back to San Francisco," she'd said, "so I cancelled my ticket and booked a cabin on a cruise ship instead. I'll be sailing from Glasgow to New York and then taking a train home from there. I'm going to use the extra travel time to get my head on straight. You understand, don't you, Mom?"

Well, of course she did. Sort of. Deep down, though, not really. Aurora came from a generation that dealt with problems head-on while working nine to five. Introspection, not partying, was the process by which people got over heart-break. Instead of trying to eat and drink away the pain—and everybody knew that's what people did on those cruises—Aurora would've preferred that Roz come straight home on the first available flight and concentrate on finding a job. Not because she was strapped for cash. She wasn't. Between the trust fund that Duncan had set up for her and a few shrewd investments on her own part, she was pretty much set for life. But being well-off wasn't the same as being well-adjusted. She needed some kind of purpose to her life.

Duncan's ghost laughed at that. *A mom-approved purpose, of course.*

No. Not necessarily. Not—

The ghost laughed again. She scowled, trying in vain to deflect the psychic mockery, and then conceded the point. "OK, I get it, you're right," she said. "But when did a mother's stamp of approval become such a bad thing?"

The telephone rang, robbing the ghost of a chance to answer. She screened the incoming call. The message was from the pharmacy in town, a final reminder for her to pick up her statin prescription. Roz would've teased her for that: "If you were any more absent-minded, we'd have to micro-chip you!" She would have shrugged such a comment off if Roz had been here to make it. In her absence, however, Aurora felt a pang of sorrow. What if she never had the pleasure of being teased by her daughter again? What if she decided to keep wandering the far corners of the world and never came home again?

A lump rose in her throat. She swallowed it immediately and then raised her eyebrows in a silent oh-dear-God. Was this what menopause was like—spurious fits of melodramatic panic? Denial was quick to dismiss the notion. She wasn't old enough to be menopausal! More likely, she was just suffering from a touch of cabin fever. She needed to get out. Talk to a few people. Socialize a bit.

Yes, that sounded good. She'd take a drive into town later— just as soon as she finished up the chapter inspired by last night's dream. The story was developing rapidly now. All of the characters were more realistic than they should be at this point, and while she still had no idea where the plot was going, she had a sense that it was heading in the right direction. She couldn't stop now; she would lose her momentum. But even as she started to hunker back down in front of her computer, the phone rang again. The voice that engaged the answering machine made her forget all about work.

"Aurora?" the message went. "This is Charles Weber. I was hoping to take you to lunch today, but apparently, you're already out and ab—"

She snagged the receiver before he could go any further. "Hello?"

"Aurora!" Charles said, sounding delighted. "So you are home."

"Yes," she replied, trying not to sound breathless. "I was working."

"Ah," he said, "again with the work. Your clients truly are slave-drivers. Does this mean you're too busy to have lunch with me?"

"Actually," she said, quashing the part of her that wanted to continue working, "I need to go into town to run a few errands. I could meet you somewhere afterward if you'd like."

"Name a place!" She did. The selection agreed with him. "After lunch," he said, "maybe we could do a little winetasting."

That workaholic in her wanted to say 'No!' to that, too, but once again, she ignored that vote. "Maybe," she said, in a shockingly flirty voice. "Let's see how lunch goes first. See you in an hour?"

"Deal," he said, and hung up.

An instant later, she was on her way to her bedroom to dress.

She was in line at the pharmacy when the hair on the back of her neck bristled. She glanced over her shoulder, expecting to see a fan approaching with one of her books in hand. But while there were people standing behind her, none of them seemed interested in making contact with her. A Spidey-sense misfire, she figured, and thought no more of it.

Until it happened again.

The second time that ticklish feeling overtook her, she was strolling down Saratoga's main drag, a ten-block strip of Big Basin Way bracketed by charming little shops and restaurants. She came to an abrupt stop in front of a high-end consignment store and pretended to eye the display while she checked out the foot-traffic in the window's reflection. Again, all she saw was people going about their business.

Stupid overactive imagination. She had been a little skittish ever since the home invasion. Granted, the experience had been more bizarre than scary, but it could have very easily gone the other way. And even though she had upgraded her security system since then, she still felt a little vulnerable at odd moments. Like now. How weird and how irritating that she didn't even have to be home for that feeling to strike.

She started on her way again, heading for the Big Basin Bar

and Grill. She was thinking about what she might like for lunch when the hair on her nape stiffened yet again. On impulse, she pivoted, a belligerent one-eighty—and almost slammed into Charles, who had a hand out as if he had been about to tap her on the shoulder. The look on his face was one of pure astonishment. She supposed it mirrored the look on her own.

"Charles!" she blurted. "What the—? Have you been following me?"

"Yeah, for the last half-block or so," he admitted. "You walked by while I was parking my car. I've been trying to catch up with you ever since. Why?"

"Oh." She meant to dismiss the matter with a breezy, 'It's nothing,' but the truth spilled out of her instead. "Someone broke into my home last week. I've been spookier than a jacked-up cat ever since."

"That's outrageous," he said, appropriately indignant. "Were you hurt in any way? Was anything taken?"

"No," she said, "nothing like that. "It was more bizarre than anything else. I shouldn't be this jumpy."

He muttered something under his breath, and then pulled himself up to his full height. All of a sudden, he seemed quite imposing. "Listen," he said. "If anything like this happens again, I want you to call me. I don't care what time of the day or night it might be. You call me and I'll be there in a flash and you'll never have to worry about your home being invaded again."

The offer made her heart flutter like a bird in a cage. Even so, she did her best to sound like a woman who preferred to be in charge of her own protection. "Thanks," she said, "but I've got it covered. I upgraded my security system and am reconsidering a dog."

"Good!" he said, relinquishing his protective stance. "I have some experience with guard dogs if you want help picking one out."

"I'll keep that in mind," she said. "But the only thing I want to pick out right now is what I'm having for lunch."

He laughed, an appreciative sound. "OK, I get it. Lunch it is."

The restaurant was just a few yards ahead of them, and as luck would have it, the hostess was able to seat them immediately. Their table was by the bar, so it was noisier than Aurora would have liked, but it beat the twenty-minute wait with which they had initially been threatened.

"Are you a fan?" Charles asked, glancing at the baseball game that was being broadcast on one of the bar's flat-screens.

"No," Aurora replied, with eyes only for her menu. "I've never been very sporty."

"Me, either," Charles said. "Never had the time or the inclination. Now that I'm retired, though, who knows? What's good here?"

"I love their burgers," she said. "With sweet potato fries and a mini-wedge salad."

He grinned at her over the top of his menu. "I'm glad you're not one of those women who live on water and tissue paper."

"Not a chance," she said, deciding at that moment to order a glass of wine as well. "I have a very healthy relationship with food."

Their waitress arrived to take their order. Charles invited Aurora to go first and then said, "I'll have the same." As the waitress headed off again, he confided, "I'm terrible with decisions."

Aurora was about to scoff at that when the two thirty-somethings who were drinking their lunch at the bar booed the ball game's plate umpire for a call that he had made.

"C'mon, Blue! Get your head out of your ass!"

Charles scowled at the duo—a darkly chivalrous look—and then looked pointedly at her. "Would you like to relocate?"

She dismissed the offer with a snort. "Thanks, but I've heard worse. Tell me how the menagerie business is going."

His perfectly landscaped face lit up like a downtown Christmas tree. "My first charges are arriving tomorrow," he said, and then leaned back to let the waitress deposit a wine glass in front of him. "I'm getting four Hartmann's zebras: one stallion and three mares. You'll have to come over and see them."

"I'd like that," she said, and meant it. She raised her wine glass. "Here's to your zebras."

In the background, the sports fans at the bar let out a raucous whoop.

"Cheers," Charles said, and then sampled his wine. "Delicious," he said afterward. "But. I've come to expect that from a Ridge. We should check out the winery this afternoon," he added casually. "You did say it wasn't too far from here, didn't you?"

"I did," she said, hoping that the bird-like flutter that had kicked up in her chest wasn't evident on her face. "And we should. But Ridge is only open to visitors on weekends."

"So what are you doing this weekend?" he asked, with a confident smile.

The fluttering in her chest intensified. She could feel heat rising in her cheeks and knew that it had nothing to do with the wine. Nevertheless, she smiled back, granting him permission to pursue her if he would. "Apparently," she said, "I'm going to Ridge with you."

Now that the elephant in the room was tranquilized, the conversation began to flow like wine. They talked about zebras until their burgers arrived, and about their favorite foods while they ate. He favored hunks of barely grilled beef. She preferred braised lamb shanks with root vegetables. Another glass of wine came and went. The guys at the bar apparently had another drink, too, for their conversation grew even louder.

"Can you believe that shit?" one of them bawled. "What a bunch of idiots."

Out of reflex, Aurora glanced at the flat-screen. Instead of a baseball stadium, she saw a local newscaster delivering one of the station's hourly updates. The TV's volume was set on low so she couldn't hear everything the woman was saying, but she could read the headline.

"Fast and furious?" she said to Charles. "Isn't that the name of a movie?"

He nodded. His expression was sober. "It's also the code name for a botched ATF sting. The idea was to sell guns to straw buyers and track the guns across the border, where they were supposed to fall into the hands of high-level cartel members who would then be busted for arms trafficking. Over two thousand weapons crossed the border with the ATF's blessing. Guess how many high-level cartel members got caught with them?" When she passed on the question with a shrug, he filled in the blank. "Zero. Absolutely none. And now there are two thousand formerly legal weapons out there in the hands of bad men. I'm telling you, Aurora, that's how the world is going to end—in a hail of bullets."

His vehemence took her aback. Seeing that, he hastened to lighten up. "Listen to me," he said, "all doom and gloom. You'd think I'd never been to lunch with a beautiful woman before! Forgive me?"

"There's nothing to forgive," she said, trying in vain not to react to his flattery. "A man's passions are the gateway to his soul."

Shit! Had she really just twittered that bit of pseudo-mystic smarm?!?

Mercifully, the waitress arrived with the check. They both reached for it at the same time, but he was quicker than she was. When she started to protest, he wagged a finger at her and then handed the jacket back to the waitress with his credit card in it. "My idea, my treat," he said. "If you ever decide to invite me to something, then you can pay."

"Well," she said, pretending to huff. "I'll have to think about that."

He laughed, showing that he could take a joke and then waxed apologetic. "Before we go, I have to hit the men's room."

"I'll meet you outside," she said, reaching for her purse. "I've heard quite enough from our friends at the bar."

"OK," he said. "But don't try to ditch me. I know where you live, you know."

The afternoon sun seemed brighter than usual, no doubt because the restaurant had been ambient dark. She stepped to the side of the building so as not to impede the flow of foot-traffic and then began rifling through her purse for her sunglasses. As she did so, the sunlight turned to shade. She looked up to see a young Asian woman standing in front of her. Her expression was one of cocky certainty, as if she expected Aurora to recognize her. And to Aurora's vast surprise, she did. This was the woman who had broken into her house!

"Naga wants to see you," Lee said in a flat, matter-of-fact tone.

"I don't care," Aurora replied.

"Look for her at this address," she said, and then slipped a piece of paper into Aurora's purse. "It is important."

"You need to stop stalking me," Aurora said, putting two and two together and coming up with an answer for where that funny feeling had been coming from. "If I see you near me again, I'll call the police."

"Go and see Naga," the woman said and then turned to leave only to be pulled halfway back by an afterthought. "The man you are with does not smell right," she said. "You should not keep his company."

A flush burned its way up Aurora's cheeks: part unease and part indignation. "Leave me—" Alone, she meant to say. But before she could get the word out, the woman disappeared.

One moment she was there; the next, Charles was peering at her with a concerned look on his face.

"Are you OK?" he asked. "You look like you just saw a ghost."

She thought to tell him about the woman and how she thought he didn't smell right, but then thought better of it. She wanted him to go on thinking of her as beautiful, not eccentric or overly dramatic. "It's nothing," she assured him. "Just a passing thought. Occupational hazard, you know."

His concern dissipated, leaving a smile in its place. "Outstanding," he said, and then took her hand as if it were a baby bird. "What do you say? Are you up for a stroll?"

"OK," she said. "So long as it's a short one. I do have to go back to work at some point today."

His smile broadened. The next thing she knew, he was leaning in for a kiss. She started to panic but managed to avoid embarrassing herself as he pressed his lips to hers. The kiss was soft and brief, a closed-mouth impression that left her a little dizzy just the same.

"Too forward?" he wondered, as he returned to his own airspace.

"Not really," she replied.

And there was absolutely nothing wrong with his smell!

CHAPTER 7

Roz lounged in a deck chair at the foot of the cruise ship's gargantuan swimming pool, nursing a tumbler of single malt and humming along to the 80's wedding tunes that were floating up from the massive welcome-aboard party down on the promenade. A month ago, she would've been in the thick of such a rage. At the moment, however, she was content to hang out by herself under a clear moonless sky and enjoy the solitude.

And not to put too fine of a point on it, but she needed some downtime after the trip from Inverness.

Brigit hadn't been boasting when she claimed to be able to jump far and wide. She could clear a mile of countryside in a single bound! The first few leaps had been fun—whee! Look at me! Mary Poppins, dragon-style! But over the course of the night, the nonstop touch-and-go's over mostly wooded ground lost their appeal. Her stomach went sour; her butt got sore. And on more than one occasion, Brigit only cleared the treetops by inches, a margin that left leafy welts on her shins. When she complained about that, Brigit responded with the psychic equivalent of a shrug.

"We have tae stay low tae avoid being seen. Try lifting yer knees up higher."

"Yeah, right," Roz fired back. "Like I'm going to do crunches all the way to Glasgow."

A hundred miles and at least seventy-five leg-lifts later, they came upon the banks of the Upper Clyde. An instant after they landed, Brigit set Roz down and then crawled into the river up to her nostrils.

"*Feck,*" she said, as she soaked in the cold water. "*A haven't traveled that far in ages. A think A'm a wee bit outa shape.*"

"I know what you mean," Roz said, trying to stretch the kinks out of her abs and quads. "The next time I offer to drive us somewhere, maybe you'll take me up on it."

"*Maybe. But like A told ye, cars tend tae break down when A'm in 'em fer any length of time.*"

"So what's next?" Roz asked. "Sunrise is still an hour away. And the ship doesn't set sail until this afternoon."

Brigit flexed her nostrils, giving off twin puffs of fog. "*A dunna know about ye, but A'm going tae catch myself sumthin' tae eat and then have a snooze.*"

"Oh," Roz said, slightly surprised that the drakena had made plans that didn't include her. "I thought we were going to go all the way to the terminal together."

"*Ye thought wrong. A've got a big swim ahead o' me, and A canna be wasting energy Changing back and forth just tae keep ye company. Find tha terminal without me. And while yer at it, find a shower, too. Yer startin' tae smell a wee bit gamy.*"

"Nice," Roz said, momentarily offended even though cleaning up was the very first thing on her to-do list once she reached her stateroom. "But just so you know, the word you're looking for is dragon-y, not gamy. I smell this way because of you."

Brigit rejected the assertion with a snort. "*Get some rest, too. Apparently, ye get a little bitchy when yer tired.*"

Roz had a snotty retort for that, too, but withheld it at the last moment when she realized that it only served to make the dragon's point. "Fine," she said. "See you tonight." She slung her grungy backpack over her shoulder and then added, "You will make sure you have the right ship before you come aboard, right?

"*Ye'll never know,*" Brigit retorted, and then submerged. With a flurry of bubbles, she was gone.

Roz smirked at the memory and then reached for her Scotch only to freeze as a fellow passenger happened into view. The first thing about him that caught her eye was his monkish robe. Who the heck dressed like that in this day and age—and on a cruise, no less! She had to admit, though: the outfit complemented his general appearance. He had a scruffy, chest-length beard, overgrown eyebrows, and a halo of mostly dark, fly-away hair. As he started toward her, she realized that he had a limp as well.

"You are wondering why I am here instead of on dance floor," he said, as he closed the gap between them. "Do not deny, I can see in your eyes."

As opening lines went, Roz had heard far worse. And his jowly Russian accent intrigued her.

"It's true," she replied. "I had you pegged as a Steely Dan fan from the moment I set eyes on you."

"What is 'Steely Dan'?" he asked, looking mystified.

"Simply the best band ever," Roz replied. "Leastwise, according to my mom. But before we go too far astray here, let's circle back to square one. Why are you here? You don't strike me as someone who spends a lot of time poolside."

"You are perceptive for one so young," he said, with a half-smile that stopped a hair short of being mocking. Then he waxed sardonic and added, "I came up here to look at the stars. Their light gives me comfort, for it comes from the Divine. But then I saw you and wondered why one so young and comely would be sitting alone when so many others are making merry below. And for me there is no wondering without asking."

"I see," she said, charmed by the stranger in spite of herself. He thought she was comely. How quaint! "And since you asked so nicely, I'll tell you. I'm by myself because someone broke my heart recently and I've lost all interest in making merry."

He sucked in a scandalized breath and then drew himself up to his full height. "Point this breaker of hearts out to me and I will see that he suffers slow and painful death."

She laughed, partly at his theatrics and partly at the mangled image of Aldo that popped into her head. Did that make her a bad person? "Thanks for the offer," she said, "but the breaker of hearts is on a plane heading back to the new world even as we speak."

"Airplanes! Yech!" he said, and shuddered. "I refuse to ride in them. I tell my colleagues that my reasons are religious, but the unadorned truth is, I simply cannot abide being confined in such a small space with so many people at such a ridiculous altitude. At least on a ship, one can step outside for a breath of fresh air and a glimpse of the stars."

"Just so," Roz said, and then was struck by an impulse. "Shall I leave so you can look at them in peace?"

The stranger fixed his dark, deep-set eyes on her as if he were trying to see through her, and for one instant, she thought she felt the feather-light tap of a thought tickle the outskirts of her mind. But even as she tried to pin the feeling down, it disappeared, and the stranger blinked.

"You are kind to make offer," he said, "but it is noisier up here than I thought it would be. I believe I will return to the privacy of my balcony to contemplate the Divine. I wish you a pleasant journey."

With that, he turned and headed back toward the lower levels. Roz watched him go with a mixture of wonder and curiosity. Such an odd man! So courtly. So last century. And yet, she had felt remarkably at ease with him, as if she knew him from somewhere. But that couldn't be. She would have remembered such a character—not to mention that accent! Oh, well. It was probably sleep-deprived delirium setting in, a by-product of leap-frogging Scotland by night. She probably should've taken a nap after showering, but she'd opted to buy herself some clean clothes instead. She gave the full-length, cold-shoulder cover-up that she was wearing a discerning once-over. It was far more glamorous than the stuff she usually wore, but glitz was the name of the game at all of your finer cruise ship boutiques. And she had to admit, she really liked the hat that went with the outfit. She pulled the brim down over her eyes, meaning to grab a nap while she was waiting for Brigit to arrive. But before she had a chance to nod off, a body reeking of beer crashed down in the deck chair next to hers.

"I hope you don't mind me saying so," a man said, "but you've got the body of a Venus. Mind if I worship you?"

It took her a second to process the accent, for she'd acclimated to Brigit's thick Scottish brogue over the last few days. When she finally recognized it as drunken American, she realized that she recognized the voice as well and her heart hit her ribcage at Mach One.

"Aldo?" she said, bolting upright. "Is that you?"

It was, gaudy Hawaiian shirt and Bermuda shorts notwithstanding. When he saw her, his slack-faced grin avalanched, leaving a façade of pure shock in its wake. He scrambled out of his slouch as if a man-eating tarantula had just popped up between his legs.

"Roz!" he squawked. "What are you doing here? You don't do cruises. You're the—" He gestured broadly, like a magician trying to conjure the right word out of a boozy fog. "You're more the expedition type."

"I thought I'd try something new," she said, in a desiccated tone. "What's your excuse? I can't believe that you'd actually pony up the price of a cabin when you had a free plane ticket in your hand."

He deflected the dig about his tight-fisted ways with a shrug. "I talked the airline into giving me credit on a future flight for the ticket," he said. "I thought I was doing you a favor."

"That's you," she sneered, "always thinking of others. If you really want to do me a favor, you'll piss off. I'm expecting someone."

"No way!" he said, chortling as he guzzled from a red plastic cup. "You hooked up with someone already? I don't believe it! He's gotta be some science geek on his way home from the North Pole who hasn't been with a proper woman in decades."

Proper woman? What the fuck? She reached for her tumbler, torn between drinking from it and smashing it against his thick skull. Before she had a chance to do either, a shrill, sing-song, "Yoo-hoo!" distracted her. "Calling Studly McStud-Muffin! Are you up there? Come out, come out wherever you are! Your Baby-Doll's getting lonesome!"

"Up here, darlin'!" Aldo crooned, sitting up straight as if that would make him look more respectable. And Roz had to admit, it did. Freaking actors. "You'll never guess who I've found."

Baby-Doll cleared the top of the stairs—an impressive feat given the six inch espadrilles that she was wearing and the amount of alcohol that she had obviously consumed. She was very blonde and very busty and at least ten years older than Aldo. Her china-doll face didn't give her away, but her hands did. They were veiny and creped like a raptor's, and looked like they were made for clutching. She half-sauntered, half-swayed her way over to Aldo and plopped down on his lap. He folded his arms around her waist and smiled at Roz, projecting not joy but smugness.

"Yvonne, my love," he said, bouncing her on his knee like a baby, "do you remember me telling you about my last girlfriend, the one I broke up with just before we met?" She nodded, a wobbly affirmative. "Well, this is her. Baby-Doll, meet my ex, Roz."

Yvonne peered at Roz for a drunken moment and then said, "You're smaller than I thought you'd be. And you look nice enough."

I'm so very relieved you think so," Roz said, squeezing her tumbler as if it were a certain person's neck—and she was pretty noncommittal about specific identities at this point. "I'm sure you'll be good for Aldo. He likes being mothered."

Aldo narrowed his eyes like a snake getting ready to strike, but Yvonne laughed like she had just heard the funniest joke ever. "Oh my God," she said, "you are so right! When I first saw him in Edinburg, he looked like a baby bird who'd fallen out of his nest. I just had to pick him up and try to keep him alive!"

She tapped on Aldo's cup, a signal for him to share. He tipped a little of his beer into her mouth and then made a move to spill her out of his lap, saying, "C'mon, lovey. Let's get back to the party. We're running low on moonshine."

"No!" Yvonne said, keeping her seat like a rodeo pro. "I wanna stay. I want Roz to tell me all about you. I bet I could learn a lot. Right, Roz?"

A whole list of Aldo classics rushed into Roz's mouth: leaving the toilet seat up, talking with his mouth full, forgetting his wallet when it was his turn to pay. But as much as she enjoyed watching the jerk squirm, she wanted him gone more, and swallowed the litany unsaid.

"Some things," she drawled instead, "are best learned firsthand."

"Oh, come on," Yvonne pressed. "You guys were together for a long time. He held you in high regard."

Roz let out a bitter ha-ha, the sound of her restraint slipping. "Trust me," she said. "The only one Aldo has ever held in high regard is Aldo."

Yvonne's jaw went slack. As she craned her head around to catch a glimpse of Aldo's face, he donned an expression that was both hurt and affronted, and said, "See? Didn't I tell you she was mean?"

"You did, sugar, you did! I'm so sorry I didn't believe you!" She shifted in his lap so she could bury her fingers in his hair and kiss his pain away. Aldo shot Roz a look of vindictive glee and then proceeded to make out with his new girlfriend.

"Jesus," Roz said, and decided to relocate to the hot tub pavilion, which was a half-level up from the pool. As she was collecting her stuff, a voice slammed into her head.

"Am coomin' up."

"Not yet!" was Roz's panicked response. *"There are people here. They'll see you".*

"A dunna care. Tha water's cold, tha ship's speeding up, and Am feckin' knackered."

"Our room has a private sundeck," Roz said, scrambling to keep the situation contained. *"Jump aboard there. I'll have the finest bottle of Scotch on the ship waiting for you."*

"Feck that!" the dragon replied, projecting outrage. *"Do ye have any feckin' idea how big this feckin' ship is? It would take me feckin' forever to find the right sundeck! All be up in a feckin' tick at the agreed-upon meeting place so ye'd best feckin' clear the area."*

Shit.

She kicked the chair on which Aldo and Yvonne were entwined. They continued to suck face like porn stars. "C'mon, you guys," she begged. "You have a room. Use it, for God's sake!" Yvonne giggled. Aldo refused to acknowledge her presence in any way. No doubt he thought he was making her jealous with his performance. She kicked the chair again and then said, "Fine, be assholes. It's your funeral."

Then she stomped up to the hot tub pavilion and tapped

into Brigit's psychic presence. *"C'mon up!"*

She heard a splash that sounded like a rogue wave breaking and then, heartbeats later, a thud like heavy metal thunder. Twin sets of claws hooked themselves over the starboard railing. Brigit's red-horned head appeared next; her teeth were bared in a strained grimace. Seeing that, Roz realized that the dragon had miscalculated her leap and was now clinging to the ship's side. She started toward the railing, thinking to help, only to be forestalled by a furious hiss. *"Stay the feck away!"* Then a furious scratching sound erupted: back claws scrabbling for a toehold. All at once, Brigit came lurching over the railing. Momentum carried her into the hot-tub-for-twenty. A tidal wave ensued, soaking Roz. She finger-combed her streaming hair away from her eyes and then slogged over to the tub. The dragon was coiled up within, and resting her chin on the rim. Her eyes were shut. The insides of her nostrils were slightly blue.

"Are you OK?" Roz whispered. "You don't look so hot."

The dragon opened one smoke-colored eye to lance her with a look. *"You try keeping up with this thing fer tha better half of a day and see how you look."*

"Roz, where'd all that water come from?" She half-turned to find Aldo standing at the top of the stairs. Their eyes met for a moment, but his slid then into the hot tub. "Jesus," he said, in a tip-toe voice. "What the hell is that?"

Shit.

"Get rid of him. Or A will."

The only plan that suggested itself to Roz on such short, unbelievable notice was to block Aldo's view with her body and pretend that nothing was wrong. "You're drunk, Aldo," she said, with as much disdain as she could muster. "Go back to your room and sleep it off."

"I'm not that drunk," he said, and then sidestepped her for

a closer, better look only to lose his beer-fueled nerve when Brigit loosed a snarl. He backpedaled several steps, slipped in a slick of water created by the mini-tsunami, and then tumbled ass over tea kettle down the stairs and into the pool area.

"Is he dead?"

"No," Roz replied, watching with a mixture of amazement and disgust as he staggered to his feet. *"They say God protects drunks and fools, and there's your proof."*

He shuffled over to his now his passed-out girlfriend and started patting her cheeks. "Baby-Doll," he said, in an urgent whisper. "ya gotta wake up! We gotta go." When she warned him off with a dream scowl, he cast a last terrified look over his shoulder at Roz, and then scrambled for the staircase that led to the promenade.

"Shit. He bolted," Roz said.

"Go after him. Bring him back here and throw him overboard. Yer strong enough, ye can do it."

"No way!" she said, appalled by the suggestion and the ruthlessness with which it was tendered.

"Then fetch him back and throw him in here with me. A'll take care of him."

"No-o!" Roz said, stretching the word into two emphatic syllables. "He may be the world's biggest jerk, but he doesn't deserve to die for that. Besides, it's too late. He's probably gibbering at a security guard even as we speak. You need to Change before he drags the poor bastard up here to point you out."

"A dunna know if A have tha strength tae Change," Brigit admitted. *"A've never swum so long or hard in me life. Am knackered, truly."*

"Well, you can't stay there as you are," Roz said, trying to listen for a commotion even as she strategized with the drakena. "If you can't Change, you'll have to go back over the side."

"Feck that. It won't be pretty, but A can take care of a couple of security guards if A have to."

A shout billowed up the staircase. Roz recognized the voice as Aldo's. "C'mon! This way!" he urged. "I'm telling you, dude, there's a monster in the hot tub."

"If he calls me a monster again, A'm goin' tae toss him overboard no matter what ye say."

"G'won! My girlfriend's up there!"

Roz heaved a sigh, venting a mental image of Aldo going over the starboard railing along with a yearning for simpler days. But speaking of Baby-Doll—

"I'm going to buy some time," she told Brigit, as she bounded into the pool area. "Use it to Change or go overboard."

Yvonne was still out cold, but Roz managed to wrestle her dead weight out of the chair and over to the top of the staircase. There, she knelt down beside the unconscious woman and pretended to give her mouth-to-mouth as someone came fast-stepping up the stairs.

"What's going on here?" that someone wanted to know.

Roz looked up to see a handsome young security guard standing over her. His name tag identified him as Kevin. He looked more perturbed than alarmed.

"Oh, thank God," Roz said, trying to sound relieved as she batted her lashes at him. "I'm not sure if I'm doing this right!"

"What happened?" he asked, trying in vain to look at Yvonne and the pool at the same time.

"She tripped and fell trying to walk in those shoes after a night of serious boozing," Roz said. "I was afraid that she'd stopped breathing."

Kevin sank into a crouch in front of Yvonne and pressed an ear to her chest. "Well," he said as he listened, "she seems to be breathing normally now. Her pulse seems normal, too." He pulled the walky-talky from his belt and requested a doctor's presence on the top deck. Then he stood up and surveyed the surrounds. "Was there anyone else here when the incident occurred?"

Roz stood up, too, and surreptitiously blocked his view of the hot tub area. "Nope, it was just me and her. Her boyfriend was here before she knocked herself out," she added, "but all of a sudden, he lit out babbling something about monsters. He was pretty wasted, too."

An indignant voice marched up the staircase. "Not that wasted!"

Kevin rolled his eyes skyward, a gesture that reminded Roz of her mother, and then muttered, "Yeah, well, you get all kinds on these cruises." Then he deftly sidestepped her and gave the pool another once-over. "Afterward, he leaned toward the staircase and announced, "You can come up now, sir. There are no monsters in the pool."

"It's not in the pool, dude!" Aldo hissed from hiding. "It's in the hot tub!"

Kevin arched a dubious eyebrow at Roz. "Is there—someone in the hot tub?"

Roz figured there was a good chance of him believing her if she said,'No.' But before she could let the lie slip, a loud splash washed her credibility away. Kevin rolled his eyes again, a silent why-me, and then trudged up the stairs leading to the top deck. Roz followed on his heels, hoping and praying that the splash they heard had been Brigit abandoning the tub for the railing. When he froze at the top of the steps and blurted, "Oh dear God," she feared the very worst.

Then a familiar female voice crooned, "Well, aren't ye a handsome devil! Have ye come tae have a soak with me?"

"Uhm," Kevin said, and Roz knew that he was blushing because the back of his neck was fiery red. "Ma'am, guests are supposed to wear a swim suit when using the hot tub."

"A seem to have misplaced mine," the voice replied, sweetly unapologetic.

"Yes, ma'am," Kevin said. "So it would seem."

Then he cleared his throat, did an abrupt about-face, and cleared out, leaving Roz to deal with an unabashedly naked changeling. She was sitting in the Jacuzzi with her arms outstretched on the rim. The water in the tub was too low to cover her breasts and she had made no attempt to hide them with her seaweed hair.

"You do know how to make an impression, don't you?" Roz drawled.

"If there's one thing A've learned over the years," Brigit said, "it's that tha sight of a pair of chebs will send most men running." She slid lower into the tub, closed her eyes, and rumbled approvingly. "Nice idea, heating tha water. A like tha bubbles, too."

"Glad you're happy," Roz said, and then strode over to a nearby cabana for a towel. "But don't get too comfortable. We need to leave before someone who isn't freaked by a set of chebs shows up."

Brigit blew a pair of lazy steam-rings from her nose. "You go. A want tae stay and get warm."

"Not a chance," Roz said, returning with the biggest towel she could find. "You'll fall asleep and forget your Shape and all hell will break loose."

She snagged Brigit by an armpit and gave her a tug, expecting resistance. She did not, however, expect to be rounded on by a changeling who was projecting fury both outwardly and inwardly. *"Dunna presume tae order me about like a child or a lap dog! A've walked this world far longer than you and dunna need a shepherd!"*

A microsecond of panic blew through Roz—a primal instinct recognizing that she stood unarmed in the presence of an apex predator. That instinct urged her to turn and run. Instead, she pushed Brigit's fuming face out of her personal space with an open palm and calmly said, "When we're in your world, you can call the shots. But when we're in mine—and this definitely qualifies as my world—you'd be wise to listen to me. And don't forget, dragon: you Called me. If you like my company, you had best mind your manners."

Brigit glared at her for a moment longer, then loosed one last petulant blast of fog and splashed to her feet. As she climbed out of the tub, Roz could not help but notice that she was sporting a tail—and not just a vestige. This appendage had to be at least two feet long, with a very twitchy tip.

"Uhm," she said, "you know you're dragging in back, right?"

"Yes," Brigit said, a dyspeptic rumble. "A'm very tired, and A had to Change in a hurry. A was hoping a soak in hot, bubbly water would give me tha where-all tae finish the job." She accepted the towel that Roz offered her and wrapped it around her torso. The towel covered all but the tip of that blue-gray tail. "Think anyone will notice?"

"Not likely given all the booze that's been flowing tonight," Roz said, trying to sound confident rather than wishful. "But just in case, let's not stop and hobnob with any of our fellow passengers along the way."

The plan might have worked if Aldo had gone back to his room like Roz had told him to. But there he was, standing next to Kevin as the ship's doctor attended to Yvonne. When he saw Roz striding toward the staircase, he grabbed Kevin by the sleeve and started yanking. "Ask her!" he exclaimed. "Make her tell you. She saw it, too!"

Kevin pulled free of Aldo's grip and smoothed out his sleeve. In a tone that only sounded patient, he said, "The lady said she didn't see any monsters, sir."

"She's a liar!" he shouted. "She'll say anything to make me look like an idiot!"

"Oh, please," Roz said. "You don't need any help from me."

H stiffened like an affronted peacock and then turned to Brigit, who was testing the pool water with a toe. "What about her?" he said. "What did she see?"

The changeling flashed him a smile filled with oversized, slightly pointy teeth. "A saw a frightened little man bounding fer tha hills like a drunken rabbit."

"Satisfied, sir?" Kevin asked, in that same pseudo-patient tone. "Alcohol can play funny tricks on people. You wouldn't be the first to see something that wasn't there."

Aldo's flush deepened. "I keep telling you—I'm not that drunk!"

"Whatever you say, Aldo," Roz said, and then winked at Kevin. "Is it OK if we leave now?"

"Of course, ladies," Kevin replied, and then gestured them toward the staircase. As they strode past Aldo, Roz shouldered him aside and cracked, "Step aside. Monsters coming through!"

"Wise-ass," he grumbled, and then did a double-take as Brigit sauntered by. "Holy shit," he said. "The redhead has a tail!"

"I think it would be a good idea if you shut up now, sir," Kevin said, and then waved Roz and Brigit on. They waved back, then hurried down the stairs and away.

Roz was lounging out on her private sundeck when someone knocked on the door to the stateroom—a discreet tap-tap, the hallmark of room service. She padded into the room, past the bed and its sprawling mound of snoring flesh, and cracked the door open. A sweet-faced Filipina woman in a starched-white uniform stood at the threshold.

"Oh, so sorry to disturb you," she said. "When would be a good time for me to return and clean your room?"

"How about tomorrow?" Roz said, the same thing she'd said for the last three days. "All I need is more towels. Sorry about the pile of dishes at the door."

"Oh, that's no problem," the maid said, smiling through the crack as she passed a stack of towels through the gap. "People seem to eat more when they're at sea. Are you sure I can't do anything else for you?"

"Not at this time, thank you," Roz said, and then firmly pulled the door shut. Afterward, she dumped the towels in the bathroom and then hovered in front of the mini-fridge, debating whether or not she wanted a nip. It was a little earlier in the day than she usually started drinking, but the fact was, she was bored. Cruise ships were like casinos—they didn't want you spending a lot of time in your room. The TV programming sucked, and there was nothing but Gideon's bible to read. What she really wanted to do was go for a run and maybe work off a little room service in the process, but she didn't dare leave the room while Brigit was asleep for fear of giving some industrious maid the OMG moment of her life.

She elected to pass on the drink—there was nothing but the sweet stuff left anyway. As she headed back toward the sundeck, she glanced at Brigit. Her color was a lot better than it had been when she had first arrived at the room, and she was much warmer. But that scaly, lake-blue tail hadn't gone away like she had hoped it would. It hadn't even gotten any smaller. One thing was for sure, though: with it hanging out and over the side of the bed like that, there was no way to forget that there was a dragon in the room.

Outside, a cool ocean wind chilled the warm summer day all the way back to late spring. Roz slung a towel over her shoulders and then went to stand at the railing. As she stared down at the choppy, white-capped Atlantic Ocean, she thought about Aurora. She had no idea how she was going to react to Brigit—or the possibility that she had a dragon of her own out there somewhere. Her mother was a lot of things: kind, generous, adventurous, open-minded. But she was not the sort who took surprises well. And irritated as she was at Roz for not coming directly home after the break-up, she was likely to be even less amenable to them than usual. Roz wished that she could call her. She'd thought about doing so at least a dozen times over the past three days. But she knew that the sound of that oh-so-familiar voice would have her spilling the beans in no time flat. That, as Brigit had noted, would probably leave her concerned for the state of Roz's mental health. People only wanted to hear about the Loch Ness Monster in the tabloids.

"Where are we?"

The query was sleepy-eyed, with notes of hunger in the background.

"At sea," Roz replied. To make it clear that she wasn't being a smart-ass, she added, "We've been sailing for three days now. We have three more to go."

Brigit rumbled. *"This ship is not a good place for sleeping. A had disturbing dreams."*

"Dragons dream?" Roz said, making no secret of her surprise. "I had no idea. What's the stuff of a dragon's nightmares?"

"Tha same stuff that darkens a human's dreams, A suppose," Brigit replied, starting to sound more awake. *"War, hoard-raiders, a steady diet of tilapia. But my dreams were more cryptic than dark. A kept getting the sense that there is danger nearby."*

"Like what?" Roz asked. "An iceberg?"

"A dunno. The Dreaming was dim and offered no clear glimpses of what it wanted me tae see."

Roz harrumphed, a prelude to a bit of snarkiness about this 'Dreaming'. Before she could say anything, though, she was distracted by the sight of a dolphin surfing on the ship's wake. An instant later, there was an entire pod wave-surfing alongside the ship. Her scowl upended itself, and she squealed with child-like delight.

"What?"

"There are dolphins in the water! Come see!"

The next thing she knew, Brigit was at her elbow. She had a towel wrapped around her, but even so, Roz could not help but notice that her tail was thrashing. She had never seen it do that before, so she had to ask, because like the old man from last night, there was no wondering without asking.

"Do you need a shot of potassium or something?"

"A dunna know what tha means," Brigit said, never taking her eyes off the dolphins.

"Just wondering why your tail has gone haywire all of a sudden," Roz said.

"A'm hungry," Brigit said, "and there is prey in sight."

At first, Roz thought Brigit was referring to her and a chill skittered down her spine. Then she realized that the dragon was talking about the dolphins and the chill shifted into an indignant sizzle.

"You can't eat dolphins!" she exclaimed.

Brigit ran her tongue over her pointy teeth, licking back drool. "Of course ye can," she said. "The meat is very lean and sweet. They're a bugger tae catch, though."

"But they're—" She was going to say 'cute', but at the last moment, came up with an argument that might have more pull with a dragon. "They're intelligent. And social. And—"

"Humans hunt dolphins, do they not?"

"Some do," Roz conceded. Before she could attach a qualifier to the admission, Brigit pressed on with her argument. "Then what is the problem? Why should it only be acceptable for humans tae eat dolphin?"

"That's the point," Roz said. "In most parts of the world, it's not acceptable anymore. No one should be eating dolphins."

"So ye think only stupid creatures should be eaten."

Roz tried to find a way to deny or at least sugar-coat that statement, but gave up halfway with a shrug. "Basically."

"That hardly seems fair," Brigit remarked. "But A'm not getting back in the water yet, so A suppose tha point is moot."

The dolphins abandoned the ship's wake then, never knowing how lucky they were.

"A will have to eat soon, though," Brigit went on, as they strode back into the stateroom. "The problem is, it's going tae take a few more days of rest tae get rid of this tail. That means A canna go foraging fer meself. Do ye think ye could bring someone back here fer me? Maybe that man who called me a monster. He seemed stupid enough."

For a fleeting moment, Roz considered the request. Two birds with one stone, that sort of thing. Then, reluctantly, she voted the idea down. "Sorry," she said, "but stupid is out of season at the moment. How about I order you some room service instead?"

Brigit cocked her head. "Room service?"

Roz pointed at the bedside phone and said, "I use that thing to call the kitchen and tell them what you want to eat. The kitchen then sends the food here."

Brigit's eyes widened, as did her nostrils. Her mouth curved upward into a vee. The only time Roz had ever seen her look this pleased was back at Loch Ness when she got ahold of Roz's bottle of Scotch. "A delightful concept," she declared. "Will the kitchen send whiskey, too?"

"That can be arranged," Roz said, and then was struck by an afterthought. "Before I put the order in, though, I'm going to go for a run. If I don't get some exercise, I'm going to burst!"

"Do what ye need tae do," the changeling said, indulging in a languid stretch. "A'm content where A am."

Roz stuffed herself into her hiking shorts and tennis shoes, then pocketed her room key. "No one in, no one out while I'm gone, okay?" she said, as she headed for the door. "There's no point in stirring up this floating anthill if we don't have to."

"Whatever," Brigit said. Then she loosed a monstrous yawn and curled up with her back to Roz.

Roz took that for a dismissal and started on her way, pulling the door firmly shut behind her and making sure the 'Do Not Disturb' sign was prominently displayed. From there, she made her way to the promenade. It was lunchtime, so there weren't a lot of people using the track that circumnavigated the deck. That suited Roz just fine. The first time around the track, she walked, warming up her muscles. The second lap, she broke into a jog. By the time she started the third lap, she was at a steady run. The sun felt good on her skin. The salt air smelled like a margarita. It felt good to be doing something physical after being sedentary for so long. Endorphins made everything feel better!

As she rounded the corner that marked the bow of the ship, a hand snaked out from out of nowhere and grabbed her by the waist. She let out a yelp. An instant later, she twisted free of her assailant and then rounded on him. Her elbow was inches away from his voice-box when she realized that she recognized the grip—and the chin.

"Aldo!" she hissed, aborting the blow but only just barely. "Are you out of your mind? I could have killed you!"

He looked a little crazy. His usually perfect hair was disheveled. His Hawaiian shirt was rumpled and stained. And she'd never seen such a frantic look in his eyes.

"I knew I'd catch you out here on the track sooner or later," he said, trying to grab her wrist. "You can't help yourself, you're compulsive."

"And you are—what?" she said, blocking his grab. "Drunk again?" She stepped back to give him a more critical look and added, "You might want to start dialing back on the booze, dude, because that semi-four-pack of yours is starting to go to seed. If you fluff up too much, Yvonne's going to dump you for someone younger and hotter."

"She already has," he said brusquely. "But I don't care. I need to know, Roz. You gotta tell me." He leaned in close, and in a half-whisper, asked, "What was that thing in the hot tub?"

She let out the breath she'd been holding as a huff, expelling as well the absurd half-hope that he might ask her to take him back. She wouldn't have agreed to a do-over, of course, even if she hadn't been sharing her room with a dragon, but she would've loved the opportunity to tell him to get stuffed. So now she couldn't resist torturing him.

"What thing?" she asked, batting her lashes at him in theatric innocence.

"You know," he said, in the same hushed tone. "I know you do. You weren't afraid of it."

"But you were, weren't you?" she said, in a sly, gloating tone. "You were so scared, you ran away, leaving your passed-out lady friend defenseless. That's why she dumped you, isn't it? She wants a boy-toy, not a lump of chickenshit."

He parried the jab with a scowl. "She doesn't remember anything about that night—not even meeting you. She just thinks I'm no fun anymore. And the sad thing is—she's right. I can't bring myself to do anything but think about what I saw."

"And you think I know what it is," she said. His hopeful little head-bob was an invitation to do her worst. So she leaned in, radiating secretiveness, and whispered, "As it happens, you're right. But you're not going to believe me if I tell you."

"No, that's not true,' he said, clutching at her like a needy child. "You know these things. I know that. Tell me—what was it?"

"The Loch Ness Monster," she said, and then grinned for all she was worth.

Surprise washed across his face, then suspicion and dismissal. His mouth narrowed, as did his eyes. "You think you're funny," he said, backing away from her. "You think you're so fucking smart. But I'll tell you what, Roz. I'm going to find out what that thing was if it's the last thing I do."

"I told you what it was," she said, stepping back onto the track. "Now stop stalking me."

As she ran her laps, her thoughts went in circles, too. She was surprised and more than a little dismayed that Aldo remembered Brigit so clearly. As drunk as he'd been, the whole night should've been one giant, possibly nightmarish blur to him. But no, the one time she needed him to forget something, he just had to go and get obsessive about it. The only good thing about him being the one who saw Brigit was his attention span, which was that of a gerbil. Something was bound to come along and distract him any moment now. In the meantime, she'd just have to make sure that he stayed well away from the changeling. Brigit's solutions to problems were much more basic than Roz's were, and despicable as he was, Roz still didn't want to see him dead.

But she was perfectly okay with him spending the next few nights alone on a deck chair.

By the time she finished with her run, she was ready for lunch, too. She jogged back to the room only to have a jolt of adrenaline spike her endorphin high when she got there.

The door was ajar.

The room was disheveled.

The changeling was gone.

The first scenario that crossed her mind involved Aldo, a squad of burly security guards, and a dragon resisting arrest. But on closer inspection, that didn't seem so likely. For one thing, there was no blood—and there would have been plenty if Brigit had been resisting. For another, there was no real evidence of a struggle. The clothes that Roz had bought for the cruise had been pulled from their hangers and tossed to the floor, but nothing was damaged. The bed was messed up, too, but it had been that way for the last three days. She checked the bathroom and the deck. No sign of Brigit there, either. Had she given up on room service and gone over the side? Please please please, let that be the case, Roz prayed, to whomever might be listening. She strode out to the deck and looked over the railing. No dolphins in the water. No dragon, either. Dammit. She didn't know what to do next. Stay here in the room? Go looking? Brigit wouldn't appreciate a search party—but what if she was in trouble? Not that Roz was going to be of much help much if in fact the dragon was out of the bag. That's why she'd wanted Brigit to stay put in the first place. Damn stubborn dragons. Traveling with one definitely had its downsides.

As she fretted, a tickle welled up in her head—an annoying buzz like tinnitus. A moment later, the tickle shaped itself into a voice. *"Where tha feck are ye? All these fecking doors look tha same!"*

Roz was at the door in one heartbeat and poking her head out into the hallway in the next. Brigit was marching down the corridor, stopping every so often to peer into a peep-hole. She was dressed in the hat and off-the-shoulder coverall that Roz had worn yesterday. Roz caught herself praying again: please say that outfit had looked better on her!

"Over here!" Roz said, an urgent whisper. Before she could add, 'Hurry!' the changeling was pushing past her to get into the room.

"Shut the door!" she said, as she rushed in. "Quickly! Before he sees me!"

"Who?" Roz said, as she did as she was told. "Aldo?"

Brigit scorned the suggestion with a snort. "A drake!"

"There's another dragon aboard the ship?" Roz echoed, unable to contain her amazement. Two weeks ago, there was supposedly no such thing as dragons. Now she was on a cruise ship with two of them? Un-freaking-real. "How do you know?"

"A caught a whiff of his musk on tha back of a sea breeze whilst A was out on the deck sunning myself," Brigit said, flaring her nostrils as if to relive the memory. "A thought he might be spying on me so A decided to see if A could track him down."

"And did you?" Roz asked.

"No," Brigit said, baring her teeth like regrets. "He were already gone by tha time A got tae tha deck where he would have been standing."

"Do you think he saw you?"

"If he did, he didn't let on."

Roz ran her fingers through her hair, hoping to comb up a useful idea. All that came to her was, "Shall I go and have a look around for him? If we can figure out who he is, maybe we can also find out what he's up to."

"No!" Brigit said. "Drakes are vicious. If he catches ye spying on him, he'll kill ye and then come looking for me. Better to lie low and let trouble pass us by."

Roz recognized the sense in what Brigit was saying. She saw the wisdom in lying low. Even so, she had an adrenaline buzz going on now and wanted to take the fight to the enemy—

especially since the enemy was someone other than Aldo.

"C'mon," she said, unable to stifle her craving for action. "There has to be something I can do!"

Brigit gave her a critical once-over, as if she were reassessing her decision. Afterward, she broke into a toothy grin and said, "Why, yes! As a matter of fact, there is something ye can do." Then she gestured at the telephone and added, "Summon tha room service."

CHAPTER 8

Grishka stood out on his cabin's coffin-sized slab of a balcony, watching as the cruise ship cut its way through the murky brown waters of the New York Harbor. It was an overcast morning, and moderately foggy. Droplets of salt-scented dew clung to his eyebrows and beard: Divine residues. The drake always felt closer to Her when he was on the vast, wild waters of an ocean. Nevertheless, he was glad that this voyage was coming to an end. 'Cruising' involved too many people and too much decadence. There had been times in his life when he had actively sought out such a combination, but these days, he preferred a more introspective lifestyle.

The ship's horn blew twice: chest-rattling, baritone blasts. Moments later, the Statue of Liberty spanned forth from the fog. Grishka had first seen the monument in the 1890s, shortly after its installation on Liberty Island. He'd admired its construction: humans could be so clever with their hands! But the concept behind the statue had never made any sense to him. A shrine to freedom and democracy? Why? It wasn't as if humans had a particular flair for these things. The powerful few had preyed on the weaker masses for as long as Grishka had been alive. He didn't object to such behavior as it was part of the natural order of things. He simply didn't understand the human need to pretend otherwise.

New York's skyline phased into view: a jagged expanse of metal, glass, and concrete swathed in skirts of morning mist. Although the city was in no way as grand as his beloved Saint Petersburg, Grishka held a certain fondness for it, especially

Manhattan. Its streets reminded him of taxi-infested canyons. And despite his limp and overgrown appearance, its residents paid him no attention at all. He liked that, so much so that he kept trying to convince Tezcatlipoca to turn the borough into a preserve when it came time to restore the natural order. The Great One was not entirely opposed to the concept.

The ship's mighty engines were powering down now; he could feel their decline through the soles of his feet. As they shut down, the sound of waves slapping against the ship's hull grew both softer and louder while overhead, gyres of common gulls began to squawk. Grishka disliked birds and their noise, and so went back into his room to wait out the first rush of disembarkation. As he sat there on the edge of his bed with his timeworn satchel ready at his feet, someone knocked on his door in passing and said, "Time to go!"

Indeed. He thought about the next leg of his journey: a train-ride to the Mexican border and then on Tezcatlipoca's compound in the Franklin Mountains. He looked forward to seeing the wyrms again and fretted about their progress. Were they developing normally? Or had Tezcatlipoca ruined them by trying to manipulate their orientation? Human magic wasn't like dragon magic; its results weren't always predictable. And so much was riding on this unprecedented gamble! If the Great One failed to produce a viable stable of breeding stock as promised, his followers would shift their allegiance to Drogo and his catastrophic vision. The fifth age would end in holocaust.

The drakena would never forgive the drakes for that.

Neither would the Divine.

Another rap sounded at the door. "Check out time! Thank you for being our guest!"

Tezcatlipoca would have bristled at such passive-aggressiveness. Drogo almost certainly would have gone in pursuit of the offender. Grishka, however, was more like the drakena in that regard: more tolerant of humans and their peculiar ways, more accepting of order and ceremony. Other drakes saw that as a sign of weakness. But Grishka was a water drake and knew that there were advantages to going with a flow.

He picked up his bag and headed toward the exit. He made no attempt at haste, so by the time he reached the gangplank, he was among the very last few who were trickling off the ship. He despised this part of any voyage, for the ramp was steep enough to make footing precarious. Had he been human, he might have used a cane to steady his descent. But he was a drake, and dragon-proud. Crippled or not, he meant to descend to the dock on his own.

What he hadn't counted on, however, was the ramp being wet.

Grishka saw the slick spot an instant before he stepped on it. By then, it was too late. His good leg slid out from under him, leaving him unbalanced. His damaged leg began to buckle. He tensed, bracing himself not for pain but rather searing embarrassment. But even as he neared his tipping point, someone caught him by the elbow and righted him again.

"Whoa," that someone said, as they both regained their equilibrium. "I guess all that talk about needing to get one's land legs wasn't just baloney."

He shifted to snap at his rescuer for daring to touch him only to realize that he recognized her. This was the young woman that he'd encountered the first night of the voyage. She'd seemed a rather delicate creature then with her distant smile and gossamer party clothes, but it had taken real strength to haul his dragon-weight out of a fall.

"No, indeed," he said, as he studied her by the light of day. "The middle ear needs time to adjust. We have met before, have we not?"

"Yes, I believe so," she said. "Are you OK?"

He patted the hand that still gripped his elbow. "Yes, of course."

She released him immediately, sputtering apologies. "I'm sorry, I didn't mean to be rude. I just forgot to let go."

He twitched her a whiskery smile. "I took no offense, child. It has been a long time since I have had the pleasure of contact with one so warm. You are stronger than you look."

"Yes," she said, as she slipped her hands into her pockets. "So are you."

"Yes," he said, intrigued in spite of himself. Perhaps it was her apparent lack of revulsion of him. Perhaps it was the way she carried herself: head up, shoulders back, confident in every regard. Whatever her secret was, it made Grishka want to charm her. "Could I perhaps persuade you to walk with me to the bottom of the ramp?" he asked. "The footing is treacherous here."

"Sure," she said, but did not offer him an arm to hold. He was disappointed by that. He looked at her intently, allowing her a glimpse of his inner dragon's eyes. Back in the days when he had been interested in doing such things, that little trick had captivated women, even a tsarina. Here and now, though, it seemed to have no effect at all. Fascinating!

"Did you manage to derive some pleasure from the voyage?" he asked, and then rolled those inner dragon eyes at himself. How banal he sounded! How specious! "Or did you languish in your cabin for the duration?"

The corners of her mouth curled upward, but he would not have called the look that she gave him then a smile but rather something more mysterious. "I ordered a lot of room service," she said. "I took great pleasure in that."

"You interest me," he said, a confession flecked with undertones of excitement. "So few people do. Where do you go from here?"

She shrugged, deliciously nonchalant. "Answer hazy," she said. "The future has yet to reveal itself to me."

Grishka's fascination with the woman ballooned. She was a student of the mystical, too! He glanced all about without seeming to, searching for an excuse to remain in her company now that they had reached the terminal. There were no cafes in sight, no interesting distractions, only a barn-like baggage claim area and a sea of taxis.

"Do you need to collect your luggage?" he asked, thinking that he could accompany her at least that far without alarming her.

"Nope," she said. "I'm traveling light—"

A shiny black Hummer limousine screeched up to the curb in front of them. The tinted rear passenger window slid down, exposing the shadowy outlines of a familiar face. "Grishka," that face hissed, "get in. We need to talk."

The window rolled back up again. The woman shot Grishka a wondering look. "Was that Drogo Channing?"

"You know of him?" Grishka asked.

"Everyone knows of him," she replied. "He's a very important man in Washington."

"I see," Grishka said. "Do you like him?"

She crinkled her nose, a gesture traditionally reserved for foul-smelling things. "No," she said. "Not really."

"Neither do I," he said, and then added, "But we cannot always choose our associates, can we?"

The window whirred down again. This time, Drogo's scowling face was in plain view. "Hurry up!"

Grishka suppressed a flash of withering resentment and then shifted toward the woman, deliberately turning his back to the other drake. "The future does not always reveal itself in ways that we expect or understand," he said, presenting her with a card that he'd pulled from a pocket in his robe. "Should you find yourself in need of answers that no one else can give you, call this number and leave a message. It may take me a while, but I will get back to you."

"Grishka!"

He caught one of the woman's strong, capable hands and stroked it from knuckle to wrist with a leathery thumb. "Do svidaniya!" he said in parting. "Until we meet again."

"You spend entirely too much time with those creatures," Drogo said, as Grishka ever so awkwardly climbed into the back of the limo. "Your weakness for them will be the death of you." He scorned Grishka's twisted form with a passing sniff and then embarked on one of his favorite situational subjects. "They tried to kill you once already. To be honest, I am amazed that they did not succeed."

"I credit the Divine for my survival," Grishka said, willing himself not to react to Drogo's overly aggressive musk. "She intervened for reasons I have yet to fathom."

"The Divine had nothing to do with your survival," Drogo said, and then tapped at the window that separated them from the driver. As the limo pulled away from the curb, he went on to say, "Your would-be assassins were simply shitty dragon-slayers."

"You were not there," Grishka asserted, "so you cannot say. Therefore, we will have to agree to disagree on the Divine's involvement."

"Listen to you!" Drogo said. "You don't even sound like a dragon anymore. Did those incompetent apes castrate you, too? I've always wondered."

"A most curious thing to have on your mind," Grishka remarked, ever so slyly, reacting to the other drake's pheromones in spite of himself. "I think it is you who have been spending too much time in the company of men. You've taken on their customs. And their trappings," he added, gesturing at the limo's luxurious interior. "Are you having sex with the females as well?" Drogo's nostrils flared, signaling a direct hit. "I thought so. When I was your age, I found them hard to resist as well."

Drogo flushed, a threat display. The cords in his neck grew taut, too. "Do not compare my actions with yours, Grishka Rasputin," he growled. "You mounted human females because you were weak and desired them. I mount them because that's what humans of my stature do. It's part of the disguise, nothing more."

"Reasons notwithstanding," Grishka said, fondling the tangles of his beard to repulse the other drake, "your sexual exploits are having an impact on your biochemistry. You're even more aggressive than usual. Your judgment may be suffering from the overflow of hormones."

Drogo leaned in close and showed his teeth. "I would kill you where you sit if you were not The Great One's court jester."

"There. See?" Grishka said, barely blinking in the face of Drogo's wrath. "You freely express your contempt for me. Yet if I am not mistaken, you summoned me into this vehicle because you want something from me. That is not clear thinking."

Drogo reared back as if to strike. At the very last moment, however, he stopped himself and lit up a cigarette instead. "Perhaps I have been a bit—edgy—of late. But for good reason, I assure you. We drakes have committed to the wrong manifesto. Creating our own breeding stock won't be enough to restore the natural order. We must be rid of the humans, too."

"The Divine does not want to see the world consumed by fire and ruin," Grishka said. "If we destroy everything, we win nothing."

"I see that now," Drogo said. "And as it happens, we don't need to use nuclear warfare to eradicate the humans. I am this close—" He pinched the air into the narrowest of margins. "—

to acquiring a cache of biological weapons. When the time is right, we can let a plague loose and let it cleanse the world!"

Grishka raked his beard again, waiting for divine guidance. When Drogo pressed him for an answer, all he could say with confidence was, "The Divine does not immediately object."

Drogo forced streamers of smoke through his nose. "Why would She? It is a good plan—better than The Great One's idea to make brood mares out of wyrms. But Tezcatlipoca will not listen to me. He only has ears for you."

Ah, so this was where the conversation was going. "You want me to talk to him for you."

"Yes! You are on your way to see him, are you not?"

Although Grishka was surprised that Drogo had a passing knowledge of his comings and goings, he kept his expression neutral. "I am."

"Tell the Great One what I have told you," Drogo said, not even trying to make that sound like a request rather than a command. "Advise him to give up his vision and follow mine instead."

Even as Tezcatlipoca's probable response to such an advisory started to take shape in Grishka's head, the limo veered to a sudden stop. An instant later, the door locks popped up.

"Get out," Drogo said. "I have a meeting at the UN. A coalition of third world countries is going to ask me to persuade the president to outlaw land mines. Can you imagine? It is going to be an exquisitely amusing afternoon." As Grishka moved to exit the vehicle, he added, "You will do as I ask?"

"It will be as if The Great One had been sitting here with us," Grishka vowed, and then climbed out of the limo. An instant later, the limo pulled away.

Although he supposed he shouldn't have been, Grishka was surprised to find himself in front of the train station. No doubt Drogo had dropped him here just to show how extensive his knowledge of Grishka's comings and goings really was. Grishka had to admit: he was impressed. And a little dismayed. He was secretive by nature, and kept a low profile despite his deformities. It came as a shock to discover that he wasn't as invisible as he'd imagined himself to be. Which was probably why the Divine had arranged this encounter in the first place. She wanted him to be more careful; more aware.

As he considered the Divine's message, an inattentive young jogger dressed in shorts and tennis shoes ran headlong into him. The human pitched backward and reeled like a drunkard. Then, when he finally realized that he had collided with Grishka rather than a brick wall, he scowled like a man offended.. "Watch it, asshole," he said, as he stuffed his ejected earbuds back into his ears. "And next time, stay out of my fucking way!"

As Grishka watched the person jog away, he thought: Maybe killing them all wasn't such a bad idea after all.

CHAPTER 9

The woman is sitting in a cramped, palm-thatched hut that smells of dry mud and stale sweat. There is a fire burning in the central pit, but neither its warmth nor its smoke has much of an impact on her. She is old now, so old that she cannot remember being young. Her longevity is a gift from Quetzalcoatl for keeping his true nature a secret. The woman believes the extra years might have been more of a blessing if the god-in-disguise had gifted her with extra youth as well, but it does not occur to her to complain because life is so much easier now. Her mate died of bad luck and a snake's bite several seasons ago so she does not have to attend to his needs. She does not have to work the chinampas, either, or venture into the jungle to forage for firewood or fruit. Her only duties involve cooking for the extended family and telling stories to the children of her children's children. These younglings are fat and well-formed, so accustomed to plenty that they laugh when she tells them how little she had in the days before Quetzalcoatl flew down from the sky. Out of all of them, only the oldest daughter of her oldest granddaughter listens to the stories with genuine interest. That girl, Quetzalli, is smarter than the other children, even the boys—an attribute that could have gotten her killed had she been born a few generations ago. But menfolk have become more tolerant of females, smart or otherwise, since Quetzalcoatl's arrival. They did not even complain much when he started inviting women to become priests. Quetzalli's mother, Quetzalpetlatl, has been a priest for many years. In the god-in-disguise's service, she has learned how to shape strips of clay into jars that can hold a week's worth of water dress wounds so they will not suppurate and blow pleasing sounds from a flute. Often,

after a day at the temple, she will join the woman by the family fire and whisper in her ear, sharing secrets that she does not want anyone else to hear. Quetzalpetlatl desires the god-in-disguise. The thought of mating with him lights a fire in her loins and leaves her aching and wet. She has never ached this way, not even in the hot-blooded throes of young womanhood. She would submit to him in a blink if he showed even a flicker of interest. But the only intimacy that Quetzalcoatl seems to crave is the thought-filled kind that exists between a teacher and his students.

The woman listens to her granddaughter's secret desires in silence. She wants to say that it is not wise to be so passionate about a god, especially one that is other than he appears, but she has made a promise and it will bind her tongue until the day she dies.

A familiar ring tone sounded, plucking Aurora out of the story. As she rifled her desktop for the phone, she realized that she was a little aroused. She laughed at the show of sympathetic horniness and wondered what would happen if Quetzalpetlatl ever managed to get with the god.

Better put some plastic down, Duncan's ghost advised.

She snickered at that only to half-choke on a giggle when she found her cell and saw the Caller ID.

"Aurora?" Charles Webber said. "Is this a bad time?"

"For what?" she retorted, and then grimaced, immediately embarrassed by her glibness.

"Well," he said, sounding completely unfazed, "since you asked, an afternoon of dancing and music."

"Elaborate," she said.

"I've got two tickets to the Aztec and Native American Dance Festival," he said. "It's being held at The Pinnacles National Park campground. Do you have any idea where that is?"

"The park is south of here," she replied, "down by Salinas.

I'm willing to bet that the campgrounds are somewhere in the vicinity."

"Would you be interested in going?" he asked. "I know it's late notice, but the tickets just fell into my lap a few minutes ago."

Although she had no intention of saying so, he'd had her at Aztec and Native American Dance. She had received a flyer about the festival in the mail a few weeks ago and set it aside as something worth looking into only to forget about it. Typical, Roz would have said, and Aurora wouldn't have disagreed.

"What a happy coincidence," she said. "I was planning on going to the festival anyway to do some research for a project I'm working on. If you don't mind me taking notes and pictures while I'm there, I'd love to go with you."

"Best news I've had all day," he said. "Pick you up in ten?"

"Make it twenty," she said. "I've got to round up my gear."

"See you in twenty then."

To her dismay, the prospect fanned the little hot spot she had going in her groin. She told herself to get over it, that the kiss they'd shared outside of the Big Basin Bar and Grill had been a one-time, experimental thing. Nevertheless, she changed her shirt twice in fifteen minutes, going sexy first and then retreating to a blue ombre pull-over that wasn't quite so tight. Then she threw a notebook and her phone into an oversized tote, grabbed her jean jacket and keys and started on her way. She cleared the front gate just as a sleek black Jaguar sedan pulled onto the side of the road. Charles got out of the car to open the passenger door for her. He was wearing a leather jacket, driving gloves, and Ray Bans. His face was clean-shaven; his hair, freshly cut. As she closed the gap between them, she tipped his sunglasses down with a forefinger so she could see his eyes and said, "Hi!"

He smiled at that and kissed her—a brotherly peck that scrambled her brains nonetheless. "Hello to you, too," he said, as he saw her into the car. "So glad you could join me." He shut her door, then went around to the driver's side. "And just in case you're in need of caffeine," he said, as he slid into his seat, "I picked you up a beverage from Rasta Roast."

Her gaze darted from him to the insulated cup in her holder and back again. Her left eyebrow arched—a look that was both playful and challenging. "That's very kind of you," she said. "But how do you know what kind of beverage I drink?"

He shrugged. "I have this knack." When she mocked him with a snort, he said, "No, really. I can usually guess what someone likes to drink. You strike me as someone who prefers tea to coffee, so I got you a chai mocha latte with a tap of cinnamon on top."

Surprise flashed across her face in the span of a blink. He must have managed to see it anyway because he laughed, one of those gotcha sounds, and then grinned at her. "I was right, wasn't I? See, told you."

Rather than give him the satisfaction of responding, she just grabbed the hot-cup and took a sip. "Perfect," she said afterward. "What other knacks do you have?"

He let go of the steering wheel for a second—just long enough to show her his empty hands. "That's it, lady," he said, "that's all there is, just one humble little knack. Sorry!" Then he gestured at the tote bag that she'd stationed on her lap. "Is that all you brought? When you said 'gear', I imagined a half-dozen cameras, a tape recorder, and a Glock."

Her first impulse was to declare that she'd never own a gun, but amazingly enough, she realized that he was joking before the words rushed from her mouth. "Used to be that way," she said instead. "But here in the twenty-first century, things are a little different. Now all I need is this—" She exposed a corner of the notebook. "And this." She held up the cell phone. "It takes pictures and video. And," she added with a flirty slyness that belied the hammering of her heart, "I've never needed a gun to get what I want."

She thought he would be intrigued by such a swaggering declaration. Instead, he looked pensive, almost wistful. "Lucky you," he said, then shifted the Jag into gear and headed for the highway. A few awkward moments passed in silence. At least, they felt awkward to her. Charles seemed quite relaxed.

"Do you know where to go?" she asked, hoping to re-break the ice.

"Got it all in the GPS," he assured her, and then gestured at the fog-shrouded world beyond the windshield. "It's like living in a cloud around here," he said. "When does the sun come out?"

"It's probably out already in the valley," she said. "Up here in the hills, we get morning fog most of the year and are glad to have it. It keeps the air cool in the summer and brings in just enough moisture to keep our mountains from drying up."

"That's another thing," he said, in a mock-aggrieved tone. "What's up with everything being fresh and green in the winter and brown the rest of the year? News-flash: that's not the way it's supposed to work."

She laughed. "By this time next year, you won't be able to remember it being any other way. And you'll think fifty-five degrees is freezing."

"Yeah, well, I never was crazy about the cold," he said, and then shifted in his seat so he could sneak more frequent glimpses of her face. "So what's this project you're working on? Are you a historian? A reporter? A Native American dancer looking to make it in the big city?"

She laughed again—shit, teen crush syndrome! "I do have some Aztec blood in me," she said, "courtesy of my mother. But I don't dance, ever."

"Not even at weddings after a couple of drinks?" he teased.

"Not even on the graves of my enemies," she replied, only to wish that she had kept her mouth shut. What the hell had happened to the filter between her brain and her mouth? He was going to think she was some kind of crazy-woman. "That's figuratively speaking, of course. I get carried away sometimes. I guess that's why I became a writer."

"Oh! You write? How interesting! Are you published?"

His surprise was genuine, as was hers. She had completely forgotten that she'd decided not to share her professional particulars with him. Now that she'd spilled her own beans all over herself, she would have to come clean—and that left her a little sad. She had really enjoyed the freedom of anonymity.

"Yeah," she said, trying to keep the admission low-key, "I have a couple of books out."

"Good for you," he said, in that jolly, encouraging way that people had with writers they did not know. "When we get home, I'm going to order the whole lot of them."

"I won't unfriend you if you don't," she said, psychically accenting 'don't'. "The stuff I have out is all YA fantasy. Young adult," she clarified, when he arched an eyebrow.

"I hope you don't mind that I haven't heard of you," he said, though he didn't look too fussed about it. "It's just that most of the reading I do is technical. I've never had the inclination or the time to read make-believe stuff."

"It's not for everyone," she said, and although there was only a hint of disappointment in her tone, he picked up on the chill immediately.

"Hey," he said, "don't write me off just yet, lady. I'm retired now, and in the process of forming all sorts of new habits. Tell me more about this book you're working on."

She had the feeling that he was trying to humor her. She

appreciated the attempt. "When I started it," she said, "I thought it was going to be the next one in the series. Much to my surprise, it's turning out to be something quite different."

"How so?" he asked, arching that perfectly manscaped eyebrow again. "Is it a romance?"

She jeered, reflexive genre snobbery. "I don't do romance."

"Pity," he said, then reached out and stroked her hand in passing. Before she could decide on a suitable response—return the touch, stay aloof, create a diversion—he went on to switch on the CD player. "I hope you don't mind," he said, as the first steamy strains of a tenor saxophone filled the car, "but this is proof that a leopard can in fact change its spots. I never had any interest in music, either, before I retired. Then a few weeks ago, I discovered jazz! This stuff could almost change my opinion of the human race. What do you think?"

"It reminds me of cool cotton sheets on a hot summer night," she said, because she could not bring herself to come right out and say that she had never heard anything so achingly sexy in her life. And damn, when had he started smelling so good? He hadn't been giving off that subtle musk this whole time, had he? Was it too cold to open the window?

He was grinning at her now, more cause for schoolgirl chagrin. "Wow," he said. "Cool sheets on a hot summer night—I think I'm going to like dating a writer."

Crap! Now they were dating? Part of her wanted to hide behind her hands and giggle at the thought. Part of her wanted to sputter: it was too soon; she wasn't ready to take that step yet! But before either of those inner voices could engage, another one stepped up to the plate. "In that case," she heard herself say, "then perhaps you'll consider attending the SiliCon Grand Ball with me next month."

He tightened his grip on the wheel and then cleared his

throat. "Did I mention that I don't do much reading?" he asked, offering her a wan sideways smile.

"I'm not asking you to read anything," she said, enjoying his discomfort. "I'm asking if you want to be my escort for an event."

"I don't have to read?" She shook her head. "And I get to spend the evening with you? Is it a fancy affair? Will I need a tux?"

"It's a masquerade," she said, "but don't worry, you don't have to go in costume. I certainly won't be. That's—" My daughter's thing, she'd been about to say. But she didn't want to talk about Roz, not yet. A thousand words wouldn't be enough, and one would be too many. Besides, she wanted him to get to know her as a woman before he saw her as a mom. "That's just not my thing," she said instead. "If you need some time to think about it, no problem."

"Thanks, but I've had all the time I need. I'd love to be your date. I haven't anyone's date in years. Just forward me the details, okay?"

The urge to hide her face and titter came over her again. At the same time, the car crested the last of the Santa Cruz foothills. The sight of the socked-in valley below was a sobering distraction.

"Damn," she said. "This could be one of those days that the fog never lifts."

"Want to turn around?" he said, cheerfully offering her the out. "We could try again tomorrow."

"I can't make it tomorrow," she said. "If you're game, so am I. But if the fog bothers you, then by all means, take us home."

He harrumphed. "You want to see fog? Check out Beijing in the winter. What you see here is just an ambitious mist. Onward we go."

The Jag surged forward. She leaned back in her seat, content to let him drive and listen to his jazz. The sensuous sounds lent the mist-shrouded roads an air of otherworldliness so intense, it seemed as if they were driving through an enchantment. An all-white stag bounded across the highway in front of them, compounding the impression. She gasped with surprise and delight.

"How cool is that?" she said, as the buck disappeared back into the fog. "I had no idea there were albino deer in the area."

"Especially an area that's so densely populated," Charles said. "You'd think that there'd be nothing but squirrels and crows between here and Yosemite."

"Are you kidding me?" she said. "Suburbia is a deer's wet dream, a smorgasbord of tasty ground-cover to eat and virtually no predators. In Monterey, you can usually see more deer on the golf courses than golfers."

"Interesting," he said. "We'll have to check that out sometime."

"Sure," she said, thrilling to the sound of 'we' even as she wondered what the hell she was doing.

The parking lot for the Pinnacles National Park campground was mostly full when they got there, proving that a little fog couldn't keep a good festival down. Charles parked next to an ancient VW mini-van that was plastered with religious bumper stickers and then flashed Aurora a rakish smile. "Shall we?"

"Let's," she replied.

The distant sound of drums and flutes greeted her as she emerged from the car. The sage-scented haze gave the music a ghostly feel. She could hear shouting, too: muffled, gull-like notes of discord that clashed with the campground's peaceful vibe.

"Are you warm enough?" Charles asked, as he closed the car door behind her. "I can lend you my jacket."

"I'm fine, thanks," she said. Then, after a moment's hesitation, she linked her arm around his proffered elbow and fell into easy step with him. As they strolled through the parking lot, the shouting became more intelligible: "Repent now! The end of the world is near!" Then a snarl of black-clad people spanned into view. They were carrying signs and haranguing festival-goers as they filed in and out of the gates. Their leader was a chubby red-haired man with piggish eyes, a bulbous nose, and a mouth that would have been the envy of a Chilean sea bass.

"Those devil-dancers will steal your souls and condemn you to eternal damnation," he bellowed at one passerby. "Go home and pray for mercy while you still have a chance. The Day of Demons is coming!"

"Amen, Brother Baine!" his acolytes trilled. "Amen!"

Aurora and Charles snuck past the apocryphal crew while it was swarming an outbound family of five, though Aurora had to admit that she did more in the way of sneaking than Charles did. He simply strode boldly past the gesticulating brother as if he were not there.

"Fools," he said, once they had cleared the entrance. "They accomplish nothing."

"True," Aurora replied, thrilling to the feel of his arm around her waist. "It's also ironic in a way."

"What is?" he asked.

"Them picketing this event," she said. "The Aztecs used to sacrifice people to their gods to prevent the world from ending."

"Wait," he said, literally stopping her in her tracks. "I'm confused. I thought the Aztecs were into doomsday events and even had a calendar that predicted the end of the world."

"That was the Mayans, who preceded the Aztecs by centuries," she said, glad that she had researched the subject. "The Mayans had a knack for mathematics and astronomy, and devised a calendar to track the passage of time through the centuries. That calendar stops on December 21, 2012. Some people believe that the world will come to an end on that date."

"Ah," he said, stretching the exclamation into a sound of comprehension. "So that's who started all those nasty rumors."

"It kind of makes you wonder, doesn't it?" When he cocked his head at her, she delivered the punch line. "Do you pay your mortgage or not?"

He looked at her askance, as if he suspected her of messing with him but wasn't quite sure. "Are you a believer?"

She laughed, delighted that she had at least given him a moment's pause. "I believe in a lot of things," she said, "but not in prophecies. That calendar is the Mayan version of Y2K. The only thing that's going to end on December 21, 2012 is all the yammering from people like that ginger-haired fool." Seized by an urge to tease him, she added, "Why? Do you think the world is going to end?"

His mouth acquired a mocking quirk. "Do I believe that a heavenly trumpet is going to sound and people are going to start floating up to heaven like helium-filled balloons? No. But I wouldn't be overly surprised if we brought the end of the world upon ourselves one day soon."

The thought sent a shiver down her spine. He drew her closer as if he thought she were cold and then shook his head. "There I go again," he said, "talking doom and gloom on a date. I'm sorry, Aurora. My learning curve seems to have grown quite steep."

"No apology necessary," she said. "Everyone's got a right to their opinion. And—oh my God, look at that head-dress! I have to get a picture of that!"

The head-dress in question was attached to one of several dancers who were working the crowd. They looked like parrots amidst a flock of domestic turkeys. Their feathered head-dresses were spectacular. Their costumes were elaborately beaded. Aurora recognized a walking photo-op when she saw one, and asked a pair of decked-out young women to press close to Charles. He played along gamely enough, but she could tell that his heart wasn't in it. She liked that about him. And when she showed him the resulting picture, saying, "Here's something for your Facebook page," he shrugged and said, "Don't have one." She liked that, too.

Vendor stalls lined the festival's outer boundaries. These offered everything from food to dolls dressed in authentic Aztec dance costumes. "That looks good," Charles said, pointing at the skewer of meat and roasted peppers that one festival-goer was carrying. "Want one?"

"Maybe later," Aurora said, feeling herself slip into work-mode. "I want to check out the Circle of Dance first."

A festival directory pointed them toward a vast green lawn. A sacramental fire burned at its center, scenting the persistent fog with wood-smoke. An array of drummers, singers, and flute players sat around the fire. As they played their ancient, eerily compelling music, dancers strode into the circle. Some danced singly. Others performed as a group. All of them mesmerized their spectators—or at least most of them. Charles watched the first few dances with an indulgent half-smile and then tapped Aurora on the shoulder.

"I'm going to get one of those skewers," he said. "Do you want anything?"

"Bottle of water, thanks," she said, and then went back to taking pictures and scribbling notes. As she worked, she drifted, following dancers at first and then whimsy. She wanted shots of everything, even the mountainous terrain in the background. She wanted to see a world where one such as Quetzalpetlatl might have lived. A stand of pink-barked manzanita and gray pine at the base of a nearby slope caught her eye and then tugged at her mind. There! That's where she wanted to be! As she hiked toward the tree-line, sporadically remembering to look out for snakes, the drumming and fluting turned ghostly again. The fog thinned out a little and acquired a spicy tang. With every step, she felt more and more like Quetzalpetlatl. She knew what the priestess was feeling as she hiked to who-knew-where: excitement! She knew what the priestess wanted, too: her god! By the time she reached the treeline, she was almost running. She took a few shots of the manzanitas and grey pines in passing, but did not linger. There seemed to be a path leading into the mountain's side. She felt drawn that way, a tug both urgent and seductive. She could not help but follow it.

Up the stony slope she hiked and into a shallow canyon. The canyon walls were rust-red flecked with beige and had the worn face of an old arroyo. She stroked a jut of stone as if it were a lover's chin. The feel of it pleased her inner Quetzalpetlatl. Clearly, this was a good way to go.

Yes! Come to me!

She blinked back surprise and a fleeting worry that she was having one of those so-called senior moments. Then the scrub-filled bend ahead rustled—a distinct shiver as if something in its midst wanted her attention. Uh-oh. There'd been a lot of mass behind that crackling. A mountain lion, maybe. Or maybe a bear or wild boar. Instinct urged her to start walking backward—slowly but steadily, showing no fear. But even as the thought crossed her mind, a piebald muzzle poked out of the brush. To her surprise, it was bubble-gum pink.

"What do we have here?" she murmured, and was answered by a testy, "Aurora! Where are you?"

She blinked, thinking, Oops, for she'd forgotten all about Charles. As she half-turned to broadcast her location, she suffered another out-of-body thought. *Don't!* But Charles was already heading in her direction. She could hear him crunching river-rock beneath his feet and possibly swearing to himself. She half-turned toward that sound and shouted, "I'm up here!" As she did so, the brush ahead of her rustled again. When she looked next, the pink muzzle was gone. Oddly enough, its absence gave her more grief than relief.

"Jesus, Aurora," Charles said, as he came marching up the arroyo. "I've been looking all over the place for you. And just so you know, it's a big place."

Even though she knew that she probably deserved it, she did not react well to his bitchy tone. She cocked her head, planted her fists on her hips, and said, "So—what? Did you think I was going to hike my way back to Saratoga?" Before he could respond, she added, "I told you I needed to work on this outing. I told you I was going to take pictures and notes."

"I know," he said, relaxing a little now that he knew she was OK. "It's just that you weren't where I left you when I got back from the food court."

She pinned him down with a full-press stare. "I don't do well on a short leash, Charles. I need the freedom to go wherever my curiosity takes me. If you can't handle that, then you had better take me home now and forget you ever met me."

To her vast surprise and displeasure, he let out an amused snort. Then, as her scowl deepened, he held up a placating hand and said, "I wasn't laughing. I swear. Leastwise, not at you. I came looking for you in the first place because I need to take you home."

"What?"

"Yeah," he said, getting his foot in the door like a seasoned salesman. "I just got off the phone with an old business associate. There's been an emergency on his end. He needs my help."

"Wow, what happened?" she said, allowing herself to be ushered toward the canyon's mouth.

He responded with a hangdog shake of his head. "Sorry, can't say. Nondisclosure issues, I'm afraid. Are you going to hate me forever for taking you away from your work?"

"Nah," she said, deciding to forgive him. "I've got enough material to start with." Then, recalling that pink snout, she added, "And I can always come back if I need more."

He nodded, signaling that he had heard her, but his cellphone was clapped to his ear and he was listening intently. With each passing second, the cords in his neck grew tauter. "Of course he's going to kill you when he finds out!" he snarled finally, and then added, "No! I'm not going to tell him for you. Just do what it takes to keep everyone calm. I'm on my way."

After that, he snapped his phone shut and then cast her a look chockful of regrets. "I'm sorry. We need to go."

"Sure," she said, and then took his outstretched hand. He set out for the campgrounds at a brisk pace. Neither one of them said a word until they cleared the festival gate, where they were swarmed by doomsday picketers.

"Seek Forgiveness for Your Unholy Affections!" one of the raggedy-Ann acolytes shrilled at Aurora and Charles. "You Doom Yourselves Otherwise!"

Aurora shooed the woman away like a flocking pigeon, saying, "You shouldn't believe everything you read."

Then Brother Baine himself stepped in front of her. "Did you not hear the Sister?" he bellowed, seizing her by the arm. "You risk eternal damnation by refusing to listen!"

"And you risk hospitalization by accosting strangers," Charles said, in a flat, steely tone that Aurora had never heard from him. "If you don't unhand the lady right this moment, you're going to know exactly what eternal damnation feels like."

The bass-mouthed preacher narrowed his eyes at Charles as if trying to see through him. An instant later, he said, "You.

You're one of them."

"Most certainly," Charles said, oozing menace.

Brother Baine withdrew his hand—slowly, as if he were pulling it through a fiery hoop. Then he backed away, never taking his eyes off Charles until he was back in the safety of his flock. "Beware!" he said then, pointing at Charles. "The end of days is coming, and his kind will light the fire."

Charles smiled at the man—a dismissive twitch of the lips. Then he draped an arm across Aurora's shoulders and led her across the parking lot. "Baine said you're one of them," she said, as they zeroed in on the car. "What did he mean by that?"

He laughed. "I have no idea. I just let him think what he would. Fools like that are always afraid of something."

"I can be a fool at times," she said, shifting back into flirty mode. "Guess what I'm afraid of!"

"That's easy," he said, and then pulled her close. "You're afraid of men like me."

In the second before they kissed, she had to admit that was true.

CHAPTER 10

The first thing Brigit said when she and Roz reunited at the cruise terminal was, "Is all of yer country like this?"

"Like what?" Roz asked, fending off a psychic wave of distress and disgust.

The changeling gestured wildly at their surrounds. "Tha water's filthy, tha air stinks, and there's naught but metal and glass and concrete as far as tha eye can see!"

"Oh. That." She understood the changeling's revulsion. On some distant, semi-conscious level, she shared it. But she'd grown up in an age where all sorts of pollution had long since been normalized, so it took an outright atrocity to raise her hackles or her gorge. "That's what happens when eight million people live together. Can you believe it? This isn't even the biggest city in the world."

"A dunna want tae believe it," Brigit said. "Why would anyone want tae live like this?"

"I couldn't tell you," Roz said, "because I much prefer country living myself. The only city I have a heart for is San Francisco. I'll take you there at some point. I think you'll like the trolley cars."

"What A'd like," Brigit said, "is a long splash in a cold mountain loch tae wash tha reek offa me. A smell like—" She sniffed at her arm as if to confirm an impression only to scowl at what she sensed. "Wait. Tha's not me." She strode closer and snuffled Roz. "That's you!" she said then. "Ye smell of drake— tha same drake A smelt on the ship. What have ye be doing?"

"Nothing!" Roz said, raising her hands as if to ward off the changeling's agitation. "I hung out at a coffee shop until it got

179

dark out and then came back here to meet you. I didn't talk to anybody and nobody talked—" To me, she meant to say. But even as the words formed in her mouth, the memory of a shaggy man in a monk's robe dispelled them. "Wait. There was this one guy. I grabbed him by the arm just as he was about to take a header down the gangplank. I don't think he was a drake, though. He had a pretty serious limp."

"A limp means nothing," Brigit said, as she sniffed Roz's forearm again. "Dragons are immune to disease but we can be injured—especially as juveniles and young adults. What else do ye remember about him?"

"He was very solid," Roz said, concentrating on the memory of that encounter, "and very hairy. I think he came from Russia. He spoke of the Divine—"

Brigit hissed, venting excitement. "Tha should have tipped ye off right there!"

"And—he gave me—this," Roz went on, and presented the proffered card with a flourish. "He told me I should call if I wanted a new path to follow. Funny thing is, there's no name on it. Just a number."

Brigit hissed again and snatched the card up. "Tha four-legged snake!" She said, between whiffs. "He was trying to seduce you into his service! This card reeks of attraction."

Seduce her? An image started to form in her mind only to be shut down by a stringent desire not to go there. But even as she shielded her mind's eye, it offered her an insight. "Yeah, well," she said. "It was probably my connection with you that he found alluring."

The suggestion raised Brigit's eyebrows first and then the corners of her mouth. "An interesting thought, lassie. A've never heard of such a thing happening, but like A said, A dunna get out much. Maybe yer mum's drakena will be able to tell us."

"Maybe. We have to find her first," Roz said, and then snatched the card back just as Brigit was about to feed it to the wind. When the changeling questioned her with a look, she shrugged and said, "You never know. It could come in handy."

"It could just as easily be tha death of ye," Brigit countered. "Drakes are not like drakena. They're killers who dunna wish mankind well. Best ye remember that."

"I will," Roz promised, only to lose track of the thought as her brain disgorged another chunk of memory. "Oh, I almost forgot! I saw my drake—Grishka, I think he's called—climb into a limo with Drogo Channing. Do you think Channing could be a drake, too?"

"Who?"

Roz didn't know whether to be thrilled or shocked by Brigit's ignorance. "He happens to be one of the most powerful men on the planet."

"Drakes tend ta gravitate toward positions of power," Brigit said, waxing thoughtful, "so A canna discount the possibility that this Drogo is a drake. Did ye happen tae see where tha two of them went?"

"Sorry," Roz said, "but I stopped paying attention as soon as they drove off. What do you think they're doing here?"

"A couldn't say," Brigit replied and then turned her face to the wind. "A dunna smell them anywhere, so perhaps, like us, they're just passin' through. There's no way of being certain about that, though, so we'd best keep tae ourselves on tha next leg of our journey."

"Whatever you say, bwana," Roz retorted, and then pointed. "The train station's that way."

The changeling glanced in that direction, then narrowed her eyes and shook off the prompt. "Not until A spend some time in a loch."

Roz rolled her eyes, thinking: dragons. They did have their priorities. "Well," she said, "Central Park has a lake, but I doubt you'll find it that nice. How about a hot shower instead?"

Brigit grimaced, grinding her desire for a cleansing swim into a paste between her back teeth. "All right," she said then, "a shower it is. And room service. Is that available on land?"

CHAPTER 11

"Where are you?" was the first thing Tezcatlipoca said, when Grishka answered his cell phone.

"En route, Great One," Grishka replied, in a snappy tone that belied his travel-induced weariness. "I should reach the borderlands two days hence and be at your compound the day after that."

"Plans have changed," Tezcatlipoca said, quick as always to get to the point of the call. "Two wyrms escaped last night. Their absence was not noted until this morning. Reports have been sketchy since, but by all accounts, they appear to be heading north toward the California coast. I want you to head west and help Carlito catch them."

"Of course, Great One," Grishka said, immediately concerned for the escapees. Having being confined since their reawakening, they would not know how to conduct themselves in the wild— or around human populations. If they were spotted, they would almost certainly be hunted down and killed. Then the conspiracy would have to find a way to explain away the wyrms' sensational existence. It was not a scenario that Grishka wanted to entertain. "I will switch trains at the next stop."

"You must hurry," Tezcatlipoca said. "The two who escaped are the most precocious of the lot and were already making rudimentary attempts to shift their shapes. If they learn how to Change before we catch up with them, we may never find them. We cannot afford to lose two potential breeders."

"No, of course not," Grishka said, only to recall a certain conversation that he had had recently. "But the situation might not be as dire as it seems."

"Really?" Tezcatlipoca said, in a jaguar-like purr. "Why not?"

"Drogo Channing was waiting for me when I arrived in New York. He was very keen on speaking to me."

"Ah, yes, so I heard," The Great One said, purring still. "I wondered if you were going to mention that meeting to me."

Grishka suppressed an irritated rumble. The fact that Drogo was keeping tabs on him had come as an unpleasant surprise. The fact that Tezcatlipoca was having him watched him as well just rankled. They were supposed to be the closest of allies! He offered up a prayer to the Divine, requesting patience. In return, She sent him a thought:

Perhaps The Great One had been spying on Drogo....

That made enough sense to mollify Grishka, so he abandoned his grievance for the nonce and said, "I'd intended to inform you of it when I arrived at the compound, Great One. But since my plans have changed, I am informing you now. Drogo wanted me to tell you that he is on the verge of gaining access to biological weapons. He wanted me to convince you to set aside your plan to secure the new age in favor of his."

Tezcatlipoca's purring slurred to an ominous stop. Suddenly, Grishka was glad that the Divine had arranged for him to deliver this report from afar. "I see," Tezcatlipoca said. "And what do you think, Grishka Rasputin? Do you agree with him?"

"I am committed to our present plan," Grishka said.

"And if I were to set that plan aside in favor of Drogo's?"

"You are the Great One, I would defer to your judgment."

The purring resumed, but there was an unhappy edge to it now. "You say that, Grishka, but I wonder sometimes. The Divine does not let you stray too far from Her holy hunting grounds.. What does She have to say about Drogo's plan?"

"She neither approves nor disapproves of it, Great One," Grishka said. "Her only thought on the matter is that biowarfare would be easier on the planet than nuclear warfare."

"True enough," Tezcatlipoca conceded. "But in the end, this plan is not for us. No matter how lethal Drogo's plague may be, there will be pockets of humanity that survive it. And humans can rebound from the brink of extinction faster than cockroaches. I know. I've seen it happen.

"And then there are the drakena. They have yet to forgive us for the last time we tried to rid the earth of their pets. If we try again before we have secured adequate breeding stock, they will make sure that we never breed again. That will spell the end to drakes. I do not believe that is the goal we should be striving for."

"Neither do I, Great One," Grishka said. "And I am sure Drogo will agree with you, too, when you explain your reasoning to him."

The purring stopped again, but this time there seemed to be no menace contained in its absence. "Always so sly you are, Grishka," Tezcatlipoca said. "I've always liked that about you. I'm sure such a quality will serve you well in your search for the runaways."

"I appreciate your confidence," Grishka said, and then paused as the Divine whispered another holy insight in his ear. "Just one more question before you disconnect."

"If you must."

Grishka ran his fingernails through the tangles of his beard as he worked through the thought. "It is my understanding that you sent Carlito to California to search for your sister."

The Great One huffed. "What of it? Finding her can wait. Finding the wyrms cannot."

"It is also my understanding that the runaways are heading for California," Grishka said. When Tezcatlipoca made no comment, Grishka added, "Three of the things that are foremost on your mind are all converging on each other. Am I the only one who thinks this seems like an outsized coincidence?"

CHAPTER 12

Aurora high-fived the garage door closer, then wheeled her suitcase and carry-ons into the house. The foyer had a stale, unoccupied smell, which meant that Roz was still somewhere on the road. Disappointment sizzled through her, then a round of irritation. How long did it take to get over a stupid broken heart?

Maybe she's like her mother in that regard, Duncan's ghost joked.

"It's a good thing you're dead already," she grumped, and then began redistributing the contents of her bags. Promo materials went back in the office, dirty clothing in the laundry, and everything else in its place. As she unpacked, she sang along to the radio. But while music made the house feel a little less empty, it could not cover up Roz's absence. In times past, her daughter would have met her at the door with a glass of wine and then quizzed her as she helped with the unpacking. Had it been a good trip? Did she have a good turn-out for the signings? Any familiar faces in the crowd? As it happened, it had been a very good trip. Seattle was a fun town and her work was popular there. She'd delivered the keynote speech at a YA writer's conference and then stayed on to do a few book signings in the area afterward. She had even had lunch at Pike Place Market with a group of fan-friends this afternoon before heading for the airport.

It was, however, oh so good to be home again; back to the land of writing, eating in, and sleeping in her own bed. She hadn't had any memorable dreams on the road, but something else had left her fidgety in the mornings: the memory of that piebald, faded pink muzzle that she had seen that day at The

Pinnacles. At the time, she had been too distracted by Charles' proximity to give the sighting the attention it deserved, but it had cropped up in her mind over and over again since then, eating at her like a bad itch. Had it been a muzzle? Really? She seemed to remember it being too big—too reptilian—to be the front end of any critter native to this part of the world. More likely, it had been a figment of her hyperactive imagination, dehydration setting in.

True or false, however, the memory still ate at her. She had seen *some*thing, dammit! But what? She had to know!

When she was finally done unpacking, she headed into the kitchen and slapped together a ham-and-cheese sandwich. As she ate, she listened to her phone messages, hoping to hear Roz's voice. Message one was from a telemarketer from Breast Cancer Research.

Save.

Message two was from a realtor who wanted to know if she was looking to sell.

Delete.

Message three was from Charles.

"Hello, Aurora. I know you're away on business but I wanted to call anyway to apologize again for cutting our outing to the dance festival short. I hated to do it, but that's life sometimes, right? I hope you'll let me make it up to you. My first preserve beasties will be out of quarantine by the time you get back. You could come over and see them. I could make you lunch or dinner afterward. And I've still got a few bottles of Ridge left. Think about it, OK? Give me a call when you decide. Bye for now."

Decision made.

But even as she reached for the phone, an image of that grizzled pink muzzle popped into her head as if to say, 'Me first!' That made a strange sort of sense to her. Best to clear up one itch before she started scratching at another.

Oh, but some itches were so hard to resist! She spent the rest of the evening trying not to think about sex.

Quetzalli is working in the temple with her mother. They are making pottery that their village will use as trade-stuff with high-landers. Although she is old, Quetzalpetlatl is still a sure hand at making sturdy, well-balanced containers. The designs that Quetzalli paints on these containers before they go into the fire are both intricate and engaging. Quetzalcoatl is the inspiration behind most of the designs. Like her mother, she feels connected to the god and loves him with all of her being. Unlike her mother, she has no wish to be his wife. She is content to serve and to learn.

As she is painting the god's pink-feathered profile on the side of a jar, a jaguar prowls into the work-room. At the sight of it, Quetzalli gasps and drops the jar. The sound of clay shattering draws Quetzalpetlatl out of her maker's trance. She looks up from a half-formed bowl and then lets out a gasp of her own. The golden-eyed jungle cat glances toward the doorway as if daring the women to bolt. When neither of them moves, it bares its moon-white fangs and snarls. The two women close ranks, but hold their ground. The jaguar screams, demanding that they run for their lives.

"We are in the house of Quetzalcoatl," Quetzalpetlatl says calmly. "The god will protect us if this is not our time to die."

The jaguar licks its chops and begins stalking Quetzalli. Closer and closer it pads, until she can see its whiskers twitching with excitement and smell its death-tinted breath. She lowers her eyes, for this is the proper thing to do so in the presence of a god. The stench of rotting meat rolls over her like a wave. Her world shrinks to the span of a jaguar's shadow. But even as that shadow rears up to crush her skull in its jaws, a voice lights up the room.

"Tezcatlipoca! Those women are not for you!"

The jaguar's jaws are so near to her head-bones, Quetzalli can feel drool dribbling onto her scalp. He purrs slyly like a cat at play and then pulses a thought at Quetzalcoatl. "There is no need to be greedy. I will take this one. You can have the other."

A fang presses against Quetzalli's temple. It feels as big as an obsidian knife. In spite of herself, she shuts her eyes and prays. Please, Quetzalcoatl, not today! As she does so, she hears the god say, "I will keep them both, Tezcatlipoca, for both of them are mine."

Saliva is running down the sides of Quetzalli's face now—at least, she hopes it is saliva and not blood. The fang does not dig any deeper, but neither does it pull away. "This is no way to treat a brother," the jaguar says, "especially a brother who has come with gifts for you."

Quetzalcoatl laughs, a warbling sound that gives Quetzalli strength. "You are not known for your generosity, Tezcatlipoca. So why would you be bringing me gifts?"

"We are kin," the jaguar says reproachfully, "and I regret the distance that has come between us. I have come to heal that gap— if you will permit it."

"Truly?" Quetzalcoatl says, a warble that could pass for either curiosity or doubt. "Then start by releasing my priestess."

"As you wish," Tezcatlipoca says, and just like that, the points of pressure at Quetzalli's temples disappear. She resists the urge to drag a forearm over her face and instead stands taller, as if nothing unusual has occurred. She thinks that prompts a nod of approval from Quetzalcoatl, but she cannot be sure because her vision is awash with sweat and tears and god's drool. "Mark my words, Quetzalcoatl," the jaguar says, as it stalks away from Quetzalli. "Nothing good will come of teaching these creatures not to fear us."

"A little fear is good, brother," Quetzalcoatl says. "But too much is boring. And in the end, it benefits no one. I would rather be respected."

"Yes," the jaguar purrs, "that has always been your weakness."

"And yours has always been hubris," Quetzalcoatl says, with a haughty riffle of his pink head-dress. "You seek to dominate everything except your own failings."

Queztalli expects the jaguar to take offense at that. To her surprise, it lets out an amused bark. "I am a god," Tezcatlipoca says. "I have no failings. But enough quarreling," he goes on, before Quetzalcoatl can respond. "I have given you back your humans. I would make other gifts to you as well. Will you not give up your grudge against me?"

Quetzalcoatl pauses, obviously weighing the offer against his grievances. Then he waves his hand as if to clear the air of a bad smell and says, "You have made an effort to repair the rift between us, brother. It would be wrong of me not to do the same." To his priestesses, he says, "Tell the people to make ready. We will celebrate my brother's coming with feasting and music and dancing and games."

"Do not forget the sacrifices," Tezcatlipoca says, starting to drool again. "There can be no celebration without an offering of blood."

Although Quetzalcoatl does not allow blood sacrifices in his own honor, Quetzalli cannot imagine him denying them to his brother on the occasion of their reconciliation. She bows her head, a gesture of deference that masks her woe for those whose hearts will be cut out and burnt. But the pink-plumed god surprises her again.

"My people need only sacrifice their sweat to us," he says.

"Your people," the jaguar says, a mocking purr. "And you accuse me of hubris. Be that as it may, however. If you say there are to be no sacrifices, then no blood will flow. I am sure I will enjoy the festivities nonetheless."

Quetzalcoatl nods, pleased and possibly surprised by Tezcatlipoca's response. "Go," he says to Quetzalli and her mother. "Make ready for the festival."

Aurora awoke with a headache, as if her own head had been clamped in a jaguar's jaws. She glanced at her alarm clock. 9:30AM? Yikes! She must have beaten the snooze button into abject submission! She crawled out of bed and into the shower. Afterward, she took a cheese sandwich out to the front porch. The fog had receded back over the mountains already, leaving a dew-washed morning behind. As she ate, the resident mockingbird went through its repertoire for her while bull hummingbirds conducted a turf war over the bougainvillea. A desire to stay home and be lazy tapped at her frontal lobe. Before it could leave a lasting impression, however, the memory of that piebald muzzle ran it off again. She had to go back to The Pinnacles and see what that muzzle was attached to. Until she did, she had the distinct feeling that she wasn't going to get anything else done.

She cast the crumbs from her breakfast onto the lawn for the songbirds, then fetched her car keys and started on her way. It was a perfect day for an adventure: sunny and warm with a cloudless blue sky, and traffic that went from light to lighter when she put Silicon Valley in her rear view mirror. As she drove, she listened to jazz on the radio and thought about Charles. She still didn't know what to call him. 'Boyfriend' sounded too high-school. 'Man-friend' felt too contrived. And 'lover' made her whole face burn! Ugh! She was too old for these kinds of self-inflicted mind games!

So why did playing them leave her giddy?

She made her way to The Pinnacles campground simply because it was the only reference point she had. The lot was much less crowded than it had been for the festival, which made it easy to spot the VW bus plastered with religious bumper stickers.

"Oh, crap," she said, when she saw it. "Not them again!"

She picked a spot as far away from the Nut Wagon as possible, but even as she shifted the Lexus into park, one of Brother Big-Mouth's black-clad acolytes emerged from the bus and came shuffling her way with a twenty-five-pound sack of rice slung over her shoulder. If Charles had been with her, she probably would have slammed the car back into gear and taken off for another lot, reference point be damned. But since she was on her own and the acolyte looked harmless enough, she decided to tough the encounter out

"Have you repented?" the acolyte asked, as she drew near. She was a scrawny, unwashed waif with hungry green eyes and matted brown hair. Aurora guessed that she was on the south side of eighteen. "The end of days is upon us."

"What's your name?" Aurora asked, feeling a sudden maternal surge. "Why are you doing this? Don't you have a home to go to?"

"My name is Bless," the woman-child replied. "My home is here with Brother Baine and my sisters." She pointed vaguely in the campground's direction. "We live over there on holy ground."

Aurora nodded cynically. "Holy ground, hmm? Sounds nice. Is that where the brother is now?" she asked. "Sacked out in a divine camp chair while you and your sisters do the heavy lifting?"

The suggestion seemed to appall Bless. Her eyes went round, as did her pale, thin-lipped mouth. "No! Brother Baine's not like that. He's up there," she said, this time pointing at a patch of mountain to the east of Aurora's destination. "He goes up there every morning to fortify himself against sin. Why do you ask?" she wondered, and then suddenly brightened. "Have you come in search of absolution? If so, I can guide you to him. I'm going that way anyway as it's my turn to bring him lunch."

"You're bringing him lunch," Aurora said, in a tone thick with brotherly contempt.

"Yes," Bless said. "Did I not say that he needs to fortify himself?"

"I've got a better idea," Aurora said, then reached into her purse and pulled out two twenty-dollar bills. "Take this, grab your sisters, and drive that hunk of junk into town for a pizza. You're kids, for God's sake. Live a little."

Bless glanced at the sack of rice on her shoulder as if weighing its gustatory value, then gave her lips a sorry lick and shook her head. "Thanks," she said, "but pizza is a forbidden food. I'll take the money as a donation to our cause, though."

"'Fraid not," Aurora said, pocketing the cash even as Bless reached for it. "You picked door number two, you live with door number two." Then, with a terse, "Have a nice day," she started on her way.

"Repent," Bless called after her, in a dolorous tone. "The end of days is coming."

"Whatever," Aurora muttered.

She strode past the campground studded with RVs and grated fire-pits, beyond the grove of manzanitas and gray oaks, and up the old wash that led into the mountain. As she walked, her irritation with poor deluded Bless gave way to a joy of being active and outdoors. She hiked up the wash, past the spot where she had seen the muzzle. Although she was no climber, her footing was surprisingly sure.

At the top of the slope, the rock-bed changed from stones to boulders, and the arroyo expanded into a small, many-creviced canyon. She started to explore the first of these cavelets only to be turned back by a flash of intuition. *Not there! Here!* She felt excited, unreasonably so, but if asked, she would have been hard-pressed to say why. Then again, who needed an excuse to feel good?

As she was working her way around a mound of nettle-studded boulders, a cloud passed in front of the sun, casting her in shade. The momentary overshadowing only registered after the fact—wait! Had that cloud circled once before moving on? She glanced up, but saw nothing but blue sky. An instant later, excitement started tugging at her again.

Just a little further now! Hurry!

Then she heard it: a strange, shrill squawk, distant but distinct, a curiosity that snapped her forward momentum. An instant later, another shadow sailed overhead, racing for a horizon that she could not see.

"What the hell was that?" she wondered aloud. But what it sounded like in her head was: *How can that be?*

The echoes of a shriek boiled into the arroyo: no wild-cat's hunting yowl, but a full-on human scream. A faint, "No! No! No!" followed and then—silence. The mountain itself seemed to be holding its breath. Aurora's immediate holy-shit impulse was to call 911. But in the midst of so much rock, she couldn't get a signal. Stupid cell service! Logic doused her indignation. What would she have said anyway—that she had heard someone cry out, somewhere? First responders needed more detail than that!

Maybe she should go and see what was going on.

No!

That was the only way she was going to know for sure if she should try and call the cops again.

No! Do not go!

But Aurora's desire to help was stronger than her instinct for self-preservation. She glanced in the direction from which the sound had come, hoping to find a quick and easy way out of the wash. As she suspected, though, the easterly rock-face was too steep and sheer for someone with her nonexistent climbing skills. Her only choice was to go back the way she had come. So back she went as fast as she could, half-scrabbling half-sliding down the stony slope and then running when she hit solid ground. As she emerged from the crack in the mountain's side, she spotted a dark-haired, black-robed woman running down the trail ahead of her. Belatedly, she recognized the woman as Bless. She started after her, but Bless was young and obviously panicked, so by the time Aurora caught up with her, they were within earshot of the campground. The unholy screech that she let out when Aurora grabbed her by the shoulder drew more than one camper's attention.

"Bless!" she shouted, spinning the girl around to face her, "it's me. Pizza-Lady! I'm not going to hurt you! Just tell me what's wrong."

The woman was flushed from running, and her thin, unwashed face was tear-streaked. "Demons," she said, a wild-eyed pant. "Demons attacked Brother Baine."

"What?" Aurora said, wondering for the first time if mental illness might be a factor in this woman's being one of Baine's followers. "Take a deep breath. Good. Now—clearly and calmly— tell me what you saw."

By then, Bless's sisters were converging on her—a swarm of black-clad women eager to re-absorb one of its own. An older Latina with bad skin and a nose ring was the first to reach her. "Que pasa aqui, mija?" she asked, as she folded Bless into her arms. "What has upset you so?"

"Demons, Luce!" Bless wailed. "They took Brother Baine. They will take us all. The end of the world is upon us!"

Luce glanced at Aurora, who deflected the unspoken WTF with a shrug, and then shook Bless ever so gently as if trying to jostle some sense into her. "Tell us what happened, mija," she said. "Tell us what you saw."

Bless sniffled, then wiped her nose on the back of her hand and said, "The Brother was sitting on his favored place of power—you know, that outcropping of boulders that looks like a man's head."

"We know the place," Luce said. "Go on."

"I was coming up the trail with the Brother's lunch when the first demon struck. It was long and black with leathery wings and stumpy legs. It came out of the sky like a streak of lightning and hit the Brother square in the chest."

The sisters sucked in a collective breath. A few of them began to moan. But Luce gave Bless another gentle shake, urging her to stay focused.

"The Brother screamed and tried to escape," Bless said, "but then the demon buried its teeth in his neck and—oh!" She covered her eyes as if to blot out the memory. "Blood spurted everywhere! I've never seen so much of it! I shouted at the demon, trying to get it to come after me instead, but it was clawing at the Brother by then and—" She whispered something into her hands. Aurora was not the only one who urged her to speak up. She let out a sob and shouted, "It was trying to have sex with him!"

The sisters recoiled at that. One of them twittered, "Oh, God! I hope he was dead!"

"As do I," Bless said, "because as the black demon was molesting the Brother, a red one swooped in and snatched his body away! The black one let out a furious hiss and then followed its diabolical cousin into the mountains.

"I'm telling you true, sisters! The end of days is upon us!"

She dissolved into tears then. Her sisters formed a human cocoon around her and started ushering her toward the campground. In no time at all, Aurora found herself alone with Luce. The sister was scowling at her.

"Why are you still here?" she asked.

Aurora glanced down at the forgotten cell phone in her hand. "I was going to call 911," she said. "But now—" She paused, stuck for a tactful word for 'bat-shit-crazy'. Before anything sprang to mind, Luce dismissed her with an authoritative wave of her hand.

"No," she said. "It is not your place to make that call. You don't believe Sister Bless. You think she is loca; I can see it in your eyes. And you will pass your disbelief on to the police, who already look down on us and our work. Bless deserves better than that. So does Brother Baine. I will call the police— and the press. The message that goes out will be correct."

"But what if the police want to talk to me?" Aurora asked, feeling absurdly reluctant to leave a possible crime scene.

"Why would they?" Luce countered scornfully. "Did you see what happened? Did you hear anything?"

"No," Aurora said, although the memory of a shadow circling overhead spiraled into her thoughts. "Not really. Just a scream and then some whimpering."

"Did you suppose that would be helpful in any way?"

"I suppose not," Aurora conceded, vainly resisting an urge to feel foolish.

"Then go away," Luce said. She started to walk away only to do a combative about-face when Aurora grabbed her by a forearm. "What?"

"Take this," Aurora said, extending one of her business cards. "If the police want to talk to me, I can be reached at that number."

"Fine," Luce said, tucking the card into a pocket without looking at it. "Now go away before the demons come back for you. Repent, for the end of days is here."

With that, the sister went in pursuit of the rest of the flock, leaving Aurora standing in the dust with cell phone in hand

and an overwhelming need to share what had just happened with a friendly ear. She scrolled through her list of contacts, meaning to stop at her publicist's number, only to find herself speed-dialing Charles instead.

"Aurora! What a pleasant surprise!" he said, upon picking up. "I didn't think you were home yet."

"I got in last night," she said. "Listen, I'm really sorry to bother you—"

"Hearing from you is never a bother. You know that, right?"

She injected a smile into her voice. "You're sweet to say so, especially given how busy you are at the moment. But I just had the weirdest experience and wanted to run it past someone to sort of ground myself."

"I'm all ears," he said.

Although his tone was inviting enough, a rogue wave of self-consciousness broke over her nonetheless. He was a sensible man, grounded in solid fact. When he heard what she had to say, he was going to think that she was the crazy one. But while the possibility daunted her, she could not quite bring herself to keep her mouth shut.

"Well," she said, "I returned to the Pinnacles this morning to finish up the research I started at the dance festival. While I was hiking up in the foothills, I heard a scream. As it turns out, it was Brother Baine—"

"Who?"

"That loud-mouthed preacher who was picketing the dance festival with his groupies," she said. "Remember? He thought you were part of some vast, end-of-the-world conspiracy."

"Sorry," he said. "That kind of stuff never sticks with me. But please, go on. What was the good brother screaming about?"

"Well," she said, trying to sound neutral, "according to one of his followers, he was attacked by a pair of demons."

"What?!?"

"I know, right?" she said. "How crazy is that?"

"Did she say what they looked like?"

The question threw her for a loop. Of all the possible responses she had imagined from him, that one didn't even make the list. "As a matter of fact, she did," she replied, letting a little of her bewilderment creep into her tone. "One was black; the other was red. Supposedly, they looked like bat-winged devils. Why?" she asked then. "You don't believe in demons, do you?"

"Of course I do," he said. "Demons. Flying monkeys. Dragons. What's not to believe?"

She let out a breath that she hadn't realized she'd been holding. Joking! He was joking! He didn't think she was crazy by association. What a relief! Now she felt free to speculate openly. "So what do you think it was?"

"I have no idea," he said. "I wasn't there. But I suppose it could've been mountain lions. Or—I hear there are condors in the area. They're predators. Maybe it was a pair of them."

The memory of that overhead shadow circled the confines of her skull again. "Yeah, maybe," she conceded. "But condors are usually scavengers rather than active hunters. And they sure as hell don't resemble bats or demons.. Why would someone lie about a thing like that?"

"Again, I wasn't there, so I can't say for sure," Charles said, "but I've been in situations where men have flat-out lost their shit after seeing things they weren't prepared to deal with. In a traumatic event, the imagination can do powerful things—maybe even make demons appear out of thin air."

"Witnessing an attack on one's spiritual leader would certainly qualify as a traumatic event," Aurora mused. "And given the conditioning that Bless no doubt received during her time with Brother Baine, perhaps it's no surprise that her brain conjured up a demon to serve as his destroyer."

"You have to admit,' Charles said. "Being attacked by demons certainly sounds more apocryphal than being attacked by big birds or overgrown cats."

She laughed at that. He was so good at putting her at ease! "Thanks," she said. "I needed that!"

"Glad I could help," he replied. "Feel better now?"

"Yeah," she said, but her hand trembled as she ran her fingers through her hair. "Still a little shaky, though

"What you need is a distraction," he said. "Why don't you come on over? I'll give you a tour of the facilities and introduce you to my new inmates. Afterward, we can have a glass of wine on the back patio and maybe even some dinner. I've been told that I grill a mean steak."

It sounded wonderful, all of it. But a little voice in her head worried that she would be imposing at an inconvenient time. "What about that job you're working on?"

He dismissed her concern with a chuckle. "You're not the only one who could use a little breather. And if it makes you feel any better, I think I just caught a break on this project. So what do you say?"

Her car-keys were already in her hand. "On my way," she said. "See you in an hour."

CHAPTER 13

A glint of reflected light from the road caught Charles' eye as he was refilling the holding pen water trough. Moments later, a car began cruising down the long, dusty driveway that wound its way through his wooded front lot. He finished topping off the trough, then shut off the faucet and retired to the shade of a towering redwood tree to wait. As the car drew closer, he noted that it was a sporty little number. He liked that. He liked that Aurora seemed to know how to handle it, too. But not even in his most fever-pitched dreams did he ever see himself falling for a woman who drove a pink sedan! For some reason, that endeared her to him all the more.

When she reached the top of the driveway, she turned toward the house, waving at him in passing. By the time he caught up with her, she was already out of the car and admiring his great white hunter digs.

"Wow," she said, by way of greeting, "this is some place you have here. I've never seen it close-up. The last owner wasn't all that sociable."

"Neither am I," he growled, drawing her into a rakish embrace. "But at least I'm smart enough to make an exception for a beautiful woman." He lip-kissed her then, harder than he'd intended. She did not seem to mind. "How are you feeling? Still shaky?"

She lingered in his embrace for a moment—a good sign, he thought. "I'm better now," she said. "The drive back settled me down. I think being behind the wheel is the best kind of therapy."

"I know what you mean," he said, and then went to kiss her again. She pulled back ever so slightly and then blushed like a schoolgirl.

"I'm sorry," she said. "It's just that I'm dirty and sticky from hiking all morning."

He laughed——a surprisingly relieved sound. "That makes two of us then, as I've been trying to catch up on all the work that's been piling up around here while I've been away." He nodded toward the holding pen and said, "Want to meet my new charges?"

"Absolutely," she said.

He ushered her over to the fence and pointed out the pair of zebras that were munching on hay in the shade of their shed. "These," he said, "are yearling Hartmann's zebras—a subspecies of mountain zebra. I got them from the owner of a hunting preserve in Texas. Made him an offer he couldn't refuse," he added, with a smile as dead as that owner was now. "As soon as I'm sure they're acclimated to this area, I'll release them to a larger pasture where they can roam at will."

"They're beautiful," Aurora said, with just the right amount of breathlessness. "Can I feed them a handful of grass or something?"

"Oh God no," he said. "They're wild animals, and meaner than spit—especially the stallion."

"Stallion?" she asked, eying the zebras dubiously.

He laughed again, a celebration this time. "He's on the other side of the shed," he said, "pestering my other female. I think she's coming into season, because he refuses to leave her alone." He was about to say more when a buzz from his back pocket cut him off. His expression immediately went flat. "I'm sorry," he said, "but I have to take this. Would you mind hanging out with these girls until I get back? I won't be long."

She sent him on his way with a flick of a wrist. "Go."

As he fast-tracked out of earshot, the phone buzzed again. He could imagine Tezcatlipoca on the other end of the line, bristling with impatience. The Great One routinely ignored calls as a show of dominance, but heaven help the fool who didn't pick up when he finally called back. Such an attitude could be wearying if not outright dangerous. Fortunately, he had the perfect antidote for it today.

"Carlito here," he said, just after the third buzz. "I have good news." That drew a moment of silence: Tezcatlipoca reining in his irritation. Charles was quick to take advantage of the shift. "The wyrms have been spotted."

"Both of them?"

"Yes."

"When?"

"This morning, due south of this location," Charles said. "I wasn't the one who made the sighting, but by all accounts, it appears that they were hunting together."

The drake hissed, venting excitement. "Good news indeed," he said. "Did it appear that they were hunting for themselves?"

The question puzzled Charles. "Who else would they be hunting for?"

"My sister, of course!" Tezcatlipoca roared. "I told you there was a chance that the wyrms might be heading your way to find her."

Charles resisted the urge to gnash his teeth. Really? A possible connection between the wyrms and the drakena? This was the first he was hearing of it! But admitting that aloud would only insult and inflame the drake. He chose to go a different route.

"Ah, yes, of course. The drakena. I was so excited about the wyrm sighting, I forgot all about her. You will be glad to hear that I am also closing in on her location." It was a flagrant misrepresentation, but one that grew smaller after factoring in this new information about the wyrms' motivations. "All of your problems will soon be behind you."

"All of them, Carlito?" Tezcatlipoca asked, in a mocking tone. "You have a gift for overstatement. But as long as you take care of the two woes that I have assigned you, I will be content."

Charles doubted that, too, but again held his tongue. There was no upside to antagonizing a dragon. "That is all the information I have for you now, Great One," he said instead. "I will call again when I am ready to trap the wyrms."

"You will not be able to do that on your own," Tezcatlipoca said. "Grishka is on his way to help you."

"What?" Charles said, but the line was already dead. His first inclination was resentment. Drake involvement in a project invariably complicated things, mainly because they were better at making work for others than they were at doing their own. But even as he started to grumble, he reminded himself that it could have been far worse. At least The Great One was sending Grishka Rasputin instead of Drogo Channing or one of that miserable lizard's minions. Grishka could be a handful with his predilections and moods, but at least Charles wouldn't have to sleep with one eye open while the drake was visiting.

But he didn't want to think about dragons of any stripe at the moment. Right now, he had another visitor on his mind.

As he headed back toward the holding pen, his gaze was all for Aurora. He liked that she hadn't stopped at her place first to tidy up; that was the hallmark of a self-confident woman. And he found that dusty, well-exercised look to be quite sexy. He could see himself doing things with her that he hadn't done in a long time. Today, maybe. The thought left him moderately aroused.

Then his stupid brain had to go and ruin it all by reminding him that he should pump her for more information about the wyrms first.

"Was it a productive call?" she asked, as he rejoined her at the fence.

"Let's just say it was a call that had to happen and leave it at that," he replied.

"Fair enough."

In his absence, the other two zebras had wandered into view. The mare was walking in slow circles, flicking invisible flies away with her tail. The stallion followed on her heels with his maleness on full display. Charles knew he should probably lead Aurora somewhere else, but wound up curling his arm around her waist instead. She tensed, once as his hand settled on her hip and then again as the stallion abruptly mounted the mare. Neither of them said a word until the stallion ejaculated, discharging an astonishing amount of semen.

"Oh my," Aurora said then, with a catch in her voice. "That reminds me of a joke I used to tell in high school."

Charles shifted, turning to stand face-to-face with her. "Let's hear it," he said, and his voice was a little raw, too.

She laughed, nervously, he thought, and then said, "What's gray and comes in quarts?" Before Charles could utter a guess, his best one being 'an elephant', she flashed him a shy smile and said, "Mayonnaise."

The erotic charge that had been building within him began to throw off arcing sparks. He pulled her tango-close and kissed her, no closed-mouth buss but an urgent, tongue-fletched press. The next thing he knew, one of her hands was knotted in his hair and the other was massaging his back pocket. Her response electrified him. He couldn't remember ever wanting a woman this intensely! He hoisted her up and onto his hips, then started shuffling toward the house. She made no move to stop him. When, a few steps later, he tripped over the hose and slammed her into the side of the shed, she let out a little gasp.

"Are you OK?"

"Getting better by the minute," she replied, and then plunged into another never-ending kiss.

He tugged the tails of her shirt free and then slipped his hands into the gap. Her skin was soft and a little sweaty. Her curves were delicious, on the ripe side of firm. She arched her back, encouraging or possibly daring him to explore where he would. But even as his hands slid over the satin rounds of her bra, the crunch and crackle of tires rolling over a dirt track distracted him. Aurora must've picked up on the sound, too, because her feet hit the ground in a hurry.

"You expecting a crowd?" she asked, as she stuffed her shirt-tails back into her pants.

"No," he said.

But he could see why she would think so. The taxi that was creeping its way toward his house was riding so low in back, it looked like it could be a loaded clown car. As it turned out, though, there was only one silhouette in the back seat.

"I don't believe this," he said, as the cab disgorged its shaggy, cloak-clad passenger. "I just got the call!"

"Carlito!" Grishka shouted to the world at large. "I have arrived!"

"Whoa," Aurora said. She had straightened out her clothing and run her fingers through her hair, but he could tell by the slight catch in her breathing that she wasn't as composed as she looked. "Looks like it's raincheck time."

"'Fraid so," Charles said, and gave her one last wistful kiss. "C'mon, I'll walk you to your car."

As they emerged from the shed's shadows, Grishka flagged them down. "Carlito! There you are!" he said, in a jovial tone. "Come and pay this man. And introduce me to your friend. I have so few opportunities to meet comely women these days."

Before she could decline the request, he steered her in that direction. "This will only take a minute," he said. "Unless he likes you. Then you might be staying for dinner after all."

"As long as you're serving Ridge," she said, "I'm good."

"Grishka, this is Aurora," he said, as they converged on the man-drake. "Aurora, this is Grishka. You'll excuse me while I pay the cab-driver."

"Aurora, is it? Such a powerful name," he heard Grishka say. "And I must say, you look like a woman of great strength. May I see your hand? One can learn so much about a person by looking at the palms."

"Some other time perhaps," Aurora replied. "I've been hiking in the hills all morning and my hands are filthy. In fact," she added, as Charles rejoined them, "I really do need to get home and clean up. Thanks for letting me see the zebras. Give me a shout when your calendar clears up." She nodded to Grishka in parting and added, "A pleasure to have met you, sir. I hope you enjoy your stay in Saratoga."

Grishka responded with a stiff, one-shouldered bow. "The pleasure was mine, Aurora. I look forward to our next meeting." As she headed for her car, he leaned toward Charles and said, "You did not have to stop on my account, you know."

"Stop what?" Charles asked, more intent on watching Aurora than conversing with the drake.

"I saw you there by the shed," Grishka said. "You could have mounted her, you know. I would not have been offended if you had kept me waiting while you conjugated."

That got Charles' attention in a hurry, and not in a particularly good way. Who wanted to locker-room talk with a dragon? "I wasn't—that is, we weren't—"

"You can fool a dragon's eyes, Carlito," Grishka scolded amiably, "but never his nose. You reek of desire. So did Aurora.

You should have relieved yourselves. I would have been content to watch. Indeed, I find watching to be rather—stimulating."

Charles' first reaction to the admission was revulsion. What kind of degenerate got off on watching an entirely different species have sex? Then he remembered the zebras and his outrage shriveled up and slunk away. "Yes, well," he said, "I'll keep that in mind. Shall we go inside?"

"Is there a room with a fire in it?" Grishka asked, as he limped toward the door. "Global warming or not, the air never feels warm enough anymore."

"The front room has a huge hearth," Charles said. "There's wood in the grate. All it needs is a spark."

"Excellent," Grishka said. "I will require vodka as well. It's been a long trip and I need to wash some of the road from my throat."

"Of course," Charles said, but what he was thinking was: and so it begins.

Happily, his liquor cabinet was well-stocked—compliments of the previous owner. He dug out a fresh bottle of Stoli, grabbed a sturdy water glass out of a neighboring cupboard, and then headed back to the front room. The drake was standing in front of the now-blazing hearth with his hands pressed against the mantel.

"I tell you truly, Carlito," he said, as Charles poured him a dragon-sized drink. "I will be immensely glad when the new age has been secured so we can all return to our own territories and stay there. Water dragons are not well-suited to be world-travelers."

"There's a swimming pool out back," Charles said, "but it hasn't been used in quite some time. If I had known you were coming, I would've called someone to come and clean it up." He set the drink down on the mantel where the drake could see it and then added, "As it happens, Tezcatlipoca only told me you were on your way about twenty minutes ago."

The corners of Grishka's mouth curved upward, making his

beard seem like a wild thing that was starting to rouse. "Yes, well," he said, "that's typical of Tezcatlipoca. One of the things he likes to hoard is information." He pushed back from the fireplace, then grabbed the drink and knocked it back all at once, Russian-style. As he held the glass out for a refill, he asked, "Why are there no pictures of Aurora on your mantel, Carlito? That is what humans do, is it not—put pictures of their mates on display?"

Oh, crap. Not this again. But if there was a good way to shut down a conversation with a drake, he sure as hell didn't know it. So as he poured Grishka another drink, he said, "She's not my mate. I don't know if she ever will be. She's quite an independent spirit."

"Yes," Grishka said, "I sensed as much. I caught a glimpse of her aura, and it was magnificent. That was why I wanted to read her palm." He tossed back his drink, then added, "I must admit, I was surprised when she refused me. Most women are quite cooperative after a glimpse of the dragon-eye."

"Yes, well, she's not like most women."

"Undoubtedly," the drake said. "And yet—she reminds me of someone. Someone I met just recently. Does she have any offspring?"

"Not that I know of," Charles said, refilling the drake's vodka yet again.

Grishka tapped at his glass with a gnarled nail as if he were trying to summon a thought from thin air. When the thought failed to materialize, a scowl ghosted over his face and then dissipated into shaggy resignation.

"I cannot identify the resemblance at the moment," he said. "No doubt it will come to me once I have spent some time in water." He sank to the floor then as if toppled by the weight of the many miles he had traveled. Despite his infirmities, he looked more comfortable sitting on the stone hearth than he had standing. "So," he said, "tell me everything I need to know. Assume I know nothing."

A dangerous assumption, to be sure, for as Grishka had noted, Tezcatlipoca was fond of his secrets. The Great One would not be pleased if Charles accidentally shared the wrong thing. But—better to offend the dragon who was a thousand miles away than the one who was staying in your guestroom, right? So rather than try to play games, he decided to be completely upfront with the drake.

"Tezcatlipoca said he was sending you to help me capture the wyrms," he said. "The good news is, they were spotted south of here this very morning."

Grishka clapped his hands and warbled. "You saw them? How do they look? Are they faring well in the wild?"

"I wasn't the one who saw them," Charles replied. "But from what my source told me, they appear to be doing OK for themselves."

"Were they on the move when they were spotted? Or did it seem as if they were settling in?"

"Unclear," Charles said. "According to my source, they attacked and presumably killed a human and then carried off the corpse."

"Curious," Grishka said, combing his beard with his fingers. "Wyrms usually eat where they take their prey."

"Tezcatlipoca thinks they were hunting for his sister."

The drake's eyebrows shot up like overgrown caterpillars. "You've located the drakena?"

"Not yet," Charles said, hoping that that more candid version of the truth didn't find its way back to The Great One. "If Tezcatlipoca is right about the wyrms hunting for her, then I've found her territory. I just need to find her lair."

"And if Tezcatlipoca is wrong?"

Then he was screwed.

But he knew better than to admit such a thing aloud. "He is the Great One," he said instead. "He is never wrong."

Grishka twitched him a sly half-smile, acknowledging and possibly even applauding the dodge. Then he climbed to his feet—a slow, staggered rise. Charles managed to look elsewhere for most of it. "I must commune with the Divine," he said afterward. "Where is your pool?"

"That way," Charles said, pointing at the wall of windows beyond the kitchen. "But as I said, it's pretty overgrown."

"I care not," Grishka said, already shuffling toward the kitchen. "Water is water. Being in it will restore me. Tomorrow I will require food. Any kind of meat will do."

As he walked, a greenish triangle appeared below the hem of his cloak. It lengthened into a tail on his way through the kitchen. By the time he reached the dining room, he was down on all fours and marching across the tile floor like an enormous Komodo dragon with a crooked leg. Charles ran to open the door, not out of subservience but rather a desire to keep the wall of glass intact. Grishka flicked a forked tongue at him in passing, then dove into the pool and disappeared beneath a thick layer of toxic-looking scum.

Charles went back inside and got to work. The sooner those wyrms were in custody, the sooner he'd have his place—and Aurora—all to himself again.

CHAPTER 14

"*Is this the* last stop?" Brigit asked, as the train pulled into the station.

"No," Roz said, thoroughly sick of that question and the one that inevitably followed.

"How many more?"

"Two," she said, barely keeping herself from snapping. "Maybe more if you keep bugging me. Now come on, let's grab a bite to eat while we're waiting for our next train. If you promise to keep the are-we-there-yets a minimum, I'll even buy you a Scotch or two at the bar."

The prospect of whiskey usually placated the changeling, but tonight, she was particularly restless. "If A had known what an enormous sprawl ur country was, A would've thought twice about making this trip. A've never been away from water this long. It's starting tae wear on me."

Ah, so that was the problem. "There's plenty of water where we're heading," Roz said. "All ya gotta do is stick the ride out for twenty-four more hours. And you can thank your lucky stars that we didn't take the bus."

"There's no such thing as lucky stars," Brigit grumbled. "They're giant balls of gas."

"How would a dragon know something like that?" Roz asked, only half in jest.

Brigit flared her nostrils as if at a bad smell. "Human arrogance can get a wee bit tiresome after a while," she said, and then cut Roz off with a hiss when she started to apologize. "Empty words, lass. In future, try tae remember tha dragons were here long before yer kind decided to climb down from yer trees. Now where's the fecking pub?"

As it happened, the station had a decent-looking bar and grill that wasn't too crowded. They passed on a table, choosing instead to stand at the bar and stretch their legs. Televisions blared on every wall, most of them broadcasting sports that didn't impress Brigit.

"What's all tha fuss about?" she asked. "It's all men trying tae hit or kick some kind of ball. Ye want tae watch something exciting? Try taber-tossing."

The man standing next to her loosed a sonic boom of a laugh—a sound to match his build. He must have been almost seven feet tall and three hundred and fifty pounds because he made Brigit seem almost normal-sized by comparison.

"That's the smartest thing I've heard all day!" he said, and then ravished Brigit with a grin. "And you're just about the most beautiful creature I've ever seen. Can I buy you and your friend a drink?"

Before Roz could warn the man, Brigit said, "Triple Dewar's, neat."

The man reared back and blinked, telegraphing surprise and disbelief. Then he laughed again and said, "Gotta love a woman who knows what she wants. What about your friend?"

"Nothing for me, thanks," Roz said, feeling antisocial. "I have to eat first."

"Suit yourself," the giant said, and then relayed his order to the bartender in a booming voice that cut through the crowd noise like an Arctic icebreaker. Afterward, he planted himself squarely in Brigit's personal space and said, "My friends call me Joe. What do people call you?"

"Nessie," Brigit replied, then leaned in close and inhaled deeply through her nose, taking in his body effluvia. His eyebrows arched as she sniffed him, but he didn't object or pull away. When she was done, she leaned back again and nodded approvingly. "Ye have a robust smell about ye."

"Well," he blurted, "that's a relief. I like the way you smell, too."

The bartender set their drinks down in front of them. He held his up in mid-air, obviously intending to make a toast. She grabbed hers and guzzled it down without ceremony. Afterward, she smacked her lips like a happy dragon and slid the empty glass toward him. "Again."

Joe reared back again as if from a sucker punch. But the look on his broad, bearded face was one of budding delight. "Well, ain't you a hellcat and a half! Barkeep! Another triple for the lady! And keep 'em coming!

"So," he said, as the bartender poured her another ration of Scotch, "what else do you like to do besides drink?"

"A swim a lot," she said, and gave her fiery locks a toss. "A like tae fish, too. Why? Did ye have somethin' in particular in mind?"

Holy shit, Roz thought, as she pretended to watch the soccer game on the far wall. The changeling was flirting with Joe! Not only that, she was actually hot for him. Roz knew because the attraction—and Brigit's carnal reaction to it—was spilling into her awareness through their blood-bond. Talk about awkward!

"Well," he said, edging closer, "I can think of a couple of things that I'd like to do with you if we had a little privacy. Do you live around here?"

"Does it sound like A live around here?" Brigit replied, but her tone was seductive rather than biting.

"I figured as much. When's your connection?"

"I dunno," she replied, uninterested as always in time. "Soon, A suppose."

Just then, the bartender delivered the sandwich and chips that Roz had ordered. Seeing that, Joe lit up like a downtown

Christmas tree and said, "Well, it'll take your friend at least fifteen minutes to finish her supper. Want to step into my office while she's eating?"

"Ye have an office?"

He smiled slyly and jerked his head in the direction of the restrooms. An instant later, a thought popped into Roz's head. *"Why would someone have an office in the loo?"*

Roz nearly blew a half-masticated bite of tuna salad sandwich out through her nose. As she coughed to clear her airways, she choked out a reply. *It's not his office. It's just a place where he does his business."*

"Makes sense, A suppose." She filched one of Roz's potato chips and popped it into her mouth like a minnow, then grinned at Joe and said, "Let's 'ave at it then."

Joe laughed. "A hellcat! I knew it!" In a lower voice, he added, "I'll go in first to clear out the place. You follow in a minute!"

An instant later, he was on his way.

Roz gripped Brigit by an elbow and hissed, "You're not seriously thinking of doing this, are you?"

The changeling freed herself with an easy tug. "Why not? He smells hardy, and he's of a suitable size. Size matters, ye know."

"I'm sure it does," Roz said, still *sotto voce*. "But Jesus, Brigit—in a public restroom? That's gross!"

"Yer just jealous. Has it been a minute yet?"

"I suppose," Roz grumbled, and then fired off a parting thought as Brigit peeled away from the bar. *"Just remember, whatever you get on you is going to stay on you for at least another twenty-four hours."*

"Dunna care!"

Well, Roz huffed to herself, that was that. But as it happened, it was not. As she hunkered over her food, a savage pang of lust erupted within her. It hit her so hard and so fast, she bolted upright and gasped.

"You OK?" The bartender asked.

She managed a feeble nod, but what she really wanted to do was lunge over the bar, tear off his clothes, and sink her nails into his chest. It didn't matter that he was skinny and bald and twenty years too old; she hungered for him with a fierce, violent passion. She clenched her jaws and then her fists, resisting urges that she did not understand. When the taste of blood filled her mouth, her excitement arced toward climax.

"Miss?" The bartender prompted, and then blurted out a startled, "What the hell," as the door to the men's room burst open. An instant later, Joe emerged, disheveled, dazed-looking, and streaming blood from a small cut on his neck. He flashed a wild-eyed look at the bartender, made a whimpering sound, and then went running out of the restaurant.

"He's nae cooming back, is he."

"Doesn't look like it."

"Feck."

The changeling came sauntering out of the bathroom with casual disregard for all of the eyes that were slanted her way. Her cheeks were rosy. Her red seaweed locks were seductively tousled. "Triple Dewar's," she said to the bartender, as she reclaimed her spot next to Roz. "No ice."

"You got a spot of ketchup right there," he said, pointing at the corner of her mouth. She licked it away with a dexterous flick of her tongue and then raised an eyebrow, inviting him to comment further. He turned an interesting shade of red, deposited her drink in front of her, and then scurried away without another word. She took a swig and then turned that arched eyebrow on Roz.

"What's this?" she said. "Ye've barely touched yer supper."

"Yes, well," Roz growled, "I was a little distracted." She paused for a moment, projecting resentment, and then added,

"You could have warned me, you know."

"A know," the changeling replied, helping herself to more of Roz's chips. "But where's tha fun in that?"

Roz leaned in close. The taste of blood still haunted her mouth. "That wasn't fun for me, dragon. You put me in a very bad spot."

"Yer right," Brigit admitted. "A should'a said something. But it's been a century or two since I last bonded with a human. A forgot that thoughts aren't tha only thing that we can share."

Mollified by the rare draconic concession and aware that she wouldn't get much more if she pressed, Roz relented. "Apology accepted," she said, even though one hadn't been tendered. "Just don't do it again." Then, as she returned to her meal, a thought struck her and she blurted it out. "The transmissions aren't that—intense—all the time, are they?"

"Feck no," Brigit said. "Over the next few years, they're going tae get worse. Dragons are very sexual beings, ye know. And the end of an age marks tha start of our breeding season. If ye thought the overflow between me and that man were intense, then ye definitely dunna want to be anywhere in the vicinity if A chance tae get with a drake."

The projection that accompanied the claim rippled with violence and lust and hints of something else that Roz couldn't believe she was sensing. "Was that dread?" she said, sharing her marvel. "Really?"

The changeling finished off Roz's sandwich in two effortless bites. "Sure," she said, as she was chewing. "Drakes are greedy and cruel, and would do absolutely anything to reassert their dominance over tha world. Yet should A happen upon one of them in the waning days of this age, instinct and chemistry would overrule my good sense, and A'd have him over and over and over again until the fever finally left me.

"Have ye never suffered an attraction to someone ye despise?"

An image of Aldo's abs flashed in Roz's mind, raising a wry half-smile. "That's the story of my life, Brigit. Story of my life." Her stomach gurgled then, a complaint that Brigit had eaten more of her meal than she had. She started to propose another round of food only to be distracted by the television over the bar. The national news was on, and the storyline on the backdrop read: 'Grisly Murder in NorCal Beach Town'.

"Hey, barkeep!" she shouted. "Can you turn that up? That's not far from where I live!"

He cast one nervous glance at Brigit and then jacked the volume just as the anchorman turned the story over to the reporter on the scene. She was dressed in khakis like a grim-faced safari guide, and had chosen the iconic Santa Cruz Boardwalk with its old-school wooden rollercoaster as her backdrop.

"That's right, Chris," she said. "Early this morning, joggers found the body of a man down on the beach. He had been decapitated. Although unconfirmed as of yet, early reports suggest that he may have been sexually assaulted, too. Police are treating the case as a homicide, but as of yet, have no theories and no sus—"

Before she could complete the thought, a wild-haired Latina clad in a black robe thrust herself in front of the camera. "A demon did it!" she asserted. "The same demon took Brother Baine! Repent, people! The end of—"

The reporter ushered the woman into the waiting arms of a crewman and then widened her eyes for the camera, telegraphing good-natured exasperation. "As I was saying, police have no theories and no suspects. Beach-goers are being urged to proceed with caution during the day, and to leave well before dark.

"This is Michelle Kelsey, reporting live from Santa Cruz."

The anchorman reappeared on-screen. He was peering intently at his teleprompter. "As a footnote to that story," he said, "our research department tells us that Justin aka Brother Baine is a Bay Area cult leader famous for picketing local cultural events and anticipating the end of the world. His followers reported him missing from their campsite three days ago, and allege that a demon took him. Neither his body—nor a demon," he added, with a fleeting smirk, "has yet been found."

Roz turned to Brigit and sneered. "What the fuck, right? Who believes in demons these days?"

Brigit shrugged. "Tha same people who believe in angels, A suppose. Is it time tae go yet?"

The changeling's blasé response disappointed Roz in some vaguely irrational way. But rather than press for a more satisfying answer, she just signed off on the subject and checked her phone. To her surprise, it was later than she had imagined.

"You can head out to the platform if you want," she said. "I have to pay up."

Without another word, Brigit took off. The bartender watched her leave through narrowed eyes and then cast an equally suspicious look at Roz. The fact that she had her credit card out did not seem to appease him.

"Is that true?" he asked, as he ran her card. "You two are from California?"

"Yep," she said, simply because she saw no point in setting the record straight.

He gave his head a derisive shake, then returned her card and said, "I should've known."

She left him a tip anyway.

CHAPTER 15

Quetzalli has fallen asleep on her feet twice already: once while carrying a plank heaped with roasted monkey meat and again while lighting the evening torches. Both times, she started awake before bad luck struck, but she does not know how much longer she can manage without rest. Yet manage she must. Quetzalcoatl will be dishonored if the festival for his brother falters in any way. She cannot allow that to happen—and not because her life is at stake. The Serpent God's honor is paramount. She drinks a cup of hot cacao spiked with fire-pepper to revive herself and then directs the next round of entertainment toward Quetzalcoatl's temple.

Dancers clad in pink-feathered headdresses go prancing past her. They are followed by a set of face-painted drummers and flute-players. As the troupe vacates the public square, a string of Mayan slaves spans into view. The oldest of them has not yet seen ten summers. Tezcatlipoca offered them to Quetzalcoatl as sacrifices, but The Serpent God decreed that they will work the chinampas instead. They look tired and hungry and utterly resigned to being livestock. Quetzalli decides to have them fed, but before she can give the order, someone shouts, "Make way! Make way, I tell you!"

The crowd that has gathered at the temple's main entryway splits like a badly sewn seam. Heartbeats later, a man emerges from the gap at a run. He's tall and well-formed and handsome as a golden eagle. Quetzalli recognizes him as her mother's youngest son, Pimotl. Like her, he serves Quetzalcoatl, and is one of the god's favored few.

"Step lively, sister," he says in passing. "The gods are in high spirits tonight."

"Where are you going?" she shouts at him.

"To fetch more pulque!" he shouts back, and then disappears.

Pulque is Tezcatlipoca's latest gift to Quetzalcoatl, an offering made just this afternoon. It is a drink of some sort. Quetzalcoatl thought it was swamp water when he first dipped a cup into the container that had been brought before him, but The Jaguar laughed and called it nectar of the gods.

"Drink," he urged. "You will see."

Quetzalli will never forget the look that came over Quetzalcoatl's face when he took his first sip. His nostrils flared. His jade-colored eyes widened into surprised circles. Tezcatlipoca laughed again and said, "Did I not tell you? Nectar! And the more you drink, the better it gets." Quetzalli supposes the pulque must be sublime now because both of the gods have been drinking it nonstop since that moment.

The troupe is performing in the central courtyard now: an exciting mélange of music and motion. The gods watch from a lavish pavilion at the top of the temple. The Jaguar has displayed a surprising appetite for music. Whenever he hears a flute, his twitchy black tail goes still and he begins to purr. The first time Quetzalcoatl saw this, he nodded approvingly. The second time, he presented Tezcatlipoca with the village's best musicians as a gift.

Serving a god in any capacity is an honor beyond compare. Even so, Quetzalli has never been happier about her relative lack of skill with the flute.

"Make way, sister!" a familiar voice shouts. "We have returned with the pulque!"

She steps to one side of the entryway. A moment later, a line of slaves files past her and into the temple. Each of them is carrying a massive jar. When Quetzalcoatl sees this, he does a double back-flip and then bounds down the side of the temple, laughing and clapping as he goes. When he reaches the courtyard, he does another back-flip and cries, "Pulque for everyone! Everyone must drink!"

The music veers off-course—a shocked, uncertain response to the declaration. For while gods routinely partake of human fare, no man has ever sampled anything intended for the divine. Nectar of the gods. The name alone makes it clear that this is not a drink for men. Overstepping that boundary will undoubtedly provoke consequences, possibly good but more likely bad—and no one is in a hurry to taste bad luck. Quetzalli does not know what to do. The idea of imbibing a god's drink makes her bowels squirm. But the thought of ignoring her god's wishes feels like a fist around her heart. She looks to Quetzalcoatl for guidance. In the face of her distress, he ruffles his pink frill and laughs.

"Fear not," he says. "Tonight, everyone celebrates. Everyone drinks and dances. Fetch cups. Pour the pulque. Let the music flow!"

Left with no choice, Quetzalli sends a slave for cups. Then she and her brother and the other favored few begin distributing the pulque. "Give yourselves extra!" Quetzacoatl says to them, after everyone else has been served. "Pouring is thirsty work!"

She does as she has been commanded. Then, as her god watches, she drinks.

The first sip makes Quetzalli's mouth water in an unpleasant way and makes her want to retch. But because the foul-tasting fluid is god-stuff, she resists the urge to spit it out and chokes it down instead. The pulque burns like the hottest of peppers as it flows down her gullet and bursts into flame when it hits her belly. She lets out a gasp and dashes a sudden swell of tears from her eyes. Quetzalcoatl laughs at her traumatized look and tells her to drink again. She takes a second sip. This time, the pulque makes her head spin. The sensation sweeps her off her feet. When she stands up again, her god nuzzles her cheek, then grabs Pimotl's hand and dances him away.

A strange fog seeps into the courtyard. It speeds some things up and slows others down. The sun sets. The moon rises. Reality wanders in and out of focus. At one point, Quetzalli sees The Jaguar drag a *child off into the darkness. At another, she thinks she sees a woman in a pink-feathered headdress kiss Pimotl. She nods off in an out-of-the-way corner only to be awakened sometime later by a terrible wailing. The sound instigates a terrible pounding in her head. She shifts onto her knees and peers out into the courtyard. Most of the torches that she lit earlier have burned out, but some few remain marginally ablaze; guttering remnants that cast restless shadows everywhere. One shadow seems more substantial than the rest. It also seems to be the source of the wailing. Quetzalli crawls that way, wanting only to silence the shadow, only to discover that the shadow is Quetzalcoatl. The Serpent God is on his knees, clutching his chest and keening.*

The sight confuses Quetzalli. What could possibly upset a god so?

Then she sees the man. He is sprawled on the ground in front of Quetzalcoatl. His naked body has been badly mauled.

"Pimotl!" she says, as recognition sets in, and then blurts out another name as an obvious conclusion presents itself. "The Jaguar did this."

"No," Quetzalcoatl says, an aching warble. "It was me."

Quetzalli wrests her gaze away from her brother's bleeding body to gape at the god. Only then does she realize his aspect has changed. He has feminine features now; a woman's fullness. Only his pink-feathered head-dress is the same.

"I desired him," Quetzalcoatl says, "so I tried to seduce him. When he resisted, thinking we would be male on male I—forced him. His resistance excited me. I lost control and—I hurt him."

"Is he dead?" Quetzalli says, sneaking a peek at Pimotl. In the near-dark, his bloody wounds look black. She cannot tell if he is breathing or not.

"No," the god says, "but he will be long in the healing. And he will never be beautiful again. I will bear the shame of that into the next age."

The admission shocks Quetzalli. How can a god possibly suffer shame when everything a god does is perfect? "My brother is yours to do as you please with him—as are we all. If he had remembered that and submitted when you first approached him, he would not be in this situation now."

"Perhaps," Quetzalcoatl says, crouching low to caress Pimotl's hair. "Perhaps not. I was not myself. I did not just lose control; I gleefully flung it aside."

"It was the pulque," Quetzalli says, a spark of insight inspired by her pounding head. "It made us all act strangely."

"Yes," the god says woefully. "I see that now. Tezcatlipoca should have warned me of its effects when he gave it as a gift. With his silence, he betrayed me."

"Where is he?" Quetzalli says, scanning the darkness for a pair of golden eyes.

"I do not know," Quetzalcoatl says. "Nor do I wish to know. My shame makes me weak. I will not be able to face him again for a time."

"How long?" Quetzalli asks, shivering in the wake of foreboding.

"I do not know," the god says again, and then stands up. From her vantage point on her knees, Quetzalli cannot help but notice how ample his breasts have become. And where has his manhood gone?

"I am female by nature," Quetzalcoatl says, sensing her thought. "You and Pimotl are the only two living humans who know this. Your brother will not remember, for I have blocked the details of our encounter from his memory. I can make you forget, too, if you want. But I would rather that you kept the secret of your own accord."

Quetzalli prostrated herself. "You know my heart," she says, happy to grovel in the dust. "I live to honor your will."

"Yes," the god says. "It has always been so with the women in your family. And now it shall always and ever be so." She grabs Quetzalli's hand and bites into her wrist, drawing blood. Quetzalli *shudders, once as Quetzalcoatl drinks from the wound and then again as she drools over it. The wound blisters and sizzles, then closes up. As Quetzalli reels from the pain and the stink of burnt flesh, Quetzalcoatl says, "We are bonded by blood and venom now. Whenever I Call, either you or one of your daughters-to-be will hear me and seek me out. Someone of your blood will always be my most trusted servant."*

Despite her headache and the pain in her wrist, Quetzalli knows a moment of pure joy. Then an uninvited thought intrudes like a floating stench. "What about Tezcatlipoca?" she says. "He must know your true nature, too."

"He does," Quetzalcoatl says. "But the Divine does not permit us to share such essential secrets with your kind. Thus, my brother seeks to unmask me obliquely."

The thought of gods living by rules boggles Quetzalli. Oddly enough, though, she is not that surprised to learn that some gods hold those rules more sacred than others. She has never trusted The Jaguar, even when he was purring.

"My brother will not yet know that his treachery succeeded," Quetzalcoatl muses aloud. "I must fly before he sees me. He can smell weakness."

"Where will you go?" Quetzalli asks, even though it is not her place to wonder such things.

"I do not know," the god says. "Someplace safe where I can contemplate my next course of action."

"What would you have of me?"

"You must stay here and nurse your brother back to health."

"And once he is well?" she says, a hopeful edge to her voice.

"You will run the temple in my absence," the god says. "You will be my high priest and continue to promote knowledge and learning in my name." When Quetzalli slumps, weighed down by massive responsibility and a crumb of undefined disappointment,

Quetzalcoatl cocks her pink-feathered head and says, "If you fail of this task, much blood will flow."

"I will not fail," Quetzalli vows.

Quetzalcoatl rewards her resolve with an approving warble. An instant later, she changes into a giant, pink-feathered serpent and launches herself into the pre-dawn sky.

Aurora woke with a start, as if she'd been ejected from her sleep. For one groggy moment afterward, she thought she could still hear the leathery flap and whoosh of serpent wings. There was a vague burning sensation in her wrist, too. She rubbed the spot, half-expecting to feel a scar even though she knew for a fact there was nothing there. Damn. She was going to have to lay off the Dragon Tea before bedtime. Because if these dreams got any more vivid, she was going to lose her grip on reality.

An exaggeration at best, Duncan's ghost drawled.

Right. As if being reassured by a ghost wasn't another skid mark on that slippery slope to lunacy.

Details, details.

She smiled, reassured in spite of herself, and said, "You sound just like your daughter."

Which reminded her of the text message that she'd received from Roz last night: C U soon! And Boy! Do I have a surprise 4 U! On one hand, Aurora was thrilled. Her baby girl was finally coming home! On the other forecasted surprises made her nervous. Most likely, Roz had picked up another souvenir for her, something big and gaudy and dragon-themed. But what if it was something else, something of such enormity that it took a cross-country train-ride to figure how to break it to a loving but sometimes critical mother?

She rejected the half-formed thought with a scowl. No. No way. Roz was on the pill. Aurora knew because she had picked the prescription up from the pharmacy on more than one occasion. But she also knew that no form of protection was fool-proof. And Aldo was an extra-strength fool. Maybe Roz had taken her time getting home so she could get used to the idea of—

Rather than finish the thought, she flung herself out of bed. She'd know one way or the other soon enough, so why torture herself with maybes in the meantime? Besides, she had a busy weekend ahead of her. Sili-Con started today. The Grand Ball was tomorrow. Charles was going to be her date. The odds of him having a good time at a masquerade ranged from slim to zero, but she had every intention of making it up to him. The thought made her giddy.

She headed downstairs for her morning coffee. She was humming a happy little tune to herself, but in the back of her mind, she kept hearing the leathery flap and whoosh of serpent wings.

CHAPTER 16

The Grand Ballroom bristled with people dressed in riotous costume: spacemen and Amazons, super-heroes and animals, quasi-Victorian courtesans, pirates, and a host of alien creatures that Charles vaguely recognized from late-night television but could not name. As he stood in line at the bar, the trio of ridge-browed men ahead of him harangued the overworked bartender in loud, guttural voices.

"What? No blood-wine?" one of them bellowed. "Are you humans so afraid of us that you will not even stock our preferred libation?"

The bartender deflected their grievance with a stony-faced shrug. "All I can do is pour what I have," she said. "If you have a beef with that, take it up with management."

"That we shall, human," the second boomed. "The entire Federation will hear of this insult!"

"But for now," the third one said in a near-normal tone, "give us three Cuervo-and-cranberries. In response his friends' *sotto voce* coaching, he jacked his voice up and thundered, "No ice!"

As soon as the trio had their drinks, they swaggered away from the bar as if they were the only ones in the vicinity. Charles reflexively side-stepped the peculiar group and sauntered up to the bar. When he offered the bartender a cursory, "How's it going," she snarled, "I told Mac not to work me tonight. I fucking hate Klingons."

"I see," Charles said, although he didn't, really. "I'll have a Stoli on ice. Make it a double."

But the drink didn't settle him the way he had hoped it

would. There were too many people at this event. There were too many doors to keep track of, and too many distractions. He would almost rather be back at home with Grishka Rasputin.

Almost.

Grishka was fairly easy-going for a drake, but he was still a drake: demanding, self-involved, eccentric. His favorite thing to do at the end of the day to guzzle vodka and talk about the Divine. He expected Charles to participate, too—in both the talk and the vodka. He also had a massive appetite, a fondness for Charles' scummy swimming pool, and an aversion to long walks. As a result, the amount of time that he actually spent wyrm-hunting was rather minimal. Fortunately, the wyrms were proving to be easy creatures to track, mainly because of the dead bodies they kept leaving behind. Just last night, there had been a report of a mauling in Monterey—the third such attack in the extended vicinity in less than two weeks.

"That's them!" Grishka had declared. "Once is chance, twice is coincidence. Three times is confirmation."

"Why are they attacking humans?" Charles asked.

"I do not know," Grishka said affably. "Normally, wyrms go out of their way to avoid human contact. But they spent a great deal of time in your company when they were younger. Maybe they are thinking of you."

"How—heartwarming," Charles said dryly, and then got down to business. "We're going to need more help capturing them, you know."

"Da," Grishka said, washing the word down with vodka, "I know. Tomorrow, I will send for Drogo Channing."

Charles groaned—to himself, or so he thought. But some little sound must have escaped him, for Grishka nodded and said, "I know. He is not pleasant company. But he desires control over things. The Great One has decided to use that desire to control him. Do you understand?"

"Of course," Charles said. "Keep your friends close and your enemies closer."

The drake laughed and cuffed Charles in the arm, a playful blow that was sure to leave a bruise. "You do understand! How delightful." He hoisted the vodka bottle and added, "Let us drink to Drogo Channing and the return of my wildlings."

"Cheers!" Charles said, but what he was really toasting was the day that he had his house and his life back. Cheers! Cheers! Cheers!

"There you are!"

Charles swiveled out of his thoughts to see a goateed man in a purple satin robe and a pointed cap striding across the dance floor with a gossamer-winged fairy in tow. These were Aurora's friends—con-kids, she had called them during introductions. Charles didn't know what that meant and didn't bother to ask for he had no intention of befriending any of these strange, strange people.

"We were afraid that we'd lost you," Mara said, with an impish titter that went well with her costume. "Aurora would have had our heads for that."

A woman after his own heart, he thought, and then scanned the harlequin crowd for a glimpse of Aurora's face. When he failed to spot her, he scowled and said, "Where is she?"

Max gestured toward the stage at the far end of the room with what Charles could only presume was a wand. As he did so, arcane, glow-in-the-dark symbols rippled into view on his satin sleeve. "The festivities are about to begin," he said, "so she had to go back-stage. She asked us to keep you company."

"How thoughtful of her," Charles said, but what he was thinking was, *crap*. As he went to douse his chagrin with Stoli, a woman dressed in a burgundy gown with drop sleeves and a split front skidded to a stop in front of Mara and twirled.

Afterward, she beamed, clearly waiting for a response. Mara was more than happy to oblige.

"It looks fabulous!" she exclaimed, hands clasped in front of her as if to provide her heart with a cage. "You're the spitting image of Lady DragonJoy!"

The woman twirled again, beaming with happiness. "Thank you! It was worth every penny! I love your costume, too. You look just like Francine the Woodland Fairy!"

"Thanks," Mara said, trying for a modest smile. "I had help, though. Max made the wings. Look, they move!" The gossamer constructs fluttered prettily—without any obvious string-pulling. Charles was almost impressed. "Aren't they amazing?"

"Very!" the woman squeaked, and then dropped into a curtsy that displayed an impressive décolleté. "Please forgive me, but I must take my leave ere my bladder bursts."

Mara tittered. "By all means, go!"

"There's a momentary lull at the bar," Max said then. "I'm going in. Can I get you something, Charles?"

"Stoli on the rocks," Charles replied, since the strange man was asking. Then, remembering that he was in the company of humans, he added, "Thank you."

Max turned to go only to step ever so slightly in front of his wife instead as a man with thinning hair and the beginnings of a paunch came striding toward them. He was dressed as Han Solo, one of the few movie characters Charles remembered from his youth. The astonishingly small Asian woman attached to his elbow was clad in a skimpy Princess Leia slave costume.

"Hey, Max. Hey, Mara," he said. "Good to see you again. Where's Roz?"

"Why?" Mara said, and Charles could have sworn that her wings buzzed like an angry bee's. "Wasn't dumping her in Scotland enough for you?"

"I didn't—" he began, only to reconsider when Mara sneered. "Yeah, OK, I guess I did dump her. It was nothing personal, though. We just didn't match up."

Mara sneered again, making Charles think that maybe she wasn't as dull as he had imagined her to be. "Now there's an understatement," she said. "Roz outclassed you on every front. You couldn't stand that."

"That wasn't it," he said. "That wasn't it at all. Roz eats, drinks, and plays like a man. That's not what a guy wants to come home to day after day after day."

Mara sneered for a third time. "Spoken like a man who calls his penis 'The Force'."

"What?" Charles asked, caught up in their squabble in spite of himself.

"'The Force'," Mara repeated, although not for Charles' benefit. "As in, 'May the Force be in you'."

Aldo's eyes bulged in their sockets. "She told you about that?"

"She told everybody," Mara said, gloating now. "Everybody knows."

"Shit," Aldo said, and then yowled as Princess Leia punched him in the thigh.

"You jerk!" she said. "You said you made that up for me!"

"You're kidding, right?" Charles said, staring at the lot of them as they had all sprouted extra heads. Drakes might be eccentric, but at least they made sense!

Aldo reared back, nostrils flared, as if to put that much more distance between him and Charles. With theatrical hauteur, he asked, "Who the fuck are you?"

"Nobody you want to mess with, boy," Charles replied, in a low, dangerous tone.

That shut Aldo up, but Princess Leia appeared to be intrigued. She looked him up and down several times, then gestured at his Armani suit and Versace tie and said, "Who are you supposed to be?" When he responded with a scowl that she mistook for confusion, she added, "Who did you come as—Doctor Who?"

"Who?" Charles echoed.

"Yes!" she said. "Exactly."

"Actually," Mara said facetiously, "he's a Terminator. You know, as in, 'Hasta la vista, baby?'"

But if Leia got the message, it didn't register on her perfect china doll face. She broke into a toothy smile as she turned her attention to Mara and clapped her hands. "Oh," she cooed. "I know who you are! Francine the Woodland Fairy! Your costume is amazing!"

Mara's wings fluttered tentatively, reflecting her surprise in being complimented by the enemy. Before she could eke out a word of thanks, though, Aldo chimed in.

"Francine's supposed to be sexy," he said. "Not fat."

"Fat?" Mara echoed, in a tone that was both incredulous and stricken. "Did you just call me fat?"

"Ahl-doh!" Leia said, punching him in the thigh again. Max looked like he wanted to slug him, too. Before further fists could fly, though, the houselights dimmed and the piped-in music that had been floating over the crowd buzz sheared off into silence. A moment later, the amplified tap-tap of someone testing a microphone called the room's attention to the stage. A large, extravagantly bearded man stood at the podium. He had the bearing of a ringmaster.

"Ladies and gentlemen," he began, "welcome to Sili-Con Nineteen. I'm Ron Wright, your Grand Master I hope you're ready to get your con on and party!" Enthusiastic applause ensued. Ron soaked the up for a few moments, then gestured for silence and expressed his gratitude to all who had worked to make the convention a success. "As you know," he went on to say, "next year will be Sili-Con's twentieth anniversary. 2012 is also the Year of The Dragon. According to the Chinese zodiac, dragons are deliverers of good fortune and masters of authority. They are the only creature in the zodiac that is considered legendary. They are said to be both intensely powerful and wise."

You have no freakin' idea, Charles thought, and then contemplated getting another drink while the rest of the room was preoccupied.

"In light of this auspicious concurrence, the board of Sili-Con did something unprecedented: we invited this year's guest of honor to be next year's Grand Master!" The announcement was met by more clapping and a modicum of whistling. Ron nodded approvingly and said, "That's right! Who better to lead us in the Year of The Dragon than the Dragon Queen herself?"

Just like that, Charles forgot about going to the bar.

"I don't know about you and your kids," Ron said, "but me and mine grew up with Ezzie and Francine. Their adventures taught us about right and wrong, and how to tell the difference between them. They offered us life lessons and positive messages, and promoted goodness and light."

A faint but persistent rustling snagged Charles's attention. It was the sound of amateurs trying to move stealthily. Without appearing to, he surveyed the room for possible threats. A fair number of people were leaving their tables for the dance floor, but for what reason, he could not tell.

"Our guest of honor's writing is both powerful and wise," Ron went on to say. "Her imagination rules the skies. My sincerest hope is that she never tires of taking us with her on her magical adventures. Ladies and gentlemen, please join me in welcoming Aurora Vanderbilt."

A third round of applause erupted. At the same time, the

dance-floor crowd hoisted dozens of pink-feathered stick puppets into the air. Mara laughed, delighted by the sight. Charles didn't understand what he was seeing and mumbled, "What the hell?"

"They're dragons," Mara said. "Effigies of Esmerelda!" When he continued to scowl, she added, "You do know that Aurora writes books about dragons, don't you?"

"No," Charles said, suffering a moment of out-of-body disconnect. Had Aurora ever mentioned anything about dragons to him? He didn't think so. A coincidence of that magnitude would have made a significant impression on him. "I had no idea."

Aurora appeared, stage-right, and strode briskly toward the podium. Her mouth was set in a professional smile—all lip, no teeth—and her posture was ramrod-straight as if she were on her way to address Congress instead of a mob of adoring fans. But when she got to the podium and saw that sea of dancing, pink-feathered dragons, everything about her lit up. Even the black dress that she was wearing seemed to acquire a lively shimmer. She stood back for a moment to take the sight and then brushed her short, mostly black hair away from her face and leaned into the microphone.

"Wow," she said. "What an incredible welcome. Thank you. Thank you so much. If you had told me thirty years ago that I'd be standing here, looking down at your smiling faces and a sea of Esmereldas, I would've told you that you were the fantasists, not me. I'm so thrilled with the honor that you've shown me that I'm going to share something with you all that I've never shared with anyone.

"Shortly after Duncan and I were married, a girlfriend and I went to San Francisco for the day. After lunch—and I'll admit, a few martinis—we stopped at a fortune teller's shop on a lark.

The fortune teller was a beefy Asian woman with green eyes and garlic breath. I wanted her to read my cards, but she grabbed my hand instead and traced a calloused finger over the lines she saw there. Afterward, she said, "You have an extraordinary future ahead of you, a life filled with adventure and learning and no small amount of peril. Dragons will whisper in your ear and their stories will change your life."

At the time, I thought it was pretty much the most bizarre thing anyone had ever said to me, and I didn't think any more of it. But one afternoon shortly after Duncan died—a cold, winter-pale day where I was missing him so badly and wondering how I was supposed to get through the rest of my life—a pink-feathered dragon popped into my head from with a tale to tell. I remembered that fortune teller's prediction then and thought, 'Why not give it a try?'

"The rest is history."

A smattering of applause broke out. She acknowledged it with a smile and a nod, and then continued. "The moral of my little story is: the next time someone tells you there's a dragon in your future, pay attention. Because you never know. Right?"

Another round of applause ensued, more emphatic this time. The sea of dragons bobbed and danced. She savored the spectacle for a moment and then leaned back into the microphone. "But enough about me already. Let's get this party started. Thank you, Sili-Con! I wish you all good things, always!"

The applause turned thunderous. She blew a handful of kisses at the crowd and then turned away from the podium. As she headed off the stage, the band came on to finish its prep-work. The lead singer looked more than a little devilish with his pointed black beard, slicked-back hair, and red leather pants.

"Oh, yay!" Mara said. "You're in for a treat tonight."

Kathleen H. Nelson

"Oh?" Charles said, still trying to process what he'd just heard. A dragon writer? Really? And how often did pink-feathered dragons just pop up out of nowhere? He was starting to wish that he had never come to this stupid ball.

"That's Simon Trinity," Mara gushed. "You wouldn't know it by looking at him," she went on, "but he's one of the most in-demand funeral singers in the Bay Area."

"What?" Charles said, suddenly worried that he was hearing everything wrong.

"A funeral singer," Marla said, happy to repeat herself. "You know—someone who sings at funerals, memorials, and the like. He and his brother pretty much have a lock on the industry around here."

"I had no idea that such an industry existed," Charles said, and then forgot all about the silly conversation as Aurora came weaving through the crowd and toward them. As soon as she made eye contact with Charles, she smiled, and the knot in his intestines melted into a vague concern in the darkest corner of his back-brain.

"There you are!" she exclaimed, then wrapped an arm around his waist as if there was no one else around. "I was looking for you at the table! Could you tell?"

"You looked perfectly natural to me," he assured her.

"What did you think of my speech?" she asked. "Was I boring?"

"Not at all," he said, and wondered if he sounded as moronic as he felt.

"You were wonderful, Aurora!" Mara interjected, unable to contain her enthusiasm—or her distance—any longer. "Do you think that fortune teller still lives in San Francisco?"

"I have no clue," Aurora said. "Why do you ask?"

"I'd love to visit her," Mara said. "I want to know if I'm going to be a world-famous novelist someday, too."

Aurora crinkled her nose and said, "A better way of finding that out would be to actually write something."

Mara laughed at that. Max joined in and then started to ask if Aurora wanted a drink. But before he could finish the question, Slave Princess Leia pushed her way into their circle. "Aurora Vanderbilt!" she exclaimed. "You are one of my favorite writers! Can I have picture with you?"

If Aurora was taken aback by the request, she didn't let on. Indeed, she looked perfectly happy to accommodate the nearly nude sprite until she dragged her boyfriend into the mix. As soon as Aurora saw him, her eyes narrowed and her upper lip pulled back. Charles could almost see her ears go flat as well. Her obvious displeasure provoked a moment of sheepishness from the man. Nevertheless, he stood his ground.

"Hello, Aurora," he said. "Good to see you again. How come Roz isn't here?"

"I don't know, Aldo," Aurora said. "Maybe she didn't feel like running into you." She peered at him then, a critical once-over, and then added, "When did you start losing your hair?"

His hand flew immediately to his receding hairline—an involuntary display of self-consciousness which he turned into a rakish, Han-Solo-like head-stroke. "Nice try," he said, with a middling smirk that made Charles want to smack him. "You just can't stand seeing me happy, can you?"

"Actually," Aurora said, "I just can't seeing you, period, so why don't you go and—"

Before she could fill in that blank, the house lights dimmed again and the band struck an opening chord. The lead singer grabbed the microphone from its stand and leered at the crowd. "Welcome to the Sili-Con Grand Ball, my friends," he said, in a silky voice. "I'm Lord MorFang The Screamer, and we're The Devil's Due. For the next three hours, we're going to do our best to keep you on your feet. If anyone has a request, bring it up—if you're willing to give the devil his due." He let out an appropriately creepy laugh and then half-turned to the band. "Ready? One, two, three," he said, and then let out a scream that morphed into a stream of high-volume lyrics.

Aurora leaned into Charles and said, "Oh, dear. I hope he doesn't keep that up all night. He's a lovely man with a lovely voice, but it's so much easier to listen to him when he isn't screaming."

Charles cupped her elbow, thinking to steer her toward a quieter corner of the ballroom so he could ask her why she'd never told him that she wrote about dragons without having to shout. But even as he started to ease her away, a group of squealing fairies came stampeding toward her, all sporting pink-feathered dragon puppets and cell phones. "Aurora! Aurora! Can we have a picture with you?"

"Me too!" Aldo's girlfriend exclaimed.

She shot Charles a helpless look and then gave herself over to her fans, pulling Mara into the mix as well. "Max," she said. "would you do the honors?"

As Lord MorFang wailed in the background, Max dutifully collected cell phones. That left Charles standing next to the Han Solo impersonator, who was watching his girlfriend cavort with the fairies with a sour look on his face. When, by chance, he looked Charles' way, his scowl deepened.

"Who are you again?" he asked.

"No one to you," Charles said, despising the man simply because Aurora did.

"You don't look like the kind of freaks that Aurora and Roz usually hang out with," he said, seemingly indifferent to Charles's scorn. "In fact, you look pretty damn normal."

"Who's Roz?" Charles said, slipping into information-collecting mode out of habit.

"My ex," Aldo said, and then hiccupped. Only then did Charles realize that the man was half in the bag. "We broke up while we were on vacation in Scotland—just couldn't take being with her any more, you know? Bitch has been messing with my head ever since."

Charles shrugged, pure indifference. What was taking Mr. Wizard so long with the pictures?

"Ever seen a monster?" Aldo asked then. When Charles didn't respond, he took another swallow from his cup and then added, "I have."

"Really," Charles said, a half-note shy of a sneer. "What did it look like?"

"I don't know exactly," Aldo said. "I was a little—intoxicated at the time."

"You don't say."

"That doesn't mean I didn't see it," Aldo said, waxing defensive. "Because I did. Roz saw it, too. One of these days, she's going to admit it."

The autograph session ended with a tinkling of thanks and well-wishes. Aurora turned back toward Charles then, but as soon as she laid eyes on Aldo, her happy smile collapsed. "Why are you still here?" she asked, and then shooed him away like a pesky blow-fly. "Piss off. You're spoiling my afterglow."

He harrumphed and then held out his elbow for his girlfriend, who seemed disinclined to take it. As he headed for the bar, he said, "Tell Roz I'm looking for her."

"Not a chance," she said, and then turned her back to him. That put her face to face with Charles, an arrangement that brought the smile back to her face. "I know," she said, before he could say anything, "this isn't your cup of tea. Are you sorry you came?"

An instant earlier, perhaps, his answer might have been different. But as he looked down into her soft brown eyes, so tender and full of hope, all he could say was, "No way! I'm getting an education!" An instant earlier, his head had been full of questions about dragons and fortune tellers and did she believe in such things or was this all just one crazy coincidence, but now, all he wanted to do was live in and for the moment. Tomorrow would find its own way. He folded her into an embrace and kissed her right there in front of everyone while Lord MorFang yowled about love in the background. Afterward, he nuzzled her ear and said, "Care to dance?"

"To this?" she asked, arching a dubious eyebrow at him. "Not a chance! Let's get a drink and go somewhere a little quieter."

"Like where?" he asked.

"Well," she said, coyly glancing toward the exit, "there's always my suite." As wonder and then comprehension swarmed across his face, she added, "I did mention that I rented a room here for the weekend, didn't I?"

She hadn't. But he sure as hell wasn't complaining and not just because the alternative was going home to a smelly, vodka-swilling drake who didn't always know when to shut up.

"Lead the way," he said, and then gladly forgot all about dragons for the rest of the night.

CHAPTER 17

The temple's central courtyard is bristling with people who have come from all corners of the city-state for the New Fire Festival. The holy fires that had burned on the temple's crown for the last fifty-two years have been doused. Sacred stars are edging toward their zenith in the night sky. When they reach their peak, The Jaguar's high priest will try to light a new fire. If he fails of the attempt, the sun will not rise and the fey Sky Spirits will descend upon the world and devour everything. The crowd is manic with suspense. No one wants to believe the world might end. But there have been signs, so many bad omens: the twenty-year drought, a dramatic rise in stillbirths, Quetzalcoatl's ongoing absence.

Quetzalli is one of the worried faces in the crowd. She is old now, a shriveled shadow of her youthful self. And while she is still Quetzalcoatl's high priestess, the status that the position once conveyed has withered, too. Not for the first time or even the thousandth, she relives the brain-throbbing, post-pulque morning that dawned after The Serpent God's shame-wracked departure.

"Quetzalcoatl had a vision last night," she announced to an assembly of bleary-eyed villagers. "He saw himself on the Great Water, sailing into the setting sun on a boat of pink serpents. He believes the vision was a message from the Divine and has embarked on a quest of discovery. He has vowed not to return until he has grasped the vision's meaning."

This was the first time that she had ever lied in her god's name. Doing it felt wrong, and she feared that the wrongness would show on her face. No one questioned her, though, not even Tezcatlipoca. Indeed, The Jaguar embraced the lie with uncharacteristic gusto.

"All hail my far-seeing brother," he said, from his perch at the top of Quetzalcoatl's temple. "I will have my priests sacrifice a hundred snakes in his honor." Then he licked his glistening white canines and added, "I shall watch over you until he returns."

The promise raised every hair on Quetzalli's spine, a foreboding both vague and potent. But her belief in Quetzalcoatl had been rock-solid back then. She believed that he would only be gone for a little while. She believed that he would return, bigger and brighter than ever. "Time means nothing to a god," she told his followers, when they began to fret about his absence. But eventually, The Jaguar's reign wore her down, too, and her faith grew fragile like a dragonfly's wings.

"Out of the way!" a voice booms, wrenching Quetzalli out of her regrets. "Make way for the Chosen."

The crowd shifts, creating a ragged fissure. Heartbeats later, a priest struts through the gap like a gamecock. His hair is matted with dried blood and detritus. His body is crusted with filth. Quetzalli's gut clenches at the sight of him and then grows queasy as the Chosen file into view. They are all well-fed young men— meaty, Pimotl would say, with a jaguar's carnivorous leer. Her brother has grown cruel over the many years since his mauling. And while he cannot remember how he came to be disfigured, he knows that Quetzalcoatl is somehow to blame and hates the god for it. His unflinching ill-will for the Serpent God has put him in good stead with Tezcatlipoca, whom he now serves.

The priest leads the Chosen up the sacred pyramid's many steps. Quetzalli follows them with her eyes. As the procession nears the top, Pimotl and his bloodthirsty god show themselves to the crowd. The Jaguar singles out one of the Chosen with a flick of his tail. Her brother lashes the man to the Sun's gore-stained altar and then takes up his sacrificial knife. Quetzalli flinches once as obsidian slams into bone and then again as Pimotl pulls a throbbing heart and heaving lungs from his victim's chest.

"For you, Great One," he says, offering the organs to the Jaguar, "so you may stand strong against the ending of the world."

The Jaguar nods, directing Pimotl to proceed. Her brother picks up a pair of wooden fire sticks and starts rubbing them together in the dead man's chest cavity. Everyone in the courtyard stares up at the altar, hoping and praying for a glimpse of a spark. Without a spark, there can be no dawn. Without a Fire, the Jaguar will not be able to keep the Sky Spirits from descending on the world and destroying it. It is dark out, so dark. Quetzalli fears that she will never see the sun again. She folds a hand over her throat as if to protect herself from a Sky Spirit's fangs. As she does so, someone grabs her other wrist and whispers, "Come with me."

Wonder leaps to life within her, brighter than any holy spark. For she knows that voice as well as she knows her own! Quetzalcoatl has returned! In her gladness, she starts to cry out. The Serpent God squeezes her wrist so hard, she lets out a gasp instead.

"Silence!" he whispers. "If my brother learns I am here, he will let the world die."

Quetzalli has never harbored any doubts about the Jaguar's brutal nature, but even so, it stuns her to know that he would kill the world rather than share it with a fellow god. Before she can say so, though, a wild cheer rises up from the crowd.

"A spark!" Quetzalli cries, singing her relief. "Pimotl must have made fire. A new day will dawn!"

She thought the news would please Quetzalcoatl, but it makes him more anxious instead. "We must be gone from here," he said, pulling her toward the courtyard's far end. "Quickly."

"Why?" she asks, forgetting in her confusion that it is not proper to question a god.

"Bloodshed is coming," he hisses, plowing through the crowd as he might a field of corn.

Now his eagerness to be gone makes sense to Quetzalli, for her *god has never shared The Jaguar's appetite for blood.* "Only ten were chosen for sacrifice," she said, wanting to offer him some small consolation. "The slaughter will be over quickly."

Quetzalcoatl hisses again. "I have spent these many years away learning how to use The Dreaming to divine my brother's thoughts. So you may believe me when I tell you that by dawn, half the city will be dead." When she stops in mid-stride, frozen by disbelief, Quetzalcoatl adds, "The Jaguar means the third age to be the last age for men."

As he says this, someone in the distance screams. It is a strange sound, familiar but not, a foreign sort of buzzing ring that repeats itself over and over and over. A need to respond washes over her. She reaches into the pouch at her waist and pulls out—

—a small, smooth, rectangular object.

She stared at the object for a moment, ignorant of its purpose. It buzzed again. Her thumb hit a symbol before the rest of her knew what she was doing.

The object spoke. "Mom?" A moment later, it spoke again. "Mother?"

"Yes," she said, and wondered how the device knew.

"It's me, Roz! Have I called at a bad time?"

The voice sounded familiar now. It belonged to Quetzal. She shook the object hoping to dislodge her daughter, but she would not come out. The effort exhausted her. "Tired," she said. Need to go back to—" *Obsidian knives glistening wetly in the night?* "Need to go."

"OK, I'll let you go. Just wanted to let you know that I'll be home tomorrow."

Home. They had no home anymore. They had abandoned it—*down the street, out of the city, into the darkened jungle?* "Run!" she said. "Don't let the priests catch you."

"Mom?"

Her thumb tapped the symbol of its own accord. The object

went dead. The next thing she knew, she was being swept back into a darkness that only seemed like sleep.

The jungle is terrifying at night, pitch-black and oppressive, silent save for the thrashing sounds of many people on the run. Quetzalcoatl has forbidden torches, so they must run blindly. Many stumble. Some fall. A few do not get back up.

"Help each other!" the god urges, from his place at the head of the flight. "But do not dally! We are not alone in the jungle tonight."

As if in response to the warning, a jaguar cries out. Although the sound is muffled by distance, it raises the hair on Quetzalli's nape just the same. She tries to wring another burst of speed from her legs and lungs, but she is old, too old for running. She slows to a walk instead and then shuffles to a stop against a mahogany tree. Quetzal is at her elbow in an instant.

"Here, Mother! Take my hand. Let me help you!"

Quetzalli waves her away. "Go," she says. "I will follow as soon as—I—catch my breath." When her daughter hesitates, Quetzalli gives her a gentle shove. "Go. Do as the god commands. I will rejoin you later."

Quetzal presses a palm to her mother's cheek, a gesture of love and farewell. An instant later, she disappears into the darkness. Quetzalli slumps to the ground and curls up in a shadow so no one else will see her and offer a hand. From there, she listens as the thrashing sounds of many people on the run recede into the darkness and then, in the span of a heartbeat, disappear.

Her breathing is steadier now, and her legs have stopped trembling. She knows that she should get up and rejoin the flight before it gets too far away from her, but she's very tired still and the ground here is well-padded and warm. The god of sleep tugs at her eyelids. Gradually, she yields to that gentle pressure. As she drowses, nearby bushes whisper a soft warning. She is not alarmed, for she knows that she is dreaming. The rustling draws closer, and then closer still. She can hear breathing now, too, the kind of throaty rasps that a jaguar makes when it is on the hunt. She realizes that Tezcatlipoca is stalking her. And still she is not afraid.

The jaguar's eyes emerge from the shadows first: cold, golden orbs that seem to deflect the darkness. Then his head appears, angled and sleek, with laid-back ears and a muzzle slicked with gore. He gazes at Quetzalli for a moment, savoring her helplessness. Then, fangs bared, he lunges. She cries out as he lands on her—the last sound she ever expects to make. But while his weight presses her into the ground, it does not crush her. And while his teeth dig into her throat, they draw no blood. She dares a peek at the god through her eyelashes. To her utter surprise, he has changed into a man! His face is a dreamy blur, but seems familiar somehow. His body stirs vague memories, too. He gnaws at her neck, a delicious sensation, and then starts to move on top of her. Suddenly, she is young again. Suddenly, she remembers desire. She arches her hips, ready to receive the god, only to be distracted as something small and fierce buzzes past her ear. What's this? A hummingbird? She knows immediately that the visit is no accident, for hummingbirds are warriors reborn, and sacred. This one buzzes her again, whispering in her ear as it passes. It urges her to fly away before this jaguar-man sets everything she knows on fire.

What?

Tezcatlipoca laughs as if he too has heard the warning. Then he swats the hummingbird out of the air and into the side of a tree. It makes a small crunching sound as it hits and then falls to the ground. The act scandalizes Quetzalli. Even gods should honor sacred things! She tries to crawl out from under the god so she can run away, but he will not permit it. He is bearing down on her again: touching, stroking, licking, pinching, compelling her to respond in spite of herself. Eventually, he sets everything on fire. She burns for what seems like forever without relief.

Aurora awoke hot and sweaty, ridiculously aroused. The first thing she did when her vision hazed into focus was check the other side of the bed for Charles. He wasn't there, of course. They had parted ways almost twenty-four hours ago in a deluxe hotel room in the city. He'd left before breakfast, apologizing for having to duck out and get back to work. Apologizing! After the night they'd had! The chemistry between them had verged on magical—her molecules resonating with his molecules to amplify intimacy. Even their first go-around, typically an awkward experience, had been shockingly good. She shivered at the memory and contemplated inviting him over for an encore. But even as the thought crossed her mind, she caught sight of the digital clock on her nightstand: 4:21AM. Hmmm. Probably not a good idea after all.

She rolled onto her side, thinking to grab another three or four hours of shut-eye. To her surprise, though, her body had other things in mind. It wanted to get up, have breakfast, and start the day! What the hell? She was never awake at this hour unless she was sick. And her head was never this clear before her first cup of coffee. Still, she wasn't about to look this gift horse in the mouth. She'd lost a lot of time to SiliCon and its sidebars; now was her chance to make that time up. She rolled out of bed, pulled on a pair of old jeans and a beat-up sweatshirt, and then padded downstairs. The house was quiet, with everything in its place—sure signs that Roz wasn't home.

The thought of her daughter reminded Aurora of—something. A phone call maybe?

I'll be home tomorrow.

She scowled, trying to wring other fragments of the call from her mind, but all she drew was a stubborn blank. She must've been dreaming of Roz, wishing her home.

And boy, do I have a surprise for you!

She turned on the radio and went to work on breakfast. As the coffee-maker did its thing, she popped half of a frozen bagel in the toaster and listened to the early morning news. None of it sounded good. The war in Afghanistan was dragging on. Syria was in turmoil. More women from Juarez had gone missing. She thought of Charles, who had said on more than one occasion that the world was going to end in a hail of fire and bullets. After listening to this litany of woes, she was tempted to agree with him.

How depressing!

Fortunately, an antidote suggested itself almost immediately. So as soon as the coffee was done, she poured herself a mug and then carried her breakfast out to the back patio so she could catch the sunrise. There were streaks of deep violet in the still-dark sky, and a fringe of lavender along the mountainous horizon. A single mockingbird was singing from its perch on the rooftop. Out on the road, she could hear the occasional whoosh of traffic: ambitious techie types looking to get a jump on the day. The air smelled of roses and hot black coffee, a surprisingly pleasant combination.

As she savored the pre-dawn peace, a shadow passed over the patio. She dismissed the darkness as a cloud right up until the moment it fell out of the sky and landed in her pasture. The crash was weighty rather than loud; the impact tremor generated ripples in her coffee mug. The half-eaten bagel tumbled from her hand, forgotten.

"What the hell?"

There was a huge, unmoving mound in the middle of the pasture now. A meteor perhaps? The possibility seemed unlikely. Whatever it was hadn't been going fast enough, and there had been no fireball. But what else might drop out of the sky and turn into a hill in her backyard? A jet engine? Had there been a plane flying overhead? She couldn't remember. Should she call the authorities?

"Come. Here."

She started and then looked around, looking for the person who'd just spoken. "Who's there?" she asked, in her most authoritative tone. "What do you want?"

"You."

Gooseflesh erupted down the length of her back, a chill inspired not only by the message but also by the realization that it hadn't been delivered out loud. Shit! What kind of craziness was this?

"You need to clear out," she said, as she glanced around for anything that might help her fend off an attack. "Leave now and I won't call the police."

By the faint light of the horizon's broadening hem, Aurora saw the mound expand and then contract again. At the same time, a sigh both profoundly weary and irked sounded in her head.

"Here—for you. Nowhere else—to go."

Having an extraterrestrial presence in her head was alarming enough. Having one that felt strangely, intimately familiar was even more boggling. Was this how a mental breakdown started?

"Who are you?" she asked, stalling for time to think. "What do you want?"

The presence flexed, becoming a psychic pressure that began to pull her forward. She dug in her heels only to find herself taking another step an instant later. How was this possible? Why was it happening to her? Her midbrain began to pump out the precursors to panic. Instinct urged her to turn and run. Yet she continued to lurch onward: across the patio, through the rose garden, and into the pasture.

"Stop this!" she shouted. "Stop right now!"

She hit the brakes again. This time, she stayed put. As she struggled to make some kind of sense out of this massive WTF moment, something began to cut a narrow swath through the waist-high pasture grass that stood between her and the mound. She watched, mesmerized, as the trough drew closer and closer. The only sounds in the world were those of grass being flattened and her own ragged breathing.

"Since you will not come—to me, I—come—to you."

Out of the grass rose a head. It was long and flat, with bony ridges over the eye-sockets that ran down the sides of its long, scaly neck. The eyes beneath those ridges were hooded. Its scaly muzzle was drawn back to show off a set of yellowed, dagger-like teeth.

"Good God," Aurora muttered.

"Have you learned—nothing? I am not—a god!"

The head reared skyward, revealing a long, muscular neck that appeared to be hooded like a cobra's. In the pre-dawn murk, the creature's reptilian profile looked stunningly familiar.

The observation sparked an oh-shit realization. It couldn't be. It just couldn't. And yet what other explanation was there?

There was a dragon in her pasture.

The dragon rumbled. The sound felt as if it could liquefy bone at a louder volume. Aurora shuddered at the sensation and then shuddered again as the dragon's massive head drew nose to muzzle with her. It smelled of carrion and vague decay. The green eyes that were now fixed on her seemed both agitated and bone-deep tired.

"Came a long—way. Must—feed."

The hair on Aurora's nape bristled to attention. Was the dragon threatening to eat her? She tried to take a step backward but found that she could not move. The chill that had raised the hair on her neck spread to other parts of her body.

"Now wait just a moment here," she said, still trying in vain to throw herself into reverse. "I am not food."

"You are not very—bright—either."

The day's first pale-pink rays broke over the horizon, colorizing her astonishment. Had the dragon just dissed her? Talk about adding insult to injury! And contrary to what the dragon might think, Aurora wasn't going down without a fight. She balled her hand into a fist, thinking to surprise the beast with a solid shot to the muzzle. With any luck, that would snap whatever hold it had on her long enough for her to break free of its spell. But even as she mustered up the nerve to slug something that was almost as big as her living room, the land beneath her feet shuddered.

Earthquake! she thought, but that wasn't right. The ground was still now. And—Roz was running toward her with open arms. The sight confused Aurora. How had she gotten here? And didn't she see that there was a dragon getting ready to eat her?

"Get back!" she said, trying to ward her daughter off with an outstretched arm. "Save—" Yourself, she meant to say, but before she could get the word out, Roz gave the dragon a friendly scratch between the eyes in passing and then swept Aurora into a crushing, confounding embrace.

"Oh my God, it's so good to see you!" she crooned, as she rocked Aurora back and forth like a rag doll. "I've missed you so much. And—how cool is this! You found your dragon, too!"

Your dragon? Too? What the fuck?

"Roz?" she asked, touching her daughter's cheek and then her shoulders and hips to make sure she was really and truly real. And she really and truly was, as far as she could tell. Questions flooded into her mouth, a roiling tangle of things she wanted to know. Absurdly, the first articles of interest that gushed out were, "Are you pregnant? Does Aldo know?"

Roz gaped at her for a moment, and then laughed as if Aurora had said something funny. "Seriously, Mom?" she asked. "A pasture full of dragons and all you can think to ask me is am I with child?"

Yes, but—wait. A pasture full?

She looked out of the corner of one eye and then the other, and then gasped as she spotted the second dragon. It was smaller and leaner than the first, and while it seemed to be mostly neck and tail, it was still a daunting sight. At the moment, it was sniffing the first dragon urgently and making soft warbling sounds.

"Brigit says your dragon is the Great One, eldest of all drakena," Roz said.

"Who's Brigit?" Aurora asked.

Roz nodded in the second dragon's direction. As she did so, the dragon cocked its head at Aurora. Its eyes glistened like polished amethysts. Its nostrils glowed like banked coals. Then it turned its attention back to the big dragon and rumbled—a low, urgent sound.

"What did it say?" Aurora asked, even though she wasn't sure she wanted to know.

"'She', not 'it', Mother," Roz clucked. "She said the Great One needs shelter and food."

"There's plenty of both in these mountains," Aurora said, glancing at the lavender-painted slopes around them. "She should go before—"

"Mo-om," Roz said, stretching the title into a reproach, "look at her. She's exhausted." Aurora didn't want to, but she looked anyway. And damned if 'her' dragon didn't look played out. Her breathing was hard and shallow. The rims of her nostrils were white. But what she didn't see was how any of this was her problem. Meanwhile, Roz said, "We can put her up in the horse barn. It's big enough. And no one uses it anymore."

Resentment flared in Aurora like a sunspot. What the hell!

Home for all of five minutes now and the kid was already trying to call the shots? Part of her recognized this as adrenaline-induced irritability. The rest of her was too freaked out to care.

"What the hell is going on here, Roz?" she asked. "Last night, dragons were a figment of my imagination. This morning, I have two of them in my pasture and you're somehow involved. Enlighten me. Please."

"I'm sorry, Mom," Roz said. "I had no idea that this is all brand-new to you. But please believe me when I say that now is neither the time nor the place for explanations. The Great One flew over fifty miles to get here. Imagine the toll that took on her at her age, and at that size. She needs our help—and she needs it before someone sees her. Please?"

Questions continued to bubble up Aurora's gullet and into her mouth. But because Roz had beseeched her, she cordoned off her teeming confusion for the time being.

"Fine," she said. "The barn it is. Can the Great One walk or should I get the tractor out?"

Brigit rumbled, a menacing sound. Aurora knew that the threat was meant for her even before Roz translated it. "She says to mind your manners. The Great One deserves respect."

"Of course she does," Aurora said, and then doubled down on her scowl as the pasture began to fill up with fog. "What now?"

"Just a little cover for the dragons," Roz said. "Brigit thought it best, given that traffic's starting to pick up."

"Seriously? These things can do that?"

When Roz made a what-does-it-look-like-to-you face, Aurora squeezed the bridge of her nose to pinch off the beginnings of a headache. "You understand how weird this is for me, don't you?" she asked. "I feel like I rolled out of bed and into the deep end of psychosis."

Roz folded her into an embrace and then rocked her as Aurora had rocked her as a child. "You're not crazy, Mom," she said. "This is really happening. You'll feel better once you know the whole story."

"I'm listening," Aurora said, savoring the comfort of her daughter's hug.

"I know," Roz replied. "But the story isn't mine to tell. You should hear it from the Great One."

Aurora glanced at the spot where the Great One had been languishing only to find it filled with fog rather than dragon-flesh. Her gaze strayed toward the barn. Through the soupy mist, she could see that the double-wide door was open and that there was some kind of commotion going on within. She had to admit: she was impressed. She hadn't expected something that massive to move so quickly—or so stealthily.

"I'll give her a few minutes to settle in," Aurora said, "and then bring her something to eat. I think I have a couple of steaks in the freezer."

Roz snorted. "A couple of steaks wouldn't even qualify as an appetizer to a dragon of the Great One's size. But don't worry; Brigit is off to hunt a proper meal for her. You can expect it to remain foggy around here until she returns."

"Oh," Aurora said vacuously, and then wondered if the fog had also infiltrated her head. "Thanks for the warning. Is there anything else I should know?"

"Scads, I should think," Roz replied. "So why don't you go and sit with The Great One while I go and grab a shower? Brigit and I have been on the road for over a week, and my stash of clean clothes ran out five days ago."

"Go," Aurora said, realizing belatedly that her daughter did smell rather cheesy. "I'll wait for you on the patio."

"Muh-ther," Roz said, gently nudging Aurora toward the

barn, "go and talk to that dragon. You're connected to her by tradition and blood. Get to know her."

"I don't want to get to know her," Aurora said, petulant as a scolded child. "She's not supposed to exist."

"Another time, another place, OK, Mom?" Roz asked, "I really need a shower."

"Yes, yes, go on," Aurora said, waving irritably. "I'll sort this out for myself."

"Awesome," Roz said, and then started toward the house. Over her shoulder, she said, "All you have to do is accept it. Everything gets easier after that."

Easy for you to say, Aurora thought, as a wave of dragon-born fog billowed over her.

The Great One was curled up in the indoor riding ring that Roz had insisted on having so she could exercise the horses even when it was raining. It had been at least a decade since the ring had last seen a horse's hooves, and in the years since then, a fair amount of junk had taken up residence there. Most of it was memorabilia: boxes stuffed with photos, newspaper clippings, and expired souvenirs. But there were other things, too—old furniture, tractor parts, a hideously ornate water fountain that Roz had absolutely adored right up until the moment the delivery van drove off. It would have taken Aurora hours to carve a dragon-sized space out of so much detritus. The Great One had simply swept the worst of it out of her way with her tail and laid down on the rest. Oh, well, Aurora thought, as she surveyed the destruction. At least the beast hadn't elected to go with slash-and-burn.

"Look—at me."

Despite her deep-seated desire not to, Aurora turned her scrutiny to The Great One. The day's first light was spilling into the ring through the skylight now, and pooling on the dragon's spiny back.

256

Her scales were a pasty shade of taupe. Her hood was collapsed and bedraggled. Were it not for that muzzle full of fearsome teeth—and the fact that she occupied most of the ring—there was really nothing to fear. So why were Aurora's knees so shaky?

"You. Know. Me."

Ha-ha. Good one, dragon. "I don't think so."

"Yes. You. Do."

The Great One's lifted her head up from its nest in her forearms. As she did so, her neck arched, her all-but-hidden wings rustled, and her hood expanded. But wait! Now that there was a measure of light to see by, Aurora realized that that wasn't a hood at all but rather a frill—of faded pink feathers. The dragon's scales were pink, too. Aurora's throat went dry. Perversely, her hands began to sweat.

"It can't be," she muttered. "It can't."

As much as she wanted to believe them, though, her denials rang false. How could she not believe when the evidence was parked right in front of her nose?

"Touch—me. Believe."

In spite of herself, she strode into the ring and then stretched forth an arm. In response, the dragon extended her neck and then nuzzled Aurora's palm. A sensation of profound age and exhaustion seeped into her awareness like sulfur-tainted fog. All at once, her bones ached. Her heartbeat was flaccid. She felt dense and hollowed-out at the same time. Yet as tired as she was, the fatigue did not own her outright. There was still purpose burning within her; a banked fire to be sure but fire nonetheless.

"Look at me."

Aurora balked at the command. Everyone knew that making eye-contact with a dragon was a perilous undertaking. A dragon's unblinking stare could beguile fools, seduce the unsuspecting, freeze all but the strongest hearts.

A wave of impatience pulsed through her: a silent command. She pushed past her fear all at once and dared to meet the Great One's gaze. Her jade eyes were flecked with gold and rheum. It was obvious that she was struggling to keep her scaly lids at half-mast. Upon seeing this, Aurora understood that all of her fears had been utter foolishness, nonsense that she herself had invented to entertain the masses. The fact was, she didn't know a solitary thing about dragons.

Except that they existed.

"OK," she said, "so you're not an extra-jalapeno-induced nightmare. Now what?"

The Great One heaved a brimstone-tinged sigh. *"Acknowledge. Me. Acknowledge the bond we have—shared—for so many years."*

And that, Aurora realized, was the kicker—the deep, dark subconscious reason she didn't want to believe that any of this was real. She'd made her name and her fortune writing about a pink-frilled dragon. But all this time, she'd just been transcribing The Great One's transmissions. That made her a fraud. That wasn't an easy thing to admit, internally or otherwise. But what else could she do when she was nose-to-nose with the living, breathing inspiration for Esmerelda?

"It's true," she said. "I've called you my Muse for many years. I simply didn't realize that there was more to you than a voice in my head."

"My fault. I have grown—weak—with age. It is hard for me to escape the Dreaming." She snuffled the crook of Aurora's neck then, and then the top of her head. *"Despite your fear, you smell stout-hearted and true. What are you called?"*

"Aurora," she replied, trying to repress her fear now that she knew it had a smell. "Aurora Vanderbilt."

"I am Quetzalcoatl."

"Yes," Aurora said, "The Winged Serpent. I remember."

The dragon constricted, returning to her original, cat-like resting pose. Her eyes, however, were livelier now, and all for Aurora. *"This is not the first time you have seen me."*

Aurora thought otherwise. But just as she opened her mouth to refute the assertion, an image of a rust-stained outcropping popped into her head. "The Pinnacles!" she blurted. "Oh my God! That was you hiding in that canyon?"

A set of psychic waves broke over her, affirmation followed by deep loss. *"I lived in those mountains for centuries. I Called for you many, many times, but you never responded. And then when you finally did come looking, something else found me first."*

An image formed in her mind: two broad-winged shadows circling high in the sky. They looked like condors to Aurora, but before she could give voice to the thought, the dragon said, *"Not condors. Juvenile dragons. The black one attacked a human. The red one brought the body to me."*

"How did they know you were there?" Aurora asked, succumbing to the lure of a story.

"I believe the Dreaming led the red one to me, though I have never encountered a wyrm with that degree of sensitivity."

"Why would it bring you a corpse?"

The next thought was chillingly matter-of-fact. *"Because it sensed my hunger."*

Even though she knew that it wouldn't do her any good if push came to shove, Aurora took several giant steps backward. Sometimes, you just had to make a statement.

"So," she said stiffly, "you eat people."

Quetzalcoatl condemned her for an idiot with a snort. *"I have never preyed on humans—you should know that. But the man was dead already and I was very hungry, so I devoured him down to the last tooth and nail. Nothing survives a dragon's digestive tract, so by eating him, I also destroyed all evidence of how he died."*

"Very thorough of you," Aurora said, but what she was thinking was: poor Brother Baine. Instead of swanning around in heaven, he was going to spend his afterlife as a pile of calcified dragon shit. Part of her wanted to dwell on the preacher's grisly fate and its karmic implications, but the writer in her wanted to get back to the story.

"OK," she said. "So you had yourself a snack and then hit the road. Why is that? My daughter says you're too big and too old to be flying."

"Your daughter is correct," Quetzalcoatl said, and once again perfused Aurora's senses with the weight of bygone millennia and exhaustion. *"As we age and grow, drakena become more of the earth than the element we were born to. But I had no choice but to take to the sky, for those wyrms drew attention to my territory. If I hadn't abandoned my den, I would've been discovered and killed."*

Aurora responded with a benign jeer. "You're thirty feet long if you're an inch. And you have to weigh at least a half-ton. Who on earth could possibly be a threat to you?"

"My brother."

An image of a malicious-looking black dragon sprung to Aurora's mind only to vaporize as the barn's double-door shuddered open. A moment later, the fog-colored dragon called Brigit came scrabbling in with something clutched in her jaws—a coarse, black tail of some kind. Then Aurora saw the rest of the animal and thought, oh shit.

"You should leave now," The Great One said, steeping the thought in hunger. *"This will not be pretty."*

Aurora didn't need to be told twice and beat a hasty retreat. As she slid the barn door shut behind her, she caught the opening sounds of two dragons tearing into a zebra carcass. It was, she thought, a sound that would stay with her for the rest of her life.

CHAPTER 18

Roz stepped out of the bathroom in a cloud of steam, aglow with the sense of being clean for the first time in what felt like forever. As she toweled off, she off-gassed the last residues of adrenaline from yesterday's goings-on. The excitement had started in Tracy, when their train hit a car. Amazingly enough, no one had been hurt, but the engine needed to be towed to the station and inspected. Had they been willing to wait, they could've overnighted in town and caught the first train out in the morning. But she had had her fill of trains and confinement and other people in close proximity, and Brigit had already threatened to eat the next crying baby. So after a brief discussion (and a ruinous visit to a nearby all-you-can-eat Chinese buffet), they headed west on foot. Then, when the sun finally went down and the world went to sleep, Brigit shifted back into dragon form and they went bounding over the Diablo Mountains. What an exhilarating ride that had been! The air smelled of hay and heat. A dry wind stroked her grimy face. Their moonlit hopscotch from one slope to the next spooked deer and cattle and even a puma on the prowl, but Brigit showed no interest in anything until they came to the Altamont windfarm. Over a thousand windmills populated that barren pass. They stood tall and still, skeletal constructs on night watch. Their sheer numbers were imposing.

"In the daytime when it's windy," she said to Brigit, "it looks like the whole mountain is waving at you."

"Ah'd like tae see that," Brigit replied, and the thought was infused with wonder.

Roz smiled at the memory. Traveling with a dragon could be trying, especially when said dragon didn't travel well and the trip was as long and circuitous as theirs had been. But moments like that, ones that took them both by surprise for different reasons, were a perfect antidote for all the aggravation.

The damp towel went in the hamper. Moments later, clean clothes topped the shower in the contest for best thing ever. Fresh underwear! Snug jeans! A tee-shirt that didn't have food or dragon drool drizzled on the front! She stuffed the beyond-grungy jeans and everything else that she'd been wearing for the past five days into the hazmat container that used to be her backpack and zipped it up tight, meaning to incinerate it at the next convenient moment. Then, bare-footed and hair still damp, she went in search of her mother.

She knew she'd been abrupt with Aurora with regard to the dragons. But what else could she have done? Coddling her wouldn't have helped. Joining her in quasi-denial wasn't exactly an option, either. The only way her mother was going to come to grips with dragons as a fact of life was to meet that reality head-on. She had no doubt that Aurora could do it. Her mom was without a doubt the bravest, most open-minded woman that Roz knew.

Or so she thought right up until she found Aurora sitting on the patio—exactly where she had left her.

"What's up, Mom?" she asked. "You're supposed to be in the barn, getting acquainted."

Aurora glanced at Roz—a haunted, slightly traumatized tone. "She's eating."

Roz winced and then sucked in a breath through clenched teeth. "Ouch. Not the easiest thing to see bright and early in the morning—or any other time of day, for that fact. The first time I saw Brigit feed in dragon form, I almost hurled. Of course, being a little hung-over at the time didn't help."

"She's eating one of Charles' zebras," Aurora said, in the same ravaged tone. "What am I supposed to tell him?"

"Beats me," Roz said, flummoxed by the conversation's oddball turn, and then blurted out a more reasonable afterthought. "Who's Charles?"

Aurora stiffened ever so slightly, and a flush crept across the shoals of her cheeks. "Oh," she said, traumatized in a different way now. "He bought the Stevenson place. He means to turn the property into a game preserve. He came over to introduce himself while you were gone."

Roz knew by the way Aurora was avoiding eye contact that there was more to the story, and intuition was quick to fill in the blanks. "Oh my God," she blurted, an instant after insight hit. "You're seeing him, aren't you!" When Aurora stiffened, Roz crowed and gave her an atta-girl clap on the back. "Check you out! I go away for a few months and you wind up with a dragon AND a boyfriend. Maybe I should go away more often."

"Maybe you should just put a sock in it," Aurora replied, with a gruffness that could not conceal her discomfort.

Roz laughed again and then tensed as if stung. A moment later, she stood up and said, "C'mon, they're done eating. The Great One wants to finish the conversation she was having with you before the Dreaming takes her. If you don't mind me asking," she went on, as they started toward the barn, "what was that conversation about?"

Aurora shrugged and said, "She was telling me about her brother."

The barn reeked of fresh blood. Aurora balked at that, but Roz took her by the hand and led her into the ring. There was a large dark spot in the dirt there and a few stray specks of gore amidst the rubble, but the only blatant evidence that dragons had just devoured a zebra on the premises were the dragons themselves. Brigit was sprawled alongside the wall across from the double-door, and there was no mistaking the bulge in her midsection for anything other than good eating. Quetzalcoatl's formerly glazed eyes glistened now and she had a rosy glow about her, but her belly still looked flaccid.

Roz shot a thought fringed with faux-indignation at Brigit. *"Jeez, dragon. It looks like you gobbled down the whole damn thing. This after you laid waste to that Chinese smörgåsbord."*

Brigit snorted. *"Chinese food is not dragon food. A was hungry ten minutes after we were told tae leave. But fear not, lassie. The Great One ate first and ate well. As big as she is, though, she'd have tae eat a whole herd of stripy things for her supper tae show."* She tipped her head in Aurora's direction and added, *"Has yer mum accepted her Calling yet?"*

"Hard to say," Roz replied, studying her mother even as her mother contemplated the Great One. *"She's not as freaked as she was a few hours ago, but—"*

Another Voice intruded on their link. *"I require your attention."*

Roz jumped. Both dragons swiveled their heads in her direction, projecting curiosity and surprise. At the same time, both of them asked, *"You heard that?"*

"Yeah," Roz said, meeting Quetzalcoatl's questioning gaze. "Loud and clear. Does that mean that Mom can hear Brigit?"

"What was that?" Aurora asked, popping out of her speculative daze. "I wasn't paying attention."

The dragons exchanged a wondering look. *"No daughter has ever had access to more than one drakena's thoughts,"* The Great One noted.

"It must be because I inherited a bond from both of my parents," Roz supposed aloud.

Quetzalcoatl pondered Roz for a long moment and then warbled like a songbird. *"It is no coincidence that a daughter of such unique ability should come of age and be Called at the end of the fifth age. She must be a gift from the Divine."*

"Wait," Aurora said, blinking repeatedly as if she were trying to clear an eyelash. "Are you talking about my daughter?" When Quetzalcoatl responded with a nod, Aurora looked at Roz as if she were trying to see something that wasn't there. "You think she's a gift from God?" When the Great One nodded again, she pressed her fingertips to her temples and said, "Seriously? Dragons believe in God?"

Brigit rumbled, a disgusted sound, and then lobbed a disbelieving thought at Roz. *"What is it with people?"*

Roz just shrugged.

Meanwhile, Quetzalcoatl took Aurora to task. *"Has the Dreaming taught you nothing? Of course dragons believe in the Divine. We have always believed in Her, even when She disowned us. Now, as the sixth age approaches, the signs suggest that She is ready to forgive us."*

"Forgive you for what?" Aurora asked, sounding as confused as she looked. "I don't understand."

Quetzalcoatl's frill bristled—an irritated display that relaxed as uncertainty set in. *"It may be that the Dreaming has not taken you back to that moment in time yet. If not, you will go there soon enough. All you need know for now is that drake cruelty against humans reached a fevered pitch at the end of the third age. Most drakena did not participate in the persecution, but neither did we do much to prevent it. The Divine punished drake and drakena alike for our callousness. For two long ages, She disavowed us. Now, as the end of the fifth age draws nigh, she has sent a pair of wonders my way: a woman who can hear two dragons, and a pair of late-stage wyrms."*

Brigit's neck arched into a disbelieving crook. *"Wyrms? How can tha be? The new age has nae dawned yet. And all the wyrms from the last age's hatch would have long since sexed."*

"Wait," Roz said. "Back up. What's a wyrm?"

"A juvenile dragon," Aurora replied, and then shrugged when Roz shot her an astonished look. "The Great One happened to mention it earlier. Apparently, dragons are born sexless and pretty much witless. They stay that way until they imprint as male or female."

Roz eyed her mother for a moment longer, inviting her to elaborate further. When Aurora declined the offer, Roz turned her attention back to the dragons and said, "So you have a couple of late bloomers. What's the big deal?"

"Dragons only breed at tha start of a new age," Brigit replied. *"Tha last age ended centuries ago. No wyrm takes that long tae 'bloom'."*

"Then maybe one of you drakena jumped the gun a little on the breeding thing," Roz said, speculating aloud. "It could happen, right? Your biological clocks can't possibly be one hundred percent in synch. I mean, take you for example. You were certainly hot enough to trot at the train station."

Brigit hissed. *"That's different! That was with a human, not a drake! And tha impetus was pleasure, not reproduction!"*

"Silence!"

Quetzalcoatl's command left both of them chastened. And the baleful look she gave them afterward filled Roz with a desperate need to apologize. As she struggled to contain the urge, the old dragon shifted irritably on her nest of debris and shamed them again.

"While you squawk like magpies over a shiny piece of glass, I cling to the waking world by a dew claw. There are things you need to know before the Dreaming reclaims me. Will you hear them or not?"

"Of course, Great One," Roz said.

"Good." The thought was brusque and fringed with grim, matriarchal satisfaction. *"Their origins are not the only curiosity that dogs these wyrms. They behave—strangely. They should be solitary at this stage, yet they travel together. They have no fear of men, either. Indeed, the black one seeks them out. When it finds one it likes, it tries to mate."*

Brigit projected a pulse of astonishment. *"Before it's fully sexed? Are ye sure? Perhaps it's just playing with the humans."*

Quetzalcoatl shook her massive head. *"I saw one of its victims firsthand. To my shame, I know what a man who has been mauled in the throes of dragon sex looks like."*

"Tha makes no sense!" Brigit declared. *"Why a human and not tha other wyrm?"*

"I do not know."

"What I can't figure out is how the wyrms knew where you were in the first place," Roz said, speaking out loud so her mother could follow along. "Did you Call them?"

"No," Quetzalcoatl replied. *"How could I when I did not know of their existence?"*

"Then how'd they find you?" Aurora pressed. "When I was out at the Pinnacles that time, I couldn't see you even when I was looking right at you."

"I do not know," the Great One said, and then yawned cavernously. *"The Dreaming may have led them to me. Or maybe it was the Divine. The important thing is—"* She yawned again. *"they found me. They know of my existence and I know of theirs."*

"If they're so important," Roz said, "then why didn't you make them stay with you?"

Quetzalcoatl rumbled, a visceral sound edged with irritation. *"The black wyrm flew away before I could make contact with it. The red one was torn between going and staying, but I drove it off."*

"Why?" Roz asked.

"Because it is a wyrm still, a creature of hunger and impulse, and its proximity would have attracted unwelcome attention."

"So," Roz said, "you sent the wyrm away so it wouldn't give away your location. But then you abandoned your territory anyway. Strategically speaking, that sounds like a lose-lose."

The Great One rumbled again, this time exclusively at Brigit. *"Is she always like this?"*

"She has her moments," Brigit replied, with a draconic smirk. *"But she also has a point. Why'd ye send the wyrm off if ye knew ye were going tae be leaving anyway?"*

The Great One shifted in her nest, projecting discomfort. *"Because,"* she replied, *"it is being hunted."*

The adventurer in Roz popped to full attention at that. "Do you know who the hunter is?"

"To be sure. He left a strong impression on the red one's psyche," Quetzalcoatl replied, and then broadcast an image of a compact black dragon with gold, predatory eyes. *"My brother, Tezcatlipoca, has an urgent interest in the wyrms. I do not know what this interest is as of yet, but I can tell you with certainty that he will stop at nothing to catch them. His agents will have tracked the wyrms to my old territory by now. They will have discovered my old lair as well. Had I still been there, they would have killed me."*

"But why?" Aurora asked, obviously troubled by the thought. "Why would your brother want you dead?"

"Because he hates me," the Great One said, and then hunkered into her nest. *"Because he would claim the next age for drakes and his so-called natural order."* She smacked her lips and then yawned. *"And because he knows that I will do what I can to thwart him."*

"Is that our mission then?" Roz wanted to know. "To stop ol' Tiger Eyes? How much time do we have before the clock on the old age strikes midnight?"

"There is no specific date for tha ending of an age," Brigit said. *"It will unfold on tha heels of a pivotal event somewhere in the next few years."*

"OK, so we've got some room to work," goal-oriented Roz said, and then tensed, stung by a thought. "Ha! Next year is *2012, Year of the Dragon.* That's gotta be a good sign. Right?"

Brigit rolled her narrow shoulders. *"Feck if A know."*

Roz laughed again and then gave the water dragon an affectionate thump. "That's what I love about you—you're always so positive." She shifted back toward Quetzalcoatl and added, "So what's the plan?"

The Great One's eyes were closed now, and her breathing had turned sonorous.

"Find—the wyrms. Keep them—away from—my brother. If they will not cooperate— Kill. Them."

"What?" Roz blurted, stunned by the drakena's ruthlessness. "Isn't that a bit—" Harsh, she meant to say. But the Great One cut her off with a doughy snore. "Go figure," she said, and then glanced across the ring to see how her mom was dealing with Quetzalcoatl's bloodthirstiness. To her immense surprise, Aurora was out cold, too. "What the hell is going on here?"

"Tis tha Dreaming," Brigit replied. *"If yer mum is susceptible to it, she will nae be able ta stay out of it this close tae tha Great One."*

"What should I do?" Roz asked, suffering a pang of panicky concern.

"Carry her into tha house. If ye leave her here, she will nae wake up until tha Great One does—and tha could be weeks from now!"

"Great," Roz muttered, as she scooped her dead-weight mother up from the ground. "And here I was, thinking that having two dragons around the joint was going to make things easier."

CHAPTER 19

Charles discovered the cave at the deep end of a crack in the mountain's side. Its mouth was obscured by a rocky overhang and a screen of scrub brush, but all things considered, it had been relatively easy to spot. He had expected more sophisticated deterrents from the greatest of the drakena. Then again, he was accustomed to Tezcatlipoca's cunning ways. Grishka had made it clear that brother and sister were nothing alike.

Lucky for him, right?

He sent the drone to scope out the situation. Until he knew how big the cave was and how many chambers it had and where, exactly, the drakena was located, he meant to stay out of sight and incineration range. The probe was fitted with a small explosive device that he could trigger remotely if the drakena figured out what was going on before he was ready to put her down, but he was hoping he wouldn't have to use that option because then he would have to dig her out and make sure she was dead. It went without saying that Tezcatlipoca would insist. And if she wasn't dead, well, wouldn't that be interesting?

The drone dipped into the cave. Charles activated its front and back lights. The blackness that had been his screen phased into a dimly lit antechamber. It was a substantial space, suitably sized for an elder drakena. The floor was bare. So were the walls, No, wait, here was something, a pictograph of horned men, deer, horses, and—a dragon. He smiled. This was the right place all right.

But where was the lady of the house?

He sent the drone ranging into an adjoining chamber. Its

forward light washed over a tall mound of rounded objects. Skulls, he thought, with a mixture of involuntary dread and boyish relish. But on second glance, he realized that he was looking at pottery: Native American work, most of it very old. Apparently, the lady of the house hoarded primitive art.

Still no sign of her, though.

The drone nosed its way into a third chamber. This space was smaller than the others, and curiously furnished. A rough-hewn bed stood against one wall. A heat-stone occupied the center of the room. There were buckets, too, for water perhaps and possibly slops, but it was obvious by their thick coats of dust that they had not been touched for quite some time. Grishka had told him that drakena sometimes took women as servants. This room must be the equivalent of servant's quarters then—and the servant must have long since passed away. Up until now, he had envied the dragons for their extreme longevity. But after seeing this, near-immortality didn't seem quite so appealing.

His cell phone buzzed once and then again. He grounded the drone for the moment and then took the call.

"I expected to hear from you earlier," Tezcatlipoca said, in lieu of a salutation. "Where are you?"

"I'm in the mountains south of San Jose," he replied, keeping his voice low. "I'm probing a cave that looks to be occupied by a dragon."

"What?" the drake barked. "Speak up, man! I can barely hear you!"

"If I raise my voice," Charles said, "your sister might hear me."

"What?" Tezcatlipoca said again, suddenly excited. "You found her?"

"I found her lair," Charles said, because the Great One was one to split hairs. "She doesn't appear to be home at the moment."

A third "What?" ensued. It was more of a roar than the first two had been and not a happy one at that. "That cannot be! You must've found one of her old lairs, one she outgrew perhaps."

"This one looks plenty big to me, Great One," Charles said, trying to ignore the knot that was forming in his guts. "And her hoard is still here and intact. I'm sure she's just out hunting. As soon as she gets back—"

Tezcatlipoca hissed, a hair-raising sound. "Fool! Drakena of her size and age do not leave their dens to hunt. She must have known that we would come after the wyrms. She has fled!"

Although he had no reason to doubt the Great One, Charles didn't want to believe him. It had taken him forever to find this lair. And from here, the drakena could have gone anywhere. Tracking a creature that had evacuated by air was going to be a bitch.

"Fortunately for you," the drake went on, "she is too big and too old to have gone very far. I'd be amazed if she cleared twenty miles."

Charles appreciated the estimate. A probable flight plan would've been better, but in this instance if no other, he was sure that the drake would have parted with that information if he had had it. He resigned himself to starting the search blind only to realize that he had something to go on after all.

"The wyrms," he said, blurting out the thought as it came to him. "They've moved north. "

Perhaps they went with her."

A moment of silence followed as the drake weighed the possibility. When he spoke again, his tone was less rancorous by a grudging degree. "The theory is not completely absurd," he said, "especially if she Called them to her in the first place. She would have known that we would track them to her old territory. So she could have led them to a new nest once they made their way to her.

"Tell me: are they still on the move?"

At first, Charles mistook the question for a random thought. An instant later, he realized how astute it really was. Free-ranging wyrms would've kited off to parts unknown by now. The fact that they were still in the Bay Area suggested that they were sticking around for a reason. It wasn't a sure sign, but it did offer some hope.

"On the contrary, Great One," he replied, with as much confidence as he could muster. "They appear to be staking out a territory for themselves. The black one has been blatant in its movements. We know where it hunts, and where it nests. The red one has been harder to track, but Grishka and I believe that we'll be able to use the black one to lure it out of hiding."

Tezcatlipoca responded with a frustrated snarl. "You know where they hunt and nest but have not caught them yet? What's the problem, man?"

"We are waiting for Drogo Channing, Great One," Charles replied, happy to throw that ill-tempered fire-drake under the bus. "It was our understanding that he was to participate in the wyrms' capture."

Another snarl, this one with Drogo's name embedded in it. "I thought he was with you already!"

Charles wanted nothing more than to back that bus up and broadside Drogo again. But when it came to dealing with dragons, it was important to know when to when to strike and when to yield. And in this case, discretion was apt to serve him better—especially when Drogo heard about this conversation. And that was almost certainly The Great One's next call.

"Drogo Channing is a high-profile public figure in this part of the world," he said. "His comings and goings are heavily scrutinized. It cannot be easy for him to get away without being seen. I'm sure he'll join us at his earliest convenience."

"Yes," Tezcatlipoca hissed, "I'm certain of that, too. In the meantime, keep hunting for my sister. Call me as soon as you find her."

"Of course, Great One."

"Do not disappoint me, Carlito. As valuable as you are, you can still be replaced."

"Of course," Charles said, but he needn't have bothered. Tezcatlipoca had already ended the call. "I'll get right on it." He stuffed the cell phone back in his pocket and then picked up the drone's control box. To his irritation, the drone didn't come when called. "Damn it," he muttered, as he emerged from his hiding place. "You'd think someone would have invented a better battery by now."

As he hiked toward the cave, he rolled Tezcatlipoca's last words around in his mouth like bits of sour candy. He'd like to see the drake try and find someone capable of filling his shoes! The poor bastard would be food for the wyrms in a fortnight! It was a damn good thing that he felt so strongly about the return of the natural order. Otherwise, he might be tempted to tell the old lizard to put his money where his leathery mouth was.

An instant after the thought crossed his mind, he laughed aloud at the sheer absurdity of it. Tezcatlipoca might not be able to fill his shoes with any alacrity, but he could sure as hell see them emptied in a hurry! No, he had made his choice a long time ago. There was no opting out of it now.

Up close, the cave was even bigger than the drone's imagery had led him to expect. Even though he had heard about dragon magic and their ability to deflect unwelcome attention, he was surprised that this place had not been discovered. Then again, maybe someone had stumbled onto it—and paid the ultimate price. Drakena were supposed to be more genteel than drakes, but they were dragons still, a thought that made him nervous about entering the lair. What if Tezcatlipoca was wrong? What if his sister had just stepped out to do a bit of hunting? What if she came home while he was on the premises? He mocked himself for his jitters even as they made him tingle. If she came home while he was here, well, she'd probably kill him and that would be that.

But Tezcatlipoca wasn't wrong. The drakena wasn't coming back. He kept telling himself that to drown out the one stubborn part of him that remained solidly unconvinced.

The first thing he noticed when he entered the cave was that old-dragon smell: ammonia crossed with brimstone and hints of decay. The floor was thick in spots with sloughed-off scales, calcified flakes that made scratchy sounds underfoot. He flinched at the sounds at first, but then muttered, "Fuck it," and strode purposefully toward the room where the drone had settled. He meant to stride right back out again and be done with this nerve-wracking house call, but as he was leaving, he caught a glimpse of the second chamber and a thought occurred to him. Why not leave with something to show for his efforts? Tezcatlipoca would not object as long as there was no gold involved. And some artifacts fetched a high price on the black market. He padded into the treasure room, stealthy as a thief. There, he used the flashlight app on his phone to survey the drakena's hoard. He did not know much about pottery, but he could tell that the stuff here was old and high-quality. One piece in particular caught his eye. It was a smallish, long-necked jar with a pot-belly. Its sides were adorned with rampant winged serpents. Aurora would love this! And after the night they had shared, he wanted a way to show his appreciation without having to resort to words. He hoisted the jar and wrapped it in his jacket for protection. On an impulse, he picked up two smaller pieces as well, thinking that he could dole them out on special occasions. As he was stashing them in his jacket's pockets, his phone buzzed, signaling an incoming text. Thinking that it might be Tezcatlipoca issuing an afterthought, he checked the message.

ZEBRA STALLION MISSING. LOOKED EVERYWHERE. CAN'T FIND. ADVISE.

He texted back: WTF?!? Then he shoved the phone back in his pocket and cleared out of the cave. As he hiked back toward civilized parts, he fumed to himself. How in hell did someone lose a half-ton of barking, braying, bad-ass zebra flesh? There must be a breach in the fence somewhere. His wayward male must be terrorizing one of the neighbors.

The next thing he knew, he was auto-dialing Aurora's number. Her phone rang and rang, which usually meant that she was writing and didn't want to be disturbed. Just as he was about to hang up, though, he heard a groggy, "Hello?"

"Aurora?" he asked, surprised to hear her so sleepy at this time of day. "Are you OK?"

"Tired," she said, slurring the word. "Can't seem to stay awake. I think I must be coming down with something."

"That's not surprising," he said, "given the size of crowd that was swirling around you at the convention. You could have gotten Ebola from that many people."

She laughed, a wan sound that tailed off into a stifled yawn. "I'm the one who's supposed to be making stuff up, not you." She mumble-laughed again and then added, "What's up?"

"Uhm—" Shit! He hadn't rehearsed how to pop this question. Now he was going to sound like a royal fool. But there was no way to go but forward now. "My groundskeeper tells me that my zebra stallion is missing. I was wondering if it might have wandered onto your property."

She coughed—choking on a laugh, no doubt. "Nope. No zebras here," she said. "Sorry." An instant later, she added,

"Maybe a predator got it."

"Maybe," he conceded, although he found it hard to believe that a solitary mountain lion could've taken down that nasty, kick-it-till-it's-dead scrapper. "I'll tell my crew to look for signs of a fight—and a large patch of gore."

"Yes, well, good luck with that," she said, and then yawned with such force that he found himself yawning in turn. "I'm really sorry," she said then, "but I just can't do this now. Can I call you later?"

"Of course," he replied. "Go back to sleep. Sweet dreams."

"Thanks," she slurred, and then hung up.

Charles continued on his way, hugging the scavenged pottery close to his chest as if the pieces could somehow transit his feelings to Aurora. 'Sweet dreams' had only been half of his wish. The part that he'd left out was a hope that those dreams would be of him.

CHAPTER 20

Quetzalli stands reeling on her feet, wearied to near death by the flight from the city. Her mouth is as dry as a year-old bean. Her heart struggles to find a rhythm it can keep. If her daughter, Quetzal, hadn't been holding her up, she would have dropped to her knees a long time ago. She feels heavy through and through, as if she is turning to stone from the inside out. She recognizes the feeling as grief: the heart-ache for things that have ended. She grieves for Pimotl, because he is stubborn beyond measure and serves a god who hates humankind. She grieves for herself, too, for she is much too old to have been so rudely uprooted. Knowing that she will not recover from the shock of such an upheaval does not make her sad, for as Quetzalcoatl's high priestess, she will be high-born in the afterlife. She just wishes she could be sure about her brother's fate. He had been a good man until the gods sank their claws into him.

A wave of dizziness rolls over her, causing her to stagger. But even as she gives herself permission to collapse, Quetzalcoatl comes floating down from the sky in all of his pink-frilled glory. Tears leap to Quetzalli's eyes, beads of joyful vindication. This is her reward for hanging on to one last shred of hope. This is a poultice for all the pain and abuse she endured at the hands of The Jaguar's fetid priests. Knowing that her daughter and her daughter's daughters will live under the protection of a wise and honorable god muffles the ache in her heart.

With a gentle warble, Quetzalcoatl tries to quiet the pool of refugees that has gathered at the base of the mountain. What he receives instead is a barrage of accolades. "Hail to Mighty Quetzalcoatl! All praise to our savior, the Serpent God!"

The god raises his hands and then extends his frill. Quetzalli has never seen him look so magnificent. "People!" he says, in a voice that travels up the side of the mountain. "Praise me not! For I have not returned to resume the old ways. I have come to deliver you unto a new age."

A confused murmur circulates through the crowd. Those closest to Quetzalli tap her on the shoulder in hopes of receiving an explanation, but she has none to give.

"For the past two ages, many of my kind have treated men with appalling cruelty," the god says. "Others, like me, did not try hard enough to stop the abuse. Our actions and inaction alike have offended The Divine. She has decreed that my kind are to be punished, one and all. She has also decreed that the length and measure of that punishment is to be determined by you."

More confusion. More murmuring. Quetzalli is so puzzled, she forgets to hold on to her daughter's arm and almost falls down.

"No longer will you be kept in the dark," Quetzalcoatl continues. "No longer will you be misled. I am here to tell you the truth." His chest heaves as if he is struggling to cough something up, but nothing comes forth. He licks his lips and warbles an apology. An apology! From a god! Quetzalli is not the only one who is scandalized by this. And his next utterance dismays her even more. "Before I enlighten you, I would have you know that I have treasured your high regard for me. And I would have you remember that I treated you well.

"You are the greatest of all the gods!" someone from the crowd shouts.

Quetzalcoatl's expression puckers for a moment and then goes hard like oven-fired clay. "And that," he says, "is the very heart of the lie. For I am not a god. I cannot hasten the end of a drought or stop the sky from falling or stave off the end of the world. None of my kind can."

"That is not so!" a woman cries, passionate in her disbelief. "At the Festival of New Fire, I saw Tezcatlipoca fight the Sky Spirits off so the sun could rise."

"*The sun would have risen regardless,*" Quetzalcoatl says ruefully. "*Tezcatlipoca is not a god.*"

"*But—we sacrificed—so many—to him!*" a man says, and Quetzalli can tell by the ache in his voice that he is recalling the list of his dead. "*Why would he have us do that?*"

"*Because,*" Quetzalcoatl says, "*he is cruel and he hates you.*"

"*We thought he was a god,*" the same man bleats.

"*You were deceived,*" Quetzalcoatl says, a rueful warble. "*And for my part in that deception, I am sorry. Farewell, people. Live free.*"

As his blessing ripples over the crowd, his body shimmers and then seems to melt away. The next thing Quetzalli knows, the man-form that she has adored since childhood is gone and she is staring at a magnificent pink-frilled serpent with wings. For the briefest of moments, it locks eyes with her. Although its gaze is alien to her now, she feels the connection just the same. The thought that blooms in her head feels familiar, too.

Our bond endures, daughter. Always.

With that, the serpent beats the air with its broad, leathery wings and takes flight. As it flaps its way toward the horizon, the ache in Quetzalli's heart returns. A lie! A lie! She has spent her whole life in service to a lie! The realization is so painful, it radiates out from her chest and into her arm. And knowing that she still loves the lie makes the hurt even worse. She thinks of her brother Pimotl and wonders how he will receive the news. Will he be devastated like her? Or relieved?

"*Mother?*"

She is on the ground now, collapsed like a speared deer. Quetzal has her by the shoulders and is shouting her name and shaking her. The rest of the world is a swirl of color and sound.

"*What are we going to do now?*" someone moans.

At first, Quetzalli thinks that someone is talking about her. Then someone else shouts, "First, we are going to find a new place to live. Then we are going to hunt down Tezcatlipoca and the other not-gods and kill them."

Savage glee blows through Quetzalli and explodes in her chest. She cries out, a garbled farewell to her god-that-is-not-a-god and then goes limp.

Aurora came awake clutching her chest. There was no pain there, only the memory of it, but that was sharp enough to make her gasp. As she struggled for breath that was slow to come, she blinked back a haze of dream tears and then sputtered a confused curse. She should've been in the barn. There should have been a giant dragon slumbering next to her. Instead, she was on the couch in her office and there were two blurs looming over her. One was larger than the other, but neither of them looked like a dragon.

"Roz?" she said, trying to squint past the teary haze. "Is that you?"

The smaller of the blurs sank into a crouch, morphing into her daughter along the way. "Yeah, Mom, it's me," Roz said, and stroked Aurora's cheek with the back of her hand as if she were a feverish child. "Are you OK? Brigit says the Dreaming can be pretty intense this close to a drakena who dreams."

"Brigit?" She peered around the room again, looking in vain for the long-necked dragon. "Is she—with Quetzalcoatl?"

"Tha Great One sleeps alone."

That came from Roz's companion, an enormous red-headed woman with smoke-colored eyes and a swimmer's lean, stream-lined body. Aurora's confusion took an irritable turn. Just what she needed—another in-the-know stranger in an already confounding mix.

"Who might you be?" she asked.

"Do ye really not recognize me?" the woman replied coyly. "Not even a wee bit?"

Nothing about her struck Aurora as familiar: not those

eyes or her long, flat face, not even that thick-as-jam brogue. And she was sure she would have remembered meeting someone who made her big, strapping daughter look dainty by comparison. Nevertheless, there was something about the woman that niggled at Aurora, a tantalizing would-be association that buzzed the fringes of her subconscious like a hungry hummingbird. And was it her sleep-drunk imagination or were the innermost recesses of her nostrils glowing?

"Can't be," she muttered to herself, and then turned to her daughter. "I give. Who is she?"

"C'mon, Mom," Roz replied. "You know."

An image of a sleek, long-necked dragon took shape in Aurora's mind. She emphatically cast it back out. "Can't be," she said again, louder this time.

"What?" Brigit asked, and then cocked her head as if she thought Aurora might be easier to understand from a different angle. "Why not?"

The truth popped out of Aurora like a Heimlich-ed chicken bone. "I don't believe in magic. There's no such thing."

Brigit snorted. "Ye have no wings, yet ye can fly all over the world. Ye can talk to people thousands of miles away. Ye can predict the weather and the sex of yer bairns. Ye can turn a slab of ice into hot food in minutes. Tha sounds like feckin' magic to me."

"That's science," Aurora argued. "All science."

"Humans manipulate matter and energy," Brigit said. "Dragons manipulate matter and energy. Call it what ye will, but it amounts to the same thing."

"Not to me it doesn't," Aurora said. "Science is real. Magic is something I write about."

"And yesterday," Roz chimed in, "dragons were mythical creatures. C'mon, Mom. You know the right of it. You're just being stubborn."

282

Aurora cast a black look at her daughter, projecting betrayal, reproach, and jealousy. How dare she take sides against her own mother? And how dare she be so damn comfortable with this bewildering turn of events? It was as if she had known all along that there were living, breathing dragons roaming the world.

Up there! In that cave! That's where it lives! Let's trap it in there and kill it!

"No!" Aurora shouted—and woke herself up. She phased back into the waking world to find Roz and Brigit staring at her with a mix of wonder and pity in their eyes. "I'm sorry," she said, rubbing her face with her hands to hide her embarrassment. "I don't know what came over me. I never nod off like that."

"It's tha Dreaming," Brigit said.

Aurora still wasn't comfortable with the idea of Brigit being a dragon in disguise, but at the moment, she was willing to let the matter slide to slake her curiosity. "I've heard this 'dreaming' mentioned several times now," she said, "but I don't understand what it is. Please explain."

If Brigit sensed Aurora's ongoing unease, she showed no sign of it. "When drakena sleep," she said, "our minds wander. Most of us stay close to our bodies, but a few, like The Great One, range far and wide, even back and forth through time. In tha Dreaming's grip, a skilled traveler can see and hear things that are happening on the other side of the world. She can even slip into another dragon's dreams in search of secrets."

"I can see how that might be a handy knack to have,' Aurora said—even if it was dragon magic. "But what does that have to do with me?"

"You share a blood-bond with the Great One," Brigit said. "When Tha Dreaming takes her, she draws you into it through that connection. Surely this isn't tha first time you've felt tha pull?"

A fresh wave of irritation welled up in Aurora, this one born of defensiveness and shame. Of course this wasn't the first time she'd felt the pull! Just ask the thousands of people that she had told over the decades that her best ideas came to her in dreams! But how was she supposed to have known that those dreams were actually a live-feed from an ancient dragon who was out on an astral walkabout? Nobody on the freaking planet would have guessed!

"Mom? You still with us?"

Her anger collapsed as quickly as it had risen, leaving a floodplain of regrets behind. "Yes, I'm still here," she said, and then forced herself to make eye-contact with the unsettling dragon-woman who was her daughter's friend. "The pull is different now—more aggressive. I can't seem to resist it like I used to."

"That's because the Great One is in yer barn now," Brigit said. "The closer ye are to her, the harder tha Dreaming will be ta resist."

The thought appalled Aurora. "But—that's not right. I've got work to do, a life to live."

"Ye could always vacant tha premises till tha Great One wakes," Brigit said. "But it's my belief that tha Dreaming is coming after ye fer a reason. Best ye surrender to yer destiny and let it take ye where it will."

"My destiny?" Aurora echoed, throwing in an incredulous sneer for good measure. "What is this? A soap opera out-take?"

Brigit glanced from Roz to Aurora and back again. "Are ye sure she's yer mother? She's awfully closed-minded."

The comment struck Aurora with the force of a blow. In its aftermath, she found herself on the other side of a fence that she hadn't been trying to clear. "No need to get bitchy, dragon," she said. "I'm just trying to wrap my head around this brand-new reality, is all."

"Well," Brigit replied, in a withering tone, "don't be all day about it. Tha end of this age is coming, and tha fate of tha next one hangs in the balance. We must be tha tipping point, not tha drakes and their agents. Our way of life depends on it."

Aurora's immediate reaction to that assertion was reflexive scorn: more hyperbole! But she didn't air the thought aloud because she was still stinging from the dragon-woman's remark about her being close-minded. Her! Of all people! And before the dragon could put her on the spot again, the home security system buzzed, announcing someone at the front gate. Grateful for the distraction, she jumped up and checked the monitor.

"Package for you, Miz V," the UPS guy said, when she clicked on the intercom. "I'll need a signature."

"Sure thing, Carl," she said, and triggered the gate. "Come on up." On her way out of the room, she frilled her fingers at Roz and said, "Don't let me hold you up if you've got someplace else to be."

The short walk to the front door felt like a reprieve. She didn't enjoy being so negative, especially in front of Roz, but the things she was being asked to accept without question were fantastical, the stuff of looking glasses and rabbit holes. There was no place for them in the real, waking world. And yet— there they were, staring her in the face, scorning her for her disbelief. And even still—acceptance felt unnatural, almost like a betrayal.

But a betrayal of whom?

The UPS truck's arrival paused her ponderings. The package that Carl then handed her made her forget everything else. It was a largish box, professionally packed, with no visible return address. Red and white 'Fragile!' stickers striped its sides. It had very little heft to it. She carried it back into her office. She was so curious about its contents and sender, she didn't even care that Roz and Brigit were still there. Roz was standing in a corner, talking on her cell phone. The dragon-woman was ensconced on the floor. Her expression was a blank.

Roz waved to Aurora and mouthed, "Mara says 'hi!'"

Aurora blew a kiss in reply and then pulled a pair of scissors from a desk drawer. Several moments and many layers of bubble wrap later, she found herself holding up a piece of pottery. "Oh my," she said, admiring it from all angles. "How beautiful! And look! It's got dragons on it!"

The next thing she knew, Brigit was at her elbow. Her nostrils were flared; her scowl, intense. "Let me see that," she said, a command rather than a request.

"Sure," Aurora said, handing the jar over so she could read the accompanying card. "'To my favorite dragon lady.'"

"Who sent this to ye?" Brigit asked brusquely.

"That's really none of your business," Aurora replied, utterly uninterested in discussing her love life with the changeling. "Why?"

"It smells of dragon," Brigit said. "It smells of tha Great One, ta be exact."

That snagged her attention. "I just handled it. And I've had contact with Quetzalcoatl. Maybe I put her smell on it."

Brigit sniffed the jar again, sucking more air in through her nose than Aurora would have thought possible. "No," she said, upon exhaling. "A cannot smell your skin oils on the clay, only tha Great One's. Her odor is ingrained, too. This jar belonged to her for a long, long time. It may be that whoever found it might have been looking for her instead. So I ask ye again: who sent this?"

"A friend," Aurora said, determined to protect Charles. "A friend who has absolutely no reason to believe in Quetzalcoatl, never mind be hunting for her. I'll tell you what, though—the next time we talk, I'll ask him where he got it."

"Do so," the changeling said. "His answer could be important."

Roz rejoined them then, looking pleased with herself. "That was Mara," she said. "She and Max are going to be in Woodside tomorrow. They've invited us to join them for lunch. Nice vase, by the way," she added, as Aurora set it down on her desk. "Who sent it?"

"She willna say," Brigit said.

A diabolical grin rippled its way across Roz's mouth. "I'll bet it's from Charles!" When Brigit cocked her head, encouraging her to elaborate, she added, "Her man-friend—the guy who raises zebras."

"Ah, yes; the stripy things. Good eating, those. A might have tae pay another visit to that paddock before long."

"Don't," Aurora said. "Don't kill any more zebras."

"Yeah," Roz chimed in, and then sniggered. "Stop eating Mom's boyfriend's pets."

Aurora rounded on her—and not just because she didn't appreciate being teased. "It's not funny, Roz. He's already asked me if I've seen the missing zebra on the grounds. If another one disappears, he's going to want to look around in person. What if he stumbled onto Quetzalcoatl? What then, huh? He'd probably be thrilled because that's the kind of guy he is, but I thought the whole idea was to keep the Great One's location a secret."

"You're right," Roz said, looking suitably chastened. "I wasn't thinking."

"You were, though," Brigit said, eying Aurora slyly. "'Tis nice ta know that ye've been paying at least a little attention tae what's being said."

That tiny jolt of approval did wonders for Aurora's confidence. Instead of bristling at the changeling, she flashed a wry half-smile and said, "I don't always react well to things, dragon, but I hear everything. Always. Now get out of here— and take my daughter with you. I want to get some work done before the Dreaming comes for me again."

Neither Brigit nor Roz protested their eviction. But even as Aurora sat down at her desk to get started, a shout rolled into the office. "Mom! Get in here! Hurry!"

She was on her feet in one instant and in the living room in the next. Roz and Brigit were staring intently at the big-screen TV. The news was on. A grim-faced reporter was broadcasting live from the Fell Street entrance to The Golden Gate Park.

"Although police say it's too soon to draw any conclusions," she said, "this morning's murder bears disturbing similarities to other recent murders in the area. In each instance, the victim was male. In each instance, the victims were attacked in remote areas. And it appears that all of the victims were mauled and sexually assaulted—"

"That's the same thing that happened to Brother Baine," Aurora said, talking over the TV. "That means the wyrms are still in the area!"

"Yes," Brigit said, hissing the tail-end of the word. "A thought tha same."

"Yay," Roz said, without enthusiasm. "We've narrowed our search parameters down to the San Francisco Bay Area. Do you have any idea how much real estate we're talking here? And it's not like the beasties are dropping clues as to their whereabouts. The attacks have taken place all along the coast."

"That might be a lot of territory for you ta cover," Brigit said, "but it's not that much fer a wyrm. And the fact that they've not kited off suggests that they're close tae sexing and feeling tha need tae nest."

"So where do wyrms nest?" Aurora asked, ever and always game for problem solving.

"They like cool, dark, out-of-tha-way places," Brigit said. "A cave would be ideal. Are there any caves in tha area?"

Aurora drew a quick blank, but Roz picked up the slack with a snap of her fingers. "Just north of the penisula at the Marin Headlands. Remember, Mom?" she went on, growing excited. "You took me hiking up there a couple of times back when I was a kid. The cliffs are riddled with caves."

"That's right," Aurora said, recalling it clearly now that her memory had been jogged. "There's lots of open space, too, and plenty of game."

"We should go there," Roz said.

"Yes," Brigit said. "We should."

CHAPTER 21

Roz drove down Skyline Boulevard at a mellow sixty miles per hour, taking her time so she could better savor the Zen-like serenity of an old-growth redwood forest. The tree-tops were swathed in fog, remnants of last night's marine layer. Their scent was both evergreen and earthy. She turned down the love song that was playing on the radio and then rapped at the truck's rear window with a knuckle to get Brigit's attention.

"So what do you think?" she asked. "Spectacular, right?"

The changeling was sprawled on her back in the flatbed. She hadn't moved so much as a muscle since they'd left Saratoga. "Oh, ai," she said, projecting reverence. "'Tis lovely country, this. We've nuthin quite like it back home. A could spend tha whole day like this."

"Sorry," Roz said, "but we've got a full dance card. First, we're meeting Max and Mara at Royce's Restaurant for breakfast—"

"Let's skip that part," Brigit interjected. "A'm not hungry."

"You'll like Royce's anyway," Roz argued. "It's embedded in the forest and has mad-crazy views. There's a trailhead in the restaurant's backyard so we can watch hikers come and go as we eat."

Brigit made a sour sound. "Why would A want tae do that? A've got no desire tae expose myself tae more people, and that includes yer friends."

"Tough," Roz countered. "They're an important part of my life, as are you. I don't want to waste time and energy trying to hide you from each other. You're going to meet them and you're going to be nice. Is that clear?"

Brigit responded with a grunt, promising nothing. Roz thumped the steering wheel with her fist, wishing it was a certain stubborn dragon's skull instead. But pressing the issue wouldn't get her anywhere but more frustrated. All she could do was shut up and hope for the best. Max would find the changeling intriguing even at her dragon-surliest just because he loved a good accent. Mara, on the other hand, did not react well to bad behavior. And if she took a disliking to somebody— fzzt, that was it, game over. She'd been that way with Aldo. Come to think of it, she'd been that way with most of the men that Roz had dated.

"One of these days, she's going to have to teach me that trick," she said, and then yelped as her truck hit a frost heave.

"What's that ye say?" Brigit said. "Tis hard tae hear over tha road noise and wind."

"You're wreaking havoc on my shocks," Roz said.

"I dunna know what tha means."

"It means you're one seriously heavy load. I think you've gained weight since we left Scotland."

"Not feckin' likely," Brigit replied. "A haven't had a single decent gorge since A—wait! Did ye see that?"

"See what?" Roz asked, glancing left and then right. "I was watching the road."

In response, Brigit launched herself out of the flatbed.

"Shit!" Roz said. But even as she went to slam on the brakes, a familiar voice bloomed in her head. *"Dunna come after me. A'll find ye later."*

Roz swore again and then checked the rearview mirror, half-expecting to see Brigit's body tumbling down the highway. There was no sign of her, though, no trace. It was as if the changeling had plunged headfirst into a hole in time and space.

"Dammit, dragon," Roz said, punching the steering wheel

again. "What the hell were you thinking? There could have been another car behind them! Someone could've seen! It would've only taken me a minute to stop!"

Then, as the microburst of adrenaline wore off, a more rational thought occurred to her: what the hell could've impelled Brigit to jump out of a speeding truck? Her aversion to meeting Max and Mara couldn't be that strong! Despite her instructions to the contrary, Roz was tempted to investigate. They were a team, dammit! They were supposed to tackle tasks together! Even as she gave herself permission to pull over and go looking for the changeling, though, the entrance to Royce's parking lot loomed to her right. Instead of pulling over, she found herself pulling in.

The restaurant was a popular roadside attraction for tourists and locals alike, so even at this hour of the day, the lot was jammed with cars, motorcycles, and bikes. Ironically, the only open space was next to Mara's sky-blue Prius. Roz heaved a sigh through her teeth, resigning herself to what was obviously meant to be, and then threw the truck into park. As she climbed down from the cab, Mara came running toward her from out of nowhere with arms open wide.

"Oh my God, look at you!" she squealed, as she closed in. "You look fabulous without one hundred and seventy pounds of conceited fat attached to your waist!"

The next thing Roz knew, she was wrapped in Mara's soft, sweet-smelling embrace. She savored the rightness of the sensation, the pure joyful hominess. Then Mara shifted, grabbing her by the arms, and looked her in the eyes. "How are you? Really?"

"I'm fine!" Roz said, laughing because Mara was making more of a deal of her break-up than she had. "Really. I cried for a while after the asshole dumped me, then went and got drunk on the foggy shores of Loch Ness."

"Ah, yes. And according to local legend, that's where you met your new friend, Brigit," Mara said. She glanced at the passenger side of the truck and then cocked her head. "Where is she? I thought she was coming with you."

Roz grimaced, a complicated dodge. "Yeah, well," she said, "something came up. She's going to join us later if all goes well."

Mara tried to look disappointed, but Roz could tell by the gleam in her eye that she wasn't entirely displeased. "Oh, well," she said, looping arms with Roz, "that gives us more time to catch up. C'mon, Max is holding a table for us. We want to hear all about Scotland—the good parts, at least. We want to see pictures, too, if you took any. We live vicariously through you, you know."

"I'm going to tell Max you said that," Roz teased.

"Please don't," Mara said. "He'd love to be adventurous like you even though he's not that guy. His knees are crap, he's allergic to practically everything under the sun, and he has a favorite chair. But if he gets it in his head that I want to do the things that you do, he'll pitch everything to the wind and do something crazy like book us a trip to Africa or the Amazon and really, Roz, all I want to do is hear about shit like that. I love my life just the way it is."

"Don't sweat it," Roz said. "Your secret is safe with me."

Their table was outdoors on the deck, shaded by an evergreen umbrella. The table next door was packed with leather-jacketed bikers. As Roz approached, one of them whistled lewdly and said, "Hey, hot stuff! Ever been with a bad boy?"

The guy had a scruffy grey ponytail and a goatee to match. There wasn't much left of his hairline. Roz stared him down like a drill sergeant until his smart-ass smirk fell to half-mast and then said, "Dude, you're not a boy. You're a man—an old man at that. So why don't you do us all a favor and act your age?"

His friends laughed and ribbed him for that. "She told you, didn't she, Kenny!" He shot her a poisonous look and snarled, "Bitch."

She gave him a thumb's-up and said, "Don't you forget it."

"Good job," Max said, as she sat down across from him. "He's been hassling women ever since he rolled in. In fact," he added, in a lower voice, "I was ready to give him a serious piece of my mind if he so much as looked cross-eyed at Mara."

Mara patted his hand and said, "Thank you, baby."

A waitress strode up to their table. She was very young and very pretty, white-blonde with frost-blue eyes and long legs that her uniform displayed to good effect. Despite her youth, she looked rather tired and foot-sore. She handed a menu to Roz and then looked expectantly at Mara and Max.

"You guys ready to order yet?" she asked.

"Sorry, Ashley," Mara said, "but we're still missing one person."

"No problem," Ashley replied. "Take all the time you want. Just so you know, though; my shift ends in fifteen minutes."

"Nice," Roz said. "You still get to enjoy the lion's share of the day."

"That was the plan yesterday," Ashley said ruefully. "This morning, however, my car crapped out. So now when I'm done here, I get to hike home and have my car towed to the garage. It's a good thing yonder trail runs right by my house."

"Yo, waitress!" A familiar voice barked. "C'mon over here and gimme some service."

Ashley clenched her teeth and rolled her eyes. Mara tried to console her by saying, "Just ignore him, sweetie. I think he's had a bit to drink. And when you get a chance, could you please bring us a round of lemonade?"

"Sure," Ashley said, then sucked in a deep breath through her nose and headed over to the biker's table. "How's it going over here, fellahs? Anything else I can get for you before I leave?"

"How 'bout I take you for a spin on my bike when you punch out?" Kenny asked. "I guarantee it'll be the ride of your life."

"Thanks," Ashley said. "but I've already made other plans. If there's nothing else, I'll get your check."

As she departed, Kenny groaned loudly and said, "You know she wants me, right?"

Mara made a sour face and muttered, "What a dick!" An instant later, she brightened back up and said, "Speaking of dicks, did I mention that we saw Aldo at SiliCon? He showed up at the Grand Ball as Han Solo—what else, right? And his new squeeze went as slave princess Leia. She must be riding him hard and fast because—"

"Mara," Max said, a polite call for discretion.

She waved him off like a pitcher wanting to throw heat. "Oh, she knows I didn't mean it like that. All I'm saying is that he's starting to look like a stretch of bad road. His hair's thinning and he's starting to get a pot. And he had the nerve to call me fat!"

"My whole life changed for the better the day he dumped me." Roz declared. "I no longer feel like I need to have a man on my arm to be complete."

"Well, hoorah for that," Max said, raising his freshly delivered glass of lemonade to that. "I've always said that being with the wrong person is worse than being with no one at all."

Mara sneered. "How would you know? I'm the only woman you've ever been with."

"And before I met you," he retorted, "I was alone. And I didn't mind being alone until I met you. Case closed."

Roz and Mara snickered at his sketchy love-flecked logic. Then Mara assumed an all-ears pose and said, "So go on and tell us about Scotland."

In response, Roz pulled out her cell phone and dialed up a

slide show. "We went to Edinburgh first. It's a beautiful city, and very friendly. This is the Duddingston Golf Club—one of the most scenic courses I've ever played. And these are shots from the Festival parade. Don't you just love marching men in kilts?" Someone tapped on their table in passing: Ashley bidding them a polite adieu. Roz absently waved goodbye and then resumed her narrative. "This is Edinburgh Castle, the place where Harry Potter was filmed—"

A flicker of movement caught her eye: Kenny, leaving his table. He was heading toward the trailhead—after Ashley. Boosted by a bad feeling, Roz shot to her feet.

"Here," she said, tossing the phone to Mara, "there's lots more. I gotta get something out of my truck and then hit the head."

"Oh," Mara said, in a knowing tone. "OK. But I've got a tampon in my purse if you want it."

"Thanks," Roz said, as she hurried off, "but I'm good."

By the time she cleared the patio deck, Ashley was already heading into the forest. Kenny was ten or so yards behind her. When the blonde dropped into a crouch to fuss with one of her shoes, Kenny turned his back to her, lit a cigarette, and pretended to admire the surroundings. A moment later, though, he resumed pursuit. Roz jogged after the two of them, intent on nipping a bad scene in the bud. Although she lost sight of them when they entered the woods, the acrid stink of tobacco smoke served as a beacon.

The trail was a well-marked path that wound from one majestic redwood to the next. The ground was carpeted with their dry dead needles, a thick, bouncy bed that muffled the sounds of her hurried footfalls. The smell of a lit cigarette drew closer, then closer still. Then Roz spotted a curl of smoke rising up from a patch of hard-pack. She crushed the butt out with the heel of her boot in passing. Moments later, she caught sight of a middle-aged man in biker leathers on the trail ahead of her.

"Hey, dickhead," she shouted. When Kenny pivoted toward her, she added, "It's fire season. Stub your stinkin' butts."

He broke into a hateful smirk and said, "Well, lookee who we have here. I guess you must have changed your mind about me."

"Not a chance," she replied. "You're still a jerk. And I'm pretty sure Ashley feels the same way. So why don't you quit stalking her and go home?"

He cast a casual glance at the trail ahead, then shrugged and resumed smirking at Roz. "I guess I don't really need her now that you're here."

"Clearly, you skipped Bad Boy School on the day Teacher delivered the 'No Means No' lecture," she said. "You really ought to read up on the concept before someone decides to beat it into your thick skull."

"And who would that someone be? You?" He jeered. "You might have a few pounds on me, but I'm pretty sure I could still take you. In fact—" He reached into his jacket and pulled out a switchblade. "I think it might be fun to go a few rounds."

Shit. What was it with men and knives?

She shifted into a fighting stance. Before she could invite him to take his best shot, though, a loud cracking sound cut her off. A microburst of redwood needles and broken branches rained down on Kenny. An instant later, a black-winged fright burst forth from the forest canopy. It looked like an Irish wolfhound with wings and clawed forearms. Bony spurs ridged its spine. It slammed into the astonished biker like a wrecking ball, then pinned him to the ground and began to violently hump him. As it did so, its features shimmered. For a second, it took on the aspect of a dark-haired man. Then it flickered back into a black-winged fright and snapped at Kenny's scruffy neck.

"Please," Kenny grated, "help me."

She scanned the ground for the switchblade that the fright had knocked out of his hand. It was nowhere to be seen so she grabbed a downed tree branch instead and jabbed the fright in the side. It swiveled its flat, narrow head toward her and hissed, spraying her with spittle that tingled when it hit her skin. Then it resumed its attack on Kenny. She struck again, swinging the branch like a club. This time, the fright abandoned its sport with a furious snarl and squared off against her. Its green eyes were wild, but not devoid of intelligence. Although it was slavering, she got the distinct sense that it wasn't from hunger.

"Fly away now," she said, thrusting the branch at it once again. "Party's over."

The fright gathered itself into a crouch, preparing to spring. Then a subliminal rumble cut through the air—a low, menacing sound. The fright let out a startled squawk and launched itself toward the treetops. A fresh round of tree debris flurried to the ground. Roz stood ready until she was sure the thing wasn't coming back and then nudged Kenny in the ribs with the branch. "You OK?"

His leather jacket looked like fringe now, as did his chaps. But aside from a smattering of tiny blisters on his face and a shallow gash on his throat, he seemed to be unhurt.

"Yeah," he said, bad boy no more but just a middle-aged schmuck who had probably crapped himself. "What the fuck was that?"

"Chupacabra," she said, making up the lie on the spot.

He shot her a mocking look. "Yeah, right."

She responded with a shrug. "Suit yourself, dude. But I think we can agree that whatever it was, it was after you. I think I can safely add that you'd be in pretty shitty shape right about now if it weren't for me."

"Yeah, I guess," he said, and then reached into the shreds of his jacket for a cigarette. As he lit up, hands trembling, he added, "Why'd you help me anyway?"

"That's what decent people do, dude."

"Yeah, right," he said, cloaking his sarcasm in smoke. "So now I owe you, right? What do you want? And just so you know, I'm broke. The second wife cleaned me out."

"Good for her," she said, meaning to leave it at that. But then she got a mental nudge, urging her not to let him off that easy. "Give me a business card. You have one, don't you? Of course you do," he added, as he pulled a holder out of his back pocket. "Everyone in California has one.

"Kenny Wayne Winters," she said, reading from the card. "'Outlaw at large'. Seriously?" She held the card up to his face. "Is this your current address and phone number?" At his nod, she tucked the card in her shirt pocket and said, "As of now, Kenny Wayne, you're on the hook for a favor. If I ever call and ask you to do something for me, I expect you to do it, no questions asked."

"It can't be anything illegal," he said.

She tsked. "Can't commit to being bad. Can't commit to being good. It must really suck being you."

"I've definitely had my low moments," he said. "This is definitely one of them."

"Boo-hoo," she said, refusing to show him any sympathy. "Maybe the next time you get it in that thick head of yours to sexually harass someone, you'll remember what that chupacabra wanted to do to you. Now make your promise to me and run along. I've got better things to do than hang out in the woods with the worst Boy Scout ever."

"Fine," he said, and then flicked his cigarette butt at her feet. "I owe you one favor. Just one. Until then, fuck off."

"Don't go away mad, little outlaw," she sneered, as he started back toward Royce's. "Just go away."

As soon as he was out of sight, Brigit stepped out from behind a nearby redwood. Her hair was littered with twigs and needles, and her kilt-like skirt was askew, but other than that, nothing about her said recently-jumped-from-a-moving-vehicle. The first thing she said as she strode toward Roz was, "I told ye not to follow me."

"I didn't," Roz said, leaving her thoughts open so the changeling could see the truth of it. "I was following that guy," she added, jerking her thumb in the direction that Kenny had gone. "Long story."

Brigit looked that way and snorted. "A canna believe ye were going ta let him walk away scot-free from his debt."

Roz deflected the mild criticism with a shrug. "He's not exactly my idea of a go-to guy."

"Even fools have their uses," Brigit said, and then glanced down at the raw patch of earth that Kenny had so recently vacated. "He could come in quite handy as bait."

A month ago, Roz would have protested that possibility in no uncertain terms. Now, she considered it without blinking an eye. "You think that wyrm would go for someone twice? That scrapper was one of the wyrms we're looking for, right?"

"Ai," Brigit said.

"And you spotted it while you were in the truck."

"Ai. A tried to make contact with it, but its mind was closed ta me so A decided tae hunt it down instead. A thought A had it when it went fer ur friend, but then ye had tae start poking at it with a feckin' stick. What tha feck were ye thinking? It would've killed you if A'd not scared it off. Did ye not see that it were in a frenzy?"

"To tell you the truth," Roz said, "I wasn't sure what I was seeing. At one point, I could have sworn that it turned halfway into a man."

"Ai, A saw that, too," Brigit said. "Tha wyrm's starting tae sex. And while it's still in tha early stages of transition, it's obviously sexing male. Which begs tha question: all other oddities aside, why's it trying tae conjugate with men?"

"Because it's gay?" Roz guessed.

"There are no gay dragons," Brigit said. "Leastwise, there haven't been until now. These wyrms are peculiar in so many ways."

"If you say so," Roz said. "What do we do now?"

"A want tae stay around here for a while and see if tha wyrm comes back. If it doesn't return, we can head north and see what we can find there."

"Let's mount our watch at the restaurant," Roz said, glancing in that direction. "All this excitement has given me an appetite. And Max and Mara must be wondering where we are by now."

Brigit reared back, astonished. "Ye think they'll still be there?"

"Oh, yeah," Roz said, starting back that way. "They're waiting for us. You can count on it."

"Feck," Brigit said, and then fell in behind Roz like a petulant child.

The bikers were gone by the time they set foot on the deck. Max and Mara were exactly where Roz had left them. Max was halfway through a plate of Eggs Benedict. Mara appeared to be on her second mimosa. As soon as she spotted Roz, she alerted Max with a thump to the arm and said, "See? Safe and sound!"

"Look who I found," Roz said, stepping aside to offer them a better view of Brigit. "Max and Mara, this is Brigit. Brigit, these are my best friends."

Mara was on her feet in one instant, and toe-to-toe with Brigit in the next. The physical disparity between the two of them was dramatic, like that between a draft horse and a pony. But if Mara was taken aback by Brigit's size, she didn't show it. "Sorry," she said, as she enfolded the changeling into an embrace, "but I'm a hugger. I'm so glad to meet you at last! Welcome to California!"

Roz held her breath, unsure of how Brigit was going to react. The last time someone had touched her without an invitation, she'd grabbed him by the shirtfront and threatened to tear out his liver. Granted, they'd been on a train at the time, the last forty-five minutes of a long, ten-hour leg, and the guy had been an obnoxious douche with a thing against big women. Still, Brigit could be unpredictable. Especially when she was hungry. Or tired. Or just in a mood. But at the moment, she seemed more bemused than anything else. She stood utterly still, with her hands at her sides, until Mara finally relented and let her go.

As soon as his wife cleared out, Max moved in. But instead of embracing Brigit, he offered her a courtly bow. When he straightened again, he had a perfect red rose bud in hand.

"For you," he said. "Any friend of Roz's is a friend of ours."

Brigit had as much use for flowers as she did for hugs, but Roz could tell that her interest had been piqued nonetheless. She sniffed the rose, not delicately but like a bloodhound searching for a scent to follow. Then she peered at Max through narrowed eyes.

"Ye didna tell me he's a magician," she said, speaking to Roz, even as she studied Max. "Magicians are valuable allies."

"Max Marino at your service, milady," Max said, and bowed again. "Anytime you need a rose plucked out of thin air, just say my name three times and snap your fingers. "But," he added, as he returned to his chair, "I do my best work with a computer."

"Interesting," Brigit said. "A have seen a computer. It is a machine. Roz's mum would have me believe that what it does is science rather than magic."

Max laughed. "That's Aurora for you: fantasist by trade, realist by nature. But I happen to know that science and magic are two sides of the same coin."

302

"A said as much," Brigit said, and then abruptly took a seat at the table. The wooden chair creaked beneath her weight. Max and Mara pretended not to notice. "Who cares what ye call it so long as it gets tha job done, right?"

"Exactly!" Max said, and then signaled for the waitress. "Sorry we started without you," he said, as she headed their way, "but we got hungry and weren't sure how long you were going to be gone. Order anything you like," he told Brigit. "It's our treat."

"In that case," she said, "A'll have a bottle of whiskey."

"Whoa," Max said, blinking back surprise and a decent dash of shock. "Good thing you're driving, Roz."

"It wouldn't matter," Roz assured him, and then tilted her head in Brigit's direction. "Really? At this hour?"

Brigit refused to be shamed. "He told me tae order anything A like. A like whiskey."

"In that case, how about a glass instead of a—"

Brigit stiffened as if insulted, then snapped to her feet and started across the deck. An instant later, everyone else was on their feet, too. "Wait!" Mara said. "If you want a bottle, you can have one! Really! We don't mind."

"It's not that," Roz said, taking off after the changeling. "She's on a mission. I'll explain later."

"OK," Mara said, in an anxious tone, and then pressed up on her tippy-toes to wave at Brigit's rapidly receding back. "Bye, Bridge! It was nice meeting you! See you again soon!"

By the time Roz caught up with the changeling, she was already ensconced in the back of the truck. "North," she said," pointing toward the road. "It's heading north."

"Got it," Roz said, and then climbed into the cab. As she fired up the engine, she shouted, "You could've said goodbye to them, you know."

"Why?"

"It would've made them happy," Roz said.

"Not my concern," Brigit said, in a tone like a shrug.

"All right then," Roz said, as she peeled out of the parking lot and down the highway. "It would've made me happy."

"A'hm not responsible fer ur happiness, either," the changeling said. "Ye've got tae find that on yer own. Now give this thing some gas!"

Not only was the wyrm fast, but the local weather conditions were on its side. Fifteen minutes into the chase, it disappeared into a resident patch of marine layer. Brigit swore like a Scottish sailor, but Roz took the loss in stride.

"It's OK," she said, glad for the excuse to slow down on the twisty, intermittently foggy two-lane road. "If the wyrm's flight path holds true, then it's either heading for San Francisco or the headlands. That's where we were heading today anyway, right? Remember Plan A? We've lost nothing."

The changeling grumbled. "And what if tha wyrm's flight plan isn't true? What then?"

"Then we lose the day," Roz said. "But we still go home knowing more about the wyrm than we did when we woke up today. Right?"

Another grumble, more grudging than the first. "Possibly. But A'hm still not happy about losing it."

Roz was tempted to offer up a dose of false sympathy, but then realized that the dragon would neither grasp nor respond to the sarcasm. So she kept her mouth shut instead and made a beeline for Golden Gate Park.

Three hours later, they found themselves deep in the park's eucalyptus-scented inner, wild reaches. Roz was hungry, thirsty, and moderately discouraged. Brigit was in hunter mode, and inscrutable. So far, they hadn't seen any sign of the wyrm. They had, however, come across an abandoned homeless encampment; a black-tailed doe and her twin fawns; and most recently, a pair of teenagers in an advanced stage of undress.

"A well-made lad," Brigit noted, as both teens went diving buck-naked into the brush.

Roz shook her head as if to dislodge a thought or image that was trying to take hold. "I don't think I'll ever get used to you ogling men."

"When in Rome," Brigit replied.

Her insouciant attitude rankled Roz. "What's the difference between you being with a man and that wyrm being with one?"

Brigit flared her nostrils at Roz—a display of mild amusement for her prudishness. "Tha wyrm takes its would-be lovers without their consent and mauls them tae death because it cannot complete or maintain a Change. My lovers have all been volunteers," she added, "and while they may walk away with a few nicks and bruises, A never cause any lasting harm."

Hardly a scintillating self-endorsement, Roz thought. But she didn't really enjoy talking about sex—not with Mara, not with her mother, and definitely not with a dragon. So rather than continue in this vein, she shifted the conversation back in a more comfortable direction. "I still say we should've tried harder to check out the grove where the wyrm attacked his second victim. We could've found a clue to help us in our search. Instead, we're stuck combing the entire interior of a National Park for that messed-up bat-winged fright."

"Too risky," Brigit said, which was exactly what she had said earlier. "That grove is still taped off as a crime scene. It attracts a fair amount of attention—none of which we can trust. In case ye've forgotten, we're not the only ones looking for that fright."

"I know, I know," Roz said, conceding the argument for

a second time. "I'm just hungry, I guess. I get impatient on an empty stomach. Any chance we can put our search for the wyrm on hold until I find a—" Hotdog cart, was what she meant to say. But before she could get the words out, they happened into a clearing that offered them a spectacular view of the park and she forgot everything else. She stood stock-still for a moment, soaking up the panorama. Then she breathed a rejuvenated sigh and said, "Hard to believe there's a city just beyond that tree-line, right?"

"Not really," Brigit replied. "Tha's not wind A'm hearing. And tha's not clean air A'm smelling. But A must admit, this view is novel enough."

"What makes it even more amazing that the park is all manmade," Roz said. "Back in the 1800s, this entire area was nothing but sand and shore dunes. Then William Hammond Hall and John McLaren got together and decided to turn it into this one-of-a-kind paradise."

"MacLaren?" Brigit warbled. "A should've known. Scots have a rare respect for the earth and growing things. Not like tha Irish. Did ye know that Ireland was mostly forest at one time? Now you can count the number of trees you see in a mile on one hand in most places."

"You've been to Ireland?"

"Oh, ai. A lived there fer a spell in my younger days," the changeling replied. "The island has some lovely rivers. But every time A found a waterway A liked, some fat-headed Irishman with a sword felt compelled to drive me out. That got tedious after a while so A moved on to Scotland. The Scots are so much more sensible about—"

She stopped in mid-breath and cocked her head to the left. At the same time, she raised a hand for silence. For one suspense-filled moment, the only thing Roz could hear was the sound of her own blood coursing through her ears. Then the muffled sounds of crunching and scraping reached her. An image of a dog gnawing on a fresh butcher bone came to mind. An instant later, the image shifted into a realization.

They'd found the wyrm.

Brigit had already begun to stalk the sounds. Unable to stop herself, Roz followed. As they waded through the brush like long-legged herons hunting frogs, the crunching and scraping grew louder and more enthusiastic. That mental image of a dog gnawing on a bone morphed into an image of a dog-sized serpent with wings gnawing on a headless corpse. She offered up a silent prayer: please don't let it be human.

Roz was so intent on her own thoughts that she didn't realize that Brigit was Changing until she shifted from two long legs to four stubbier ones. A heartbeat later, she had a stretchy neck and tail too, and was charging through the bush with a speed and agility that Roz could not match. First the dragon vanished from sight. Then she passed beyond earshot, too. Fortunately, she left a trail that a toddler could follow. As Roz made her way down that battered and bruised track, she stumbled over a mess of darkly gleaming remains. An instant later, the smell of blood rose up from the carcass like a host of flies. The smell gagged her. The possibility of the remains being human brought the threat of tears to her eyes. She forced herself to look anyway—because that was the only decent thing to do. To her vast relief, the carcass was recognizable as a deer.

A few yards later, the trail came to an abrupt end. There were signs of a struggle: freshly turned leaves and detritus, claw-marks in the exposed earth. Brigit was coiled up beneath a tree, panting a little. The ground beneath her hindquarters was an alarming shade of red. Roz let out a curse and started toward her, saying, "Are you all right," only to skid to a stop as the patch of red sprouted a head and hissed at her. Its face was narrow, almost birdlike. It even had a beak.

"Oh," she said. "I see now. You're the other one."

The wyrm hissed again and tried to scrabble free of Brigit's backside. The vehemence of its struggles, futile though they were, impressed Roz. She shared a look with the dragon and said, "Feisty little shit, aye?"

"*Ai,*" Brigit replied, and then abruptly deepened their mind-link. The next thing Roz knew, she could sense not only the dragon's thoughts but the wyrm's as well. Its mind was a maelstrom of fear, confusion, and fury. When a passing breeze brought the smell of blood back to its nose, it grew excited, too, and redoubled its efforts to escape. That irritated Brigit.

"*Be still!*" she commanded. "*Elsewise, I will crush you and eat your kill.*"

The wyrm went immediately limp. Roz got the sense that it was more concerned for its supper than its own well-being.

"*Better,*" Brigit said. "*Now tell me ur name if ye have one.*"

"*Saidhe,*" the wyrm replied, sullen as a teenager. "*I am Saidhe. You go now. I want eat.*"

"*Questions first,*" Brigit said and then shifted, giving the wyrm an inch more of breathing room. "*Where is the black wyrm—The one who preys on humans?*" When the wyrm did not reply, she directed its attention to Roz. "*Human. Like her. Understand?*"

Saidhe hissed, projecting resentment. "*I know human.*"

"*You prey on them, too?*"

"*No! That is the other's doing.*" The accompanying image was of the fright that Roz had confronted back in Woodside. "*That one is disturbed. That one has—urges.*"

"*Where is that one now?*" Brigit asked,

Saidhe hissed. "*I do not know. Go away now.*"

Brigit remained unmoved. *"Not just yet. Do ye know where can we find the other?"*

"No! I hide from that one. You let me go. I hunger."

"If A release ye," Brigit said, *"will you fly away?"*

The wyrm's mind-set turned suddenly sly. *"What will you promise me to stay?"*

"A will let ye keep ur kill."

Saidhe considered the offer for a moment and then broadcast its decision. *"Then I will stay until the kill is gone."*

To Roz's surprise, Brigit made no effort to haggle for more time with the wyrm. Instead, she rumbled her approval and shifted her hindquarters. As soon as Saidhe was free, it bolted for the carcass and began eating as fast as it could. Roz thanked her lucky stars—once for not being able to see the frenzy from her vantage point and then again when the gnashing, crunching, and slavering came to an end. Afterward, the wyrm rolled in the detritus where its kill had lain and then shook itself—a shudder that started at its head and rippled all the way down to the tip of its scaly tail. There was a bulge in its midsection now, a bulge that it did not seem to notice until it tried to launch itself skyward. When it belly-flopped instead, it let out a surprised honk and then swiveled its head in Brigit's direction.

"You knew I would not be able to fly if I ate it all. That is why you did not take it from me."

"You are smart for a wyrm," Brigit noted. *"While you digest, tell me about your clutch and where it was hatched."*

"What will you give me to do so?"

Brigit bared her teeth. *"Yer life."*

Saidhe snorted, twin puffs of irritation. *"You bargain with things that are not yours to give."*

"On tha contrary. A bargain with things that are mine fer tha taking. So if ye want tae go on living, ye'll mind urself and answer my questions."

The wyrm snorted again, venting disgruntled resignation. Then it curled up around its distended belly and lobbed a sullen thought at Brigit. *"What would you know?"*

"Tell me of your clutch. Where did it hatch?"

"We hatched twice," Saidhe said, a puzzling claim. *"All I remember from the first time we came alive is snow and cold and the world collapsing all around us. The second time we awoke, we were underground and wearing hurt-things."* It projected an image of something that looked like a horse-collar. *"These things gave us great pain when we displeased our keepers. In spite of this, most of my clutch-mates were content to remain in that underground place, for there was always plenty to eat and places to play. But the black one and I longed to see the sky again, so I chewed off his hurt-thing and he chewed off mine and away we flew.*

"Why does your human stare at me?"

The question startled Roz, and it took her a moment to realize that she had indeed been staring at a curious little patch at the top of the wyrm's throat. At first, she thought it was gore because it was shiny and slick, but on second and third glance she decided otherwise because the patch was perfectly symmetrical.

"She has something right here", she told Brigit, touching her own throat in approximately the same area. "It doesn't look natural."

When Brigit relayed the thought to Saidhe, the wyrm traded the menacing gleam in its eyes for something more resentful. *"It is another thing the keepers made us wear. This thing does not hurt. But I still do not like it."*

"These keepers sound like a bunch of creeps," Roz remarked aloud. "Does it know who they are?"

"Dragons," Saidhe replied, when Brigit relayed the question. *"Like you, only different."*

A swarm of images followed the thought: an astonishing jumble of dragons and dragons-in-human-form. Roz recognized one man-drake in particular: a cloaked, hairy figure who walked with a pronounced limp.

"That's the drake from the cruise!" she exclaimed. "He's the one who got into a limo with Drago Channing in New York."

When Brigit relayed an image of the drake to the wyrm, it let out a lukewarm warble. "*That is Dyadya. He treated us better than the others. But he still made us feel pain when we disregarded him.*"

"*Tha Great One believes that yer keepers are on tha hunt for ye and the other,*" Brigit said. "*She thinks ye should come with us.*"

Saidhe bared its teeth and hissed. "*The Great One drove me away, even after I offered her tribute. She told me to go away and never come back.*"

"*That's because She didna want ye tae lead yer keepers tae her lair. She's flown since then. We can bring ye tae her in a way that willna compromise her safety.*"

"*She told me to go away and never come back.*"

The insides of Brigit's nostrils flared an irritated shade of red, but she strove to keep the tenor of her thoughts neutral. "*We cannot protect ye if we dunna know where ye are.*"

"*I do not need your protection!*" The wyrm declared, rearing back to make itself look larger. "*I am fast, fast as the wind! I will fly far, far away and protect myself!*"

Brigit growled, a frustrated sound that no sane creature wanted to be on the wrong end of. In an aside to Roz, she groused, "*Feckin' stupid wyrms. No wonder the drakes used hurt-things on them.*"

"Now, now," Roz said, hoping to shut down that kind of thinking before the wyrm picked up on it. "That attitude isn't going to get us anywhere. Let's try honey instead of vinegar."

"*Vinegar? Have ye lost yer fecking mind? What's vinegar got tae do with this?*"

Roz suppressed a chuckle to and instead, said, "Just ask it if it would like me to remove that patch."

When Brigit relayed the offer, Saidhe snuffled in Roz's direction—a suspicious display if Roz had ever seen one. *"What does she want in return?"*

"Nothing but the patch," Roz said.

Saidhe sniffed again, winnowing the air for traces of treachery. Then, almost grudgingly, it extended its neck, exposing the patch. *"If she tries to trick me, I will bite her head off."*

Roz's faith in the honey-versus-vinegar axiom took a sharp, sudden dip. But her trust in Brigit and the dragon's ability to protect her remained intact, so she started toward the wyrm. She walked slowly, holding her hands up and open. "It's OK," she said, as she approached. "I mean you no harm."

"You should not talk," Brigit advised. *"The sound of yer voice agitates it."*

Great. Just great.

Up close, Saidhe reeked of blood and rancid meat and offal mixed with hints of sulfur. But its eyes were quite pretty, pale gold flecked with obsidian. And despite its fierce expression, it could not stifle a nervous tic on the underside of its jaw. Only then did it occur to Roz that the wyrm might be afraid, too. The thought calmed her.

"It's OK," she said again, as she extended a hand, "I won't hurt you."

The patch peeled off without incident or upset. It was slightly larger than a Post-it note. Its backside was uniformly sticky. As Roz examined it, trying to divine its purpose, the wyrm warbled.

"It says having it off feels the same as having it on."

"Good to know," Roz said. She folded the patch in half and tucked it into a pocket. "I'll have Max take a look at it. Maybe he can give us some insight into what it's doing on a wyrm's neck."

Brigit rumbled approvingly and then fixed her foggy gaze on the wyrm again. *"Are ye sure ye will nae come with us?"*

"I will not," Saidhe replied, drawing itself into a compact

knot and averting its eyes. *"You cannot force me."*

"Drakes use force," Brigit said haughtily. *"Drakena use reason. If ye will not listen tae reason, then we have no use for ye anyway. Hopefully, your clutch-mate is smarter than you."*

The wyrm disparaged that hope with a hiss. *"That one is stupid! It knows nothing beyond its urges."*

"Then tell us where we can find it! Tell us, and A'll give ye a gold coin fer ur hoard." The wyrm wavered between loyalty, uncertainty, and greed. Brigit pressured it from a different angle. *"Or maybe ye'd like yer keepers tae find it first."*

Saidhe hissed again, an eruption of spite and despair. Then it went limp with resignation. *"That one is restless, and spends most of its time ranging between the mountains and the sea. But on moonless nights, it can be found in the hills beyond the orange metal sea-span. There is good hunting there, and many places to sleep. I believe it may be starting to build a lair."*

"And now," the wyrm added, glaring at Brigit, *"you are going to drive it away. Because it has—urges."*

"Perhaps," Brigit said, cold as a San Francisco fog. *"Perhaps not. At this point, our only aim is tae save it—and you—from yer keepers."*

"Save us?" Saidhe mocked the thought with a snort. *"Dyadya used to talk about how he saved us. He said we would all still be dead if not for him. But he kept us confined in a place without a sky. He hurt us for having fun. How is that better than being dead? How was that saving us?"*

The bitter diatribe rattled Roz. She was about to say, "We wouldn't do that," when Brigit stopped her with a thought: *"Dunna make promises ye canna keep."*

The wyrm snorted again, making it clear that its suspicions had been confirmed. *"Save the black one if you must, for it is disturbed. But leave me out of your plans. I am going to fly far, far away. You will never see me again."*

CHAPTER 22

Aurora was upstairs packing for her Portland trip. The conference wasn't until next week, but the four cups of black coffee that she'd had over the course of the afternoon insisted that she keep busy. She'd cleaned the house already, roasted a chicken for dinner, and run out to the barn at least a dozen times to check on the Great One. Next up on the docket was an evening power walk.

The rumble of a pick-up truck rolling up the driveway caught her attention. Shortly thereafter, the front door creaked open and then slammed shut. "Hey, Mom!" Roz shouted. "We're back! Are you home?"

"Hello!" Aurora shouted back. "Be right there!"

In the minute or so that it took her to hustle down the stairs, Roz and Brigit managed to eviscerate her fridge. Brigit was scooping day-old tuna salad out of a container with her fingers and chowing it down. Roz was nibbling at leftover chicken and sipping white wine. There was a jar of pickled eggs on the counter, too, as well as a package of deli ham, two blocks of cheese, and an open can of sardines. Roz looked up and smiled as Aurora joined them, but Brigit just kept on eating.

"Goodness," Aurora said, in lieu of lecturing them on the perils of a low fiber diet. "Did you guys visit a pot dispensary on your way home?"

"Nuh-uh," Roz said, sawing off a chunk of cheddar for herself. "Just hungry. Didn't get a chance to eat all day." She held up a freshly opened bottle of sauvignon blanc and added, "You want some of this?"

"Yes, I'd love a glass," Aurora replied. "Anything to cut the caffeine a little."

"How much did you drink?" Roz asked.

"An entire pot," Aurora replied, wincing at the confession. "I had to do something to keep the Dreaming at bay. But enough about my day," she added, as Roz handed her a glass. "How did your hunt go?"

"Mixed bag," Roz said, between bites and sips. "We had a close encounter with the wyrm that's been killing people, but it took off before we could subdue it. While we were trying to pick up its trail, we stumbled onto its clutch-mate, Saidhe. That one seemed fairly sane—"

"Fer a wyrm," Brigit interjected, and then waved a drumstick in Aurora's direction. "This chicken's a wee bit dry. Do ye have any whiskey tae help it go down?"

On some other occasion, the blunt critique of her cooking might've stung Aurora's pride. At the moment, however, she was too wired and distracted to take offense. "In there," she said, with a dismissive gesture at the liquor cabinet. Then she returned the whole of her attention to her daughter.

"We tried to convince Saidhe to come with us," Roz said, "but it didn't want anything to do with us thanks to the Great One's previous scare tactics. Before we parted company, though, it did allow us to relieve it of this." She fished a snack-sized latex rectangle from her back pocket and set it on a napkin, then slid the napkin toward Aurora. "What does that look like to you?"

Aurora studied the rectangle for a moment and then flipped it over with a fingernail. As she did so, she saw that it had been folded in half.

"Is the bottom side sticky?" she asked.

"Yep.

Aurora flipped the rectangle again and then scowled. "It's

too big," she said, "but otherwise it looks like a birth control patch to me."

"That's what I thought, too," Roz said. "But why a sexually immature wyrm need something like that?"

"Could it have gotten on the wyrm by accident?" Aurora asked.

Roz denied the possibility with a sour shake of her head. "That was drake handiwork. According to Saidhe, there's a whole conspiracy of them. They somehow got their hands on a clutch of wyrms and are holding them captive in some underground compound. They're using shock collars to control them."

"So maybe the patch is a form of control, too," Aurora mused. "A time-released sedative or psychotropic drug. That could explain the rogue wyrm's behavior."

"But not Saidhe's," Roz was quick to counter. "Why would the patch make one of them crazy and not the other?"

"I don't know," Aurora said, and then snapped her fingers as an idea occurred to her. "But I know someone who might. He has connections to a pharmacology lab. He could have the patch analyzed for us."

"Would that someone happen to be Charles?" Roz said, in that smirking, sing-song tone that smacked of hazing.

"It would," Aurora said, determined not to let her daughter pull that chain anymore. "And as it happens, I have a lunch date with him tomorrow."

"Is that tha man who gave ye tha jar that belonged tae tha Great One?" Brigit asked, working the words around a logjam of half-masticated eggs.

"It is," Aurora said primly.

"Did ye ask him where he got tha vase?"

"I'm going to do that tomorrow—when I see him for lunch. I could give the patch to him then, too."

Brigit rejected the idea with a fiery shake of her mane. "I dunna like the smell of it. Tha man's too much of a cypher."

Aurora skewered the changeling with a look and then half-turned to eyeball Roz, who had suddenly lost her appetite. "Well," she asked archly. "What do you think?"

Roz scrunched up her face the same way she used to as a child when Aurora tried to feed her eggplant. In an equally conflicted tone, she said, "I dunno, Mom, I'm kind of with Brigit on this one. I mean, what do we know about Charles?"

"Quite a lot, actually," Aurora said. "We talk about everything. He cares about the same things I do."

"Do you trust him?" Roz asked.

"Absolutely," Aurora said, as if she were taking an oath.

But that, apparently, wasn't good enough for Roz. She made another face, washed it away with a gulp of wine, and then started to pace. "I'm sure Charles is an amazing human being," she said, "but like Bridge says, he's an unknown in our book and that makes us uncomfortable. I'm going to ask Max to analyze the patch. We've known him forever and he's as trustworthy as the day is long."

Although Aurora couldn't argue with her daughter's decision or the reasoning behind it, it left her feeling slightly out of sorts—displaced, superfluous, supplanted by a whiskey-guzzling dragon. She thought about digging her heels in just on principle, but then realized that she was just being petty. All mothers had to let go of their children at some point.

"Well then," she said, raising her glass in a mock-toast, "that's settled. What's next on the agenda?"

"I'm going to go and call Max," she said, already heading toward her room with her cell phone in hand. "After that, I'm going to go outside and practice the Dragon Form for a while. I need to get back into fighting form."

"And what about you?" Aurora asked the changeling, as Roz disappeared from sight.

The counter looked like ground zero now: nothing but containers had survived Brigit's appetite. The changeling surveyed the wreckage with rueful eyes, then looked up and said, "Is there anythin' else ta eat? Jumpin' back and forth between shapes always leaves me famished."

"I suppose I could thaw a steak or two for you," Aurora replied. "It would only take a few minutes if I tossed them in the microwave."

Brigit curled her upper lip. "A dunna like the way meat tastes when it comes out of tha thing."

"Then I guess you're out of luck," Aurora said matter-of-factly. "I'm going to pick up a side of beef for the Great One before I leave for Portland, but that's still a few days out."

"In that case—" The changeling polished off the rest of the Dewar's in a one massive glug, tossed the empty into the sink, and then started toward the patio door. "Tell Roz not tae wait up. A might be late."

"Where are you going?" Aurora asked, purely out of reflex.

Brigit grinned, a toothy display. "A'm not in tha habit of sharin' my comings and goings with others. But because yer Roz's mum and bonded with the Great One, A'll make an exception just this once. A'm going fishing in tha lake that's up tha road from here."

"It's a reservoir, not a lake," Aurora said, flustered into inanity by the drakena's reproach. "Lexington Reservoir."

"Whatever," Brigit said, a response that she had clearly acquired from Roz. "It's filled with tasty fish."

"Oh. OK," Aurora said, and then reached for her wine glass again only to be struck by an afterthought. "Just be careful."

Halfway out the door already, Brigit stopped and glanced

back at Aurora. Her eyes were narrowed; her mouth, a flat line. "Do A strike ye as the careless type?"

"Not particularly," Aurora replied, refusing to be intimidated. "But the other day, I heard a local deejay talking about a Nessie sighting—quote—in our own backyard."

"What of it?"

"I'm not the only one who listens to the radio."

The changeling thought about that for a moment, and then nodded approvingly. At the same time, her expression relaxed. "A hear you," she said. "A will be mindful while A hunt."

"Good," Aurora said. "Because if I get a call from Animal Control, I'm going to deny knowing you."

"Funny," Brigit said dryly, and then continued on her way. As the patio door closed behind her, Roz stepped back into the kitchen.

"Where's she going?" she asked, as she refilled her empty wine glass.

"Fishing," Aurora replied, and then slid her glass across the counter. "Me, too, please."

Roz grabbed the glass only to have it slip through her fingers. An instant later, it hit the tiled floor and shattered. "Shit!" she said, and made a beeline for the garage. A moment later, she returned with the vacuum cleaner.

"Here, let me," Aurora said, before her daughter could get to work. "If I don't move a little, the Dreaming will catch up with me again."

"That must be kind of weird, huh?" Roz said, shouting over the vacuum's roar and the chinkety-clink of glass pieces being sucked into the machine. "Where do you go when you're in it?"

"So far, it's only taken me to the past," Aurora said. "I don't know if that's Quetzalcoatl feeling nostalgic or the Dreaming acting on its own or some combination thereof. Whatever it is, it's interesting. And exhausting." She switched the vacuum off.

As she emptied the cylinder into the garbage bin, she added, "I have to say, I'm looking forward to my trip to Portland. Five days of complete and utter normalcy!"

Roz cracked a wry half-smile. "I'm sorry, Mom. I know that all of this dragon stuff hit you pretty hard. How are you doing with it? Honestly."

"Well," Aurora said, after giving the question a moment's thought, "the good news is, I'm not reeling from the shock anymore. I can admit that dragons do in fact exist without rolling my eyes. And the idea of dragon magic doesn't freak me out as much so long as I don't dwell on the particulars. But— every time I think I've come to grips with everything that needs to be handled, something new pops up."

"Such as?" Roz prompted, even as she handed Aurora a new, brimming wine glass. Aurora took a sip to rinse a tickle from her throat, and then continued.

"Well, this afternoon for instance, while I was out checking on the Great One, it suddenly dawned me that she's here for good. You know, for ever and ever, amen? This may sound whiny and I suppose it is, but the fact is, I'm not prepared to house a dragon in my property indefinitely. I don't know how to take care of Her. I don't know what She needs. And what if somebody sees Her?"

"I wouldn't worry about that," Roz said. "From what I've seen so far, dragons are kind of like hobbits: if they don't want to be seen, they probably won't be."

The glib reassurance made Aurora bristle. "That's not funny, Roz! Quetzalcoatl isn't some barn cat that can be easily overlooked. If someone stumbles onto Her, who do I protect— Her or the someone? In either case, how far should I go? The Great One and I share a bond, but it's not as intense as the one between you and Brigit. I just don't know if I could harm another human being to keep Her presence a secret."

"I've struggled with the same concerns," Roz admitted, in a far less cavalier tone. "And to tell you the truth, I've got no answers. I simply have to believe that when the time comes, I'll do the right thing. I think that's all any of us can do."

"I suppose," Aurora said, a grudging concession. "I guess I'll just rest easier when we put all of this drake conspiracy business behind us. Speaking of which, what did Max say? Will he analyze the patch for us?"

"Yeah, he said he'd do it," Roz said, "but the lab is being audited this week, so he won't be able to run the tests until the inspectors finish up and clear out."

"Fair enough," Aurora said.

"Maybe," Roz said, "but I don't want to wait that long for the information. So—" She tugged two white envelopes from her back pocket and presented one to Aurora. "Here's what I'm thinking. We give one half of the patch to my guy and the other to yours. The first one to get back to us wins a prize. Plus, we'll have two sets of results. We can compare and contrast. What do you say?"

In reply, Aurora tucked the envelope in her own back pocket. "You got a deal," she said, then gestured at the trashed countertop and added, "But only if you clean up after your dragon. They should call her Messy instead of Nessie."

Roz laughed and folded Aurora into a hug. "I love you, Mom. I've really missed hanging out in the kitchen with you."

That touched off a tidal wave of warm-and-fuzzies in Aurora. She gave Roz a squeeze and said, "I've missed you, too, baby." Then, hoping to ward off a sudden crush of sentimental tears, she added, "But at least I haven't had to put up with Aldo. I haven't missed him at all!"

Roz laughed again—a liberated guffaw. "I know, right? I can't believe I actually thought he was Mr. Right." She eased out of their embrace and began gathering up discarded containers. "I also can't believe you thought I was pregnant!"

The sip of wine that Aurora had just swallowed almost came shooting back out through her nose. "Yeah, well," she said, as her abused sinuses sizzled, "you have to admit that your behavior was damn peculiar. The theory suited the situation. I'm just glad I was wrong."

"First time I've ever heard you say that!" Roz teased.

"First time I've ever been wrong," Aurora teased back, and then started for the patio. "I'm off to check on Quetzalcoatl. If I'm not back in twenty, come and get me. Bring a wheelbarrow cuz I'll be dead to the world."

"Will do," Roz said. "And if you're not passed out, you can practice the Dragon Form with me. We need to be prepared for anything, right?"

"Right," Aurora said, and continued on her way. As she headed for the barn, the tender glow that Roz had ignited in her morphed into a similar sentiment for the drakena. When she realized this, she broke into an amazed smile. How much her attitude had changed in the past few days! That had to be a kind of dragon magic, too!

CHAPTER 23

The bistro was quiet save for the soft, jazzy stylings that were being piped in from the bar. The last vestiges of the lunchtime crowd were lingering over their cappuccinos and checks. Charles spied on these people from his booth at the back of the dining room, feeling nothing but contempt for their soft, selfish lives. Did they care that whole swathes of jungle had been mowed down so industrial agriculture could grow their coffee in full-sun? No. Did they lose so much as a wink of sleep over the resulting loss of habitat? Not likely. He bared his teeth in a feral grin, projecting an equally feral thought: enjoy yourselves now, you wasteful fools! Because things were going to change in a big way when the drakes reclaimed the world!

The thought of his co-conspirators wiped the grin from his face. For while he supported their ascendancy whole-heartedly, working with them toward that goal was rapidly wearing his nerves down to twitchy little nubs. Tezcatlipoca wanted his every order, no matter how complex, to be fulfilled instantly— and bellowed threats when his expectations were not met. In contrast, Grishka was as patient as an iceberg and did nothing without consulting the Divine first. And Drogo Channing? Ugh! That vile-tempered drake had been doing his best to make everybody miserable from the moment he turned up on Charles' doorstep. In the field, he kept his plans to himself and then excoriated Charles for failing to read his mind. At home, he constantly tried to dominate Grishka even though Grishka slyly mocked him for his efforts. Charles spent most of his meager downtime outside so he wouldn't have to walk on the minefield of eggshells that the drakes had laid down. And he dared not complain to Tezcatlipoca about the situation because he had yet not found his MIA sister and the Great One would be savage with incredulity. How could such a huge, ungainly creature simply disappear? How far could one who had long outgrown her wings possibly have gotten? What kind of hunter was he? Charles didn't need to hear such questions voiced. He'd asked them all himself a hundred times already.

The bistro's front door swung open. An instant later, Aurora strode in, backlit by a flash of afternoon sun. She moved with confidence and grace, like an athlete half her age. He could have caught her attention with a wave but chose instead to sit back and watch as she strode over to the hostess's station. Her cheeks were flushed; her hair, tousled. The smile she shared with the hostess positively glinted. As the two women turned toward his table, he popped to his feet like an anxious bridegroom.

"There you are!" she said, as they approached. "I didn't see you hiding in the corner."

He meant only to take her hand or maybe give her the briefest of hugs. But the closer she got, the more alluring she became. As soon as the hostess turned her back to them, he pulled her close for a kiss that left both of them flustered afterward.

"My!" she said, flushing with what he could only hope was pleasure. "You sure know how to make a girl feel welcome!"

"I'm sorry," he said, as he ushered her into her side of the booth. "I usually despise public displays of affection, but I was just so taken by the sight of you, I couldn't help myself."

She laughed, self-consciously it seemed. He liked that she didn't know how attractive she was. "It's been awhile since I've overwhelmed anyone's sensibilities," she said, as she sat down. "But I must admit: I'm happy to see you, too. It's been awhile, hasn't it?"

"It has," he replied, then scooped up her hand and stroked it like a kitten. "Too long."

A waiter appeared with menus, glasses, and a bottle of wine. "I hope you don't mind a second presumption," he said, as the waiter showed the bottle off.

Her eyes widened with surprise as she read the label. "A 2007 Monte Bello! What's the occasion?"

"Lunch with you," he said.

The waiter poured for them and then departed without asking if they were ready to order. Charles made a mental note to tip him well. He slid one glass her way and then hoisted the other. "To you," he said. "And to many more outings like this."

"I'll drink to that," she said, and then did so. The smile that crept across her face as she savored the sip made him want to kiss her again. "Does this mean you're done with the project that's been eating up all your time?"

"Almost," he said, trying to give the word more finality than it actually had. "And it can't happen soon enough as far as I'm concerned. My associates are driving me crazy."

"Associates can do that," she said sympathetically.

He reclaimed her hand, turning it palm-side up so he could nuzzle her pulse-point. "Nice fragrance," he said. "Is it new?"

She rewarded his perceptiveness with a throaty little purr. "It's called 'Flight'. My daughter bought it for me."

Just like that, the happy little hum in his head skirled to a stop. "You have a daughter?" he said, too surprised to keep the thought to himself. "How is that possible? I've never heard you mention her."

"Really?" Aurora said, looking surprised in turn. "How curious. I feel like I talk about her all the time. Her name is Rosalyn. She's bright and beautiful and good at everything she decides to do. It could be that I didn't mention her because she was in Europe on an extended vacation and talking about her made me miss her too much. Or," she added, catching and holding his gaze so he could see the genuine vulnerability in her eyes, "it could be that I didn't say anything because I wanted you to think of me as a woman rather than a mom."

That made sense. Talking about something you missed only made you miss it more. And it pleased him to think that she had wanted to make just the right impression on him because he felt the same exact way.

"It doesn't matter to me if you have children, Aurora," he said, capturing her hand once again. "When I look at you, all I can see is the most amazing woman on the planet." He planted a kiss on her knuckles and then gave voice to an impulse. "How about we skip lunch and go back to your place for—" He gave his eyebrows a suggestive waggle. "Dessert."

Regret flashed across her face: a heart-stopping look. "I'm sorry," she said. His cheeks flared hot and red as if she'd just slapped him. He almost didn't hear her when she added, "My daughter has friends over and I'm just not ready to have dessert while they're downstairs. How about we go to your place instead?"

His heartbeat kicked back in—a wild, ecstatic rhythm. He was so thrilled to realize that his proposal had been deflected rather than rejected, he almost agreed to her counter-offer. But even as the words flooded into his mouth, an image of his dragon-trashed cabin, reeking of pool scum and Drogo's testosterone-laden musk, came to mind. That wouldn't do, no, not ever.

"I have company, too," he said sadly.

"Then maybe we should just get a room," she said.

His jaw started to drop; he caught it just in time and then wrung his gob-smacked smile into something closer to overjoyed. "You are the most amazing woman," he said. "I wish I had met you sooner."

She laughed, a nervous little titter, and then fanned herself with a hand like a flustered Southern belle. "Oh, my. How you do go on," she said. After a dramatic pause, she added, "No. Really. Go on."

The joke relaxed him. "I like you, Aurora. If more people were like you, I'd—well, I'd like more people. Yes, let's get a room. Let's go someplace nice like the Fairmont. We can make a day of it—and if we're lucky, a night."

"I can't do an overnighter," she said ruefully. "I'm leaving for Portland in the morning and I haven't finished packing yet."

"Ah," he said. "Another convention?"

She nodded, and then, in a dangling tone, added, "You could come with me. I won't be working all of the time."

"Sorry," he said, trying not to oversell the lie. But if he never attended another science fiction and fantasy Grand Ball in this lifetime, he'd still be able to say that he'd been to one too many. "I'm on call. How about I pick you up at the airport on Sunday and take you to dinner?"

"Sorry," she said, "but I don't get in until late. And after four days of nonstop mingling, I really like to get in my car and drive to clear my head. 280 is great for that. But I'm free all day on Monday," she hastened to add. "You could come over for lunch. I'll make sure my daughter and her friends aren't around."

He perked up, a whole-body rebirth. Even his fingertips felt more energized. Amazing, he thought, what a little hope could do. "I'd like that," he said, and then started as his phone buzzed in his pocket. He pulled it out, hoping against hope that it wasn't who he thought it was only to be disappointed. "Sorry," he said, as the phone buzzed again, "but I have to take this."

"Go on," she said, shooing him away. "I'll just help myself to more wine."

"Thanks," he said, and then stepped out into the brilliance

of another sunny California day. "Yeah," he said. squinting like some subterranean creature that had just been dragged topside. "I'm listening."

"Sundown. Marin Headlands. A place called Spencer Battery," Drogo said. "Get rid of any humans who might be lingering there and wait for us. Bring whatever you think you might need to subdue and transport at least one wyrm."

"Will do," he said, unnecessarily, since the drake had already hung up.

"What's up?" Aurora asked, when he returned to the table. "You look preoccupied."

"Duty calls," he said, looking at her with a mixture of longing and regret. "I've got to go."

"Such a shame," she said, with a surprisingly wicked gleam in her eye. "I was so looking forward to dessert." As he reeled from the cock-tease, she signaled the waiter, saying, "Let's get you something to-go before you go riding off into battle."

"Many thanks, lovely lady," he said, taking the opportunity to plant a courtly kiss on her hand. "Unfortunately, my time is no longer my own."

The waiter arrived with menus in hand. Aurora said, "There's been a change of plans. Just bring me the check and a cork for the bottle, please."

Charles started to protest, but Aurora wouldn't hear of it. "I'm drinking most of it so I'm paying for it." As she pulled her wallet out of her purse, an open white envelope slid out. As it hit the table, it semi-disgorged an opaque square. The sight tickled his curiosity.

"What's that?" he asked.

"Oh," she said, one of those stretchy sounds that often accompany a long story. "It's just something I was going to ask you to have analyzed for me. But I don't want to bother you when you're so busy. I'll get it done elsewhere."

"No, wait," he said, catching her forearm as she went to tap the square back into the envelope. "What is it? What's it got to do with you?"

"My daughter's idiot boyfriend is a CSI freak and he talked her into checking out that terrible crime scene in Golden Gate Park—you know, the one where that poor man was mauled to death? While they were poking around, they found this--"She tapped the patch with a forefinger. "—stuck in some brush. She wanted to go to the police with it, but he insisted on having it checked out first, because, quote unquote, 'If it's not relevant to the case, then they'll ding us for trespassing on a crime scene.'

"So they came to me."

"Because—?" he said, inviting her to fill in the blank.

"Because I know people who know things," she said, "or who can find things out for me. I like my books to be authentic."

"Ah, of course," he said, jarred out of his hydroplaning thoughts. "You're a writer, you have sources."

"Bingo," she said. "And I can consult with someone else about this little conundrum."

"No, please," he hastened to say. "I'd like to do this for you. It won't be a problem. Really."

"Are you sure?"

In response, he snatched the envelope up, tucked it into his shirt pocket and then patted it as if he were making a promise from the heart. "It'll take me a day or two to get the results," he said, "but I'll definitely have something for you by the time you get back from Portland. What time did you say you were getting in?"

"The plane lands ten-thirtyish," she said. "I should be home by midnight, but feel free to wait until morning to call me."

"I'll keep that in mind," he said, and then scooted out of the booth. "I have to go."

She stood up, too. For a moment, they stood there staring at each other, two awkward adults indulging in a teenage moment. Then he caressed her jawline, a gesture both tender and wistful, and said, "I really do wish that I had met you earlier."

Charles sped down the highway with a fist around his heart and a knot in his intestines. His every thought looped back to the square in his shirt pocket. The analytical side of his brain wondered: what did Aurora know? The emotional side cried: nothing! Otherwise, she wouldn't have brought him the damn patch in the first place.

But his analytical side didn't trust coincidences. Trust was for chumps—or chimps, as the drakes liked to say. Trust was not a good counselor.

What did she know?

Why hadn't she told him about her daughter?

Most mothers couldn't shut up about their children unless they were addicts or convicts and sometimes not even then. The bright and beautiful Rosalyn apparently didn't fall into the Offspring Hall of Shame category. And—the bright and beautiful Rosalyn had found the patch. So why the secrecy? Why no word of her at all until today?

He drove over a giant pothole that caused his F-250 and the large-animal trailer that he was towing to pitch like a rodeo bull. The buck caused his thoughts to skip and then spurred an insight. Maybe the daughter was involved in things that she ought not to be. Instead of finding the patch, maybe she had obtained it. From a drakena, maybe. *The* drakena, maybe. Maybe she was the reason that he had not yet located The Great One.

Maybe, maybe, maybe. Drogo would sneer at so much conjecture. Grishka would twist it into a philosophical discussion about the Divine. And yet—

And yet, an alliance between Aurora's daughter and The Great One consolidated a lot of would-be coincidences. Quetzalcoatl had had contact with the wyrms. She could have acquired the patch and then given it to Rosalyn when she got back from her European holiday. If, in fact, she had actually ventured across the pond. She could have lied to Aurora about that so she could sneak around for Quetzalcoatl. Hell, she had probably spent the time delivering the old drakena to her new lair! That would explain why he hadn't been able to find her. It would also explain why Aurora had been so ingenuous about bringing the patch to him. Her daughter was using her as a dupe!

The theory eased his mind, for he had it bad for Aurora and his brain rejected all thought of giving her up. Tezcatlipoca had promised him wealth beyond his imagining for his help in securing the sixth age, but the only treasure he desired was her. He couldn't wait for all of this footwork to be over and done with so he could begin pursuing her in earnest. He would win her over and make her his own.

As for her daughter—

He thought about having her killed. One phone call, and she would disappear forever. But he worried about the impact such a sudden and profound loss would have on Aurora. Grief might make her turn inward, away from him. And he did not want to risk that—not while there was a possibility that Rosalyn wasn't involved with the drakena. He had no solid proof yet, nothing but a loose-fitting theory. As unsettling as they were, flukes did happen sometimes. Maybe Rosalyn and her idiot boyfriend really had stumbled onto the patch while nosing around that kill zone. Maybe Charles ought to be figuring out a way to reward them rather turn them into fertilizer. If the patch had wound up in a regular lab, it could've raised a lot of questions that were better left unasked. Questions like: what kind of estrogen was this? Who had synthesized it? Why such a massive dose? As it was, Charles could make up whatever nonsense he liked about it and no one would be the wiser. Aurora would be safer that way. So might her daughter—if she checked out OK. And he most definitely meant to have her checked out.

His cell phone buzzed. The call went through on the truck's Bluetooth. A very creepy rendition of Drogo's voice slithered forth from the sound system. "Where are you?"

"Approaching San Francisco," he said. "But rush hour's in full bloom and I expect traffic to start backing up any mile now. My estimated time of arrival is slightly after sunset."

The stereo hissed, draconian feedback. "If our prey gets away because of your torpidity," Drogo said, "I will know the taste of your heart's blood, no matter whose pet you are."

"Fuck you," Charles said, knowing full well that the drake had already terminated the call.

Up ahead, a river of tail-lights flared red, signaling the onset of his prediction. So many cars, so many people! He preferred wilder spaces, far wilder even than the Saratoga foothills. As he crept along, his thoughts drifted back to Aurora. She didn't seem all that fond of urban living. He wondered if she'd be interested in relocating to a more remote site, someplace in Romania or Bolivia or—

"Seriously, Charles?" he said, equal parts annoyed and dismayed with himself. "You're thinking about nesting? Now? Snap out of it!"

But now that his temporal lobe had dragged Aurora back into the limelight, he could not think of anything else. If things went the way he hoped they would, he'd have to tell her about his affiliation with the drakes at some point. She wrote about dragons, so coming to terms with them as living, fire-breathing entities probably wouldn't be too great of a stretch for her. The sticking point was: would she also be able to accept their vision for the next age? She shared his love of nature and the natural world. But—would she be willing to sacrifice a significant portion of her modern lifestyle to see the planet's former grandeur restored? What would make a woman more inclined to make that kind of sacrifice? A declaration of love? A promise to protect and take care of her? He believed that he could make such a promise. As long as he served Tezcatlipoca well, the Great One wouldn't care if he took a mate. Indeed, he'd consider something so mundane and human to be entirely beneath his notice.

But what would Aurora say?

San Francisco was socked in. The fog was so soupy, it turned the city's distinctive skyline into a fuzzy gray jag of refracted light and shadow. The headlands would be fogbound as well, he supposed. Which was fine by him. The more fog, the less tourists. The less tourists, the quicker he and the drakes could get the job at hand done.

The Spencer Battery was perched on a cliff overlooking the mouth of the San Francisco Bay. Even in its heyday, it would have been a desolate place, as warm and inviting as Alcatraz. In its second life as a tourist attraction, it offered little beyond an amazing view of the Golden Gate Bridge. As Charles had hoped, the dirt parking strip that hemmed the park's outskirts was empty. The weather and nightfall had done his work for him. He backed the trailer up to the park's main entrance— just in case he had to load one or both of the wyrms in a hurry. Hopefully, their capture would play out on less rugged terrain, but it was better to be prepared than sorry.

A gust of wind scented with sea salt and fennel crashed over the ridge, raising gooseflesh on his arms and neck. Damn! So much for summer! He'd planned to swap the leather jacket for his chain-mail shirt, but on second thought, he decided to wear both. He grabbed the shirt from the truck's locker and pulled it on. The extra layer made him feel bulky but well-protected—and not just from the wind. Even a small wyrm had a nasty bite, and there was no telling how big the escapees had gotten while frolicking in the wild. Next, he withdrew a knapsack from the locker. It contained the evening's party-favors: duct tape, syringes filled with ketamine, and his heavy-duty flashlight-taser. He fished out the light, slung the pack over his shoulder, and then started on his way up the stone stairway that was the park's main entrance. The going was slow, even with the flashlight, for the steps were heavily eroded and slick with fog. To his left, the terrain sloped into a steep embankment. To his right loomed rocky hillside. And then there was the wind: great, billowing gusts that crashed into him like waves. If he slipped and injured himself at this juncture, Drogo would probably gut him out of pure irritation.

As the stairway began to level out, the concrete outbuildings that formerly supported the battery came into view. These were flat-topped cement structures, riddled with gaps where once there had been windows and doors. Charles could think of worse places for a pair of dragons to wait out his arrival. He shined his light into their shadowy depths, whispering, "Drogo! Grishka! All's clear, come on out." All he saw, though, was darkness. And all he heard was heavy surf breaking against the headland cliffs.

At the top of the hill, the terrain flattened into a large apron of graded slate. The circular base of an old artillery cannon occupied the forefront of this apron. Beyond that—more darkness and fog and ocean sounds. As he wandered out that way, a gust of wind exposed the blinking red tower lights of the Golden Gate Bridge. The sight made him think of dragon eyes even though no dragon that he knew of had red eyes.

The sound of claws scratching against stone snagged his attention. "About time," he muttered, and then pivoted toward the battery. But what came scrabbling out of the fog-laced shadows was not a pair of dragons. Nor was it human. It walked upright like a man, but had leathery wings and a devil's pointy tail. Its arms and legs were stunted. It was also naked—and very excited.

"Shit," Charles said, and thumbed the flashlight into stun gun mode.

The changeling launched itself into the air. As it soared toward Charles, its form guttered like a fatty candle. One instant, it looked like a man; the next, a winged demon. He jabbed the taser into the changeling's chest as it slammed into him, but it absorbed the jolt with a furious yowl. The taser went flying. So did the backpack. The next thing he knew, he was on his back on the ground with a snapping, clawing, humping wyrm on top of him. He fought off the jaws that were straining for his neck, but could not otherwise defend himself. Talons raked his mail-shirt: a savage, washboard sound. Moments later, the right inner thigh of his jeans fell apart. He hissed at the pain that welled up in the rents. The wyrm hissed back, splashing his face with flecks of venom, then let out a startled squawk and abruptly vanished.

"What the—?"

Charles scrambled up and onto his elbows. As he did so, he saw a blur of movement: the wyrm writhing beneath the weight of a full-grown, blood-red drake. It looked like the drake was trying to subdue the smaller wyrm—leastwise until he swung his great, horned head around and savaged the wyrm's throat. The wyrm shuddered, then collapsed into a steaming heap. The drake licked his gore-stained muzzle with gusto and then sidestepped the carcass, trampling it in the process.

"You're hurt," a familiar voice noted, in a tone that was more irritated than concerned. "How bad is the injury?"

Charles pulled himself into a sitting position, grimacing at the pain, and then had a look at the gouges in his thigh. Two of them were deep—and bloody. He'd be lucky if all he needed was stitches. He looked up. Grishka was standing over him, bundled in his buffalo robe and looking perfectly composed. Nothing about him suggested a recent transformation. His lack of Change-symptoms triggered a realization in Charles: the drakes had used him. As bait. And he couldn't take them to task for doing so without appearing whiny and weak. Drogo would despise him for that. Grishka would pretend not to notice. And Tezcatlipoca wouldn't care one way or the other as long as the job got done.

"It's bad enough," he replied, not bothering to hide his pain. "Explaining it to a doctor is going to be a challenge."

The drake extended his neck in Charles' direction and then snuffled at his leg. Afterward, he bared his teeth and rumbled.

"Drogo says you smell good enough to eat," Grishka reported, deadpan as always. "He says you are lucky that he is not hungry."

"I rejoice in my good fortune," he said, and then nodded at the wyrm's corpse to change the subject. "I thought the plan was to bring it back to Tezcatlipoca alive."

"Plans change," Grishka said, but while his voice was level, there was a tinge of grief in his eyes. "When we saw how degenerate it was, we decided to destroy it. The Divine sanctioned our decision."

"I see," he said, and then yelped as Drogo began to drool on his torn flesh. "What the fuck! That hurts!"

"He is cauterizing the wounds," Grishka said. "He says the smell will overwhelm his good sense otherwise."

"Well then," Charles said, forcing the words past gritted teeth, "by all means, proceed."

By the time Drogo was done sealing the wounds, Charles' vision was swimming and he was one tiny bad smell away from barfing. Grishka clapped him on the back, congratulating him on his fortitude, and then bent down to have a look at Drogo's handiwork.

"Nice," he remarked. "By morning, it will be good as new. Now let us burn the wyrm and be gone from this place. I have no affection for the cold anymore."

Drogo inhaled deeply, drawing up a fiery breath.

"Wait!" Charles blurted, and then rushed to speak the thing that had popped into his head before the drake decided to turn that fiery breath on him. "I need to see if it's wearing a patch."

"Why?" Grishka asked, more curious than indignant.

"Tell you in a—second," he said, wincing as he climbed to his feet.

To his surprise, walking didn't hurt as much as he thought it would. Even so, he hobbled over to the wyrm's corpse. He had no light, so he had to run his hands up and down the tattered throat like a blind man. Nothing here, nothing here, nothing here, the right side of his brain kept chanting as he fingered his way through the shredded tissue and gore. Then, on the underside of the wyrm's jawline, he felt it: a pharmaceutical patch, sister to the one in his pocket.

"Shit," he said, and then came limping back to the drakes, more broken now than he had been a few minutes ago.

"Well?" Grishka asked, a curious warble. "Was it?"

"Yes," Charles said, opening his hand to show them the bloody patch. "It was wearing one."

"Why is this significant?" Grishka asked.

For one brief, conflicted moment, Charles thought about lying to the drakes. He did not want Aurora to be involved with this. He did not want her to be on the wrong side. But there was no denying proof that had been manufactured in one of Tezcatlipoca's own bootleg labs. Almost of its own volition, his hand retrieved the envelope from his pocket.

"Because," he said, displaying the patch, "I have this."

Both Drogo and Grishka hissed. Then Grishka snatched the patch from his fingers and held it out for Drogo to sniff. Moments later, Grishka said, "He wants to know where you got this."

Again, his first impulse was to lie. He didn't have to bring Aurora into this. He could lay all the blame on her daughter and no one would be the wiser. He'd been thinking of having her killed anyway—

Drogo rumbled: a prompting perhaps or a warning. Either way, it was not a sound to be ignored.

"A woman I know gave it to me. She said her daughter found it at one of yonder wyrm's kill sites," he said, trying for a neutral tone. But Grishka must have heard the subliminal strains of grief anyway.

"Ah," the man-drake said in a tone flecked with woe, "this is Aurora you speak of."

Before Charles could either confirm or deny the guess, Drogo rumbled again and began to thrash his tail. "Yes, I know," Grishka said to him, and then looked at Charles. "This wyrm was the man-slayer. Therefore, Aurora lied to you. Why would she lie if she wasn't somehow involved with the drakena?"

"I don't know," Charles said. "It's possible that she's being duped by her daughter."

The red drake grew even more agitated. He hissed. Grishka scowled. A moment later, his lopsided shoulders slumped forward and he turned to Charles again. "He says now is not the time to indulge in possibilities. I concur with him. We cannot afford to be compromised. Both Aurora and her daughter must be eliminated."

"I understand," Charles said bleakly. "I'll see to it."

CHAPTER 24

Roz was in the kitchen, cooking for the first time in God only knew how long. The house smelled of roasting pork and garlic. The glass of cabernet that she had poured for herself smelled like black pepper and cherries. She savored the richness of the aromas and the glorious sensation of having a moment to herself. Aurora was in Portland. Brigit was basking in the backyard. As much as she loved her mom and the drakena, she was happy to have a bit of time and space to herself. She sipped at her wine and then switched on the radio. Music erupted: a bass-driven tune that she didn't recognize. Feck! How out of touch she had become! Before she left for Scotland, she had been up on all of the latest releases, most of the up-and-coming bands, and a respectable amount of music-related gossip. Now she was as clueless as a golden oldie. Her world revolved around dragons and their business these days.

The thought provoked a snort from her, half amused and half incredulous. Six months ago, who would've guessed that she and the Loch Ness Monster would be BFFs? Or that she'd be colluding with the mother of all dragons to determine the constitution of the next age? Her life had definitely taken a strange and wondrous turn! She pulled out a half-dozen potatoes from the pantry and tossed them into the sink like grenades. As she scrubbed their thick brown skins, the music gave way to the hourly news. One of the stories prompted her to jeer. As she did so, Brigit came strolling in through the patio sliders.

"Ye almost sound like a dragon when ye do that," she said. "What's tha occasion?"

Roz curled her upper lip—a look to match the sound. "Vern Pendragon. The man is a rich, narcissistic, toxic-waste dump with delusions of grandeur."

Brigit shrugged. "Sounds like a lot of rich men tae me. Why do ye care about this one?"

"He was talking about running for the presidency earlier this year. Happily, someone changed his mind for him."

"Probably decided tae work on his golf game instead," Brigit remarked, and then inhaled deeply through her nose as Roz began tossing spuds into the oven. "That pig smells uncommonly good!"

Roz was quick to close the oven door. "I thought you went fishing last night. Didn't you catch anything?"

The changeling bristled at the question as if insulted. "A'm a water dragon. Of course A caught something. But tha fish in yon reservoir are tiny! A'd have tae eat every last one of them tae truly get my fill. An' those juicy pig smells are making me keenly aware of just empty my belly is."

"Maybe you should run out to the woods and bag yourself a deer before Max and Mara get here," Roz said, "I'm fairly sure that they're not ready for the sight of a hungry dragon at the dinner table."

"Ye did say ye were thinking about letting them in on our secret."

"Yeah, but not like that!"

The land-line rang, disrupting their conversation. In the few seconds that it took for Roz to get to the hand-set, she managed to convince herself that it was Max calling to bail on dinner. He had a track-record of last-minute cancellations, and the habit drove her nuts. "If you're not coming," she barked, in lieu of a greeting, "I swear I will never play 'Dungeons & Dragons' with you again! And I mean it this time!"

"Excuse me?" the voice on the other end of the line said. "Do I have the right number? I'm calling for Aurora."

"Oh!" Roz said, immediately red-faced. "Sorry. Yes, this is her number. But she's out of town for the weekend."

"Ah, yes, of course," the caller said. "I'd forgotten. You must be her daughter."

"The one and only," she said. Then, because she was still embarrassed, she tried to make him feel uncomfortable, too. "You must be her new boyfriend, Chuck."

"Charles," he said, both polite and firm. "Could you take a message for her?"

"Sure," she said. "Fire away."

"Tell her I got the results back on the patch." He paused for a moment and then added, "You were the one who found it, right?"

"Guilty as charged," she quipped. "What's the scoop on it?"

"My friend said he couldn't be sure," Charles said, "but he thought it appeared to be some kind of hormone patch."

"It's estrogen," Roz said, taking a perverse delight in one-upping her mother's man-friend. "A massive dose. My guy said—"

"Wait. Your guy?"

"Yeah," Roz said, realizing after the fact that she might have been a bit too forthcoming. But now that the cat was out of the bag, all she could do was go forward. "I cut the patch in half and gave my piece to a friend who has access to a lab."

"You what?" he asked, sounding shocked. "Why would you do that?" An instant later, he added, "The police could charge you with tampering with evidence."

"They could," she retorted. "If they knew about it. Since they don't, I think I'm safe."

"I wish your mother had told me about this," he said, shifting into a pissier tone. "I had to jump through several hoops to get this favor done for her."

"Mom didn't know," Roz lied, instinctively shielding Aurora. "She thought she was giving you the whole thing. But I thought it would be better to divvy the thing up—you know, so we'd double our chances of getting some kind of data that we could take to the police."

"Very smart of you," Charles said, a grudging compliment. "I like to hedge my bets, too. So your friend said he found estrogen in the patch?"

"Yep. Pure, concentrated human estradiol."

"What?" The line fell silent again—another shocked sound. An instant later, he said, "I'm no expert on the matter, but that doesn't sound like anything that anyone should be wearing."

"I know, right? It must've driven its wearer right out of its mind," Roz said. "Maybe that's why he killed all those people in such a gruesome way."

"Maybe," Charles echoed, and while his tone was level, it was on the tight side now as if she had said something to offend him. "Maybe not. I'm sure someone will figure it all out sooner or later. I've got another call coming in, so I'll leave you to your evening."

"Thanks," Roz said. "I'll tell Mom you called."

"Please do. Oh," he added, before she could sign off, "when is she getting in?"

"Sunday, 10:40PM, on Alaska Airlines," she said. "Bye now."

"Who was that?" Brigit asked.

"Mom's boyfriend," Roz said, vaguely unsettled by the conversation.

"Really? What's he like?"

"Nice enough, I suppose," Roz said, as she replayed the conversation over in her head. "In an old-dude kind of way. He got kind of bitchy about the patch, though—as if he was ticked that Max's analysis was better than his guy's."

"Mmmmf—Wait! He—mmmf—knows about tha patch? A thought we—mmmf—decided against showing it tae him."

"We did," Roz said, head-down over a cutting board loaded with vegetables so she would not have to look Brigit in the eye and expose her chagrin. "But then the lab audit thing with Max came up and I wanted information fast, so I cut the patch in half and gave one piece to Mom to give to what's-his-name just in case the audit ran long."

"And how is it tha A'm just—mmfff—hearing about this now?"

All at once, Roz processed the sounds that had been impinging on her subconscious. She pivoted to find Brigit standing in front of the open oven door. There was a chunk of half-cooked meat in her fist and an equal amount in her maw. "Hey!" Roz shouted. "That's for dinner!"

"A'm hungry now," Brigit said, and shoved the rest of the purloined meat into her face all at once. As she chewed, she said, "Ye should have—mmmff mmmf—told me about this. Mmff. It could be important."

"I know," Roz said, truly remorseful. "It slipped my mind, is all." Then, as the changeling went to tear another hunk of pork from the roast, her rue flared into indignation. "Get away from there, dammit!" She tried to shove Brigit away from the oven. When that failed, as she should've known it would, she inserted herself between the roast and Brigit instead. "Shit!" she said, as she surveyed the damage to her main course. "This looks like this has been savaged by dogs!"

"Now, now," Brigit clucked, "no need tae get nasty." Her mouth and hands were slathered with grease. Her expression was one of supreme satisfaction. "There's plenty left."

"That's only because I started with a whole freaking loin," Roz said, and then gestured at the roast's ravaged remains again. "I'm going to have to do cosmetic surgery on this thing before Max and Mara get—"

Bing-bong!

"Here," she finished woodenly. "Figures. First time ever that they arrive on time." She pointed Brigit toward the front door. "Go and greet them. Take your time letting them in."

Brigit wiped her mouth with the back on her hands and then her hands on the backside of her skirt and then sauntered toward the door. As Roz sawed the remnants of the roast into crude double-thick chops, she listened for the sound of her friends' voices. What she heard instead lifted the hair on the back of her neck.

"Well, who have we here?" Aldo said. "I know all of Roz's old friends. It's about time she started making new ones."

"What do ye want?" Brigit asked, a query as flat as a floorboard.

Aldo laughed—an insincere, chauvinistic chortle. "Easy there, Red. I don't bite."

"A do."

He laughed again. "I'll just bet you do. Now be a sweetheart and step aside. I need to see Roz." Scuffling sounds ensued: him trying in vain to side-step Brigit. "Roz!" he shouted then, in his most authoritarian voice. "Call off your door bitch! We need to talk."

"I've got nothing to say to you," Roz shouted back. "If you're smart, you'll leave now and forget you ever knew the pass-code to the front gate."

"Not until I get some answers," he countered. "I want to know what I saw that night on the ship. You know what I'm talking about. I know you do."

"Oh," she heard Brigit warble, "A kin help ye with that."

At which point, Roz bolted toward the front door, projecting a vehement, *No!* But she was too late. Aldo was already hightailing it for his car.

"Shit!" Roz barked. "What did you do?"

Brigit displayed a grin that was entirely too toothy for her face. "A gave him a glimpse of what he thought he wanted tae see." When Roz continued to gape at her, she added, "Don't worry. He won't quite remember it."

"Which means he won't quite forget, either," Roz said, scowling now. "Right?"

Brigit's only response was a sly smirk. Which was as much of an admission of guilt as Roz needed. "You jerk," she said, thumping the changeling's arm, a blow that left her knuckles spangling. "The last thing we need right now is Aldo poking his nose around here."

"A can make sure he goes away permanently if he shows his face again," Brigit said, and there was no hint of playfulness left in her tone. "He's bound tae taste better than he looks."

"'Don't even think about it," Roz said, as she stomped back to the kitchen. "Around here, we don't eat people just for being a pain in the ass."

"There may come a day when ye feel differently," Brigit said mildly, and then retired to the patio, snagging the evening's sacrificial bottle of Scotch in passing.

"Dragons," Roz grumbled. "Can't live with 'em. Can't kill 'em."

"Don't ye forget it!"

An instant later, the front door burst open and Mara came charging in, singing, "Oh my God! You will never guess who went speeding past us as we were pulling into the driveway!"

"Aldo," Roz said flatly, and then laughed as her friend's scandalized grin deflated. "He was just here," she went on, a consolation of sorts. "Brigit gave him the bum's rush."

"Oh, yes. Brigit," Mara said, turning a little wistful. "I'd forgotten that she was going to be here." Then, when Roz scooped her into a welcoming hug, she perked back up and said, "So what did the ass-hat want?"

"He wanted to talk about old times," Roz said, regretting the dodge but what else could she do? Until Brigit decided, if ever, to out herself, Roz was obliged to keep the secret. "I think he's a little wrong in the head."

Max snorted as he came up behind them. "You're just figuring that out now?" He helped himself to a hug and then handed her a bottle of wine. "Sorry we're late."

She gave his bewhiskered cheek an affectionate pinch. "You're not late," she said. "You're right on time." She glanced at the bottle's label, made a happy sound deep in her throat, and then added, "What say we crack this baby now and drink it out on the patio? Dinner's still at least a half-hour away."

"Sounds like a plan," Max said, always easy-going when it came to dining and drinking. "You pop the cork; I'll get the glasses."

"We'll only need three," she said. "Brigit prefers grain to grape."

"I remember that about her," Max said. "I also seem to recall that she prefers it by the bottle."

"And here I was, thinking all you mad scientist types were absent-minded," Roz quipped, as she applied the cork-pull. "Your memory's just fine."

"So how long is Brigit going to be here?" Mara asked. "Doesn't she have a life to get back to in Scotland?"

"She's on a sabbatical of sorts," Roz replied, wondering at the slight edge to her friend's voice. Granted, Brigit hadn't gone out of her way to be nice during that outing at Royce's. Then again, she hadn't been particularly unkind, either. She had just been her usual aloof self. "I'm not sure when she'll be leaving."

"Oh," Mara said, and the edge in her tone wilted into disappointment. "It must be nice to have that kind of flexibility in your life."

They migrated out to the patio to find Brigit sprawled

on the ground in front of a blazing fire pit. The changeling nodded ever so slightly at Mara and Max, and then flared her nostrils at Roz. Roz invited the Marinos to park themselves in the Adirondack chairs that she had set out for them and then settled down in the grass alongside Brigit. The Marinos exchanged a look, but Max refused to give voice to the eyebrow-arching thought that passed between them.

"Thanks for having us," he said instead. "It's a pleasure to see you both again." Then he raised his glass and added, "Hey, Brigit. How about starting us off with a Scottish toast?"

The changeling hoisted the whiskey bottle high and said, "Here's tae us; wha's like us? Gey few, and they're a deid."

"What?" Mara said, crinkling her nose as if at a bad smell. But Max said, "Here, here!" and sampled the wine. Afterward, he tipped his head at Roz. "So? What do you think?"

"Nice," Roz said. Very smooth and fruit-forward." She swirled the glass under Brigit's nose. "Want to try?"

"Feck no!" Brigit replied, and then swatted at Roz when she continued to tease her. "Feck off!"

Roz laughed and thought to goad the changeling again only to freeze when Mara blurted, "OK, I'm just going to come right out and say it!"

"Mara," Max said, *sotto voce*. "Don't."

But she would not be shushed. "I'm sorry," she huffed. "I'm not going to spend the whole evening trying to talk around the elephant in the room."

Brigit loosed a curious warble at that, then sat up and looked all around. "Elephant? What elephant? Where?"

"I'm not sure," Roz said, "but I think it's a metaphor." She cocked her head at Mara and said, "Spit it out, girlfriend."

Unable to contain herself, Mara did that. "Are you two lovers?"

Max hid his face in the palm of his hand. At the same time,

Brigit leaned in closer as if to see Mara better. "Why do ye ask?"

"It's obvious that something's going on between you two," she replied, in a serrated tone that Roz belatedly recognized as jealousy. "I mean, look at you—curled up together on the grass, all cozy-like. And you're always around these days. Always! I can't even talk on the phone with Roz without you hovering around somewhere in the background. So are you together or what?"

Mara was red in the face now. Roz could feel a little burn in her own cheeks, too. It had never occurred to her that her behavior had been out of the ordinary. Now that she saw herself through Mara's eyes, though, she had to admit that things looked a little—intimate. But if Roz was shaken by the question, Brigit remained stalwartly composed.

"Yer a Seer," she said to Mara. "A should have known ye would sense the truth."

That seemed to stun Mara. "So it's true then. You're—gay?"

"No. Ye See, but ye do not understand."

A voice popped into Roz's head. *What will they do if A reveal my true nature?*

Roz shrugged. "I think they can handle it."

"Handle what?" Mara asked, looking confused as well as irritated. "The truth?"

"Ye are a Seer," Brigit told her. "And ye," she added, looking pointedly at Max, "are a Magician. A am a wee bit—unusual—too."

"Oh, please," Mara snapped, in no mood to play nice. "We're all just ordinary people."

Brigit grinned. The insides of her nostrils flared red. "Do A really look ordinary ta you?"

When neither Max nor Mara responded, she shifted into a sitting position and thrust a hand into the depths of the firepit. Mara yelped. Max lunged to his feet. But even as he started toward Brigit, Roz forestalled him with an upraised finger.

"No," she said. "Wait."

As the Marinos gaped, mesmerized by horror, Brigit picked up a chunk of burning wood. Flames engulfed her hand and then surged up her forearm. Her skin glimmered in the fire's light, but did not burn or even singe.

"My God," Mara said, and her hand rose up to cover her mouth. "That's not—possible."

"Oh, but it is," Brigit said. There was a reptilian cast to her eyes now, and her grin was toothsome.

"There's more," Roz said softly, and then stood up to get out of Brigit's way. "You don't have to watch if you don't want to," she added, as Brigit began to Change. "But trust me when I tell you that what's happening is completely and utterly real."

Neither Max nor Mara said a word until Brigit the woman was gone and a lavender-eyed dragon stood before them. Max looked tempted to bolt, but Mara stood there gaping in awe. "Oh my God," she croaked at last. "I never would've guessed." She raised a hand toward Brigit's outstretched head. "May I?"

"Yes," Roz said, "but on the neck, not the face. She doesn't like being petted."

Slowly, with a sensible degree of trepidation, Mara reached out and pressed her knuckles to the dragon's scaled neck. A moment later, she let out the breath that she had been holding and broke into an incredulous half-smile.

"I thought her scales would be rough, but they're not. They're smooth, almost soft. Max," she said, gesturing at her still spooked husband with her free hand, "c'mon over here, babe. You need to check this out."

Almost in spite of himself, he joined his wife at the dragon's side. As they caressed her throat, she rumbled approvingly. They mistook the sound for irritation and quickly jerked their hands away. Roz hastened to put their minds at ease.

No need to freak," she said. "She likes having her throat stroked. She likes a good belly rub, too, but I wouldn't recommend trying that just now. She ate a lot of pork not too long ago and that gives her the most ungodly gas."

Brigit narrowed her eyes and snorted twin licks of flame that landed at Roz's feet—a playful warning shot. Max and Mara stomped out those little tongues, exchanged another look, and then collectively lost their shit. Max began pacing back and forth in front of the firepit. At the same time, Mara lapsed into a giggle-fit. When Roz called her out with a dubious, "What?", she broke into hysterical laughter. In between guffaws, she gasped, "I can't believe—I thought you—and her—were a couple!"

"Well," Roz said, "in a way we are."

Mara howled at that, a release so profound as to be infectious. Roz joined in first and then Max and they belly-laughed themselves all the way to the ground. Afterward, as they lay panting in the grass, Max said, "Only you, Rosalyn Vanderbilt. Only you could have stumbled onto a living, breathing dragon. Where on God's green earth did you find her? And what the hell is she doing here?"

"We met on the shores of Loch Ness on the night Aldo dumped me," Roz said, smiling as she and the dragon flash-shared the memory. "She came here to save mankind from the drakes, who want to rule the world as they did in ages past."

Mara started giggling again. Max hauled her into a comforting embrace and then said, "Don't mind her. She's just a little overwrought." As he patted Mara's back, he added, "Does Aurora know about this?"

Roz and Brigit ducked into their link for a private side-bar. How much should they say? How much could Max and Mara take? As they weighed their choices, Max crinkled his nose in a very unflattering way. "What's that smell?"

Roz's first thought was: shit, she'd burned the pork. But

that wasn't it. The smell that he was talking was gamier, almost rancid—and oddly familiar. As she flared her nostrils, trying to distill a name from the stink, something fell from the night-time sky and landed in Aurora's rose garden. An instant later, that something let out a shriek. By then, everyone was on their feet: Max in front of Mara. Roz in front of Max; all of them behind Brigit. The drakena rumbled. A shadow the size of a wolfhound came prowling out of the darkness and toward them. Its iridescent hide reflected the fire's light like a disco ball.

"What is it?" Mara whispered, peering over Max's shoulder.

"Juvenile dragon," Roz whispered back. "They're called wyrms."

"What's it want?" Max asked.

"I don't know," Roz replied.

Brigit rumbled again. In response, the wyrm sank into a crouch just beyond the patio and panted like an anxious dog. A moment later, Brigit said, *"It seeks The Great One."*

"How did it find us?" Roz wondered aloud. "Did you leave a trail for her?"

"No. It says the Great One Called to it."

"Oh? Then I guess it's time to pay the old girl a visit." When Brigit rumbled agreement, Roz turned to her friends and said, "As it happens, we have one more surprise in store for you if you're up for it."

"Is it bigger than that one?" Max asked, glancing in Brigit's direction.

"Yes," Roz said, resisting the urge to modify the truth for easier hearing. "Definitely."

Both Max and Mara swallowed hard. But when Brigit nosed the wyrm to its feet and toward the barn, they joined Roz in the rearguard without further prompting.

"This is either the weirdest day of my life," Max said, "or the most amazing. I can't call it yet."

"I have a feeling that this is just the tip of the iceberg either way," Mara said.

Then they stepped into the barn and fell into slack-jawed silence.

Quetzalcoatl was still curled up in the riding ring, but her rheumy jade eyes were open to slits now, and her weathered frill was unfurled. She was peering at the wyrm, who had parked itself in front of her.

"My God," Max said, as the Great One studied the juvenile. "Are you seeing this, Mara? It's—it's a pink dragon. We've stumbled into the flesh-and-blood version of one of Aurora's stories."

"Yes," Mara said, unable to look away from the ancient dragon. "I can see that, my love. Whatever you do, don't pinch me. I don't want to wake up."

When Quetzalcoatl finished her inspection, she scooped the wyrm into the cradle of her forearms. The wyrm snuggled up against her massive chest without hesitation. Roz took that to mean that it was okay for her to start asking questions.

"So what's it doing here?" Roz asked. "It told us it was going to fly far, far away."

"Not 'it'," Quetzalcoatl said. *"'Her.' The youngling has sexed. She is here because I visited her in her dreams and convinced her to seek us out."*

"Why?" Roz asked.

"The Dreaming took me to the future. I saw her there. She was—useful."

"How?" Roz asked.

"Who are you talking to?" Max whispered.

Roz silenced him with an upraised hand so she could concentrate on Quetzalcoatl's reply. *"I may not speak of things which have not happened yet,"* the Great One said. *"But I am free to tell you something of use that the youngling just shared with me."*

"And what would that be?"

"The black wyrm is dead."

"What? How?"

"Killed by two drakes and a man. The youngling witnessed the murder."

Roz rounded on the wyrm, who hissed a warning at her. "You little liar. You said you were going to fly far, far away."

Brigit nosed her out of striking distance and then rumbled, urging her to not to agitate the wyrm while she was nesting with The Great One. *"Juveniles are secretive creatures,"* she said, *"and dunna share much of anything willingly. My guess is tha she had every intention of fleeing—just as soon as she tracked her clutch-mate down and persuaded it tae leave with her."*

"Did those slayers see her?"

"If they had," the Great One replied, *"she would either be dead now—or on her way back to my brother's compound."* Her neck frill quivered then as if tickled by an afterthought. She nosed the now-cozy wyrm and said, *"Can you show me where Tezcatlipoca's compound is?"*

The wyrm loosed an incredulous warble which Brigit was quick to translate. *"She thinks tha Great One is too old and too fat to fly that far."*

Quetzalcoatl rumbled, a voluminous sound that could have served as either a reproach or a stream of amusement. *"If we use the Dreaming",* she said, *"we can go there and back without ever raising a wing. But you will need to lead the way."*

The youngling squirmed in her comfy bed, a display of grudgingness. When the Great One nosed her, pressing for a response, she let out a plaintive bleat.

"Typical wyrm," Brigit said. *"She wants tae eat first. A'm not hunting fer her, so she'll have to make do with whatever ye've got on hand."*

Roz was quick to see what Brigit had in mind: her pork

chops! Sometimes dragons could be so nervy! But she couldn't say no, not when it was for the cause. So she turned to Max and Mara. They had the shell-shocked look of people who had wandered into a fun-house only to find themselves trapped on the set of a live sex show.

"Sorry, guys," she said, pitching the apology on several different levels, "but dinner has been cancelled. The little one needs to eat."

Max raised his hands as if in surrender. "You'll get no argument from us," he said, "not when there's a hungry dragon involved."

"Good choice," she said, and then shifted toward the exit. "Hang tight, I'll be back in a tick with the roast."

"No, wait!" Mara said. "We'll get it."

"We will?" Max warbled, wide-eyed with surprise.

"Yes, of course," Mara said, batting her lashes at him. "Unless you'd rather stay here with the hungry dragon."

He coughed up a clot of air. "Good point," he said, and then grabbed Mara by the hand. "Anything else we can get while we're in transit—the bottle of whiskey for Brigit, perhaps?"

"Such a thoughtful man. He must be Scottish!"

"I think he's Italian, actually," Roz replied, and then cast Max a look of grateful regret. "She can't drink while she's in dragon form. Her arms are too short."

"Oh. OK," Max said, in a leery tone, as if he suspected her of teasing him. "We'll be off to fetch the meat then. Come along, dear."

They headed for the door at a pace just shy of a run. As Roz watched them scurry away, Brigit impinged on her thoughts. *"Think they'll be back?"* Which was, of course, exactly what Roz had been wondering.

"Yeah, probably," she said, although she was equally sure that they would at least talk about bolting while they were out of earshot. "They're braver than they think they are. Plus, I think they're hooked." She turned her attention back to the wyrm. She was snugged up against Quetzalcoatl's breastbone, dozing like a Komodo lizard in the sun. "What are we going to do with her?"

I dunno. She's nae going tae tolerate being cooped up in yer barn—especially since she's been confined for all but a few weeks of her life. But we have tae keep her somewhere tha drakes won't find her.

"Why do they want her?" Roz asked. "Have we figured that out yet?"

"Nae. Not yet."

Max returned with the roasting pan in his mitted hands, looking both triumphant and a little timid. Mara was right behind him, watchful as a mother goose. As the succulent smell of roasted pork infiltrated the barn, the wyrm roused from her lazy drowse. Her nostrils flared first. Then her eyelids twitched. Then, as she lifted her head up from the pillow of her forearms, she let out a distressed honk and morphed all at once into a woman-child. She was pretty and petite, with cinnamon-colored eyes and skin that seemed to sparkle. She also sported a miniature set of gossamer wings.

"Oh!" Mara exclaimed. "She looks just like Francine, the woodland fairy!"

A heartbeat later, the fairy was gone, replaced by a slavering wyrm whose eyes were all for Max. Roz elbowed him in the ribs and said, "I think you'd better give that to her. She looks kind of ravenous."

He blinked like someone who'd just been snapped out of a hypnotist's trance and said, "It just came out of the oven. Won't it be too hot?"

Roz rolled her eyes at him and sing-songed, "Dra-gon."

When he didn't get it, she added, "As in, 'fire-breathing'?"

"Oh, yeah," he said, flushing a little underneath his facial hair. "Of course."

He shuffled toward the wyrm as if she were an open flame and then gingerly set the pan down in from of her. Before he had a chance to stand back up, the chops were gone.

"Whoa," Max said, and scrambled back to the relative safety of Roz's shadow. "And I thought you ate fast!"

"Ha-ha," Roz drawled.

The wyrm licked its lipless mouth, then curled back up against Quetzalcoatl's chest and shut her eyes. The Great One snuffled the youngling, then snorted a dismissal and let her eyelids droop, too.

"That's our cue to move along," Roz said. "Let's go back to the house and find ourselves something to eat."

"Eat?" Max echoed. "I'm all for a good stiff drink."

Brigit rumbled approvingly. *"Ar ye sure he's not a Scot?"*

CHAPTER 25

The hair on the back of Aurora's neck bristled as she rode the escalator that bottomed into the baggage claim area at SFO. The feeling was so intense, she felt compelled to glance over her shoulder. She saw lots of travel-weary faces, but none that she recognized. And no one appeared to be the least bit interested in her. Her imagination must be stuck in hyperdrive, she decided. It happened sometimes, especially after socializing with hardcore science fiction and fantasy fans for extended weekends. The only known cure was a king-sized dose of domestic down-time.

The thought of home triggered a cascade of mental images: Roz, her bed, Charles, a glass of red wine, Quetzalcoatl. It came as no surprise that Roz topped this list of cravings, but the fact that the dragon claimed a solid second place amazed her. Who would've guessed that that frowsy old behemoth would come to own that much psychic territory in such a short span of time? And without attempting to be endearing! Aurora missed the dispassionate intimacy of their bond, and the astounding impact that it had on her dreams.

But she had to admit: it had been nice to fall asleep and wake up on her own terms rather than the Dreaming's!

Her baggage had yet to make it to the designated carousel, so like everyone else on her flight, she pulled out her cell phone to pass the time. To her surprise, she found a message from Roz waiting for her.

"Mom, hi, it's me. Just wanted to let you know that Brigit and I won't be home when you get there tonight. Sadie coughed up a scrap of information—Quetzalcoatl will fill you in on the details. Anyway, Brigit and I are on our way south to check the intel out. We ought to be home again in a week or so. See you when we get back, Love you! Bye!"

Aurora replayed the message twice. As she did so, questions swirled around in her head, an eddy both intrigued and irritated. Who was this Sadie and what was she to Quetzalcoatl? When had the Great One woken up?

And—what was this business about Roz and that fire-haired she-dragon heading south? How far south, exactly? What were they going to do when they got there?

The carousel alarms went off, cacophonic blasts that jarred her out of her thoughts. A moment later, the conveyor belt lurched into motion. Luggage began tumbling down from the carousel's upper reaches then. As she waited for hers to appear, a nearby flat-screen caught her eye. It was streaming CNN. At the moment, the newscaster was talking about yet another murder in Juarez. According to local authorities, the victim had worked in a bootleg pharmacology lab just south of the border and had been found in a shallow grave in the desert minus his head and various other parts. The backdrop picture was of a high desert wasteland. The mountains in the background looked like The Pinnacles only bigger, more rugged, desolate. As Aurora peered at them, a peculiar sense of déjà vu came over her. Even though she had never seen that section of the Sierras before, some visceral part of her recognized those mountains—not just in general, but intimately.

That's the place!

The balding, middle-aged man standing next to her pressed a hand to her shoulder-blade and asked, "Are you OK?"

Fuddled in the aftermath of that psychic jolt, she mistook his concern for something more sinister and responded with suspicion. "Who are you?" she asked, as she recoiled. "Why are you following me?"

"Jesus, lady," he said, making a production out of backing off, "I was just trying to be nice."

That was when she realized that several other of her fellow passengers were staring at her as if she were drooling blood. Apparently, that psychic jolt had come with both an inside and an outside voice.

Embarrassment attempted to flare across the shoals of her cheeks, but agitation kept it at bay. Echoes of that feeling were still rippling through her! There had been a definite connection to it, and it had been fitted with a sense of urgency. The only time she'd ever come close to such a sensation was when—oh. That two-plus-two moment dismayed her far more than her outburst had. Of course! That had been Quetzalcoatl, not déjà vu! She must be wearier than she thought to not recognize the Great One's touch instantly.

At the sight of her luggage tumbling into view, she shifted out of her thoughts and back into airport auto-pilot. But on the shuttle ride out to long-term parking, she replayed the episode in her head and decided that she wasn't losing her grip after all. Quetzalcoatl's presence had been different this time: more urgent and direct. Contact had been made from a considerable distance, too. She was tempted to fret about the possible reason behind these anomalies, but then shrugged the urge onto her back-brain's back-burner. The answer to her questions was a little less than an hour away. She could wait that long.

She loaded her bags into the trunk of her car and then headed for the highway. By the time she hit the on-ramp, she was one with the road: relaxed, content, at peace in her four-wheel isolation chamber. Roz didn't understand why Aurora always insisted on driving herself to the airport and back. "Your Lexus will be a sitting duck for vandals and thieves," she argued. "Let me drive you. Or hire a limo. It's not that expensive, you know."

But there was nothing like a drive to clear the head after an afternoon of low-grade stress. When the car keys were in her hand, the only schedule she needed to contend with was her own. As Duncan used to say, 'Trust is good. Control is better.'

The thought triggered a random memory: him ringing the doorbell to her apartment and then flashing a smile when she cracked the door open to peer at him. He had been handsome in a western European sort of way, dressed for date night and possessed of a bouquet that came from an honest-to-God florist rather than the grocery store. She was dressed in flip-flops and rags, and was disappointed to see that he was not the delivery guy with her celebratory, post-finals double jalapeno pizza.

"Good evening," he said. "Would you happen to know if the woman in 4G is home?"

"Her doorbell's broken," she said. "Try knocking." Then, propelled by an inexplicable whim, she reached out with ninja-like precision and plucked a single rosebud from the bouquet. "For my trouble. Have a nice night." she added, and then hip-checked her door shut.

Nothing about that encounter would have led her to suspect that he'd be ringing her bell again the very next day with a dozen roses in hand all for her.

She sighed, one of those heart-shaped sounds that contained at its core an if-only. If only he hadn't been on the road that night.

As she breathed that wish for what had to be the millionth time, a truck barreled past her: a steel-gray semi that could have been a twin to the one with which Duncan had collided. Over fifty cars had been involved in that foggy I-5 pile-up; fifty cars and nine casualties. Duncan had been the worst, DOA with massive head trauma. Back in the early years, she used to rage at his ghost for not pulling into a roadside motel when the fog got bad, but eventually she was able to admit that she had wanted him nowhere but home that night. Both she and Roz had been sick all weekend, and Roz wouldn't stop crying for him. "Dah-Dee, come back!" As if she had known all along that they were never going to see him alive again.

A reflected flash of bright white light jarred her back to the here-and-now. She glanced in her rear-view mirror to see a black SUV closing in on her in a major hurry. Figures, she grumped to herself. Open highway for as far as the eye could see and this bozo still had to hog her lane. As she shifted to the right, the SUV pulled even with her. An instant later, it slammed into her front fender. The Lexus veered toward the guardrail. She wrestled it back toward the road. As she did so—BAM! The SUV sideswiped her again. Her car skittered through a slick of gravel and into the guardrail.

"What the fuck?" she shouted at the truck, as she struggled to regain control. "Are you out of your mind?!"

The SUV crashed into her a third time. This time, instead of veering away, it pressed into the Lexus, muscling it against the guardrail. Distressed metal shrieked. The car's chassis shivered and bucked. Then the scrub growth on the far side of the railing gave way to a patch of dark open space. Although Aurora couldn't see the sixty-foot embankment that spanned below that space, she knew it was there. She also knew that her sporty little sedan wouldn't survive such a plunge.

Do something, Duncan's ghost urged her.

In response, she punched her car horn as if it were the other driver's face. Then she hit the brakes.

The SUV fishtailed back onto the freeway. Her car bounced off the guardrail, did a full three-sixty and then slammed back into the rail. Her airbag deployed, smashing her into her seat.

Her world became a blinding mass of billowing whiteness. For one dazed moment, all she could do was sit there and gasp for breath that was slow to come. Then a metallic groan burrowed into her awareness. It was followed by a slo-mo crumpling sound and then the dull snap of a guardrail giving way. An instant later, her car lurched toward the embankment.

Shit!

Instantly energized, she clawed her way past the deflating airbag and grabbed the door handle. But the door refused to open, and when she tried to force the issue, the car rolled closer to the edge of the world. Shit! What now? Her frantic gaze settled on the giant spider-web crack in the windshield. Maybe she could kick the glass out and crawl to safety! She shifted, meaning to do just that. As she did so, the front of the car pitched forth into thin air and then hung there like an unfinished thought. She sucked in a breath that reeked of airbag propellant and tasted like blood.

"Aurora Vanderbilt!"

The shout was accompanied by a rap on the driver's side window. Aurora shifted that way, hoping beyond hope to see a big, burly fireman or cop getting ready to mount a rescue. Instead, her eyes locked with those of a young Asian woman. "You must get out!" The woman shouted. "Hurry!"

"I can't!" Aurora shouted back. "The door's jammed."

The car's grill slanted downward. The back-end elevated. Then, as gravity began to assert itself, she felt the car's underbelly snag on something—the guardrail's stump perhaps?

"Get out now!" the woman urged. "Use the passenger door!"

"No way!" Aurora said. "There's a shitload of thin air between me and the ground on that side."

"Do it! You will be safe. You will see."

The woman's pushiness punched through Aurora's shock,

triggering a pang of recognition. "Lee?" she blurted, stunned in an entirely different way now. "Why did you run me off the road? Are you trying to kill me?"

"If that had been my intent," Lee replied, "you would be dead already. Now get out of the car! Naga cannot support it forever."

That made no sense to Aurora. Naga? Hold? Instinct urged her to dismiss the woman and her babble as the byproducts of a concussion. But—the car did in fact seem to be suspended in mid-air. And—there really didn't appear to be any other way out of the car. She took a deep breath, prelude to the biggest leap of faith ever, and then scrambled over the center console. An instant after she pushed the passenger door open, she found herself contemplating the possible side-effects of a concussion once again. For instead of a gloom-filled void, what she saw below her was a pair of gleaming bronze eyes set in a head filled with pointy teeth.

"Shit!" she shouted. "There's a dragon down there."

"Yes," Lee said. "And she grows impatient. Jump, before she decides to release the car and let you fall to your death!"

"Where am I supposed to jump to?"

"Just jump!" Lee barked, sounding more than a little impatient herself. "She will preserve you!"

The drakena rumbled then, encouragement perhaps or perhaps the draconic equivalent of a weight-lifter's grunt. An instant later, gravity began to drag the car over the ledge. Aurora swore again, then pitched herself out the door—and into free-fall. Her stomach lurched. Her heart-rate tripled. She flailed at the darkness, trying to slow her descent, and then squawked with surprise as a scaly, tuft-tipped tail wrapped itself around her waist. The next thing she knew, she was being airlifted back toward the road. A pair of headlights dazzled her eyes in passing. Moments later, a deceptively soft crash rose up from the bottom of the ravine. Aurora suffered a sentimental pang of loss and regret, then let out a squawk as the dragon dropped her onto the pavement.

"Quiet!"

She turned to demand a little consideration from Lee only to come face-to-face with the business end of the dragon instead. It blasted her with twin gusts of heated air and then nosed her toward its backside. When she balked, unsure of what she was being told to do, Lee closed in on her and none too gently grabbed her upper arm.

"Hurry!" she hissed, dragging her like a petulant child. "We must be gone before we are seen."

"But—ow!" Aurora said, irritated now as well as confused. "What the hell is going on?"

"Not now!" Lee snapped, as she monkey-climbed her way onto the dragon's back. "You are still in danger. That endangers us as well. Hold your tongue and get up here!"

Aurora didn't understand. Why was she in danger? What had she done? And why would a strange dragon be coming to her rescue? As she rolled these questions around in her mouth like pieces of hard sour candy, she doggedly hoisted herself onto the dragon's waiting elbow and then onto the span of its narrow shoulders. An instant after she was seated, the drakena dove into the ravine. Aurora's heart jumped into her throat. Her only thought was, 'Shit!' Then the drakena's trajectory leveled out and twin beams of debris-flecked light caught Aurora's attention. Hey, those were the sedan's headlights! The sight excited her. Where there was light, there was hope, right? Maybe the car wasn't completely trashed. Maybe she could get a crew out here to salvage her beloved—

The drakena sucked in a massive breath, distracting Aurora

from her musings. An instant later, she sent a coruscating stream of white-hot flame into the space between the two headlights. Aurora heard a violent thud and then a whoosh. An instant later, the car exploded.

"Jesus!" Aurora sputtered, as the drakena soared over the burning wreckage. Before she could rebound from the shock of seeing her car fire-bombed, the burning remains of an entirely different wreck spanned into view. "Jesus!" she sputtered again. "What the hell is going on?"

"That was the man who tried to force you over the cliff," Lee said, keeping her face to the wind. "Naga attended to him before she attended to you."

Aurora's shock intensified. "There's a—man—in there?" she asked, twisting around on the bones of her butt to try and catch another glimpse of the second wreck. When Lee nodded, Aurora swallowed hard and said, "Shouldn't we go back and try to help him?"

"Why would you want to do that?" Lee asked. "He meant to kill you."

"You don't know that," Aurora said, aware that she wasn't being exactly rational but unable to say exactly why. "He could've been drunk or something. Besides," she added, when Lee refused to acknowledge the possibility, "It's fire season! Those two wrecks could touch off wildfires up and down the peninsula."

Lee sneered. "The fire will only consume what it was meant to consume. Do you know nothing?"

"I know I should call 9-1-1," Aurora fired back, feeling her shock starting to give way to annoyance and a desire to be annoying in return. "Do you know their number?"

"Put your cell phone away," Lee said, without bothering to see if Aurora was just joking or not. "You can never use that one again. It would be best if you didn't use a phone at all."

Aurora made a disparaging mouth sound. "This phone cost me two hundred dollars. There's no way I'm dumping it."

Between one flap of her wings and the next, the drakena rumbled. It was not, Aurora noted, a happy sound. Lee replayed the message in her trademark monotone. "Naga insists. She says you have been compromised."

Compromised? The word raised the hair on the back of Aurora's neck even as it confused her. "I don't understand," she said. "Compromised how?"

The drakena rumbled again. Once again, her companion was quick to translate. "It may be that a drake knows your name."

Once again, Aurora's nape hairs leapt to attention. Her hankering for belligerence turned into a grudging sense of dread. "How is that possible? I haven't said anything to anyone."

"Naga does not know how you came to be known. No doubt the Great One will tell you when we reunite you with her."

It took Aurora a moment to process that statement, but when she did, a microburst of excitement momentarily displaced her unease. "You know Quetzalcoatl?"

"Not in the flesh," Lee said. "But she and Naga have ridden the Dreaming together on more than one occasion. Just this morning, they went that way. When Naga returned to the waking world, she knew your peril as well as where and when to find it. "

Aurora's first impulse was to dismiss Lee's testimony as a big fat bowl of bullshit. But—here she was on the back of an unfamiliar drakena who had snatched her from certain death just in the nick of time, apparently at her own dragon's behest. It was all so fucking fantastical! And yet—here she was. Compromised. Exposed. Targeted for death.

It may be that a drake knows your name.

But who could this drake be? Someone passing as a fan?

That seemed like a reasonable possibility, given the number of people that she came into contact with in that context. But how could that theoretical faux-fan have discovered her association with Quetzalcoatl? No one but friends and family had been out to the house, and only Roz and Brigit had been to the barn. Neither of them would have let the drakena out of the bag.

The thought of her daughter spawned an oh-shit moment. If a drake knew Aurora's name, there was a good chance that he knew Roz's as well. All of a sudden, she was extremely thankful that she and the water-drakena were heading south. Yet even as that wave of dread drew back out to sea, a fresh one broke over her.

What about Quetzalcoatl?

If that drake in the know knew who she was, he wouldn't have to work very hard to find out where she lived. And while some part of her wanted to believe that the information wouldn't matter to him now that she was supposedly dead, the rest of her mocked her for her hubris. She was merely collateral damage in this contest for the next age. Quetzalcoatl was the grand prize. Damn straight that drake was interested in her address! She leaned forward and shouted in Lee's ear.

"We need to get to Quetzalcoatl as fast as possible!"

If the woman was startled by Aurora's outburst, she made no show of it. "The Great One guides us to her lair as we speak," Lee replied, still facing forward. "Naga cannot fly any faster while bearing the weight of two people."

"When we get there," Aurora said, her thoughts scrabbling like a long-clawed dog on ice, "we're going to have to move her!"

An instant later, the enormity of such a task caught up with her. They would need a semi to transport the mountain of flesh that was Quetzalcoatl—assuming that they could get her aboard one! Even awake, she was nearly dead weight. Maybe this mystery drakena could help in some way. Maybe she knew

Kathleen H. Nelson

some kind of anti-gravity magic. Maybe—

An image of fire erupted in Aurora's mind: a violent conflagration that bore a pink-frilled dragon in its center. The vision was so personal and intense, she broke out in a sweat. The sense of urgency that accompanied it made her cheeks burn. She bellowed the Great One's name. At the same time, she flung her mind open in the frantic hope of improving her reception.

"Why do you shout?" Lee demanded of her.

Aurora made no reply. She could feel Quetzalcoatl straining to synch up with her. The first impression that came through was familiar: all-consuming fatigue. That was followed by a flash of frustration and then a futile yearning to be young and mobile again. Redness seeped into her thoughts like blood. A moment later, she felt the drakena's spirit sink into a deep, dark pool of resignation. Aurora instinctively knew what the Great One was preparing to do.

"Hang on!" she said, projecting the thought like a shout. *"We're coming!"*

"No. Stay away. I am lost."

A vision of hungry yellow fire rose up in the wake of that thought. It started out as a stream and then expanded into a river. As it crested, so did her fatigue. Her thoughts began to spiral. Her lungs grew weak. As she gasped for breath that was slow to come, a sharp, jagged pain erupted at the base of her throat and then exploded. Aurora's hands flew to her neck, but it was intact, seamless, dry. Nevertheless, she choked on phantom blood.

"Hurry!" she croaked. "She's dying."

In response, the drakena banked—in the wrong direction.

"No!" Aurora said, urgently pointing them toward her home even though no one was looking. "I live over there."

"Not anymore," Lee said, inflectionless as ever.

CHAPTER 26

Charles autodialed Aurora's cell phone for the third time, and for the third time, the call went straight to message. "Just wondering if you were home yet," he crooned, even though he'd already heard about her 'accident' via the police scanner. Apparently, she'd taken out his hitman even as he did her in. *A woman after his own heart.* "Call me when you get in."

Not that anyone would suspect him of having anything to do with her tragic death. He was just thorough out of habit. That, and it kept his mind from wandering into untowardly tender spaces. *"What's grey and comes in quarts?"*

Next, he called Aurora's land-line. He had a big, fat, crocodile-y, "Is she there yet?" ready for the daughter, but that was too was just camouflage. What he really wanted to know was if the daughter was home. It was a relatively minor detail in the grand scheme of things, but he wanted to be adequately prepared when he came calling later.

Unfortunately, he got the answering machine. The sound of Aurora's no-nonsense voice missed piercing his heart by the narrowest of margins. He swore and cut the message off in mid-greeting.

"Well?" Drogo growled, from his seat on the floor in front of the blazing hearth. "Is she home?"

"Unclear," Charles replied, shoving his grief into a shallow grave in his back-brain. "She didn't answer, but that could just mean that she's sleeping or feeling uncommunicative. It doesn't really matter one way or the other, though. If she's there, I'll dispatch her. If not, I'll arrange a hit-and-run for her in the near fu—"

His cell phone cut him off with an urgent buzz. He responded immediately even though or possibly because he knew that doing so would irk Drogo. The text message that awaited him floated the corners of his mouth into the semblance of a smile. The accompanying photo raised his eyebrows.

"What is it?" Grishka asked, from his 'territory' on the fireplace's far side.

A report from one of my agents," Charles replied, still focused on his phone. "It would appear that tonight is our lucky night." He flashed the photo to the drakes. It was of a silhouette in the moonlit sky.

"The wyrm!" Grishka exclaimed. "Where was that taken?"

Charles' upper lip curled, seemingly of its own accord. "Less than two miles away," he replied. "On the fringes of my own property. It would appear that the little dickens has taken an interest in my zebras." He slid the cell phone back in his pocket and then started toward the front door. "That photo was just taken. If we hurry, we can catch it before it attacks one of them."

"Stay!" Drogo commanded, even as he rose to his feet. When Charles cocked his head at him, projecting an exasperated WTF, the drake mocked him with a snort. "If the wyrm makes a kill, it will gorge itself and be unable to fly afterward. That will make it easier for Grishka and me to catch and subdue it."

"But—!"

"We will attend to the youngling," Drogo said, drawing himself up to his full, belligerent height to discourage further challenge. "You will go to that woman's house. Kill the daughter if you find her there, then search the property for signs of the Great One."

"What am I supposed to do if I find her?" Charles asked, trying to keep his irritation in check. "Put a shotgun to her head?"

Drogo snorted again, a draconic as-if. At the same time, Grishka snapped, "No! She is a Great One! She must be preserved and treated with respect."

"Yes," Drogo said, a poisonous croon, "you would be wise to respect her. Old as she is, she could still reduce you to cinders if she saw you coming. If you find her, ping Grishka's cell phone and stay out of sight. We will come and take care of her, too."

Charles did not like the plan; it felt too nebulous, too cavalier. He voiced the first concern that came to mind. "But—how will you be able to find the right house?"

The question provoked a sneer from Drogo. "Fool. We are dragons. We have exceptional navigational instincts."

"And I've got GPS," Grishka added slyly.

Drogo swiveled his head toward the other drake and hissed. "You are an even bigger fool than the human, Rasputin. If you have any sway whatsoever with the Divine, you should pray for this to be our last night together."

"It is a prayer I have repeated daily since your arrival," Grishka said, in a tone that was both tragic and dignified. Then he climbed to his feet and hobbled out of the room to Change in private. Drogo bared his teeth at his retreating back and then turned his snarl on Charles.

"You should pray for success tonight, too," he said, and then rubbed cheeks with Charles. "Disappointment makes me hungry."

Yeah, yeah, Charles thought, as the mandrake made his way out of the house. But that did not mean he wasn't afraid.

On the drive to Aurora's place, Charles tried to clear his mind of everything but the task at hand, but his thoughts kept spinning like tires stuck in axle-deep mud. There were things that he had not told the drakes. Like: the agent who had spotted the wyrm had been assigned to watch Aurora's house. And: the wyrm had been spotted leaving her property.

Damn it! Why couldn't he have met her earlier? He might have been able to ward off this regrettable collision of alliances! He might have been able to—

A sedan passed him on the right. As it sped off, tail-lights glaring in the dark, an image of a mangled pink Lexus cropped up in his head. The contents of that Lexus were mangled, too, and bleeding out on the otherwise spotless upholstery. Damn it! They had had so much in common: the same outlooks, the same concerns for the world and its man-made decline. If only the drakena hadn't sunk their claws in her.

Still, there was no point in crying over spilled milk—or blood. The drakes had wanted Aurora dead and he had made it happen. Next, he was going to murder her daughter. Because the drakes wanted that, too.

The driveway to Aurora's estate loomed to the left. He killed the truck's headlights and coasted to a stop in front of the gate. He buzzed the house once and then again, thinking that it would be easier to be let in than to break in. When no one within responded, he resigned himself to doing things the hard way and pulled the truck into the shadows on the side of the road. Then, murder kit strapped to his back, he scaled the fence. There was no razor-wire to contend with and no embedded glass, but still, he struggled a little going over the top. Getting old, he thought, as he jumped to the ground. Getting soft. Drakes didn't admire softness in humans. Their word for it was 'tasty'. Time to toughen up again.

As he stole his way toward the house, he took in details: no vehicles in the driveway, no lights on inside, nothing to suggest that there was anyone at home. But—the porch light was on. Maybe the daughter had gone out for the evening and hadn't come back yet. Or, maybe she had simply grown tired of waiting for her wayward mother and gone to bed. At this point, he wasn't taking anything off the table.

He prowled around to the back of the house. To his delight and amazement, the patio doors were unlocked. An instant after he let himself in, a swarm of house smells engulfed him: roasted fish, some waxy floral scent, the lingering aromatics of whiskey. Then he caught a stray whiff of Aurora's perfume and his heart clenched so hard, he had to press a hand to his mouth to keep himself from crying out. The depths of his weakness appalled him. Drogo would've bitten his head off for such a display, and rightly so! He pulled the shotgun from his pack. The weight of it shored up his mental defenses. As he stole from room to room, he tapped its trigger-guard, telegraphing his intentions.

He found two bedrooms downstairs. One of them was almost certainly the daughter's; he could tell by the youthful décor and the clutter. There were shoes all over the floor, and lumps of discarded clothing. There was something else, too—a distinctive brimstone smell, somewhat dissipated but still recognizable. Son of a bitch! The daughter had recently been in close contact with a dragon!

The realization sparked a wildfire of apprehension within him. Had he killed the wrong woman? Had he just made the biggest mistake of his life? His stomach knotted. The air in his lungs turned to lead. What had he done, what had he done, what had he done? Yet even as panic threatened to set in, a stern inner voice marched him back from the edge. It didn't matter if she was the Great One's primary agent or her daughter's dupe. That business with the patch had confirmed her involvement and sealed her fate.

As he poked through the daughter's things, searching for clues as to her whereabouts, he heard the muffled whir of a garage opener. His pulse spiked—a grim, predatory quickening. Ah, there she was! He thumbed the shotgun's safety off. An instant later, a door slammed open and a man shouted, "Rise and shine, Roz! You're going to talk to me or else!"

Dammit! Not the daughter!

"You hear me? You've got some 'splaining to do!"

Footsteps sounded in the hallway outside of the daughter's bedroom. Then the intruder barged into the room and swatted the light switch in passing with a precision born of familiarity. As the overhead light came on, he started to sing-song, "Wakey-wakey," only to cut himself off when he realized that he was staring at the business end of a shotgun. "Easy there, dude," he said, as he raised his hands over his head. "I got no gripe with you."

"What are you doing here?" Charles asked, stalling for time while he tried to decide how he wanted to play this unexpected turn of events.

"I was hoping to talk to my ex," the man said, glancing at the neatly made bed on the far wall, "hopefully without that ball-busting girlfriend of hers around. I guess she isn't home after all."

"Any idea where she might be?" Charles asked casually.

"Probably with her geeky friends," he said. "They won't answer my calls, either. Say," he added then, peering at Charles with dawning awareness, "I know you, don't I? You attended the Sili-Con Grand Ball this year with Aurora. You went as Doctor Who, right? I was Han Solo."

Charles tapped the trigger-guard, a negative reaction to the positive ID. An inner voice that sounded very much like Drogo urged him to kill the fool and be done with him already, but Charles resisted the urge because the fool happened to know more about Aurora's daughter than he did.

"Where do these friends live?" Charles asked. "Could you take me to them?"

The fool shrugged, seemingly unaware of how much danger in was in. "I suppose. But why would I? What's your interest in Roz? And why are you poking around here in the dark with a shotgun?"

"Aurora called me," Charles said, a shameless and unflappable lie. "She was afraid that there might be an intruder in the house and asked me to investigate. She also wanted me to make sure Roz was OK."

The last part of the lie provoked a bitter snort from the man. "Trust me, if Roz had been home and someone broke in, you would've found him splattered all over the floor. That woman might borderline geek, but she can definitely handle herself in a fight."

Good to know, Charles thought, and then gestured toward the door. "Just the same," he said, "I'd like to find her and see for myself. Aurora's peace of mind is important to me." When the man balked, Charles prodded him with the gun and said, "I could shoot you instead. I'll tell the cops I caught you burgling the place. I'm pretty sure they'd call it justified homicide. You good with that?"

"No," the man grumbled, "Not really."

"Then let's pay a visit to your ex's friends."

His new guide led him out of the house through the garage and then up to an ancient VW bug that looked like it was being held together by rust and duct tape. "Seriously?" Charles said, as he gaped at the junker. "This is your car?"

"It's a loaner," the man said, as he looked up and down the driveway. "Where's yours?" A moment later, he let out a happy little gasp. "Look!" he said, pointing out a small gleam in the darkness beyond the pasture. "There's a light on in the barn! Maybe that's where Roz is! When we were dating, she used to practice her karate stuff out there."

Charles scowled in that direction, irritated with himself for failing to notice that glimmer earlier. He'd forgotten that Aurora owned a barn! It looked to be good-sized, too—large enough to house something more substantial than horses. Maybe the daughter was out there doing katas. Or maybe, just maybe, she was consorting with the drakena. Either way, he was good.

"This is your lucky day, friend," he said, prodding him toward his POS. "You get to get in your car and go home."

To Charles' vast surprise and annoyance, the man ignored this incredibly generous stay of execution. He seemed suddenly twitchy, as if he'd stepped on a downed electric fence. His hands in particular were all aflutter. "You think there's a monster in that barn, don't you?"

Charles' annoyance dissipated. His surprise took a different tack. He lowered the shotgun that he had started to raise and peered at the man, taking in details that he had not cared to glean earlier. He was a young man already going to pot, with thinning hair, a thickening waistline, and a slouch. Although Charles preferred his hirelings to be older and more hardened, mentally and physically, this fellow struck him as both malleable and malicious—traits that might come in handy under the right circumstances. Charles was willing to explore the possibility, leastwise to a certain degree.

"What's your name?" he asked, in a semi-avuncular tone.

"Aldo," the man replied. "Aldo Whimsey Baker. Maybe you've heard of me. I'm an actor."

"Good for you," Charles said. "What makes you think there's a monster in that barn?"

"I've seen it," he said, with enticing confidence.

"Where?" Charles asked. "Here?"

"No," Aldo said, eager to tell his tale to a willing ear. "On a cruise ship heading to New York from Scotland. I admit, I was drunk at the time, but I know what I saw, dammit! Freakin' Roz saw it, too, but she won't say so—not yet, anyway. But one way or another, I'm going to get the truth out of her."

Charles did not respond immediately because he was trying to puzzle out the huge discrepancy that was Scotland. Prior to her flight from the Pinnacles area, the Great One hadn't left her territory for at least a century. There was no way that Aldo could have seen her on that ship. However, it was clear that he had seen *some*thing that he couldn't explain. For that reason alone, Charles decided to string him along for a while longer.

"All right," he said, "here's the deal. As it happens, I do think there's a monster in there. I'm going to have a look. If you want to come with me, I'll permit it—"

Aldo puffed up like an affronted game-cock. "You'll permit it? Now see here—"

"No," Charles said, in a soft, serrated tone. "You listen. I'm in charge here. If you can't accept that, you can leave now and I'll forget you were ever here. Trust me, that's a gift—and a one-time offer. If you decide to come with me, however, you will do what I tell you to do when I tell you to do it from now on or I'll kill you. It's as simple as that. So what do you say?"

Aldo's gaze flitted from the shotgun to Charles' unsmiling face and back again. He licked his lips like a nervous dog. Then, driven by obsession, he choked back his pride and reservations and committed himself to Charles' service with a nod.

"So be it," Charles said, and then gestured for Aldo to follow him. "Let's go and have a look-see. Stay behind me."

Charles cleared the pasture fence in one easy vault. Aldo chose to climb over it instead, but at least he did so quietly. As they waded through the calf-high timothy, they happened onto a well-worn path that seemed to run directly from the house to the barn. The discovery encouraged him, for a trail as ingrained as this suggested regular foot traffic rather than the occasional jaunt. He followed the seam all the way up to a side-door and then motioned for Aldo to press himself against the outer wall.

"Wait here," he whispered. "I'll be back."

Presuming Aldo's unconditional obedience, he then eased his way into the barn.

The air smelled—not of horses or hay or leathery tack, but of recently charred flesh and musty brimstone. Any doubts that he might have harbored about being this being the right place disintegrated. He oriented himself in the direction of the light. It was coming from his left—not the barn proper as he had originally assumed but rather an annex of some kind. As he stole that way, holding tightly to the shadows, the light expanded, revealing an old riding ring. And there, in the center of that ring, curled up around a swath of household junk, slept a dragon. It had to be the Great One. Had to. Neither Tezcatlipoca nor Drogo came close to rivaling her in size. Huge as she was, though, she didn't strike Charles as particularly fearsome. More than anything, she looked faded, worn out; painfully, excessively old.

But that wasn't his problem.

He backtracked then, retreating from the barn so he could ping Grishka. An instant after he stepped outside, Aldo was at his elbow. "Well?" he whispered. "Is there a monster in there or what?"

Charles gave him a critical once-over, assessing his readiness for a close encounter of the draconic kind. He looked both anxious and eager, like a kid expecting a pony for his birthday. If Charles didn't green-light him, he'd probably have a meltdown. That alone wasn't reason enough to give him the go-ahead, but it did act in concert with his desire to contact the drakes in peace.

"Go and have a look," he finally whispered back. Slowly!" he added, as Aldo scrambled for the door. "And be quiet! If you wake her up, she'll save me the trouble of killing you."

The warning seemed to do the trick, for Aldo turned hyper-stealthy, almost comically so. Scant minutes later, however, he came galloping back from the barn all wide-eyed and pasty-faced.

"Son of a sea-biscuit!" he gabbled. "That thing is huge!"

"Quiet!" Charles hissed, and then modified his tone as he grasped what Aldo was really telling him. "That's not the monster you saw on your cruise?"

"Hell no!" Aldo said, making an effort to control both his volume and his agitation. "The one I saw was smaller and darker and wormier. This one looks like—" He scowled as if trying to wring a connection into being. "It looks kind of like a giant version of Esmerelda. Is that—" He paused, daunted by the leap of faith he was asking himself to make. "Shit! Is that a dragon?"

Charles had every intention of confirming the suspicion, but before he got the chance, something came streaking out of the darkness. It touched down in the pasture, but then caught sight of Charles and launched itself back into the night-time sky with a warning squawk. As it flapped its way over the barn, Aldo knotted his hands in his hair and said, "Oh my God! That was another one, wasn't it?"

Charles didn't answer. He was busy tapping out a message to Grishka. Yet even as he hit 'send', a muscular red drake descended from the starless heights. An instant after he landed in the grass, a deformed grey drake joined him. Aldo clamped his hands to his forehead as if to keep his brains trapped in his skull and said, "Jesus! They're coming out of the woodwork!"

"The wyrm went that way!" Charles said, pointing at the barn's weather vane. "The Great One is inside!"

Drogo swiveled his head at Grishka and rumbled. In response, the grey drake vaulted into the air and over the vane. Without so much as a sideways glance at Charles, Drogo then stormed into the barn. A furious exchange of roars ensued.

"What's happening?" Aldo said, straying toward the barn door in spite of himself. "What are all these—"

Another round of roaring cut him off. He exchanged a disbelieving look with Charles and then darted into the barn like a teenaged boy who has just heard someone yell, 'Fight!' Although he knew that it was unwise to do so, Charles followed him. As Tezcatlipoca's agent, he had witnessed numerous territorial squabbles between drakes, but those involved more posturing than action. The conflict between Drogo and the drakena would be a full-fledged battle to the death.

Charles joined Aldo behind the broken remains of an outlandish fountain on the outskirts of the riding ring. By then, the two dragons were at each other's throats in earnest. Drogo was smaller than the drakena by a magnitude, but what he lacked in size, he made up for in agility and savagery. He darted in and out and in again, striking at her eyes, throat, and underarms with teeth and claws. She deflected the attacks with her heavily scaled neck and tail, but the efforts left her staggering on shaky legs. When the drake slammed into her heaving side, she collapsed with a pained roar and could not regain her feet. Drogo lunged for her tender under-throat then. Out of desperation, she breathed a stream of fire at him. The stream bounced off his chest and splattered against a barn wall. The wall ignited with a whoosh. An instant later, the fire was racing toward the rafters.

Charles grabbed Aldo by the shoulder and whispered, "Time to go!"

"Just a sec," Aldo said, riveted by the spectacle of draconic savagery.

The drake had the Great One by the throat now. She tried to shake him off—to no avail. She tried to slash her way free of his jaws, but he ignored her flailing claws and held on. Her breathing became frantic: terrible, strangled sounds that shifted into a liquid gurgle as his teeth finally pierced her flesh. He tore her throat apart then. For one devastated moment afterward, her head remained upright. Then, in slow motion, it sank to the floor and did not move again.

"Time's up," Charles hissed, as Drogo began to roll around in the drakena's blood. "Move!"

"One more minute!" Aldo begged.

"Suit yourself," Charles said, already starting toward the smoke-clogged door. "But when that dragon's done there, he's likely to do the same to you if he finds you here. That is, if the fire doesn't get you first."

Grudgingly, Aldo abandoned his front-row seat to the carnage. As he followed Charles out of the burning barn and across the pasture, however, he kept looking over his shoulder and shaking his head.

"Holy shit!" he said, when they reached the relative safety of Aurora's patio. "That was insane! Why were they fighting?"

"Philosophical dispute," Charles replied, in no mood to elaborate further. Tezcatlipoca would regard tonight's proceedings as a job well done and reward him handsomely for it, but Charles took neither pride nor pleasure in the work. Precious things had been lost this night, things that couldn't be replaced. It would be wrong to take joy in such losses. A grim sort of satisfaction was the best he could manage.

"Uhm, dude?" Aldo gulped then. "Something's comin'."

Charles emerged from his brooding thoughts to see a two-legged figure striding across the pasture, shedding gouts of fire as it went. It had a saurian-shaped head and body at first, but as it drew nearer, its skull rounded into a dome, its torso lengthened, and its arms dropped to its sides.

"Oh my God!" Aldo gabbled. "That looks just like—"

"Do not say his name," Charles warned, through gritted teeth. "In fact, if you want to live, you will keep your mouth shut until I tell you to open it again. And don't stare!"

Not staring was easier said than done, though. The mandrake was naked, and his body glistened in the barn-fire's light like a gilded statue of ruin and might. His muscles rippled. His penis was hard. As he closed in on the patio, he let out a laugh that raised the hair on Charles' arms.

"What a spectacular kill that was!" he exclaimed. "Old as she was, she had power still. I could taste it as her blood spilled into my mouth! Such an invigorating flavor! You'll never know the like, human; I almost feel sorry for you for that." He stretched, showing off his fell physique, and then licked his teeth as he noticed Aldo for the first time.

"What's this?" he asked, leaning closer for an extended sniff. "A snack? How thoughtful of you."

"He is not for eating," Charles said, although he didn't intend to argue the point too strenuously if Drogo decided to make a fuss. "He has information that might prove useful."

"Really?" Drogo said, helping himself to another snuffle. "Are you sure? He doesn't smell very useful."

"Smells can be deceiving," Charles replied, trying to sound blasé. "Speaking of which, someone is bound to smell the smoke from yonder fire at some point and call 9-1-1. It would be best if we weren't here when the fire engines arrive."

"You do know how to spoil a party, don't you?" Drogo said, which was by his standards a remarkably good-natured riposte. His gaze flicked, reptilian-like, from the barn to the house and then to Aldo. "You," he said, flicking a gore-flecked hand at him, "go and fill the house with fire. See that it gets in every room."

When Aldo balked, Charles was quick to shove him toward the house. "The Great One gave you an order. See to it!"

Aldo bounded off like a spooked hare. Drogo watched him go with a predatory gleam in his eyes. "Are you sure we need him?"

Charles responded with a rueful nod. "If nothing else," he said, "I'll make sure that he gets blamed for the fire."

"Clever monkey," Drogo rumbled facetiously, and then rubbed his hairless midsection. "All of this excitement has left me famished. I will hunt now. If Rasputin contacts you while I am gone, assist him in securing the wyrm. Tomorrow or perhaps the next day, we will transport it back to Juarez."

"Of course, Great One," Charles said respectfully, taking extra care to stay on a hungry dragon's good side. "Just one more thing before you go."

The drake's eyes narrowed, signaling an end to his good humor. "What?"

"What I should do with the drakena's remains?" Charles said. "Tezcatlipoca would not be happy with me if I were to let the first responders find them."

"Such a good pet you are," Drogo sneered, and then started to walk away. Over his shoulder, almost as an afterthought, he added, "Dragons turn to ash when they die."

An instant later, the drake was gone.

There were lights flickering in the house's upper windows now. As Charles watched, they grew larger and brighter. Then Aldo came galloping out of the house with a maniacal grin on his face. "We should go," he said, "cuz this place is going to blow when the fire hits the gas!" As they ran toward the driveway, giving the house a wide berth, he added, "Dude! Most exciting day ever! Thank you!"

Charles had never felt more alone.

CHAPTER 27

From his hiding place in the woods, Grishka Rasputin watched Quetzalcoatl's lair burn. His heart ached. His jaws hurt from clenching. He knew that the drakena was dead. The Divine had made that clear to him. He knew too that Drogo had killed her—this, in spite of the Divine's wishes. This, no doubt with Tezcatlipoca's blessing, for as bold as he was, Drogo would not have dared such a killing without the Great One's approval. The both of them were fools, unwilling to evolve beyond their power-hungry instincts and ambitions. Grishka had tried to encourage them toward change, but to no avail. In that regard, he was responsible for tonight's tragedy, too.

And the Divine held him to a higher standard.

Sirens rent the still night air. Soon after, flashing red lights gave the smoke a bloody hue. Hoses came out. Water spurted. But they were too late; the fire was too far gone. Neither house nor barn would survive the night. Not that he cared. He had watched thus far only to honor the Quetzalcoatl's passing.

Now he needed to go and find some water. He needed to immerse himself and connect with the Divine and figure out what to do next.

Made in the USA
Monee, IL
17 December 2019

18922616R00224